THE
WARSLAYER

BAEN BOOKS by ROSEMARY EDGHILL

The Warslayer
Beyond World's End
(with Mercedes Lackey)
Spirits White as Lightning
(with Mercedes Lackey)

THE
WARSLAYER

The Incredibly True Adventures of
Vixen the Slayer,
The Beginning

ROSEMARY EDGHILL

Copyright © 2002 by Rosemary Edghill

A Baen Books Original

Baen Publishing Enterprises
P.O. Box 1403
Riverdale, NY 10471
www.baen.com

ISBN: 0-7394-2612-5

Cover art by Carol Heyer

Distributed by Simon & Schuster
1230 Avenue of the Americas
New York, NY 10020

Production by Windhaven Press, Auburn, NH
Printed in the United States of America

Dedications

To the Troops of Oz:
Barry Cadwigan
Allen Hazen
Andrea Hoseth
Sylvia Kelso

And the Home Guard:
Greg Cox
Elektra
Doris Egan
Nancy Hanger
Jim Macdonald
Sarah Thompsen
Toni Weisskopf

*And Most of All, to the Men
Behind the Legend:*
Russ Galen
Jim Baen

Contents

"GOD'S TEETH!"
The Making of a Cult Phenomenon
(from *Vixen the Slayer:*
The Unofficial Journeys)

BY GREG COX

From the start, she made an indelible impression
on everyone lucky enough to catch her startling debut:
charging out of the misty English (or was it Australian?) countryside astride her magnificent chestnut
stallion, her silver rapier catching the moonlight, her
scarlet tresses dancing in whistling wind like the very
fires of Perdition. "Evil wakes!" she warned us hus-
kily, as her unsheathed blade swiftly dispatched what
would turn out to be merely the first in an endless
parade of hell-spawned ghouls and revenants. For those
of us who tuned into that first episode out of curiosity, or even by accident, it was clear at once that this

was a woman to be reckoned with—as millions of devoted fans would soon discover.

Who would've guessed that the first great TV heroine of the 21st Century would be a feisty, indomitable demon-hunter straight out of the Elizabethan era? Certainly not Gloria McArdle, the incandescent former Olympic gymnast who brings "Vix" thrillingly to life every Friday night, or so it seemed from the shell-shocked expression on Glory's face when she received a standing ovation from a veritable horde of adoring fans (many decked out in full 16th-century regalia) at the first official Vixen the Slayer Convention in New York City. I was there myself, frantically scribbling notes on the back of my program book, and can testify that the sheer amount of devotion, excitement, and, okay, out-and-out lust that filled that crowded convention center when Glory took the stage was enough to fuel a full-fledged crusade against the forces of darkness, or at least sell out every piece of licensed merchandise in the dealers' room. The Beatles may have been more popular than Jesus Christ, but Vixen has certainly got Lucifer beaten hands-down.

But if McArdle was slow to realize the full enormity of her kohl-eyed counterpart's impassioned fan following, then she was probably the last person on the planet to do so. All you need to do is look on the Internet, where you can quickly find enough evidence to fill even Father Diavolo's *Book of the Damned.* Fan-generated Vixen web pages abound (despite the pernicious efforts of Full Earth's over-zealous legal department), with even Adrian the Wonder Horse receiving a score of tribute sites. Pseudo-scholarly web magazines like *Camrado: Ye Olde Journal of Vixen Studies* publish earnest treatises on such provocative topics as "Vixen: An Inspired Fusion of Red Sonja and

Solomon Kane" and "Whither the Beast?: Biblical Imagery in 'Vixen'."

Speaking of provocative, let's not forget all the fan fiction out there, an endlessly growing archive of semi-apocryphal "Vixen" adventures that are generally a whole lot steamier (and more explicit) than the exploits that actually air on the television series. Not surprisingly, the vast majority of these unsanctioned narratives have Vixen and her arch-nemesis, Lilith Kane, the Duchess of Darkness, taking their love-hate relationship to a whole new level. (Sometimes Sister Bernadette joins in as well, vows or no vows.) And don't get me started on all the "Mary Sue" stories out there, in which thinly-disguised versions of the authors are mystically transported through time to join Vixen the Slayer in her never-ending battle for truth, freedom, and the way of the ninja. (I refuse to comment on all those anonymously authored stories teaming Vix with "Gerg Xoc," journeyman scribe.)

Meanwhile, in dozens of chat rooms and newsgroups, Vixites from around the world argue incessantly about what *really* happened in the infamous "dream" episode, or who would win in a three-way fight between Vixen, Xena, and Buffy? (The general consensus on the latter was that Buffy would win, but only if she was allowed to import a missile launcher from the 20th century.) In all, there's enough Vixen material on-line that, in theory, you could spend 24 hours a day in the world of our favorite ninja vampire hunter without ever watching the show! But who in God's name would want to do that?

Every fan has their own favorite episode, of course. Some prefer the nonstop demon-fighting action of such classics as "To Hunt the Hunter" or "Thirteen Minutes to Doomsday," while others groove on moodier, more atmospheric fare like "The Haunter of

Crimson Cove" or "Behowl the Moon." Hardcore romantics pine for more episodes like "A Slayer in Love" (with Christopher Marlowe, no less!), while still others (you know who you are) can't get enough of such, er, stimulating episodes as "Corsets and Catacombs" or "The Duchess's Delights." From a strictly historical standpoint, few shows are more fascinating than "Across the Veil of Worlds," in which the ever-frugal folks at Full Earth Productions incorporated footage from the original, never-aired pilot for *Ninja Vampire Hunter* starring Doreen Liu, thus providing an intriguing glimpse of an alternate reality featuring a very different Slayer.

Granted, there are a few episodes that most of us would prefer to forget. Did we really need to watch a sixty-minute flashback to Sister Bernadette's halcyon days at the nunnery in "The Trouble with Anglicans"? Or watch our usually fierce Slayer baby-sit that obnoxious urchin in "Mother for a Day"? Oh well, I guess even the Anointed Champion of the Light can have an off day. Or two.

How much longer can the Vixen phenomenon thrive and flourish? From where I'm sitting, the sky's the limit. As of this writing, the first official Vixen novel, *The Warslayer* by Rosemary Edghill, is sitting atop the *New York Times* Bestseller List, while First Lady Tipper Gore just cited Vixen as "an outstanding role model for America's youth." Not bad for the bastard child of an English lord and a Japanese geisha!

Now you'll have to excuse me. It's nine o'clock and a brand new episode has just begun. On my TV screen a full moon is rising, the Duchess and her fiendish lackeys are plotting new devilment, and justice, in the form of a flame-haired female privateer, is riding into the dark and unholy night.

I may never go out on Fridays again.

GREG COX is the author of numerous books, including *Vixen the Slayer: The Unauthorized Journeys.* He has never missed a single episode.

CHAPTER ONE:
Leather and Steel

✳

The troll was enormous: eight, maybe nine feet tall. Its skin was a mottled bluish-purple, covered with coarse black hair and warts the size of dinner plates. Its knuckles nearly brushed the ground when it walked, and its wrists were as big around as her thighs.

Vixen the Slayer bared her teeth in a feral smile, tossing her sword from hand to hand as she moved backward in a fighter's crouch. The monster had to be stopped here, and there was nobody who could do it but her. She was just lucky that something that big was also slow. . . .

The troll tottered forward another few steps, then wavered and fell flat on its face, exposing the two puppeteers who had been inside and the tangle of trailing air-hoses that led back to the rest of the crew.

"Cut," Megan said, sighing. "Rennie—"

"He tripped me!" Rennie said, pointing at his partner Roald, on whose shoulders he'd been sitting a few moments before.

"Maybe we should try it the other way around," Roald suggested snarkily. He was six feet three and outweighed Rennie by a good ten stone.

"It was nobody's fault," Megan said, putting on her "soothing mom" voice. "Vix, honey, we're going to have to go again. Everybody take ten!"

Vixen the Slayer, ninja-raised do-gooder and scourge of the Satanic legions that plagued the Elizabethan countryside, stretched and sighed, her hand on the small of her back. That knife-fighter's crouch looked great on camera, but it played hell with the vertebrae.

"Sure, Meg," she called back. "I'm going to be in my trailer, okay?"

Megan nodded, distracted, and Vixen—aka Gloria Emmeline McArdle—walked off. She knew from long experience that ten minutes was going to be at least forty-five, what with getting all the air-hoses and electrical cables untangled so that Truxton the Troll would be ready to go again. He was really just a nine-foot All-Purpose Creature Armature that could be dressed in any number of foam latex monster disguises; otherwise, he'd have been far too expensive for the budget of a syndicated TV series, even one filmed in The Wonder Down Under.

She walked past the camera and craft services until she got to her trailer. Closing the door behind her, she tossed her sword on the couch and sat down in front of the mirror. Vixen's masklike makeup and kohl-lined eyes stared back.

This time last year, she'd been plain Gloria "Glory" McArdle, ex-Olympian, red-headed teacher of girls' gymnastics and physical education at Ned Kelly High School in Melbourne, Australia. She'd been good enough to be on the Australian team that went to Seoul, and not good enough to medal and garner tempting offers from top coaches and sportswear manufacturers, and that was that. When her final growth spurt hit late that summer, taking her from five-five (pretty tall for a gymnast even at that) to six foot in her stocking feet and built like a Vargas pinup, it thoroughly put an end to any possibility of ever competing again.

She'd been wise enough not to go into coaching—better a clean break than being tormented with constant reminders of "might have been." She'd gotten her teaching certificate instead, and while she was relieved to find that she enjoyed teaching—molding and shaping impressionable little minds and bodies—as she settled into her new life, she found she was still hungry for . . . something.

Boredom is a dangerous taskmaster. Out of boredom Glory had gone to an open audition for a straight-to-cable series called *Ninja Vampire Hunter.* The ad had mentioned that gymnastics training was a plus, but Full Earth Productions had really just been looking for extras to stand around in the background while Doreen Liu, their Asian martial arts star, bounced off trampolines.

So she'd started fooling about, and found that a six-foot redhead who could do back flips, layouts, and walkovers had gotten the casting director's attention. She'd been hired on the spot, spent the Long Vac on the set, and thought that was the end of it. She wasn't a professional actress, and other extras with more experience had told her that most pilots didn't get picked up.

But *Ninja Vampire Hunter* had tested well, and with a little tweaking had gone to series, following in the fertile footsteps of such disparate role-models as *Xena:*

Warrior Princess and *Buffy the Vampire Slayer.* And that was when Barry Doherty and Full Earth had offered her the lead.

"Doreen doesn't want to spend a year in Melbourne, and anyway, you look a lot better in a black leather corset," he'd said winningly.

It wasn't one of Life's Tough Choices. Playing "Orcs-and-Bush-Rangers" as Vixen (neé Koroshiya) the Slayer (even with a whoppingly sexist leather corset) was more fun—and more lucrative—than teaching high school. She signed a three-year contract with Full Earth to star in the re-christened *The Incredibly True Adventures of Vixen the Slayer* (*TITAoVtS* for short) and entered the glamorous world of show-biz on the spot. On an eighteen-hour shooting day and an average six-day-per-episode shoot, Vixen the Slayer and her sidekick Sister Bernadette wandered the villages and hedgerows of England in search of supernatural evil and religious intolerance. The Australian exteriors gave viewers a peculiar idea of the English countryside, not that anyone particularly seemed to care.

Veteran stage actress Anne-Marie Campbell was playing her co-star, the doughty ex-nun Bernadette, and American soap villainess (and former Southland Studios child star) Romy Blackburn had the plum role of Vixen's recurring foe: Lilith Kane, the Duchess of Darkness. By the time the first six episodes had aired, *Vixen* was international front-page news, captivating millions of UPN Network viewers every Friday night and generating hundreds of column inches. Glory became a Star overnight, and discovered that she was suddenly somehow terribly important and publicity-worthy. The usual news story portrayed *TITAoVtS'* star in mid-backflip beneath a banner headline saying something like: "Is this Today's Woman?"

Well, only if today's woman needs to be able to slay trolls and vampires at need, Glory thought, and kept her thoughts to herself.

When the publicity hit, Barry realized that it was important to strike while the *zeitgeist* was hot and had taken advantage of owning the Flavor of the Month to book the regulars for a promotional tour of the U.S. during hiatus: interviews, photo layouts, talk shows, personal appearances, the whole enchilada. The moment the season's filming wrapped, Romy, Glory, Anne-Marie, Dylan (the Duchess of Darkness's lackey, the venal Jesuit Fra Diavolo), and even Adrian the Wonder Horse (a burly chestnut with a tendency to overact) would be shipped Trans-Pacific to fame, frenzy, and a general blurring of the lines between fantasy and reality.

Such is fame, Glory thought wisely to herself, unimpressed. *I wonder how long this is going to last?*

Two months later:

I wish this were over. Glory sighed, and began to put on the makeup that would hide her thousands of pale-gold freckles. There were deep circles under her tiger-yellow eyes, and she looked haggard. *This isn't what twenty-six and famous is supposed to look like. And this is supposed to be my vacation. . . .*

Six weeks. Three dozen American cities that all looked alike. They'd done ShoWest, Letterman, Leno, Oprah, six media conventions, dozens of local shows and special appearances, and interviews for everyone from *Movieline* and the Sci-Fi Channel to *Cosmopolitan.* As the show's star, Glory bore the brunt of the publicity: she'd signed copies of *TITAoVtS* tie-in books at chain stores across America and schmoozed with every UPN executive they threw at her. Every single one of the people she met wanted just one little piece of her, but a million little drops added up to an ocean, and a million little pieces added up to more than one Glory "Vixen" McArdle.

Everything they've ever told you about fame is true, Glory told herself sagely. She'd had a taste of it in her Olympic days; she'd known it wouldn't be all gravy— but somewhere deep inside she'd assumed the TV star business wouldn't be that much different from the Olympics. She'd been right . . . and wrong. The Summer Games only lasted two weeks, and a promotional tour went on forever.

I want out, she thought forlornly.

But if you get out, where will you go?

That was the real question. It wasn't so much that Fame had changed her. It had just changed everybody else, to the point where they yelled for Vixen and Glory answered, and she wasn't really sure how much of a difference there really was. She knew this couldn't last forever, but she didn't know if she could just go back to being a Phys Ed teacher again once it was over, and she knew she didn't want to. But if not this, and not that, then what?

She mascaraed her pale lashes and slathered on the kohl, and finished up with a liberal application of blood-red MAC lipstick. When she was done, the masklike face of Vixen the Slayer stared back at her from the mirror, yellow eyes gleaming out of Goth-black rings. She sighed, and reached for Gordon, resting her chin on his head. The big blue elephant had traveled everywhere with her since she was six and attending her first out-of-town gymnastics competition. At least he was a familiar face in a town full of strangers.

And a room full of strangers as well: her dressing-room was filled with an ever-growing collection of licensed Vixen tie-ins. The eighteen-inch stuffed Vixen doll—the full set of action figures (including the very rare Lilith Kane, the Duchess of Darkness)—the Franklin Mint limited edition sword and stake (of genuine English rowan!)—the cups and mugs and keychains and T-shirts and caps blazoned with the show's logo and her picture. She would have stopped collecting them long ago, but people kept giving them to her. When she'd started, it had all been fun.

But now . . .

This is not fun. I have had fun, and this is not it.

She cuddled Gordon harder and picked up the copy of the script that was on the corner of the table. She was in Hollywood, California, to tape an MTV special *en persona* as Vixen the Slayer. Christina (her personal publicist, and, as far as Glory was concerned, personal devil) had set it up, as she set everything up, usually without consulting Glory. Still, Glory knew just what Christina would have said: *Hey, Vix, easy money. Show up, do some shtick, a few back-flips, everybody's happy.*

Everybody but Vixen the Slayer, scourge of the soundstages.

She dropped the script unread. What did a bunch of cues and stage directions matter? They wanted Vixen. That's what they'd get.

Except that Vixen the Slayer would have cut their idiot heads off by now, and I'd be safe in a nice warm jail cell.

Although she was too sensible to think that would be really appealing. And trying to outface the cameras in jeans and a T-shirt certainly wasn't. If she was going to be Vixen, it was time to get dressed.

Her costume was laid out neatly on the couch: a fantasy in black leather along vaguely Elizabethan lines . . . assuming, of course, that the Elizabethans had been into serious bondage. The main part of the *Vixen* costume actually came in two pieces. There was the black-leather corset (it looked as if it laced, but that was an illusion; the laces were elastic, crossing over an inset panel of stretchable scarlet brocade that allowed her to breathe and move in the thing, and entry was actually accomplished through a set of concealed speed-release clasps on the sides) with the flared mock-pannier fabric-gathers over the hips, and then below that, the puffy leather slashed-look faux Elizabethan slops, or shorts (hotpants, really, and back in the day an item of strictly male attire), because their costume designer had seen *The Six Wives of Henry VIII* one too many times. Thank God the costume designer hadn't been let to keep the ruff—not after the dress rehearsal, anyway. Once she had the rest of it on she could wrestle with her elbow-length handless gloves at leisure—double bracers, really, upper and lower arm, leather and studded, with another of those idiotic slashed poofy things in the middle. Had the costume designer thought her elbows were going to get cold? Or be the focus of intense perverse lust among the males of cable TV? At least the neckline of the costume—what there was of it—made sense from a ratings standpoint, if not from a martial one. Add the sword, and the stakes sheathed along the outsides of her thigh-high leather boots (there was a spike-heeled pair for the publicity stills and the odd shot of her sitting down in the show, but thank God cooler heads had prevailed when it came to the boots she actually had to move in), and she was a sound technician's nightmare.

She squirmed into her costume with the ease of long practice. She'd just pulled one boot into place and was reaching for the other when there was a knock on the door.

Oh, Christ all bloody mighty!

Glory wriggled quickly into the second boot and staggered to her feet. Christina never knocked, and it was too early for them to want her in front of the cameras. *Something's hit the fan*, she told herself wisely, and opened the door in a rattle and creak of leather armor.

When she registered what was waiting for her, her mind went blank. She stared.

There were three androgynous entities standing in the doorway. The tallest of them didn't even come up to the top of her shoulder. They looked kind of like Classic Trek aliens—the weird, meddling, superpowerful kind—or maybe like really, really tall Munchkins. They were all wearing stiff shiny long-sleeved floor-length embroidered robes in virulent candy-colors—turquoise, green, and pink—and the one in front, whose receding hairline dipped into a killer widow's peak, was carrying a long stave with a glowing purple crystal on the top.

When it became obvious to both of them that she wasn't going to say anything, the staveholder spoke.

"We have come seeking Vixen the Slayer," he said.

After the last six weeks, she answered as easily to one name as the other. "Yeah, sure," Glory drawled in her hard-learned American accent, tossing her long red hair back over her shoulders and stepping back. She'd thought she was doing a solo act today, but it looked like she'd been wrong. Just like Christina not to give her all the gory details. Well, from their rig-outs, these guys looked like pros. They'd manage.

She turned back to the dressing table, reaching for her script again. If it involved strange men in pink dresses, she'd better actually read it.

"We have journeyed far from the plains of Serenthodial, through many perils, seeking you, O great warrior," the staveholder continued, stepping into the room. His companions followed, shutting the door behind them. "I am Belegir, and these are my co-Mages, Englor and Helevrin. We follow Cinnas the Warkiller, and I pray that we are not too late to seek aid for the Allimir."

"What the fu— *heck* is the Allimir?" Glory demanded, dropping her script.

"We are," the little one in the green robe—Englor— piped. Suddenly Glory had a terrible suspicion that this little delegation wasn't intending to appear on MTV at any time in the immediate future, and when she saw what Englor was holding, she was sure of it.

I will get somebody for this. I don't know who, but I do know that it will be very painful for them when I do.

"Look, I really love meeting fans," Glory lied, "but—" *But how the hell did you get back here dressed like that without anyone stopping you? I thought Yanks were all paranoid.*

Short as he was—even in a silly pink robe and wearing mascara—there was something enormously *dignified* about Belegir and his two companions, and weary as she was, Glory couldn't bring herself to step on that. Besides, in some sense she owed Belegir and the others: it wasn't as if millions of viewers had been sucked in by her acting ability. If the show hadn't attracted followers and a fandom, if people like these hadn't liked the show, none of this fame and fortune would have happened.

Take that how you like.

And anyway, how could it hurt her to be nice? This couldn't go on for more than a few minutes. When they were ready for her in front of the cameras, Christina would certainly appear to drag her out there and send this lot packing. And Christina had a ruthless streak to which Glory could only aspire.

"Okay. What can I do for you?" she asked, carefully stifling a sigh. *If I find out this is one of Barry's practical jokes, my mate Bazza's a dead man.*

Belegir drew himself up proudly.

"A terrible power has been unleashed in the land of Erchanen. Long was it prisoned upon the peaks of Grey Arlinn, until foul mischance freed it once more. Now it stalks the plains of Serenthodial, and Great Drathil is no more than an abode of shadows. We are a simple gentle people, without the arts of war, and we knew that only the greatest warrior who ever lived could help our people in their hour of greatest need. You are she."

Great grammar, Vixen thought automatically, though the rest had gone on far too long. *"Terrible power"? "Foul mischance"? "Greatest warrior"? Oh, no, mate. You've come to the wrong address. I get* PAID *for acting out other peoples' fantasies. . . .*

From surfing the Net, she knew there was a bumper crop of Vixen fan-fiction out there, most of it centering on unlikely encounters between her and Romy, but some of it indistinguishable from one of the show's storylines. And from the chat-rooms, she knew that there were people who took the show's slogan—*Live the Legend!*—far too much to heart. She'd seen the homemade props and costumes herself, and a lot of them were better than the real thing—or what passed for real in front of the cameras.

But how could she really blame them? She'd felt the allure of doing just that herself. It was just luck that made her one of the few who could turn her playgames into a living.

"I'm really sorry," she said to Belegir as gently as she could. "I'd like to come to your . . ." Convention? Asylum? She abandoned her search for *le mot juste.* "But I'm afraid I don't have any free days this year. If you want to write to the Publicity Department at Full Earth, I reckon Barry could . . ."

She stopped.

The little man was crying. He did not argue or beg. The look on his face was one of utter despair. Englor was weeping as well, and Helevrin's face was set in a stony mask.

"You're really serious, aren't you?" Glory said helplessly. Though the situation was implausibly weird, she found that she was upset for these people rather than irritated by them. She couldn't believe that such an open display of grief was faked.

But if it was not . . .

Deep inside her, a tiny spark of warning woke to life. That these three were honestly sincere was something she did not doubt for a moment—but what they were showing her was the utter sincerity of madness. Glory had been famous for six months, long enough to know the dark side of it: the obsessed, the stalkers, the people dazzled by the bright images on their movie or television screen into believing those images were real people who could see them back. So much belief could *twist* people in ways they never would have chosen for themselves: twist them and change them into weapons pointed at the celebrities they worshipped. These three truly believed that they needed Vixen the Slayer, but all she had to give them was Glory McArdle. When they realized the difference—when they realized there *was* a difference, things were going to get . . . ugly.

"I'm not what you need," she said, very quietly. *I couldn't even medal at the Games. I'm a too-tall Phys Ed teacher who got lucky!* "It's not like I— You shouldn't believe everything you see on television. I mean— You've got the wrong person. I'm an actress. Not even all that good an actress, I reckon. Romy's better. She plays Lilith, and . . ." *Cut the grizzling, Glor.*

"You were our last hope," Belegir said, his voice choked with hopelessness. "We have sought through all the worlds, gone to each hero—kings, barbarians, warrior-maids, and doomed princes. Always the answer is the same: they are too busy, they will come later. *But there is no later for us, Slayer! We are dying now!*"

"And so we came here. This is not a world for heroes—but we did our research," Englor said despairingly. He thrust the book he carried toward her.

Glory looked down at the well-worn paperback copy of *Vixen the Slayer: The Unofficial Journeys* by Greg Cox. She'd spied it a moment ago and thought it meant they were fans, but if they were, they weren't the same kind of fans she'd been meeting all summer. Not by a long chalk.

"Your life imitates art," Englor added with forlorn dignity. Mascara made grainy tracks down his face as well. "We have read it." Then he sobbed outright, and Helevrin enfolded him in her arms. The turquoise-clad woman glared accusingly at Glory as she comforted her comrade, and in that instant Glory understood completely how love could turn to hate.

"We will go," Belegir said with quiet dignity.

Oh, God, yes. Just open the door and go.

The intensity of her fear made her feel angry and ashamed. How could they do this to her? What *right* did they have to do this to her? Being Vixen was a part, a role, a really expensive *game*. It wasn't life!

She clenched her hands at her sides and concentrated on what she was going to say to Christina when she got her hands on the lazy little tart—and flinched back as Belegir raised his staff. It was of some straight fine-grained wood, silvery with exposure and handling, and banded and capped in shining copper. Strange symbols graven in fine spidery lines seemed to dance over its surface, and the strange violet jewel on its end glowed with cool radiance.

"*Neddhelorn, Hambrellorn, Gathrond Megnas!*"

Belegir chanted in a deep impressive voice. He thumped the staff on the floor as he did, and with each blow the purple crystal glowed brighter.

"Hey, Vixy? C'mon, you're up next." Christina's voice, calling through the door. There was a rattle as she tried the knob.

The door was locked. Glory hadn't locked it.

"—Lergethil, Gwainirdel, Algoth-Angras!"

"Yo! Vix*en!*" The knob rattled again.

Glory lunged for the door, forgetting she was spooked by the weirdos, forgetting to be afraid that one of the "Allimir" might be armed with more than the strength of his convictions. Christina could set things right. Everything would be fine.

Just as her hand touched the doorknob, there was a loud pop, a flash, and a wave of intense scent like burned perfume. Glory screamed and flinched in shock, but an instant later she realized she wasn't hurt—yet. She grabbed the knob tightly and jerked at it as hard as she could, willing the door to open, to let her escape.

The knob slipped from her hands, pulling and twisting until she lost her grip. The door fell free, hinges first. Could she have torn it loose in her momentary panic? She blinked. It hadn't made a "bang" as it hit the floor. Christina hadn't screamed.

And for a very good reason, so it seemed. Christina wasn't there, and neither was the hall outside her dressing room.

A wave of cold, damp, forest-y air rolled into the room, and through the now-open doorway, Glory could see trees—a birch forest that stretched into the infinite distance. She could hear the rustle of the branches as the wind passed through them, and watch the flicker of sunlight. The forest floor was covered with bright yellow leaves that began sharply as her doorway ended. As Glory stared in wonder, the leaves rustled and disgorged a chipmunk. It dashed up to her feet before realizing where it was, then turned and dived back into the leaves again.

"God's teeth!" she gasped, and just-too-late remembered it was a line from the show. Vixen's favorite oath.

She turned back into her dressing room, still blinking away afterspots from the flash that had somehow put this outside her door. When her vision cleared, she saw all three of the short guys were still standing in the middle of her dressing room, staring at each other in confusion.

"This wasn't supposed to happen," Belegir gasped. The purple crystal on his staff was slagged and melted, like the remains of an old-time flashbulb.

"It *has* happened," said Helevrin. "The magic went awry and took that which it ought not have. But she hasn't agreed to help us. We have to send her back."

"*How?*" Belegir cried in anguish. "This is the forest of Duirondel—beyond it lies Serenthodial the Golden—home! The stave's power is expended, and the rest returns to Erchane's embrace." He let go of the staff. It hit the tatty green linoleum floor in pieces, crumbling into a line of dust as Glory watched in relieved disbelief.

This is real. They were telling the truth. This is all real, or . . . or I'm going to break Bazza's jaw, is what.

"We'll have to get more," Englor piped up bravely. From the way the other two looked at him, Glory got the impression that getting more magic wasn't going to be all that easy.

She felt a pang of relief so strong it was almost painful. These people weren't nutters. She knew what special effects could do, and they couldn't drop a Hollywood dressing room into the middle of a birch forest that looked and smelled and felt like a birch forest, even for a goof. The forest was a real forest.

But that meant a delegation of wizards really had come to her for help.

"I reckon that I— I just— I'm glad this is all . . . " She leaned against the doorway, fighting a wave of dizziness born of shock. "What did you think I could *do?*"

"We did not know," Helevrin said simply. "All we know is that only a hero can save us."

If she didn't sit down soon, she was going to fall over and probably squash a couple of her guests. Glory staggered over to the couch and collapsed, breathing as deeply as she could under the circumstances. Gordon tumbled from his perch and she clutched the stuffed elephant reflexively to her chest.

This is wackier than all of last season's scripts put together.

"What will we do? What will we do?" Englor was actually wringing his hands in panic.

"We must . . . we must ask her to come with us. As our guest. We will consult the Oracle of Erchane to see why this has happened and how best to return the Slayer to her own place," Belegir said.

"Just like that?" Glory heard herself say.

The fact that she always got into some kind of trouble because of it had never kept Glory from speaking her mind. Today, the unreality of the whole situation made shooting off her mouth even easier. This was all so real that her mind insisted it couldn't be happening.

All three of the Allimir turned to look at her.

"I mean, you asked for my help, and now you've got me here, and you're just going to turn around and let me go?"

"The Allimir," said Helevrin stiffly, "are people of honor. Your presence is an accident. You have not offered to aid us. We have no claim on you."

If that's their idea of begging for help, no wonder everyone else turned them down.

"Look, I— I reckon you've really got the wrong person. There isn't anything I can do about whatever it is. But I can come and take a dekko, maybe give you some advice, hey? No promises." *This is SUCH a stupid idea. God's teeth, gel, doesn't your mouth ever get tired of writing checks your body can't cash?*

"'No promises,'" Belegir echoed, as if the words puzzled him. "Come, then." He held out his hand.

Glory got to her feet, clutching Gordon reflexively. By now the temperature of the room had dropped to that of a crisp fall day, and she grabbed a sweatshirt— grey with a picture of Vixen on the back and the show's logo embroidered on the right front—and knotted it around her shoulders. After a panicked moment— knowing she ought to pack for this adventure but without the faintest idea of what to bring—she grabbed a large logo tote-bag and stuffed her street clothes, her makeup, her purse, and her script into it. She tucked Gordon carefully into the top. He was her mascot, and she wasn't leaving him behind.

"Okay," she said breathlessly. "Let's go."

The Allimir turned and filed through the doorway. Glory hesitated, then hitched her bag over her shoulder and followed them.

Her feet scuffed through a thick fall of yellow birch leaves, and the bite of the air made her glad she'd brought the sweatshirt. She would have liked to change back to her baggy T-shirt and jeans before going off with these guys, but she'd felt an odd reluctance to suggest it. While she wore the costume, she was Vixen the Slayer, and groundless though the conviction was, wearing the costume made her feel protected.

Protected or not, her arms and the tops of her thighs

tingled with the cold while the rest of her sweltered under several layers of squeaking, creaking, and jingling leather, buckram, and steel, and after a minute she knew she was going to get the usual raw place under her right arm where the shoulder-piece always rubbed. At least her feet didn't hurt. Her armor was a pain in the ass to march in, but the boots were comfortable.

"Hey guys, you know what? I reckon I'd better go back and change clothes after a—"

She turned back. She'd been expecting to see the dressing room, or at least the doorway and a chunk of wall. But there was nothing there. Only a square raw spot on the forest floor where *something* had been.

Glory felt her stomach clench with panicky nausea. Suddenly she felt trapped, though she was in precisely the same situation that she'd been in the moment before. But now even the *illusion* she could leave was gone. Nothing was left but the forest, her strange companions, and her idiotic bravura.

They were staring at her again.

"Oh, well. Never mind. Look. Why don't you . . . um, tell me about yourselves, hey?" She still didn't know what Belegir and company thought she could do for them, but whatever it was, it had to be easier than being a Media Personality. And if somehow this still turned out to be a joke, at least it was one of the elaborate interdimensional kind.

"We are the disciples of the great mage Cinnas the Warkiller," Englor began proudly. "In every generation . . ."

" . . . there can be only one," Glory finished automatically.

"No. Three," Englor corrected her kindly.

She'd caught up to the others, and they'd started

walking again. Helevrin kept glancing at her suspiciously, but Englor was frankly worshipful.

"Um. Sorry. Go on."

She'd have to remember that these people didn't
watch a lot of television, though apparently they'd seen
enough to have gotten her into real trouble.

"For a hundred generations the legend of Cinnas
the Warkiller has been a beacon to his people. Though
he died in the moment of his greatest triumph, his
works live on!"

"That's reassuring," Glory muttered. *Dead, then, is
he? Precious little use to you now.*

"Only now—"

"If she isn't going to help us, she doesn't need to
know," Helevrin interrupted brusquely. It didn't look
like she was going to forgive Glory for making Belegir
and Englor cry any time soon.

"I— But— Well— Oh, yes, of course. You're right,"
Englor faltered, glancing from Glory to Helevrin.

The journey continued in silence.

Two hours later they were still walking through the
same forest, and if not for the consistent presence of
the sun on her left hand, Glory would have been willing to swear they'd been walking in circles the entire
time. She could feel the tendons in her legs thrumming
like a plucked guitar string, and her back ached, but
despite her physical discomfort, Glory actually felt better
than she could remember feeling in months. All the
grinding weight of the show and the media spotlight had
been lifted from her shoulders, and she was no longer
surrounded by people wanting her to be perky and pho-
togenic when she felt grumpy and dull. And if these
people had her confused with Vixen, at least they were
innocent and up-front about it—not a bunch of supposed media-savvy grown-ups who ought to know better.

Helevrin hadn't thawed, but Glory had stopped worrying about it, because it was taking all she had to keep up with her. The three mages might be short, but they scuttled through the forest at an amazing rate.

The sun had been high overhead when they'd first started out of Duirondel. Now the shadows were long and the light had a twilight ruddiness, but at last Glory began to see signs of change in her surroundings—the trees began to thin, and grass began to poke up through the drifts of leaves, the stalks growing longer and the clumps thicker until Glory realized she wasn't walking through a forest with occasional grass, but a grassland with occasional trees.

"Are we there yet?" she muttered under her breath. She'd thought she was in good physical shape from the show, but cross-country hiking used unfamiliar muscles.

She looked up, watching something besides her own feet for the first time in hours, and the vista had the impact of a blow.

There was nothing before her but kilometers of flat open plain covered with golden autumnal grasses. It stretched on in an unbroken sweep until it passed over the shoulder of the earth. She could *see* the wind as it gusted across the prairie, making dips and shadows in its grassy surface. If a wheat field could be a thousand miles wide it would look like this: so vast and featureless that for a moment the placid blue sky seemed close enough to crush her like an open hand. She staggered back, throwing up an arm to shield her eyes from the glare of the westering sun. A grass ocean, with no place to run to, nowhere to hide . . .

She spun around, looking back wildly the way she'd come.

Behind her was the forest through which she and her companions had walked. The birches were bright autumn gold against the midnight green of a dense pine forest that seemed to stretch for miles, climbing the lower slopes of mountains that thrust blue and jagged into the evening sky. The setting sun turned the patches of snow on their higher slopes a pale shell-pink. It was a scene as beautiful as a painting, reminding her of nothing so much as pictures she'd seen of the Canadian Rockies.

The other three had stopped.

"Behold, Vixen—Serenthodial the Golden!" Englor said, gesturing toward the plains ahead.

This is really real. This is really happening. You're not in Kansas anymore, Glor, let alone Oz. Christ— what were you THINKING? You should have stayed on that couch and screamed until somebody showed up with a rubber tuxedo!

"There is the camp of the Allimir," Belegir said, pointing off into the distance. Glory squinted in the direction he was pointing. Halfway to the horizon she could see the smudges and dots of what might be . . . something. A thin spiral of white smoke rose into the sky, the only vertical in a horizontal landscape. Something with a cook fire, then, but whatever it was, it was miles away, and she'd already walked miles today.

"Since the destruction of Great Drathil, we have become refugees, outlaws in our own land, hunted for the sport of Cinnas' once-prisoned foe," Belegir added, as if that were some sort of an explanation.

She wished she'd paid better attention when they'd been talking back in her dressing room. She knew they'd been looking for someone like Vixen the Slayer, but she was hazy about the reason why. The trouble with Belegir was that he talked like a script before rewrite, and she was afraid that asking a bunch of questions now would only give him the idea she wanted to help.

But you do, don't you? And crikey, look at these

guys—a housecat would give them trouble, wouldn't it? All you'll have to do is show up and fetch what ails them a good kick in the goolies, do a backflip or two, and everybody's happy.

"Outlaws?" she said cautiously.

"Oh, he doesn't mean *real* outlaws," Englor assured her hastily. "Nothing involving, you know, *peacebreaking.*" His voice dropped on the last word, as though he were saying something indecent.

"Driven from our homes. Hunted like mice in a granary—with the Warmother the cat!" Helevrin said harshly.

"Do not speak of *Her* here," Belegir said, glancing up apprehensively toward the sky. Glory followed the direction of his gaze, but she saw nothing but sky and a collection of very large mountains. Nevertheless, the expression on his face sent a chill up her spine.

"Send for Ivradan," Belegir said. "Best we be within bounds by the time night falls."

Not unless this Ivradan has a lorry, Glory thought.

Her feelings must have shown in her face, because Belegir smiled. "Fear not. Ivradan will bring horses, and we may ride back to our people in state—bringing a hero."

Helevrin reached into her sleeve and withdrew a little red bird. At least, it looked like a bird to Glory— she caught only a glimpse of it before Helevrin flung it into the sky. Whatever it was, it flew like a bird as well, cutting through the sky in darting swoops, its body a scarlet spark against the vast blue and gold emptiness. Glory lost sight of it almost at once, but the three Allimir stared after it as if they could still track its flight.

When nothing happened immediately, Glory dropped her tote-bag to the ground and sat down beside it with a sigh. She didn't care if she never got up. She was

tired of standing. At once the world retreated behind
a veil of grass that crackled as she shifted her weight.
The sword on her back poked her in the ribs as it
always did, while the leather corset held her in an
implacable embrace. But those discomforts were
homely and familiar, and her current circumstances
were not.

It just didn't seem *likely* that she was here. Even
if somehow, somewhere, there was such a thing as
magic, how had the Allimir found her? How could they
have confused her with Vixen? What if there were a
real Vixen the Slayer somewhere and Glory was impersonating her? What if the real Vixen found out?

If there is and she does, I'm dead meat.

It was almost more comforting to worry about that
than about what she was going to do when Belegir and
company found out she didn't measure up to their
hopes. Vixen won her battles each week because the
scriptwriters were on her side. There weren't any
scriptwriters around here—just a bunch of mini-mages
making cryptic pronouncements.

And looking up at the sky as if they expected something to come diving out of it.

Something nasty.

"Ah," Belegir said suddenly.

Glory twitched, startled.

"They have seen us. We should reach the camp
before dark—and tomorrow we can go to the Oracle,
who will tell us what we must do to return you to your
home," he added, turning to Glory.

"Yeah. Right." Reluctantly Glory floundered to her
feet again. Her eyes were beginning to adjust both to
the light and the enormous scale of this place, and now,
when she looked in the direction of the smoke plume,
she could see a disturbance in the grass arrowing
toward them. It didn't take a rocket scientist to figure

out that what was making it was Ivradan and the
horses.

A few moments later she could even make out
figures—five dun-colored critters that looked like
brumbies, one with a rider, nearly invisible against the
tall grass—and then she could hear the pounding of
their cantering hooves. But her eyes had played tricks
on her again, between the vastness of the plain and
the lack of local referents. From a distance they'd
looked like full-sized horses, but when they got closer,
she realized they were more like ponies. All five beasts
were virtually identical: black mane and tail and muzzle,
long black socks, and faint grey bars along shoulders
and rump, as though there were some tabby cat in their
backgrounds. From a dozen yards away, you would not
be able to see them in the tall grass.

As Ivradan rode closer he slowed down, and Glory
could feel him staring at her. His skin was the dark
tan of a man who lived his life outdoors—next to him,
the three mages looked as pink and white as a bunch
of roses. His eyes were black, and his hair was brown,
bleached to chestnut by the same harsh sun. He looked
as if he might be about Englor's age, perhaps a few
years older, but she wasn't sure.

He tapped his pony's shoulder, bringing the entire
string of animals to a halt before Glory and the three
mages. Ivradan glanced from Glory to Belegir, his
expression wary.

"Behold!" Belegir boomed in theatrical tones, gesturing toward Glory. "For it is written in the Prophecies of Cinnas, that there shall come . . . a hero!"

Even the sound of the word made her stomach
flinch. With each passing moment she was getting in
further over her head, she knew that much. Oracle or
no Oracle, sooner or later Belegir was going to tell her
his problem, and what was she going to say then?

Ivradan touched his forehead, bowing deeply from the back of his mount. He must be an ordinary Allimir instead of a mage, because he wasn't dressed anything like the other three. Instead of being bareheaded in long robes, he wore a soft cap—a Phrygian cap, Tricia, the wardrobe mistress on *TITAoVtS* had called it—tunic and leggings, and high soft boots that looked as if they were made of heavy felt. The garments were violently colorful, and Ivradan looked like a jockey who'd been dressed by a color-blind bag lady. If he and the three wizards were any indication of the general run of Allimir, she must be the tallest person he'd ever seen (not to mention the best dressed): Ivradan couldn't be more than five feet four on a tall day. The expression on his face was a mixture of joy and wariness.

Englor began to sing in a clear pure tenor. "'In days of old was darkness bold and Evil stalked the hearthside/A hero came with hair of flame to guard the light within us/Sing hey! for our lady/Her sword and her stake/Who saves us from trouble and strife/Sing Hey for our Vixen who's Evil's affliction and will be the rest of her life!'"

It was the *TITAoVtS* theme song, in all its creaking mis-rhymed glory.

"It is she!" Ivradan said in awed understanding. "You have brought us Vixen the Slayer!"

Well, sort of.

Now was the time when Belegir or at least Helevrin should have piped up to say: *Nope. This is just her inept twin. This is just a peculiar accident. She isn't the hero we're looking for, and besides, she hasn't agreed to help.* But oddly, neither of them did.

"Welcome, Vixen the Slayer," Ivradan said, bowing from horseback. He looked from Glory to the ponies, his face plainly indicated that he'd never expected to have to arrange transport for such an enormous creature. The only tack Ivradan rode with was a braided leather loop hooked over his mount's lower jaw, and Glory saw no sign of a saddle. None of the other ponies were saddled either. *Oh, this just gets better. Horseback I can manage, but bareback? Wearing THIS?*

"Um . . . hiya," Glory said inadequately. She didn't know what Vixen would say in a situation like this. Usually Vixen just growled and let Sister Bernadette handle the talking.

"Well, come on," Helevrin said brusquely. The other two mages had already moved toward the beasts, unknotting the leading-rein around their necks and using it to bridle their diminutive mounts.

"There is bad news," Ivradan said. "*She* came again last night."

All at once Belegir seemed to shrink, as if someone had stuck a pin into him. Though he had never looked like a young man to Glory, in that moment he looked terribly old.

"How many are left?" Belegir said.

It was only a long time later that Glory would realize what had struck her as so odd about the question. Belegir didn't ask about dead or wounded or whether their side had won the fight. He only asked how many were left.

"Yesterday runners came from the other camps, bringing the New Moon tally. We are four great-hands now, and that is all. Of all the Allimir nation!" Abruptly Ivradan buried his face in his pony's mane.

"Four hundred," Helevrin whispered. She stared, shocked, at her companions, and even forgot to scowl at Glory.

Four hundred people? Out of how many?

"I reckon—" Glory's voice squeaked, and she took a deep breath and tried again. "I reckon you better tell me what you brought me here to do."

It was as if the other four had forgotten her presence until she spoke. Englor emitted a faint distressed peep.

"*We* did not bring you here," Helevrin said harshly.

"Someone did," Glory pointed out. "And you're not going to deny you came looking for me, right?" *Or at least for Vixen the Slayer?*

"But you said . . . she isn't here to help us?" Ivradan asked in disbelief.

"She . . . we must consult with the Oracle before we proceed," Belegir said hastily.

Glory saw Helevrin and Englor exchange glances, and knew that Belegir's little white misdirection wouldn't hold up for long. But the pink mage obviously didn't want to talk about it out here, and as the shadows had grown longer, all three of the mages had become twitchier and twitchier, to the point where Glory, too, would be just as happy to get out of here rather than press the point. She unknotted the sweatshirt tied around her shoulders and walked toward the pony whose rein Ivradan was holding.

But there's going to be a reckoning real soon now. You can take that to the bank.

"Well, Slayer?" Helevrin said brusquely. She and Englor were already mounted, and now even Belegir was climbing aboard his mount. The mages' robes were gored in back to permit this, and now Glory could see that they wore high felt boots dyed the same bright colors as their robes.

Glory sighed, squaring her shoulders. Feigning an assurance she did not feel, Glory settled the sweatshirt on the pony's back, shrugged her tote-bag firmly onto her shoulder, and took a tight grasp on the animal's mane. Then she bounced up and swung her leg over.

The pony sidestepped. But Glory had not spent an entire shooting season being bumped, jostled, and

otherwise upstaged by Adrian the Wonder Horse to no
purpose. She went with it, gained the animal's back,
and gripped its ribs tightly with her thighs. Her feet
hung inches from the ground.

When she was settled, Ivradan turned and started
off. The other ponies—including Glory's—followed.

The Allimir camp looked rather like a diorama
depicting "Barbie's Malibu *Vardo*"—a collection of
ornate, fantastically painted and carved diminutive high-
wheeled wagons that were drawn in a circle around
a central fire. The dense grass for acres all around them
had been grazed down to bristle by the Allimir's
assorted livestock—large dun-colored oxen with wide
glistening horns, a wary herd of striped ponies with
their mounted wranglers, and the ubiquitous goats and
sheep. It was dinnertime, and Glory could smell the
aromas of baking bread and roasting meat, reminding
her of just how very long it had been since breakfast.

The men and women of the Allimir seemed to dress
very much alike, in tunics, trousers, caps, and felt boots.
Some of them wore aprons, and some wore kerchiefs
instead of caps, but Glory wasn't prepared to distin-
guish men from women on that basis just yet. As the
riders approached, they stopped what they were doing,
stepped down out of the wagons and away from their
tasks to await the party's arrival.

Glory was so caught up in the improbable wonder
of what she was seeing that she didn't remember until
Belegir dismounted that they were going to be expecting him to announce that he'd brought them a hero.

And instead of a hero, he had her.

Everyone gathered around him, all talking at once,
and several of them began pointing at Glory. She
waved, not knowing what else to do.

Belegir raised his hands for silence.

"My friends—" he began, but they weren't listening. They'd hurried past him, to where Glory was trying to decide how stiff she was from a long jog on a short horse, and if she could dismount gracefully. All of them began talking to each other even louder than before, pointing at her and nudging each other and staring with wide round eyes.

A cold lump of anger began to grow in Glory's chest at the sight of them. These people looked to be in pretty good shape, but they were desperate all the same. Whether they had a reason to be spooked or not, they were terrified of something, and it was Glory's steadfast conviction that nobody should have to be that afraid.

What was it Belegir had said? Something about how he'd tried everyone else, and nobody else would come. Well, bugger that for a game of soldiers.

"Uh . . . hiya," she said. "My name is Vixen the Slayer, and I'm here to rescue you."

The Allimir cheered wildly, some throwing their caps in the air. After that, the celebrations began, and it was impossible to get Belegir alone.

The Allimir were gracious hosts. They'd provided Glory with a wagon for her own use, and she'd taken the opportunity to change out of her costume and back into jeans, T-shirt, and sneakers, and to scrub most of the Max Factor off her face. Changing clothes in the cramped confines of the *vardo* had a number of things in common with crocodile wrestling in a phone booth, and when she came out she was hot and sweaty. Englor was waiting for her as if he were her personal assistant. He thrust a mug into her hand, and Glory discovered that no matter how short the Allimir might be, they weren't teetotalers. They brewed a strong ale (a nice change from piss-pale American beer) and an even stronger mead, as she found out when Englor led her back to where the casks were. Walking all those miles today had left her with a powerful thirst, and all of the Allimir (if Englor were any indication) seemed to have been born with a hollow leg. By the time it was fully dark and food was being served, Glory was sitting on a bench feeling pleasantly relaxed.

The Allimir, out of kindness or shyness—she wasn't sure which—were staying out of her way, but at least that meant they weren't asking questions she couldn't answer. Englor had wandered off when she wasn't looking—she could hear him somewhere in the distance; it sounded as if he were trying to teach the rest of the Allimir to sing the *Vixen* theme song.

She wasn't so relaxed that she wasn't keeping an eye out for Belegir, though. The two of them were going to have words. She'd found herself a nice vantage point a little distance away from the main campfire but in sight of her wagon. There was a lantern hung from the edge of the *vardo's* roof, and suicidal moths were flinging themselves at the small gold flame. The rest of the camp was, well, *bustling*. It was a peaceful moment.

"So you've decided to help us." Helevrin sat down beside her on the bench, with a quart mug of mead clutched in her sturdy fist.

Well, you are offering me this lovely free vacation and all . . .

"I reckon I can at least fill in until one of your heroes shows up," Glory answered.

"No one else will come," Helevrin said flatly.

"Then they aren't much in the hero department," Glory answered solemnly, and drank. "Look here," she added, as new inspiration struck her. "*You* don't know what's going on here, do you, mate? Old Belegir's shy as a goat."

"He fears that to speak of *Her* will summon her.

Myself, I don't think it makes any difference. I think *She* will come as *She* pleases, no matter what we do."

One of the children—at least Glory was guessing this was a child; it was much the shortest Allimir she'd seen so far, anyway—hurried over to them, carrying a large painted earthenware platter filled with roast meat, pancakes, and vegetables. As Glory seemed to be the largest person they had ever seen, they were feeding her accordingly: there was enough food for a family of six on the brightly painted platter.

It's like being held prisoner in a crafts fair.

"Thank you," she said, struggling not to drop it as it was passed to her. "Run along now."

The child—Glory was more certain now—giggled and scurried off. Glory rested the hot platter on her knees and picked up a handy chunk of meat.

"So," she said, turning back to Helevrin. "Why am I here?"

"Belegir told you that when he asked for your help."

Bitch. "Well, I wasn't exactly listening. Care for some dinner?"

Helevrin was not shy about accepting. She dug in lustily, picking up one of the flat soft pancakes and using it to hold meat and onions. "You don't know why you're here—and you still agreed to help?" Helevrin asked around a mouthful of food.

"I'm stupid that way." It was a line from one of the shows, and Glory felt a guilty thrill of impersonation before quashing it ruthlessly. "But you can't deny you need help. So tell me what's going on, why don't you? It'll save me having to chase down Belegir."

Helevrin seemed to be willing to take Glory at her word.

"Five years ago we were a rich and happy people. Serenthodial was ours, from the High Hilvorns to the River Baurod. We had no reason to believe there was

anything in all the world to fear—oh, there are always
wolves, and winter, and a bad harvest, but those are
the will of Erchane, and all must suffer them. We had
no true enemies, for Cinnas the Warkiller had
destroyed them all long ago . . . or so we thought. We
did not then know that the Warmother was about to
waken from her long sleep. How could we know? She
had been a tale for children, to frighten them into bed,
since the beginning of time. No one knew. No one
believed . . . save Belegir.

"He had read more of the Prophecies of Cinnas than
any of us, and for years he had warned us that the stars
foretold that on the thousandth anniversary of Cinnas'
great battle, Evil would stalk the earth once more."

Helevrin fell silent, staring into her mead.

"And did it?" Glory prompted after a while.

"Drathil burned," Helevrin said, as if that were an
answer. "I was not there to see it, but that is what I
heard. Great Drathil burned, and then the outlying
villages, the markets and the towns, until all our people
found themselves wanderers. We could not bring the
harvest in from the field. We could not husband our
flocks. All we could do was flee from the fires that
sought us out, harrying us across the face of
Serenthodial the Golden. We starved, we sickened, we
died of a thousand causes. The Traveling Folk took in
as many as they could, and taught us to build wagons,
for the first thing we learned was that each time we
tried to rebuild our villages, we made ourselves *Her*
prey. Only so long as we move are we safe—safe to
glean grain from abandoned fields and fruit from
abandoned orchards, and tend such stock as remains
to us, and so we have not died of hunger and lack. But
when the last store of grain is gone, if any of us are
left, we will die then.

"I do not think we will survive so long as that. *She*

comes, like a wolf in the night, to take our children and our hope. *She* will have us all, for what Cinnas did."

"But who is she?" Glory asked.

"The Warmother," Helevrin's voice dropped to a hiss. "She whom Cinnas chained upon Elboroth-Haden of the Hilvorns a thousand years past, who now walks among us unfettered once more."

"What does she look like?" Glory asked, hoping for more information.

"Look like?" Helevrin echoed, sounding puzzled.

"Look like. Is she tall, short, what?"

"No one has ever seen the Warmother," Helevrin said, as if this were self-evident.

Glory stared at her. "You're out here running around in circles to get away from something you've never seen?"

The disbelief in her voice made Helevrin get stiffly to her feet. "You think that we are foolish children, running from shadows, yet it was no shadow that reduced Great Drathil to ash. Bide here with us, Vixen the Slayer, and you will have all the proof you require, to the last full measure." She stalked off, leaving Glory alone.

Carefully, Glory removed the half-empty platter from her knees and set it on the ground. Several of the camp dogs—big animals that looked half wolf, their golden fur stippled and barred with grey—had been sitting a few feet away, watching them as they ate. Seeing that Glory wasn't going to chase them away, they quickly made short work of the remains of the food, grumbling and growling amiably among themselves as they licked the platter clean before wandering off again.

Helevrin had left her mug behind, so Glory prudently finished off its contents, then drained her own.

This just keeps getting better. The Allimir were being

chased by a monster that none of them had ever actually seen. And better yet, a monster out of their old nursery rhymes.

And exactly how am I supposed to square off against Mother Goose, hey?

There didn't seem to be much of an answer to that.

Soon enough thereafter, the combination of a heavy meal and a long walk did their job. Her head started to droop, and Glory caught herself nodding off. Time to hit the sack. And maybe, if she were lucky, she'd wake up in some nice California hotel room tomorrow and this would all have been a really weird dream.

The wagon that the Allimir had reserved for her use had four shelf-beds, none of which was long enough for six feet of red-headed ex-gymnast to occupy comfortably. She stripped the bedding from all four and made herself a satisfactory nest on the floor. She'd slept rougher than this, God knew, back on her Dad's old sheep station. This was no hardship. She fell quickly asleep, clutching Gordon tightly to her chest.

She awoke in the middle of the night. The ground was shaking, as if beneath the impact of many hooves. *Earthquake?* she wondered, mind still muzzy with sleep.

Then the screaming began.

She reacted instinctively, struggling out of the wagon before she remembered where she was. The sight of the gathered *vardos* made her reel with the shock of recognition, as though she'd tried to mount a step that wasn't there. But the screaming—a polyphony of shouts and unearthly howls—galvanized her. She ran toward it, her bare feet pounding against the earth: six feet of red-headed gymnast wearing a *Vixen* T-shirt and very little else.

The night was bright with enough starlight to make
it possible to find her way, and the flickering lanterns
hung on the ends of the *vardos* provided additional aids
to navigation. All around her the sleeping encampment
was coming to life, but she was the only one moving.
Everyone else seemed to be staying inside their wagons.

She dodged aside as one of the ponies came running at her. It had neither saddle nor rein and was
running blindly, eyes wide and rolling, coat foamy with
terror. When she reached the outside boundaries of the
camp she saw that the herd's nightriders were all clustered together, working hard to control their frantic
mounts. Some had given up trying, dismounting and
freeing their animals. All were staring off into the
darkness beyond the range of the torches, their bodies rigid with fear. The screaming continued now on
a single maddened note; the sound a badly wounded
animal might make.

Ivradan was one of those who were still mounted.
A-horse, he was just above Glory's eye-level. She
grabbed the front of his shirt, compelling him to look
down at her.

"What's going on?" she demanded.

"*She's* returned. She's taken the king-stallion." She
could feel him shuddering with fear, but his voice was
steady and low.

"Well, aren't you going to *do* something?" Glory
demanded. The screams were fainter now, farther apart,
as if what made them was exhausted and dying.

Ivradan stared at her blankly.

Hissing with frustration and fury, Glory grabbed the
torch out of his hand. If she couldn't save the beast,
she could at least chase the predator away from its
meal. She had no doubt that was what it was—
catamount or dingo, either one capable of hamstringing
a pony and then devouring it alive. She released

Ivradan with a jerk that made his pony lunge and sidle, and ran toward the sound. She wished, now, that she'd asked him for a knife—she'd have to do something to put the poor beast out of its misery.

On the short-grazed grass it was easy to spot the body as soon as the light from her torch fell on it. And what she saw then stopped her in her tracks.

The gallant little pony stallion had fought—the churned earth around the body was testament to the battle it had lost. It was dead now beyond doubt.

And someone had flayed it alive. Nothing else could account for the sounds she had heard. She stood over the body. Its skin had been pulled away as a woman might remove a glove. The exposed flesh bore no mark at all, no other wound to account for its death. And the body was completely intact.

No animal killed like this. No person, no matter how twisted, could skin a healthy horse alive and leave no trace of how it was done—not in the time that had passed since she heard the first screams. There wasn't a drop of blood anywhere, just as there was no wound on the body. And around the body, nothing but hoof marks. No predator's tracks to let her know what had killed here.

Glory stood staring down at the body, her mind empty with shock, until the torch burned low and spit fat sparks onto the back of her hand. The pain made her startle and wince, and she looked back over her shoulder, to where the nightriders were clustered anxiously, staring out at her unmoving.

Her senses returned: she heard the call of an unfamiliar night-bird, the rustle of the wind through the grass. She smelled wood-smoke and dung and the ripe meaty scent of the stallion's flayed body. The world seemed vast and empty and very quiet. She glanced up at the sky, at the unfamiliar bright wash of stars, and saw, with a slow spasm of disbelief, the chain of toylike pastel moons that arced across the sky. How could she possibly know what kind of monsters stalked the night in a world where all the ground rules of Reality could be rewritten this way?

She looked back at the nightriders again. Belegir had joined them, his pink robe a bright splash of pale color. This was their world. They knew its rules. Why hadn't any of them come out to see what was wrong? They had knives—she'd seen them earlier—so they must have swords. Spears. Arrows. Some way to protect the herd animals.

But at the first sign of trouble, they'd . . . run. Bolted for the safety of the wagons and left the animals to fend for themselves.

It made no sense. Any stockman worth his salt would guard his herd—and from what Helevrin said, these animals were all they had. They were precious beyond price. And they had herd-dogs. She'd seen them earlier. Yet she'd heard nothing bark. Where was the rest of the herd? Where were the other animals?

Scattered from hell to breakfast, more than likely, and the devil's own job to round them up again with the few mounts they had left. But that wasn't her problem.

Was it?

She shrugged, and began walking slowly back to the ring of wagons, the guttering torch held well away from her body. All they needed to round out the evening would be a nice grass-fire, she didn't think. It was cold out here—she noticed it now—and the grass stubble was slick and sharp beneath her feet. She hadn't thought when she'd been so rudely awakened. She'd just gone barging in without a backward thought. It was just what Vixen would have done—but of course, Vixen slept fully clothed, in deference to the tender sensibilities of Broadcast Standards and Practices.

Ah, well. Likely they've seen a naked sheila in their time, Glory thought philosophically. *And as for you, gel, do try to remember that you AREN'T a superhero. You just play one on telly. You keep trying stunts like this and someone's going to prove it to you sure.*

When she got back to the riders, Belegir came forward to meet her. He looked desperately afraid—and guilty, like a man who knew too much about what had just happened.

"Something got your stallion. Skinned it like a rabbit," she added brutally.

Belegir winced. "*She* toys with us," he said mournfully. "But you—you would have remonstrated with her." He gazed at her in wonder, as though running into the night half-cocked was right up there with Gallipoli.

"You're not right in the head," Glory told him simply. She turned away and headed for her wagon. She'd been thinking before that the Allimir had just been spooked by a run of bad luck, but now she wasn't so sure.

Belegir followed her, babbling like a man who hopes he won't be asked hard questions. "Does this mean . . . ? You've said you would help us, but it isn't right that you should face such peril as this without— We must go to the Oracle at once, as soon as it is light—we must discover Erchane's will in this before something bad happens to you."

"Something bad's already happened," Glory said, stopping. But it wasn't her, it was *Vixen* who turned back and smiled at him, lips stretched back in a mocking grin.

"Sure, I'll go see your oracle," she drawled. "And then I'm going to find whatever was out there tonight

and peel it like a onion. If you're a good boy, I'll let
you help."

Belegir uttered a small dismayed bleat and reached
out as if to soothe her.

Vixen smiled. "Aw, c'mon, Belegir. You wanna live
forever?"

CHAPTER TWO:
Earth and Sky

Glory didn't even try to get back to sleep after that. She pulled on her jeans and her sneakers and her sweatshirt and sat in the doorway of the wagon, her feet on the ground, clutching Gordon and doing her best to *deal*, as Christina might have put it.

This hallucinatory world was still here, and she was still in it. Her faint hopes of waking up back in her own life were gone. She was stuck here for the duration, and the Allimir's problems seemed somehow more immediate now than they had before she'd seen the slaughtered stallion. She was going to have to solve them—or someone was, and the Allimir didn't look like being the ones to do it.

Item: they'd gone looking for a hero to save them from a bogeyman who'd taken down their entire civilization and was now hunting them slowly to extinction— horse by horse, if tonight's attack was any clue. Helevrin had said *She* was toying with them. Glory'd discounted that as empty rhetoric at the time, but it seemed more reasonable now. And that meant their monster was a smart monster, able to think and plan and not gulp its pleasures.

That wasn't good.

Item: the Allimir mages had gone looking for a hero to slay their monster, and had come up dry. They'd come to her. She'd explained their mistake (where had Englor gotten a copy of the Cox book anyway?) and they'd been going to leave without her, only something had gone wrong with that and she'd ended up back here with them by accident. After all she'd seen, Glory couldn't believe they'd lied to her about that. She didn't think the Allimir *could* lie, any more than they seemed to be able to stand up for themselves.

And that was odd, wasn't it? But she didn't have enough information to give the matter proper consideration, and there were a lot of other things that seemed much more important right now—like Belegir's plan to take her to the Oracle (whatever that was) to find out what to do next.

He'd said—or at least implied—that this Oracle had the power to send her home, which would probably be best all round, but she wasn't completely comfortable with the notion. She was the Allimir's last hope. They'd been really clear about that. And while she wasn't much of a hero, they were obviously doing a piss-poor job of coping on their own.

Around her, in the predawn darkness, the encampment slowly roused to greet a new day. She could hear the murmur of low voices from the nearer wagons as the word of this latest disaster spread, and listlessly the Allimir drifted together, clustering around their central fire.

"Slayer, are you all right?" Englor asked.

Glory yelped. He'd come around the back of the *vardo*, quiet as mice, and she hadn't seen him. He jumped back, gazing around himself wildly for the source of her distress.

"I was," she growled. It was Vixen again—Vixen's attitude, Vixen's dialogue—and Glory cringed inwardly. Being Vixen felt too much like lying, and she didn't want to lie to these people.

"I brought you something to drink." In each hand, he held one of the leather quart-jacks. Steam rose from them. She took one and sipped cautiously. Hot spiced beer. Not bad, though not what she'd choose to replace morning coffee with.

"You were so brave," Englor said sighing happily. "It was just like something out of one of the Unofficial Journeys."

Glory shook her head. "You do know that everything in that book of yours isn't real, don't you, mate? It's all made-up?"

Englor regarded her tolerantly. "The Prophecies of Cinnas tell us that every story, no matter how seemingly fabricated, is yet woven around a kernel of essential truth. And I have seen you rush valiantly forth into the darkness to do battle against an unknown foe. You would have *remonstrated* with *Her*."

I would have been dead, Glory thought.

"And you have a sword," Englor added, as if that were a deciding factor.

"And you don't?"

"Oh, no." Englor sounded horrified and intrigued at the same time. "Swords are instruments of war and aggression, tempting people to try to solve disputes by force. Violence never solved anything."

"It certainly solved the question of what that bloody nag was going to be doing come Saturday night, I reckon," Glory growled. "Englor, this doesn't make

sense. You keep going on about how you are a harmless gentle people who abhor violence. You don't have
a single weapon in this entire camp so far as I've seen.
But you came looking for me, because you reckon
I'm—" *A homicidal maniac with poor impulse control,
that's what he thinks.* "Well, anyway. You came looking for someone to be violent *for* you. Isn't that a
little—" *Hypocritical?* "—inconsistent?"

"We sought a hero because we have lost the arts of
war and cannot learn them," Englor said sadly. "Without a hero, we will all die."

Glory sighed and took another swig of her drink. The
sky was starting to lighten. The sun would be up in a
few hours. Then they could start trying to get the
animals back.

"And there wasn't anyone local you could call?"

"Serenthodial belongs to the Allimir, from the
Hilvorn to the Carormanda," Englor said, as if that
were an explanation. Glory sighed again. The trouble
with having a meaningful conversation with any of these
people was that you couldn't. They took their world
for granted, and any time she wanted to know something, she had to cross-examine one of them. It was
a pain in the ass.

"So what do you know about this Oracle?" she said
at last.

Englor smiled, obviously happy to tell her everything
he knew. "The Oracle of Erchane is revered throughout
the land. Even we mages bow to the wisdom of the
Oracle of Erchane. Since before time began the Oracle
has served the Allimir."

"Nice, but a bit vague," Glory said. "But what *is* it?
Have you ever been there? What do you see?"

"Indeed I have been there. Every child of the Allimir
visits the Oracle before his tenth birthday, to see what
path his life should take. By the Oracle's grace, I

became a mage, bound to the study of the Prophecies, and so served many years within the Temple as well."

"Um." Glory thought that over. "But what if you hadn't wanted to become a mage?"

Englor stared at her, with the blank expression she was coming to know too well. "But why would the Oracle tell me to do something I didn't want to do?" he finally said.

Right.

"Tell me about being a mage," she asked, trying again. "I guess you've got to be a pretty bright lad to manage that, hey?"

"There can be only three," Englor said proudly. "It takes years of study to master the Prophecies and understand all the signs and portents, so that all we do is in accordance with Erchane's will. Until Fadril died, I was Belegir's apprentice, because of course we all thought he would die first. Aldien was Helevrin's apprentice, but he . . ." There was a long pause. "He was in Drathil the night *She* came," Englor whispered.

Glory reached out and patted him awkwardly on the shoulder. Every time she started thinking of these people as the inhabitants of some kind of weird sitcom, something like this happened. No matter how peculiar they were, they felt pain. They grieved.

"I'm sorry," she said.

Englor bowed his head, then looked up, smiling through his tears. "But now we have hope once more. You have come. You will hunt *Her* and save us all— just as you saved Queen Elizabeth from the werewolf!"

"I didn't—"

"I know," Englor said, smiling gently and holding up his hand. "They are only stories. But every story contains a grain of truth. *Ay reckon* this one does too," he added, in a fair approximation of her nasal Melbourne accent.

"I reckon," Glory echoed. "Look, if I'm going some-where today, I'd better get dressed. Thanks for the beer, mate." She handed him the empty mug and fled to the safety of her wagon, closing the door behind her.

It was dark inside the *vardo*, though the light of dawn was seeping through the chinks in the closed shutters. She bundled the bedding up off the floor, and found that the bed-benches folded back. With three of them pegged out of the way and the fourth hold-ing the bed-gear, she had a little more room to maneu-ver. She groped for the hanging lantern in the middle of the ceiling—she'd rung her head on it more than once the night before—and took it down, setting it atop the tall chest at the front wall, next to her purse and tote-bag. She rummaged around in her purse, locat-ing first a flashlight key-card and then a disposable lighter, both stamped with the show logo. After a few tries, she got the lantern lit, then sat down on the remaining bench.

What am I supposed to do? What in God's name am I supposed to do?

She hadn't felt this inadequate in years. You trained for years for the Games, but once you got there, you had one chance to do your best, and a thousand bad-luck things might happen. In television there was a different kind of pressure: you got as many tries as you needed to get it right—or nearly—but each try cost money, and there was so many peoples' livelihood riding on one person's ability that every failure hurt.

This was like an unholy amalgam of both. Every-thing was riding on what she did. And there was one chance to get it right, and no ground rules.

That isn't true. That can't be true. I wouldn't be here if that were true, she told herself desperately.

No matter that the Allimir mages had made an error in contacting her in the first place, the fact remained that a power greater than theirs had brought her here. Important Great Powers didn't make wrong choices of that magnitude (she hoped), so either they'd picked the right person for the job, or the job itself wasn't so much of a muchness. Left to herself, Glory would happily have chosen Option B—but she thought about the flayed stallion again, and shuddered. No matter that she thought the Allimir twitchy and sometimes outright weird: there *was* some sort of monstrous monster out there on the plains of Serenthodial the Golden.

But was there? Maybe it was disease. Maybe it was underachieving army ants. Maybe. . . .

It was almost a relief when Belegir finally knocked on the door.

"Slayer? Are you within?"

Glory opened the door, wincing slightly at the dawn light. Belegir was standing there in his long pink robe, looking very much as if he hadn't slept for the last several years.

"Wozzer?"

"We must depart now for the Oracle, if we are to reach it before nightfall," Belegir said. He regarded her civilian clothes dubiously.

"Right." She could take a hint. "I'll change."

She closed the door again and picked up her armor.

Getting kitted out had all the charm of trying to put on a diving suit in a phone booth, but she managed. She rolled up her jeans, T-shirt, and sweatshirt into a tight wad, preparing to stuff them into the tote-bag duffle, and hesitated. Something was missing.

The makeup. The painted mask that turned her from Glory McArdle, ordinary person, into the hieratic Vixen, scourge of evildoers. It was silly, but she just didn't feel like Vixen without the war paint. And though it felt very much like unlawful impersonation, she suspected the best thing all round was to at least *seem* to be the hero they'd ordered. She set the clothing aside and rummaged in her bag again.

The pancake went on in a few swipes, covering plain Glory McArdle's pale-gold freckles. Then mascara, the soft kohl crayon around her eyes, then more mascara. Last of all, a good slather of blood-red lipstick. It was hard to manage with the tiny mirror and the dim light, but she'd done this so many times over the past months that it was almost second nature now. As she worked, she felt the Vixen *persona* settle into place, a soothing ghost.

When she was finished, she bared her teeth at the compact mirror and admired the effect before stowing everything away all right and tight. She stuffed everything into the tote, slung the bag over her shoulder, and picked up Gordon and her sword.

"Easy money," she muttered under her breath, and pushed open the door.

Belegir was still patiently waiting.

She stepped down onto the grass and looked around, then swung her sword up over her shoulder and into its sheath with a practiced flourish. It had taken her and Bruce, the swordmaster, hours to perfect that little gesture, but she had to admit it was damned impressive.

"Where's everyone else?" she asked. Belegir looked blank. "The rest of the people going to the Oracle—you know, the armed escort?"

Considering how terrified they all were of the Warmother, she'd thought Belegir would be bringing the biggest army he could field, or at least bringing his co-Mages Englor and Helevrin.

"It is only we two," Belegir explained. "The others remain to aid our people. We have no 'armed escort' to offer you, Slayer. The Allimir are a peaceful people—"

"Etcetera, etcetera, and so forth," Glory finished. "Yeah, I get it. So how are we getting there? We walk?"

"The others are bringing in the animals now. Come, I will show you."

Belegir led her to the edge of the camp. Most of the Allimir, children included, were gathered there, gazing out at the plain. Those who still had horses were holding fast to their manes; the others carried the simple riding tack of the Allimir. Glory looked, but didn't see the dead stallion's body anywhere, and made a mental note to refuse any stew she was offered this morning.

Early morning mist still hung over the grass, and the sky was the palest blue of dawn. She was warm and comfortable beneath her leather, and chilly everywhere else—later in the day, the situation would be reversed, and she'd be glad then of her sweatshirt, odd as it might look with Elizabethan S&M leather.

Helevrin and Englor stood about a hundred yards away from the camp, also facing outward toward the plains. They held their hands before them, heads bowed as if they were looking at something.

It was close to full light now, and so Glory could see—beyond the two mages, on the perfect flatness of the vast Serenthodial—scattered dots: the routed livestock of the Allimir.

"They use the Calling Tools to bring the flocks and herds back to them. It is Erchane's gift to the Allimir from ancient times, held in safekeeping by the Oracle against necessity such as this. Never did I think they would be required again."

"Good thing you lot don't throw anything out," Glory commented absently. She craned her neck, trying to see what they were doing. Just as she thought nothing was going to happen, she began to see that the dots on the horizon were moving—toward the mages.

The dogs arrived first, bounding up to the two mages, brisking and fawning, pink tongues lolling, but came away quickly as their owners whistled for them. A couple of them stopped to investigate Glory and Belegir in a quick professional way, before returning to their masters.

Next came the ponies, trotting along as briskly as if someone were rattling an invisible oat-pan. As they clustered about the mages, nuzzling and pawing the ground, the herdsmen sent the horse-dogs out with a volley of whistles. The dogs quickly bunched the horses and began moving them away from the two mages. The mounted Allimir rode up to help, cutting out mounts and bringing them back to their brethren afoot. Soon all of the herd-riders were mounted. They rode out, dogs at their heels, toward the other beasts still drifting toward the mages' call.

It was all accomplished with a minimum of fuss. Whatever else might be true of the Allimir, they weren't afraid of a little hard work.

"What happens now?" Glory asked, impressed in spite of herself.

"Ivradan will bring us horses, so that we may depart. Helevrin and Englor will Call until the herds are re-gathered. Once the oxen have returned, the wagons can move—perhaps tomorrow, as the beasts will be exhausted from their flight. And we will see what stock survives."

Belegir sighed. "I fear we have lost many to this night's work. Even if *She* has not slain them, there are many deaths that roam Serenthodial the Golden. The wolf and the lion grow fat upon our misfortune." He shook his head, rousing himself from his melancholy with a visible effort. "I shall miss Helevrin and Englor. They will go from here as soon as they can, to return to the other camps of our people. We dare not stay together—it would be too easy for *Her* to slay us all with one blow, and in these dark times that would be a perilous loss, for Helevrin's apprentice is but a child, and was to have stayed safe at the Oracle for many summers yet—and I do not know where an apprentice for Englor may be found, now that we may not approach the Oracle as we once did."

Glory was surprised to realize how much she'd miss Englor and his weird combination of pragmatism and starry-eyed hero-worship. She guessed the three of them had only gotten together to go looking for a hero. She wondered what the other two would tell the rest of the Allimir when they caught up with them.

"I'd like to take a closer look at this magic of yours," Glory said. Belegir motioned her forward.

When she reached them, Glory could see that each of the mages was holding a faceted crystal sphere. The gems glowed with the same violet light that Glory remembered from the crystal that had topped Belegir's staff.

"Where do those come from?" she asked Belegir.

The pink mage looked uncomfortable, as if she'd touched on a sensitive issue. "Erchane sends them at our need."

"Hm." Another conversational dead end. "So what else do they do?" She had a vague idea in the back of her mind that this stuff might prove useful later on—but only if she knew what it did.

"These are for Calling only. There are others for other purposes—to tell the weather, to find water, to light a fire. They are the masterworks of generations of mages, all stored up against a time of great need."

Like now.

"Don't any of them do anything useful?"

"All these things are useful," Belegir said in surprise.

"Why would someone take Erchane's gifts to make that which was not useful?"

Glory sighed. "But maybe there are some that would be *more* useful right now. Like something that could fling a lightning bolt, say."

Belegir regarded her with a mixture of distaste and admiration. "But such things would be dangerous. Their use could lead to destruction and war."

"Like you don't have that going on now," Glory muttered under her breath. She glanced sideways at the other two mages, but each seemed to be rapt in concentration on their crystals. "Oh, well. Just a thought."

"Let us go back," Belegir urged. "Ivradan will have made all ready for our journey. And we must arrive ere night falls."

Ivradan was waiting for them when they returned. Two dogs sat at his feet, pink tongues lolling happily. He had three ponies with him. Two were bridled and had thick fleece saddle-pads (Glory was relieved to see) on their backs. The third carried a wooden packsaddle, its contents an anonymous canvas-wrapped bundle, but had no bridle or leading-rein.

"These are Felba and Fimlas," Ivradan said, indicating the two riding horses. "They are brothers, and will wish to stay together. Marchiel will carry your supplies, and Kurfan will keep him honest." The dog looked up at the sound of his name. "You need carry nothing, Slayer, while Marchiel is here to do it for you."

He reached for her tote-bag, hefted it for weight, and expertly lashed it to the packhorse's load with plaited leather ropes. Glory realized she was still clutching Gordon, and reluctantly surrendered the stuffed elephant as well. Gordon looked incongruously gay perched atop the bundle on Marchiel's back.

"I will ride with you a little way," Ivradan added. "If it is permitted."

There was a pause, and Glory realized that both men were looking at her. "Oh, sure, ta very much, mate," she said quickly. It occurred to her to wonder just what Belegir had told his people. Last night he'd brought them a "hero," and today he was taking her away. But maybe the Allimir were as incurious as they were passive—Ivradan didn't ask questions, anyway.

Ivradan mounted his pony as Glory contemplated her own mount. Fimlas was a bit larger than the pony she'd ridden yesterday—probably one of the largest animals the Allimir had. It was still ludicrously under-sized for its rider—about the size of a large Shetland pony—but there was nothing to be done about it. It was this or walk. She took a firm grip on its mane and bounced up onto its back.

She was relieved to note that either Fimlas was naturally quiet, or the night's exertions had taken the kinks out of his temper. He stood steady as a rock while she settled herself, whisking his scraggly black tail meditatively.

Seeing them both mounted, Ivradan clucked to his mount and moved off, one of the dogs at his side. The other horses followed. Kurfan circled back and encouraged the packhorse with a few growls and a rush at its heels. Apparently the Allimir ponies were used to such treatment, for Marchiel only seemed to sigh, and wandered sedately after the others.

The Allimir camp was small, its wagons seeming as if they were constructed on three-quarter scale, but Glory was uncomfortably surprised to realize how exposed she felt once they'd ridden away from them. As if she'd ventured from concealment into exposure, like a cockroach wandering across a kitchen table. Her nervousness embarrassed her—it was the height of un-Vixen-ishness. Her alter ego had no nerves to speak of, and was as phlegmatic as your average granite rock. Sister Bernadette had taken care of all of the screaming and marveling required, which had been a blessing to Glory's limited acting abilities.

But this wasn't television. This was reality, and she wasn't sure how to behave.

The day brightened into full color as they rode westward, the last of the mist vanishing from the long grass. The sun turned the sky violet, then to a blazing pink behind them (she looked) and then slowly began to ripen into a deep and limitless blue. Glory was relieved to find that the thick padded fleece beneath her made riding relatively comfortable, though she expected she'd still be sore come tomorrow. They rode through scattered livestock—goats, cattle, a few loitering horses, and several of the (now) placid, plodding oxen, all moving purposefully in the direction of the encampment. The dogs whined hopefully at the sight of so many things to chase, but not receiving any encouragement from the riders, continued following in the horses' footsteps.

When they had ridden a little way, Ivradan stopped.

"Here I must leave you," Ivradan said. "There is much work to be done to repair this latest incursion, but I do not envy you your part. Each of us has a task to perform—and may Erchane's grace defend you on your journey!" Setting heels to his mount, he sent it pelting back the way they'd come, wheeling in a wide arc toward a nearby clump of sheep. His dog put on a frantic burst of speed and circled wider, barking authoritatively. Between them, dog and rider managed to get the wooly beasts moving faster and in reasonably good order. The familiar sight woke a pang of homesickness in her.

Stupid beasts. I suppose this Call of the Allimir's

needs a brain to work on, which means they'll be looking for the witless brutes until Kingdom Come, Glory thought sourly. Sheep weren't as stupid as cabbages, but just barely.

Kurfan woofed hopefully, looking after the sheep, but seemed to resign himself to the task at hand, encouraging Marchiel to close up with the two riders. Glory and Belegir rode on for a while in silence, until Glory finally broke it.

"You know I'm not a real hero," she said lamely. "You know I'll do what I can for you—but I'll need your help. You need to tell me about your world—what it's like. What I should expect. You can start with this Oracle of yours, for one. Why are we going there?"

Belegir thought carefully and hard before he answered. "The Oracle of Erchane first told us we must find a hero to save us—that was when Evesal was still alive to tend the shrine. I do not know how she survived as long as she did," he added musingly. "*She* moved quickly against any who might defy her."

Which seemed to leave Belegir and his mates right out, if truth be told.

"So this Evesal's dead now and there's nobody home. So why are we going there?" Glory asked. In her admittedly limited experience, oracles were run by collections of women in sheer draperies, who either read their prophecies out of dusty old books or made them up on the spot.

"The Oracle itself is undamaged, of course. Its magic remains. And perhaps it will explain why you are here and what we must do now," Belegir said, sounding hopeful.

Glory realized with a sudden sinking feeling that Belegir had no more idea of what to do in this situation than she did.

"And what if this Oracle of yours dummies up?" she asked.

"Do you think Erchane will withhold her grace from us?" Belegir asked, sounding so horrified that Glory hastened to assure him that no, nothing could be further from the case, of course she wouldn't. And Belegir believed her, which only made Glory want to scream louder as soon as the time for advanced screaming rolled around.

She tried a few more questions, but they all seemed to lead immediately into conversational dead ends. It wasn't that Belegir didn't want to help her in any way he could, it was just that he seemed so convinced that there was nothing he could do. Figuring out what was going on here was like trying to solve an Agatha Christie with half the pages missing, and doing the Sherlock wasn't something that Vixen would have done. Vixen never borrowed trouble—just waited for it to show up and hit it with her sword. Eventually Glory stopped prodding him.

The journey settled into a quiet rhythm—ride for an hour, walk the horses for a while, then ride again. At least the frequent dismounts kept her from stiffening up, though Glory knew she was going to be sore by tomorrow morning.

After a while she realized she was straining her ears to hear traffic noises, or the sounds of planes flying overhead, and that she wasn't going to hear either one. Except for the sound of the horses, the wind through the long grass, and the distant calls of unfamiliar birds, everything was quiet in a way that a truly inhabited place could never be. The only things in the sky were the black shapes of high-wheeling birds—hawks, she supposed, or eagles. Serenthodial stretched out around her like a sleeping golden lion, leading her eye toward a horizon as infinite as the ocean's. In the distance ahead, she could see the mountains towering skyward, their lower slopes clothed by the forest she'd come through only yesterday, though so many strange things had happened since then that it seemed a very long time ago.

At last they came to a road.

It was pounded earth, two wheel-ruts with a hummock of brittle dispirited grass running between. Its presence changed the scope of things immediately. Roads implied traffic to run on them, cities for them to run between, but this haunted land seemed to hold neither. Belegir turned his pony onto the road with a small grunt of approval.

"This will take us past Mechanayas. It is halfway to the Oracle and I believe that the well there is still good; we should stop there to eat and give the horses a longer rest."

Glory nodded without speaking.

The first sign they had of the village was the trees— orderly plantings of fruit trees, their branches full and heavy with bird-pecked autumn fruit. The ground at their roots was littered with windfalls that soured the ground, and the horses slowed, nosing among the bounty. Even Kurfan gave one of the apples an experimental bite. Glory dismounted and stood, stretching, looking around.

Beyond the orchards were a series of patchwork gardens, the earth straggly with the green leaves of plantings untended for many seasons and intermixed with the tall stalks of opportunistic weeds. The poles set in the middle of some of the gardens leaned crazily in the buckled earth. Some of the whirligigs of folded paper that had been tied there as scare-crows still dangled from them, drab and draggled by the rains.

Surrounding the garden plots were a series of low

stone walls, no more than two feet high, and as Glory's
eyes adjusted, she could see that in many places the
walls were buckled and charred. Here and there half
a brick wall stood, or some tumbled timbers, and Glory
realized that some of the "walls" were the foundations
of buildings, and that there had once been a large and
prosperous village here, now gone.

She wanted to ask where the village was, but that
would be trivial and stupid. Her eyes could tell her
where the village was. It was here, all that was left of
it. It was just that part of her hoped that by asking
the question she'd get a different answer than what she
knew to be the truth.

She didn't understand at first why so many of the
gardens had been dug up and replaced with neat
tamped mounds over which weeds and grass ran anar-
chic riot, but it was only a moment before she saw the
place where a pit had been dug and not refilled. These
were graves, all of them, mass graves, dug to house
too many dead. The Allimir of Mechanayas had been
laid to rest in their own gardens.

She left her horse to browse among the apples, and
walked through the orchard toward the village beyond.
She did not look back to see if Belegir followed. She
did not walk over the mounded gardens, or near the
last still-open grave. She had no desire to see what it
contained, nor to know why its dead remained unbur-
ied.

The sun was warm on her back, illuminating the
landscape with a shadowless noontide glare. Much of
the village had burned, it was true, but as much more
looked as if it had been simply blasted out of exist-
ence. One building was nothing more than a spray of
bricks scattered on the ground, as if some giant had
just come along and shoved it over. From what she
could see and imagine, Mechanayas looked as if it had

started life as one of those doll-sized ideal English villages that Anne-Marie liked to collect. Everything was built to Allimir scale, giving the remains of the tidy little houses around her the air of having been built for hobbits. Dead hobbits.

A sudden movement startled her, and she squealed and jerked in surprise, but it turned out to be only a lean and suspicious chicken startled into flight by her presence. The Allimir had gone to their gardens, but it seemed their livestock had been left behind, to fend for itself as best it could. Those wary and clever chickens that had survived seasons of freedom and predators still haunted their ancestral homes.

Here and there some things remained, untouched by what had slain Mechanayas. A gate in a stone wall, carved and painted blue. A tile stove, half-sunk into the earth and surrounded by poppies, with no sign of the house that should have contained it. A building's interior wall, the exposed beams shaped and polished, the small-paned window of colored glass, unbroken in its painted carven frame, casting pools of green and blue, gold and red, upon the weeds that grew up through the stones of the floor.

She kept seeing movement out of the corner of her eye, but every time she turned it was gone. Trick of the light? More chickens? Survivors? She stopped and listened, but heard nothing other than scraps of birdsong and the whistle of wind over the stone. After a pause, she walked on.

The Allimir village had been built along medieval lines, with what must once have been shops and houses set around a town commons with a well and a watering trough beside it. Unconsciously she'd expected the destruction to get worse the closer she got to the center of the village, but instead there were more partially intact houses—as if whatever had come for the villagers had worked its way inward—and the central green itself was untouched, though the grass had gone weed-choked and yellow. There was a tree growing beside the well—an enormous tree, of village smithy proportions. It looked enough like an oak to be one, and its bark, as far as she could reach, was smoothed and polished by generations of caressing hands.

Again Glory had the creepy sense of being watched and measured, but saw nothing. She certainly had nothing to fear from the Allimir, if Belegir and the others were any indication, and if there were anything in all the Land of Erchanen capable of even using harsh language in an adversarial situation, Belegir would certainly already have enlisted it in the fight to save his people.

She turned back to the well. Belegir said they'd need to water the horses here. She might as well see what kind of effort that was going to take.

To her surprise, the well was pump-driven rather than bucket-and-windlass, though if you wrestled the wooden cover off the well, you could probably get a bucket down it. She did pull the cover off before she started pumping—no point in going to all that work for foul water—but when she'd dragged the heavy lid from the wellhead and leaned in, all she could smell was moss and wet stone. She picked up an acorn from the ground and dropped it in. It fell for several seconds before she heard a faint plash.

So there was water down there, and odds were it was drinkable. Now to get it out. She turned to the pump. The handle had slipped free and was lying in the weeds. After a little trouble she located it and slipped it into place.

The rusty, iron-bound wood gritted against her hands as she worked the pump-handle up and down, wondering how long it had been since water had flowed through these underground pipes. Finally, thick black sludge began to ooze from the spout, splatting into the hollowed stone catch-trough. The bottom of the trough was covered with dried ooze, and windblown seeds had taken root only to die. In a few more generations, some chance-flung acorn would grow up through the stone, breaking it into anonymous bits and crumbling it away to sand, just as every stone and timber of this village would crumble. And then nothing would remain but the endless golden grassland and the wild herds of animals that had once been tame.

The image was eerie, apocalyptic yet strangely mesmerizing. *Not with a bang, but with a whimper, hey?*

Finally the water came, stuttering and spraying in a frigid rainbow mist from the half-clogged spout, propelled by gouts of bright clear water that even smelled cold. Glory ducked her head under it, forgetting her makeup and her public persona for one shining moment, and reveled in the shock of cold. She pumped until the trough ran over, knowing that next time— would there be a next time?—it would be that much easier to start the water coming, and then went to duck her face and head in the filled trough. No Wardrobe wrangler stood over her worrying about the safety of the precious leather costume, no Makeup artist stood ready to repaint her face while some hairdresser stood by to make her pretty for the money shot. It was just . . .

Real.

No retakes, no second chances, no script. Everything counted the first time.

When she blinked the water out of her eyes, Glory was staring at a wolf.

No, a dog. Several dogs, which had approached while she was pumping and now stood staring at her. Their leader was a huge black animal who regarded her from a sitting position, head cocked and tongue lolling. But where Kurfan and the other animals she'd seen at the caravan were sleek and happy, these animals were gaunt and watchful, obviously in business for themselves. As she stared, only slowly coming to realize how much trouble she was in, he got to his feet, lazily, and took a step forward. The others began to pace to the sides, flanking her. Glory backed up, feeling the warm stone of the wellhead at her back. She could run, but they'd pull her down. She could stand, and sooner or later they'd rush her. These dogs had been companions once. They had no fear of Man.

She wondered if she could get her sword out without looking away from the leader. "Good boy," she said in a husky whisper. He cocked his head again, listening. In a story she might be able to win him over, but he didn't look well-fed enough for that. He took another step forward, lowering into the crouch that was the prelude to a spring.

A rock whizzed by her head, striking him in front of his ear. He yelped and jumped back, turning to run as other stones flew around her, hitting the flanks and haunches of the pack with a series of audible thuds.

Glory spun around. Belegir was walking toward her, a sling in his hands, a sack of stones slung over one shoulder. As she watched he loaded his sling once more and sent a last missile flying after the retreating pack.

"Forgive me, Slayer, I should have mentioned the dogs," he said apologetically. "I did not think you would wish to sully your sword upon such unworthy prey, so I followed you."

"Damn skippy you should've mentioned the dogs, mate!" she said hotly. Her heart was hammering and her mouth was sour with fear, and beneath it all she felt a vast betrayed indignation. *"The-Allimir-are-a-peaceful-people." Yeah, right. Tell that to White Fang there.*

But a nation of farmers that couldn't even scare crows out of their fields would soon starve. Apparently the Allimir could chastise the animal kingdom—someone after all must have slaughtered whatever had been made into the pot roast she'd eaten last night—but that still didn't mean they could do much about the gods and demons that were giving them their current problems.

Seeing the pack was gone, Belegir whistled. A few minutes later Kurfan arrived, herding the horses before him. Just as well they hadn't been left to graze their fill in the orchard; they'd be colicky, or drunk, or both, and nursing a drunk horse was not Glory's idea of a good time. When they smelled the water, they hurried toward it, shouldering each other aside at the trough and blowing bubbles through the water.

Belegir looked almost guilty, as though he'd done something more than chase off a pack of dogs that were about to have her for lunch. Or maybe it was just her nerves being on edge. The sight of this place—thoroughly dead, thoroughly empty, half picked over by scavengers on two legs and four—was unsettling in the way that nothing before it had been. But it wasn't as if he'd sprung things on her. Belegir'd said they were coming here, and they'd come here. He'd already said the Allimir had been hunted from their homes. This was what it looked like. There was no point in asking by what, or who, or how. By now she'd had variations on that conversation with Belegir so many times that she could run it by herself at will.

—What happened here?

—*She* came, to wreak destruction on the Allimir.

—Why?

—Because *She* has been released.

—Who's she?

—She is the Warmother.

—Who's the Warmother?

—She is that whom Cinnas the Warkiller, greatest of the Allimir Mages, chained upon the peaks of Grey Arlinn a thousand years ago.

And round and round and round, and if she asked "how" rather than "who," she'd get to hear about how it was dark, and how She came in the night, and how the Allimir knew not the arts of war.

Glory sighed heavily. "So what's for pudding, then?"

She watched as Belegir lifted the pack from Marchiel and began to empty out supplies. She plucked Gordon and her tote-bag from the top of the pile and retreated, watching as Belegir removed the tarpaulin and stacked a series of bags and baskets on the ground beside the well, until he'd assembled a tidy little mound of picnic gear, then led the three horses around to the far side of the oak to graze. Kurfan paced around the edge of the green, sniffing and posturing, but Glory doubted the wild dogs would come back any time soon.

Glory leaned against the tree, feeling as if she ought to help, but with no idea of what to do. Belegir spread the tarp as a groundcover and opened a well-worn leather bag, from which he removed a small metal stand, a round pottery bottle with a protruding wick, and several metal hoops and stakes. Obviously the wick meant a lamp of some sort, but she couldn't see the point to the rest. It was broad day; they hardly needed light.

With the ease of long practice, Belegir assembled the object, producing a ring held by metal rods about six inches above the wick.

I've got it now.

When he turned back to the bundle of supplies,

she'd anticipated him, plucking out an irregular tin jerrycan and dipping it full of water at the trough. She handed the container to him, and was absurdly pleased to see him smile and set it carefully above the lamp. She'd figured right, then.

Belegir leaned forward and snapped his fingers. The wick burst into sudden light, settling to burn with a strong yellow flame. Glory blinked, disconcerted. She managed to forget about the magic between the times it was shoved in her face. It just didn't seem likely that people could be so ordinary and still do things like light a fire with a snap of their fingers. Being able to do something like that ought to make you different, some-how. More different than a little old man whose stron-gest resemblance was to a pink-cheeked Kewpie doll, and not Gandalf the Grey.

She sighed and shook her head. Shouldn't magic solve your problems? And if it should, why wasn't it?

"There is ale if you wish it, Slayer," Belegir said, catching her look. "I know that a great hero—"

"Button it!" Glory snapped. She closed her eyes for a moment, fighting to hold on to her temper. "See here, Belegir. I reckon we'll both get on a deal better if you don't confuse me with *her*—" God's teeth, now he had *her* talking in italics! "With, um, the Slayer, I mean. Vixen. Her. I'll do what I can, but just . . ." her furi-ous guilt evaporated, along with her point. "Don't call me a hero, hey?"

"As you wish," Belegir agreed, sounding baffled.

As the water heated he turned back to their sup-plies. Glory knelt on the sun-warmed tarp with the grace of many hours of practice at moving with five feet of live steel strapped to her back. Fortunately the costume's scabbard was hung to rock up and sideways, or wearing the sword would have been like being tied to a stake.

Lunch was cold meat pasties and apples gathered from the orchard. Having had not-much for breakfast, Glory tucked into her share with a good will. The meat was tough and stringy, as free-range protein tends to be, thickened with boiled grain instead of root vegetables, and unexpectedly filled with raisins—or something rather like raisins—as well, giving it a sweet-vinegar tang. Kurfan returned from his explorations and sat at the edge of the groundcloth, alert and watchful for scraps. Glory shied a few bits of crust his way. He snapped them gracefully out of the air and looked hopefully at her for more. Belegir tossed the dog a whole pasty, and Kurfan retreated behind the tree with his prize.

By then the water had boiled. Belegir took a brightly painted tin box from another of the ubiquitous baskets and shook some of the contents into the boiling water, then extinguished the flame beneath the pot with another snap of his fingers. When the liquid had turned peat-dark, he poured it out into a pair of wooden mugs and added several lumps of something dark and gritty-looking to both. When she sipped, Glory realized the lumps had been some kind of sugar; the tea itself was bitter, an unfamiliar mix of herbs. She only hoped that none of them had embarrassing side effects, but she'd always had the constitution of a horse. Besides, last night's dinner hadn't killed her.

John Carter of Mars never has to worry about things like this. But then, he's got the writer on his side. And you don't. Not here.

Soon enough the sun began moving visibly westward. As Belegir began to repack their supplies, Glory finally remembered her makeup. A quick check of her mirror in her bag convinced her of the need for repair. Her eyes were ringed with shadowy grey smudges where the kohl and mascara had run, and her freckles showed plainly through the pancake. She sighed, and pulled out her stuff. She might not look like a cover-model, but she could at least look like Vixen.

After all, if Belegir believed in the Slayer, then maybe the Warmother did too. Wouldn't that be a kick in the head?

By the time she was done with her repairs, the supplies were all bundled back together. She held the packhorse while Belegir built the pack into place, lashing it down firmly. As before, she tucked Gordon onto the top. The little stuffed elephant looked absurdly surreal, and once again Glory felt a pang of angry guilt. She was a Phys Ed teacher who still slept with stuffed animals—what right did she have holding out even the most tenuous sort of hope to these people? She didn't have any experience dealing with something that could whip through a village like turbocharged Black Death and peel a full-grown pony stallion like a banana. She wasn't a hero. She wasn't even a cop. She wasn't *anybody!*

Maybe this Oracle of Belegir's would see that, and send her home before she could get anyone into any trouble by believing she could help. At least she wouldn't have to *choose,* and wonder forever if she were being a coward or just a realist.

And if it says you should stay?

She shook her head. If the Oracle thought she should stay, then it wasn't much of an Oracle, that was all.

They rode away from the village. As the day wore on, she could feel a prickling on her neck and shoulders—and on her bare upper thighs and exposed and cantilevered chest—that promised a ripe sunburn tomorrow, and wished she'd thought to get out her T-shirt when they'd stopped—it would cover some of her at least. Belegir was more than usually pink as well, though his mage-robes covered all of him except his hands and feet. Soon he'd be as brown as the rest of the Allimir.

And you should have asked for a tube of sun cream before you went off on this wild goose chase. Sun cream, and a big hat, and a dozen other things these people probably didn't have. This wasn't weekend camping or a Cable TV game of Let's Pretend. It was real, no matter how much she might keep forgetting that. There was no referee to whom she could appeal for a Time Out when she didn't like the way the play was going.

And she wasn't her character. Why did she keep coming back to that, as though she were arguing against some unseen audience? God knew Vixen's was a tempting lifestyle—nobody gave you a lot of lip when you had a large sword and a bad temper and a host of spear-carriers to clean up after you—but it just wouldn't play in real life. The rules were different for heroes, and maybe that explained why there weren't any heroes anymore, except in popular fiction.

But it was tempting. Was that her problem? That she was tempted by the chance to *be* Vixen in something that passed for reality, translating every passing mood and pang of wayward conscience into backflips and sword-blows? Only she was smart enough to know it wouldn't work—and still wished it could.

But not enough to get real people hurt. *Fun's fun until people start dying.* She flashed back to the mass graves she'd seen at Mechanayas, and shuddered. Dead, all dead, and Belegir said that no one else would come to save them. The inarticulate anger she'd felt before woke again into sullen life. It wasn't *fair*, by God—the Allimir had played by all the rules of fairy tales, and by those rules they should have gotten a proper hero to sort out their mess, not a pack of apologetic refusals.

Still brooding, she rode after Belegir.

They reached Duirondel in the late afternoon. The light was golden, but the trees were casting long shadows back the way they'd come and there was already a hint of evening chill in the air. She squinted up at the sun. If they were going to reach their destination before night fell, it'd better be no more than two hours away at the outside. Reflexively, Glory touched one of the "rowan" stakes sheathed on the outsides of her thigh-high black leather boots. They were cast resin— more durable than wood and able to be lit up nicely for the money shots—and sharp, but she'd hate to try to defend herself with one. Come to that, being in a situation where she had to defend herself at all from anything other than bad press was really low on her list of fun ways to spend an afternoon.

"Are we there yet?" she called to Belegir.

"Soon, I hope," was the less than reassuring answer.

It was okay while they were still riding among the scattered birches—the road vanished beneath drifts of golden leaves, and Glory no longer knew whether they were following it or not—but when birch gave way to pine, the sun-drenched gold gave way to cool blue shadows. As soon as the sun dropped behind the Hilvorn Peaks, it would be dark. In direct sunlight, her chrome-and-black-leather costume had been almost too hot to touch, but now the metal was only barely warm, and she was starting to feel chilly again. *Freeze or fry, it's always the way.*

"Say, Belegir, what have you got round here that comes out at night? You've got sheep, you must have something that eats sheep."

"Wolves, of course, and in these dark times, dogs that have lost their masters. If it has been a long winter, sometimes bears will come down off the mountain, but only in spring, when they are hungry. The rock-cats do not bother the herds, unless they think they may take a lamb or kid easily. It is fall, so I do not think we need fear for the horses, even here, and besides, Kurfan will warn us should anything draw near."

Glory glanced over her shoulder, and saw the shadowy shape plodding along at Marchiel's heels. The dog's eyes flashed silvery-red in the dimness.

"What about dragons, then?" she asked. *Or bandits, outlaws, that kind of thing? Except I'm betting you don't have any of those here in the worker's paradise, do you? Not going by what Englor was saying earlier.*

Surprisingly, Belegir laughed.

"Slayer, dragons belong to the Age of Legend, when Cinnas walked the earth! You need not fear meeting such creatures today."

But how do you KNOW? she wondered. Helevrin had said that none of the Allimir had ever actually *seen* the monster that had driven them out of their homes and was slowly killing them, only its effects. Now she'd seen some of those effects, too, and she had to admit they were pretty daunting. But couldn't there be another explanation—or a whole collection of other explanations—than a demon out of legend? Maybe a dragon, and a few volcanoes, some plague, and . . .

You're guessing, gel. But here in the woods in the dark was no place to be asking—just in case Belegir was right, and there *was* a Warmother. But sooner or later they were going to have to have a nice long chat about *Her,* and what she was, and what she could do— why the Allimir feared her, and why this Cinnas had locked her up in the first place.

And what I can do about it. Just to add a little farce to the mix.

But maybe it IS a dragon. The thought made her feel better. A dragon was just another predator, and she'd seen today that the Allimir could fight back against predators. If she could prove to Belegir that it was just a dragon, then the Allimir could—

"Just" a dragon? Just a DRAGON? Are you listening to yourself, Gloria Emmeline McArdle?

"Yeah, right," she muttered under her breath. "A dragon. Easy money."

CHAPTER THREE:
Iron and Fire

First it was gloomy under the pines, then it was dark. Then it was *really* dark, as the last of the light faded from the sky. *We were supposed to be there by now.* They stopped to remove the reins from the riding ponies and to link the three horses together with a coil of rope taken from the pack-pony, then led them all along on foot. Belegir had taken a crystal from his pocket at the stop. It glowed with an intense purple light, enough to show them the upward-slanting track through the pines.

Enough to bring any monsters interested in a hero snack running. Glory drew her sword and walked with it in her hand, not feeling stupid about it at all. Every sound seemed unbearably, pointedly loud, from the scuffing of their steps through the leaves and twigs of the forest floor to the unearthly cries of hunting owls. Kurfan walked close at Belegir's side, ears cocked alertly.

"There," Belegir said, pointing.

Glory looked, and for a moment saw nothing. Then Belegir raised the crystal in his hand higher, illuminating a sheer wall of rock, and the pitch-dark opening of a narrow cave.

"This is it?" Glory said, torn between relief and disappointment. From the way Belegir had talked about the Oracle of Erchane, she'd expected something fancier than a hole in the wall.

"Yes. Hurry."

She needed no more encouragement. Belegir's tension was catching. Kurfan bounded ahead, disappearing through the cut in the rock. The ponies lugged forward as though they scented home and mother, breaking free of Belegir and scrambling up the last sharp incline into the cave, still roped loosely together, followed closely by Glory and Belegir.

She was relieved to see that the cave was tall enough inside that she could easily stand upright, as well as wide enough that she could shoulder past the ponies to look around. It looked pretty much like a natural cave to her, maybe the kind that had gotten a little primitive help. The walls were smooth and cool; the floor, when she scraped the leaves aside with the tip of her sword, was hard rock beneath wind-blown detritus, all illuminated by the weird black-light glow of Belegir's crystal. It seemed to go on for some distance—at least, she couldn't see the far end.

"Is this it?" she asked again. "All of it?"

Belegir chuckled, his voice sounding shaky with relief at having reached sanctuary. "Hardly—though I do not blame you for doubting, seeing us reduced to a nation of ragged wanderers as you have. But come, Slayer. Let me show you Erchane's wonders!"

He strode jauntily past her. Glory shrugged and followed, leading the string of ponies. After a few steps,

the passage was filled with the echoing clatter of
unshod hooves on stone, blotting out all other sound.

Well, I reckon they'll know we're coming.

The cave-corridor broadened, the walls becoming
vertical and even. After a few moments, she realized
she could see perfectly well, and when Belegir dropped
his crystal back into a pocket of his robe, she realized
that the light was coming from the cave itself, though
she couldn't see any light source.

Glory stopped to carefully re-sheathe her sword. It
was heavy, and there didn't seem to be any reason to
brandish it in here. Belegir obviously thought they were
safe.

She stopped. When she looked over her shoulder,
she could still see the entrance, far behind her. The
passageway ran straight as an arrow, directly into the
guts of the mountain.

"Belegir, where are we *going?*" *I'm asking questions
again. I know I'm going to regret this. But I can't help
it.*

"To the Oracle," he said, for all the world as if that
were an explanation. "Soon we will reach the Outer
Courtyard, where once all the Allimir nation came to
receive Erchane's wise counsel. We can leave the horses
there for the night at the Pilgrim's Fountain—I do not
think Erchane will mind."

"So this place is safe as houses, hey?" Glory said.
Belegir nodded. "And big, from the looks of it, I
reckon. So why didn't you just bring everybody here
when the balloon went up?"

Belegir gazed at her in polite incomprehension.

"Bring them here? For safety?" *So they wouldn't all
DIE?*

"We could not do that," he said at last.

At the look on her face he recoiled, and added
hastily, "It would not have worked, Slayer! It is true—

many of the Allimir nation could have been housed here, and *She* would not dare to approach this holy place. But they could not be fed. Evesal sent all the acolytes away when Great Drathil burned for just that reason—it was Drathil that supplied the Oracle with food. There is no food here, nor could it be brought, and stored, without making those who carried it targets for *Her* wrath."

"Hmp." The explanation sounded reasonable, not that that counted for much. "And you say she's dead now, too—so who are we going to talk to?"

"We come to speak to no one, Slayer. We have come to consult the Oracle." Belegir reached out and took the ponies' lead-rope from her slack hand, then turned and walked away.

Glory growled—not caring at the moment if she was stealing one of Vixen's lines—and followed him sullenly. *Come here to talk to somebody, only we're not going to talk to anybody. I reckon all wizards must get a course in talking in riddles along with the wand and the pointy hat.*

The corridor was like one of those M. C. Escher drawings where a bird turns into a fish by such slow stages you barely notice. As Glory followed Belegir, the hall about her slowly changed. The clatter of the horses' hooves—and of her flat-soled leather boots—was muted when the rock floor was replaced first by coarse gravel, then by fine sand: first white, then colored sand fine as sugar, poured in intricate patterns as bright and elaborate as a woven rug. Just as the floor changed, so did the walls. Decoration appeared: first simple geometric designs, then more elaborate botanical paintings augmented by carvings, as the corridor slowly widened and the ceiling rose, until without any clear sense of transition Glory found herself walking soundlessly over a floor of intricately patterned colored sand through the center of a huge hall a dozen yards wide whose walls were carved with monumental colored bas-reliefs inset with jewels.

Glory had to admit she was impressed. This was light-years more posh than a string of raggle taggle gypsy wagons-O and some smelly sheep. This was *Civilization*.

She'd dropped further and further behind Belegir, gawking at the paintings, trying to imagine living in the world that they showed. Here were the Allimir as they must have been before the disaster (whatever it was)—a gentle, happy people, as Belegir had said, and a pretty well-off lot besides. It all looked sort of high medieval, if you assumed a medieval artist who'd discovered true perspective. Everything was in scale, so they didn't look like a pack of midgets. No churches, and nothing much she recognized as religion, but everyone looked cheerful and well fed. If it was propaganda, it was still an attractive line of country. There were depictions of villages, of planting and harvest, of hunting and horse-racing, of shepherds with their flocks.

Of war.

It took her several seconds of staring at a quite nicely painted battle with banners and a lot of foot soldiers with long spears before she realized what she was looking at. Bloodshed. Battles. Conflict. Strife. Peace-breaking, in fact. And all the figures were obviously Allimir, the folks who were allegedly so clueless about this sort of thing they'd got an Aussie school-teacher to do their fighting for them.

"*Belegir!*"

He came running when she bellowed, looking frightened and out of breath, dropping the lead-rope and leaving the animals behind. She pointed accusingly at the wall with its pictures of battles.

"What is this? Is this you? You told me you and your

mates were pacifists! Englor got all queasy at the thought of fudging a traffic ticket! You weren't even willing to bully me into sticking around to help you— and now this? Looks like you can stage a good and proper barney when you want to. God's *teeth!*"

Belegir stared at the wall, where several Allimir spearmen were engaged in graphic and bloody violation of one another's civil rights and personal space.

"But that was long ago," he said weakly. "We no longer—"

Glory turned on him with a low growl, clenching her fists. If this was getting in touch with her Inner Vixen, at the moment she welcomed it. She'd been frustrated, frightened, and guilty for too long. Now she wanted to break something.

"You—told—me—you—didn't—do—things—like— that—" she growled in a low husky feline rumble, leaning over until she was staring right into his eyes. "You said you didn't know *how!*"

"I said we had forgotten the arts of war," Belegir whimpered, tears welling up in his eyes. "And we *have!* Oh, please, Slayer, do not hit me! I beg you—"

Glory straightened up with a gasp, stepping back and raising her hands to her face. Her heart hammered. The line between being a bully and an action hero was a fine one, and she was afraid she'd just crossed it. "Sorry," she muttered, stepping back further. "I'm sorry. Belegir— Oh Lord, please don't *cry*. I'm sorry I scared you. Please. But you have to explain this. I don't understand." She closed her eyes, wishing the ground would open up and swallow her, or that Erchane were a proper Goddess-sort who could rise up and smite her dead. Was this what she'd come to? Beating up on someone she was dead sure wouldn't fight back?

"If you can do this, if you have pictures of this, why aren't you. . . ?"

"These walls show stories of long ago," the Allimir mage said in a low trembling voice. "Long before Cinnas, in the morning of the world, the Time of Legend. That the pictures are true is a secret only the mages know—the people who once came through these halls saw only something they knew could not be, a nightmare to frighten children, but we who are of the Temple know the truth. It is no myth. Once this was so, as real as the wind and the sky. In the long ago, the Allimir had conquered the world, enslaved the nations until they were no more, until there was nothing in all Erchanen but the Allimir. But War was like an old love that would not be set aside, and so, in our folly, we still courted her, turning at last upon our own people to set upon them in lieu of other foes. It was an age of madness. The Allimir would have been swept from Erchane's embrace forever, swept away like the snows of winter when spring once more rules the land.

"But Cinnas came to save us. Cinnas brought peace to the Allimir, may his name be revered forever."

Belegir hung his head, as though he had told her something so shameful she'd hate him forever.

Glory looked back at the painted walls. King Arthur and the Norman Conquest, Ivanhoe and the Wars of the Roses; the sort of endless hearts in armor brawls that had been a staple of cartoons and comic books—and syndicated TV series like *TITAoVtS*—ever since people had started telling each other stories. So ordinary, so inevitable, that they were kiddie fare where she came from, instead of the stuff of repressed nightmare.

"How?" she said at last.

"He banished War from Erchanen, chaining Her upon Elboroth-Haden of the Hilvorn, once called Grey Arlinn. In relief at their deliverance, his people believed

She was gone forever, but when I began my studies in this very place, I realized that was not what Cinnas had said to the people when he descended the mountain. No magic—no ensorcelment—endures forever. Why should this of all the great magical workings of history have been different? Discovering those time-lost details became my obsession. I became distant, ungracious, even rude."

"Fancy that," Glory muttered under her breath.

"I taught myself disciplines that no mage had seen a use for in centuries. I mastered ciphers that had lain fallow since Cinnas' day. And I discovered that Cinnas' magics had indeed possessed a term. On the thousandth anniversary of her binding, the Warmother would go free of her chains unless—until—a hero bound her once again."

Belegir heaved a sigh of despair, staring at the floor. His shoulders drooped.

"I tried to warn them. But how could I, when no one, not even Cinnas in his age, had known what would happen then? And things did not stand as they did in Cinnas' day, when all the world looked to the mages for guidance and advice. Even Helevrin thought my studies had addled my mind. Englor, I know now, would have believed, but in that time he was but an apprentice, an untried lad, and I hope I would have hesitated to set mother against son so."

"Wait a minute," Glory said, grasping at the only thing in all of this she clearly understood. "Englor is Helevrin's son?"

"But of course he is," Belegir said in surprise. "He and Ivradan are brothers, and they are Helevrin's sons. Have you not remarked the close resemblance? The magery runs in only a few families among the people, though it is rare for the Oracle to choose two so closely related. Though there was the case in Sinintil's time, when the twins Menegoth and Menelor were chosen. . . ."

Belegir roused himself from the digression with an effort. "But you will not care to know about that part of our history which does not concern itself with the Warmother. As I have said, I alone had penetrated to the heart of Cinnas' riddle, and could convince no one of the truth of my discovery. And to my horror, the thousandth anniversary of our deliverance was drawing swiftly near. Barely could I nerve myself to decide to climb Elboroth-Haden, whom the ancients name Grey Arlinn, to see if in that way I could find some proof to convince my fellows that our darkest, most secret legends were truth. But the records were old, and the day I had set for my endeavor was too late. *She* rose from her chains before that day, and all the questions I had posed during my foolish years of innocence were answered in full and hideous measure."

"Um. And that was five years ago, was it?" Glory said, still staring at the murals to keep from having to face Belegir. Out of the corner of her eye, she caught the mage's nod of assent. "And no one's actually *seen* this . . . *Her*?"

"It is the only mercy," Belegir said in a low voice. "That we have been spared that."

Glory shook her head. She'd almost thought she had a notion, but whatever it was it had slipped away while she was listening to Belegir's tale. Maybe it would come back again later. And anyway, it could wait. They had this Oracle to get through beforehand.

But at least she was finally learning some facts. She wasn't sure what use they were, but facts were always nice to have. Maybe when she had enough of them she could . . . knit a tea-cozy, or something.

"Well, cheer up. You've got me, now. When *She* sees that, She oughtta wet herself laughing. C'mon."

Side by side, they walked up to the animals, and then on through the hall of the Oracle of Erchane. As they went backward through Time, the scenes of warfare gave way to depictions of the Allimir fighting against skin-clad barbarians, and then against creatures that Glory hoped were either mythical or extinct: large long-toothed spotted cats, and—yes!—dragons, or something looking a lot like them, sailing through Serenthodialian skies spraying smoking death on harried villagers below. The dragon flame had been depicted with great care, and so it was easy to see that the dragon did not actually breathe flame, but jetted a spray of venom from its mouth which burst into flame as it evaporated.

God's teeth, maybe the Allimir's problem is just a dragon after all! Great Drathil—they said—burned. And SOMETHING happened at Mechanayas. And the stallion, back at the camp . . . you wouldn't have to flay it if you sprayed it with acid—maybe old Belegir knows just what it was those things used to spit. Maybe some earthquake opened up a cave full of them. Now how, I wonder, do you take out a dragon . . . ?

She was preoccupied with her thoughts, taking little notice as they traversed the rest of the hall and passed through the great golden doors that stood open at the end of the Hall of Murals.

"Here the Oracle's domain properly begins!" Belegir announced proudly.

Roused from her dragon-slaying reverie, Glory looked around at the interior cavern. Its pale fine-grained stone walls were carved with heroic figures in deep relief, standing side-by-side in characteristic attitudes, as if caught attending the longest cocktail party ever. Band after band of these figures, their scale impossible to judge, covered the walls all the way to the distant, domed ceiling.

They'd come at least a mile, maybe more to reach this point. This was the heart of the mountain, and so she should have some sense of being planted deep in the heart of the earth, of the tons of rock suspended above her head.

She didn't. The chamber was too large. It was big enough to trick the senses, to convince her body she was outdoors.

Had this ever been an natural cave? Or was it, first to last, an engineering project that made the Great Pyramid and the Great Wall look like a game of Pick-Up Sticks? Done with magic? Done with mirrors?

She could hear the faint sound that caves made— it was like holding a seashell to your ear, only in this case the seashell was a lot bigger, and she was stand-ing inside—and, somewhere in the distance, Glory could hear the faint, definitive plashing of water. Looking down the length of the cavern, she saw a flight of steps that led up to a doll-small temple set at the end of the cavern. The structure glowed with opales-cent fire along its pillared face, and at the foot of the stairs was the source of the water music. A wide round fountain, its bowl glowing with the sun-saturated green of a butterfly's wing, splashed and rang with falling water.

She turned to say something to Belegir, but the Allimir mage was already striding toward the temple and fountain. Glory followed reluctantly. She'd expected, maybe, a touch of claustrophobia when she'd decided to go caving with Belegir. Agoraphobia had been the least of her worries.

The temple was farther than it looked, and as she trudged toward it, the whole scale of the place shifted in the weird mutable way of something without any built-in reference points. Things that she'd thought were small surged and billowed like a Disney cartoon

on acid. The doll's-house temple became enormous, its
smallness an effect of distance and her inability to put
it into perspective, then shifted again; looming and
dwindling as her mind fought to make sense of its
surroundings. The effect, while not frightening precisely, was dizzying.

Finally they were close enough to it that their own
bodies provided the perspective cue, and Glory realized why this place looked so naggingly familiar. Either
the Allimir mages had used their dimension-hopping
powers back in the Time of Legend to take in a large
number of Busby Berkeley musicals, or it was another
of those wacky trans-universal coincidences, because
the wide shallow half-moon stairs leading up to the
portico built in no Earthly style were surely designed
for bevies of sequin-clad lovelies to dance down. And
whatever they'd been carved from, they sparkled now
as if they'd been dusted with sugar.

The travelers stopped at the fountain.

"Here we will leave the animals, and go on alone,
into the Oracle's inner sanctum," Belegir told her.

"You're sure it won't mind?" Glory asked uneasily.
It had been easy to dismiss talk of the Oracle as primitive superstition on the plains above, in the daylight.
Here, in the middle of stupefying proof of Allimir
skill—at magic or engineering, it didn't really matter
when you came right down to it—it was a lot harder
to disbelieve, or to take the Oracle's power lightly.

"She who called you will hardly object to your
presence," Belegir answered with easy faith. "And we
must have answers."

Damn right, Glory thought grumblingly. She drank
from the fountain, then helped Belegir unsaddle the
packhorse, unrope the animals, and strip the other two
ponies of their remaining tack. He tossed Kurfan the
last of the cold pasties, and left the horses with a meal

of grain and some of the windfall apples gathered from the orchard at Mechanayas. Apparently the beasts were to be left to wander as they chose in the chamber, but with Kurfan to guard them, they shouldn't wander out.

He made a neat bundle of the tarp and several of the larger baskets and left it tucked against the side of the fountain. The remaining bundle—the tea-kit and a few other items—he rolled into several blankets crisscrossed with ropes, making a sort of crude back-pack.

"You ought to let me carry that," Glory said. She had her bag slung over one shoulder, and was holding Gordon.

"It is no trouble, Slayer," Belegir answered, shrugging it onto his shoulders as he straightened up. "A warrior, so say the old chronicles, does not labor like a beast of burden."

"Nice work if you can get it," Glory muttered under her breath. She was still humiliated about losing her temper with Belegir earlier. She had tarnished some heretofore-unsuspected good opinion she had held of herself, and was feeling ashamed. It wasn't a pleasant feeling, and like so many unpleasant things, could easily turn itself into anger if she let it. Anger would make her feel better, for as long as she could fool herself, only she couldn't fool herself forever, and then things would be worse.

Too bad I can't find something around here that deserves to be hit. Because when I do. . . .

The steps were harder than the whole rest of the day had been. Fine for making grand processions up and down, scaled to Allimir legs, they were hell for someone Glory's size to get up briskly. And there were a lot of them. Eventually, puffing more than a little, she got to the top.

Belegir, of course, wasn't even breathing hard.

Must be the damn corset. Has to be. If I thought I was actually going to have to be doing any dragon slaying, I'd be worried.

She looked around. This was a pillared portico suitable for the making of grand pronouncements. Near the fountain, the ponies dozed, looking bored. She could look across the square and see the ribbon-friezes of heroic-scale Allimir all marching toward the open bronze doors.

She could see something else, too. All over the enormous floor of the cavern, there were thin silvery lines, inlaid against the dark stone, that she'd crossed before without noticing. She'd thought they were just meaningless random decoration, but from here, they were more than that.

They made a map.

"Belegir?" she called, taking care this time to keep her voice soft and friendly, "Tell me what you see," she asked, pointing at the cavern floor.

He came and stood beside her, looking where she pointed. "I see a map of the world," he answered, sounding faintly puzzled. "There is another inside, in color, and I think there may still be some maps on velum here as well."

Oh.

She gazed down at the shapes laid out on the ground below—continents, oceans, which were which? She couldn't tell. But somehow seeing them did as much to make the Allimir real as this whole temple had. With every image she saw, the world became wider and more vivid, more *real.*

More dangerous.

A fantasy couldn't hurt you. In proper stories, the hero always won—and certainly Vixen came out on top in every episode of *The Incredibly True Adventures.* But Glory wasn't fool enough to imagine those rules held true for real life. She supposed that somewhere in the back of her mind, for sanity's sake, she'd been holding on to the hopeful notion that this was all some sort of role-playing, with everyone improvising their way toward a foreordained outcome that let the hero win.

But despite magic, despite long pink robes and funny-sounding names, despite weird-looking livestock and strange Oracles, there weren't any certainties. The only thing that was looking more certain with every heartbeat was that stupid unfair things could happen just as easily here as in the world she'd left.

Which meant she could die. And as far as she could tell, the Allimir were the only ones in this brave new world who'd taken an oath of pacifism.

She sighed, feeling tireder than she had a right to, and followed Belegir into the temple.

She'd expected to see a lot of pomp and circumstance—thrones and altars and whatnot—but what there was instead was a large anteroom that led immediately into a sort of hiring hall space. Here the walls were unornamented, covered with a plain coat of homely whitewash, the worn stone floor set with rows of polished wooden benches soft and smooth with age and use. At the top of the room there was a dais with two deep stone cisterns (now empty) flanking it. Obviously, everyone who entered the Oracle Temple came in here. But where did they go *from* here?

Along the sides of the room ran a series of narrow archways. Glory ducked into the nearest one and looked around. It led down a long close hallway. Along one side there were rows of small cubbies, each barely large enough to hold (as it did) a meager Allimir-sized bed.

"On his tenth birthday, every Allimir child comes here to the Oracle to drink her waters and dream of his purpose in life. So also come those troubled in spirit, or who seek counsel only the Oracle can give.

All sleep—slept—here, and took the dreams sent by the Oracle's waters," Belegir said from behind her.

"I hope you don't reckon I'm going to," Glory said dangerously. "Sleep here, I mean."

Belegir chuckled. "Of course not. We go to the living source itself."

With one last look at the series of tiny sleeping cubicles, Glory followed Belegir back out into the hall. The wall behind the dais was cleverly carved—from straight ahead it appeared solid, but in fact its face concealed a passageway . . . one wide enough, she imagined, to accommodate endless rounds of Allimir apprentices carrying the buckets needed to fill the two cisterns. She and Belegir eased through it, and found themselves in a much larger and more elaborate space, as different from the asceticism of the hiring hall as a Quaker meeting house from the Vatican.

From the central court, passages (built God knew when) led off in a dozen different directions. Though there could have been no particular need for them from a structural perspective, the courtyard space was ringed with pillared archways. The pillars were colored marble, which she was pretty sure hadn't grown down here naturally, and the floor underfoot was a mosaic done in brightly colored stones—its center another map just as Belegir had promised, a circle about five meters across, with greens and blues for water, and golds and white and greens for land, and a bright border of gems set in gold. There were ships (out of scale) on the water, and coiling sea serpents, and small golden towns set at various places on the land. The whole effect managed to transcend weird, alien, and unearthly and move right along to vulgar, garish, and over-the-top. Tastes must have changed (and improved) for the Allimir to have moved the paying customers out to the other set-up she'd seen.

"Here is where those who lived at the Oracle had their place," Belegir said wistfully. "But in the Time of Legend, it was otherwise, and in this chamber the pilgrims to the Oracle once gathered. The outer complex is a later addition, built after Cinnas' day—I could talk until the seasons changed, and not exhaust the wonders of the Oracle's building."

And it would probably be chock-full of helpful useful information, Glory reflected, if she were only the right kind of hero. But she just wasn't the anthropological ancient-cities-finding sort, who could figure out the answers to riddles from antediluvian tomb-carvings and whatnot. She wasn't really sure what sort she was, but she wasn't that. And so, things being what they were, old Belegir could natter on until Doomsday about outer complexes and carved pilasters and it wouldn't tell her a thing.

She looked around, hoping for inspiration.

"Here is the world," Belegir said, gesturing at the floor. "Serenthodial, the High Hilvorns, the Great River Baurod, the Sea Carormanda. Beyond it, the Arkarthane Pelagio, where once the finest dyestuffs in our Empire were woven, and beyond that, the Infinite Ocean which circles the world. To the West, beyond the Hilvorns, the Cold Lands: Nirahir, Kirthim, and Ithralay. Oh, Slayer, once the world was wide!"

"Until *She* came," Glory said, knowing the responses in this particular catechism.

Belegir's shoulder's slumped. "I think *She* must go among the barbarians when she turns her attentions away from us, and I shudder to think what she may do there, for surely they are as helpless as we?"

Glory frowned. She thought there must be a flaw in Belegir's reasoning, but couldn't put her finger on it, and decided to save thinking the matter through until later.

"How big is this?" she asked, gesturing at the map in the floor.

"How big?" Belegir asked blankly.

"Where are we? And where were we this morning?" She wanted to get some idea of the scale of the Allimir world, though she wasn't sure why.

"Here is the Oracle." Belegir stepped forward, and bent down to touch a pale triangle of amethyst set into the base of one of the silvery-grey Hilvorns. "Here is— *was*—Great Drathil." A gold city-shape a few fingers-widths away. That made sense; he'd said that Drathil had supplied the Oracle, so it had to be close. "This is Elboroth-Haden, once called Grey Arlinn." His finger swept upward from the gold city-shape, to a symbol in delicate chips of vivid red stone inlaid upon the flanks of another mountain.

He studied the map for long moments, lips pursed. "Here is Mechanayas. Here is Duirondel the Golden Forest. And here is where we began. The scale of the map is not exact, of course."

Less than a good handspan. Glory stared down at the map, converting the hours on horseback into a rough approximation of kilometers, and the kilometers of travel to millimeters of map, and coming up with a size for Serenthodial and the Land of Erchanen that made her blink. You could drop all of Australia into the middle of the Serenthodial without it making much of a splash.

She looked at all of the little gold crowns that had once been towns, five years ago. And now, according to Belegir, there were four hundred people left in the whole place. She shook her head, as close to panic as she'd yet gotten.

"Once the world was wide."

Yeah. And once the world WAS.

"Okay, mate," she said gruffly. "Let's move on."

᳅   ᳅   ᳅

Belegir hadn't said so right out, but Glory got the sense that back at the beginning of the Troubles, a lot of stuff had been brought here for general safekeeping, before people realized they were going to have to devote all their energy to staying alive. A lot of the siderooms that they passed were full of things stacked in the haphazard fashion of things that people hadn't had time to put away properly. As if in acknowledgement of that fact, the rooms weren't charged up with the wizard light, the way every other place she'd seen here had been. She saw their contents in shadowy glimpses as the two of them walked by, the clutter making it impossible to tell what the original use of those rooms had been.

Not that she was overfamiliar with alien oracles and their interior design at the best of times.

They were still moving in a straight line, and Glory was starting to sincerely look forward to the time that they'd stop. It'd been a long day, and a long ride, and on top of all that, she thought she'd been walking for several kilometers by now. If she'd got some kind of high-powered cannon, the kind that could throw a shell for a dozen klicks at a go, and fired it at the outer opening of the cave, back in the forest, she'd lay good money it'd come straight through here. What kind of nuts laid out an underground temple in a straight line like a runway at Sydney International?

Or (for that matter) *could*?

Educated, really adept nutcases with a strong engineering background, that was who.

And that was what was really bothering her about all this. Because they were a bunch of folk who could build something like this—who HAD built something like this, and then had been rolled out like pastry dough by a villain. . . .

Whom they expected her to put under heavy manners for them with a nice sword, a fancy costume, and some B-movie dialogue.

Her.

The final results are in and it's definite: the universe is without reason or sense.

"How very odd," Belegir said suddenly.

"Wozzer?" Glory said, startled. She dropped her totebag, her hand going to her sword in a gesture that was starting to become automatic. It wasn't as if she thought she could actually *use* it on someone in cold blood, but it certainly looked intimidating. And she could certainly give them a good discouraging whack with the flat.

"That door oughtn't be open."

As though it had grown as tired as she was, the ornament and the cyclopean scale had both dwindled slowly and unnoticeably away, until Glory and her companion now stood in a passageway little different than the one they had first entered: a bare corridor of grey rock about twelve feet in every direction. Directly ahead, the passage ended. In the end wall, three steps led up to a plain wooden door secured with a drop bar.

To the right of the steps, on the level they were on now, another wooden door—the one that bothered Belegir—stood open. Bright purple radiance, as harsh and strong as desert sunlight, illuminated the room within and spilled out into the corridor.

"What's in there?" Glory asked, drawing her sword as quietly as she could. A random thought came to her: she wondered why the scriptwriters on *TITAoVtS* had never given the thing a name, like Bonecruncher or Headknocker or something. Maybe they'd been saving it for Season Two.

"Artifacts of the Time of Legend," Belegir said.

"Great. You wait here." She set Gordon carefully

down beside her bag, and tiptoed cautiously toward the light.

Why am I doing this? she wondered in the part of her mind that was still bothering with anything beyond listening intently for sounds from up ahead. The answer was patently obvious. Because Belegir was a helpless old man. Because he was doing his best for her, and so she ought to do her best for him. Because good harmless people did not deserve to play the victim for villains and frighteners. And because she was the one with the big sword.

She got to the door and peered cautiously around the edge. If this had been an episode, she'd have done a forward roll and come up fighting, but it was a stone floor and she had no idea what the inside of the room looked like. If it was as full of junk as the others they'd passed had been, she could do more damage to herself than the villains could, assuming there were any in there.

She peeped cautiously around the edge. No sound. No movement. Just a whole room full of . . .

Armor?

And the purple light was coming from a giant neon sword that was hovering in midair.

Glory gave up on stealth, walked in flat-footed, and stared.

She realized after a moment that the sword wasn't all that giant, and it wasn't neon. But it did seem to be hovering, and it did seem to be the source of most of the light in the room. She stared at it for several seconds before she could tear her gaze away and look quickly around the rest of the room.

It looked pretty much like the Wardrobe and Props Department at *TITAoVtS:* racks of armor, racks of shields, racks of weapons. Nothing else. Nothing that looked like a threat or menace.

"Ah, Belegir? I reckon it's safe to come in," she said sheepishly. She went back to staring at the sword.

It was—radiance or no radiance—purple. No, *PURPLE*. The blade had that dull satiny sheen and pale grape color of that weird posh metal they made hypoallergenic jewelry out of. It looked sharp. She couldn't quite bring herself to touch it, even if she could have figured out how, with the thing hovering point-downward in the middle of the room eight feet off the floor. She craned her neck to look up.

The helve and quillons (she knew these terms courtesy of Bruce, the show's swordmaster, who was a real bug on all things edged and pointy) were of the same color metal as the blade, though glossier, and very fancy in a curved and scrolled fashion. Quillons and pommel were inset with large fuchsia crystals that looked just like the one that had been on Belegir's staff when he'd come to see her in Hollywood. They were the source of the light bright enough to read Bible print by. The whole effect was rather gaudy and alarming, really, but somehow Glory wasn't alarmed. It was more like she'd gotten to the money shot in the latest summer blockbuster and was marveling at the cool special effects.

"It is the Sword of Cinnas, with which he chained the Warmother and brought peace to the land," Belegir said, awestruck.

"Izzit?" Glory said, trying to sound intelligent and well-informed.

"Long has it lain dormant," Belegir said, indicating a slotted stone pedestal in the middle of the floor, directly beneath the hovering sword.

"Now at last it wakes," Glory said, trying to be helpful and enter into the spirit of things. She stared up at the sword. It was really rather pretty, in a lurid kind of way.

"Yes!" Belegir said, pleased that she understood. "The sword wakes as evil wakes, and waits for a hero to claim it."

There was a pause. Belegir was looking at her again.

"I've already got a sword," Glory said at last. *Leaving aside how I get The Sword of Cinnas to come down from there if it doesn't want to.* A glowing purple sword might be pretty, but it was also creepy. And how much of what she'd just heard was take-it-to-the-bank truth, and how much myth, wishful thinking, or just the usual game of telephone-through-the-centuries? Maybe the sword hadn't ever really belonged to Cinnas at all. And probably it wasn't waiting around for a hero, and even if it was, the smart money said it wasn't waiting around for her.

"But do you not want to . . . ?" Belegir sounded confused.

"No," Glory said decisively. "Bazza and his mates paid a lot of money for this sword," she said, wagging the one in her hand. "It's the real deal, forged and everything. The least I can do is actually hit something with it." *If it comes to that.*

"Well then." Another weird thing about the Allimir was that they never argued. God only knew how they got anything done. But Belegir simply took her at her word, and that was that. When they left the armory, Belegir pulled the door shut behind him, shutting out the violet radiance.

"Behind this door is a place which few among the Allimir have ever seen," Belegir said proudly a few moments later. "The waters of the Oracle of Erchane Herself. It is from the Well Itself that I and my co-mages journeyed across the worlds in search of aid—and found you."

Lucky mages.

He paused to set down his pack and excavate a small metal lantern from it. He opened the lantern and lit the candle within with a snap of his fingers.

"There is no magic beyond that door save what Erchane bestows, not what we choose. Stay close beside me."

"Too right." She slung her bag over her shoulder and held Gordon close.

Belegir left the pack and strode confidently up the steps to lift the bar from the door. The thought took strong possession of Glory's mind that anyone following them would only need to drop that bar into place again to put an end to anything the two of them could do to set the situation here to rights, especially if Belegir was right about not being able to use magic beyond that door. With an effort, she dismissed the notion. Who could do that? The rest of the Allimir were cream puffs and the Warmother (whether she existed or not) couldn't get in here. Who did that leave?

Belegir pushed the door open and stepped inside. Glory followed, having to duck for the first time since she'd entered the temple in order to get through the door. Suddenly she was surrounded by the suffocating dark of deep underground, and for the first time she could feel every kilo of the living rock above her pressing down. Even the wan light of Belegir's candle seemed compressed by the weight of the rock above. She drew a quick shaky breath, glancing longingly over her shoulder at the corridor outside. Belegir was going to shut the two of them in here with the dark. She just knew it.

Belegir crossed the small chamber as easily as if he were in his own living room and set the lantern into a shallow niche carved into the wall. With the new angle of the light she could see that the circular chamber was small, smaller than the corridor outside. The walls were rough and curved, resonant with age. In the center of the floor, round and smooth and still as a black mirror, was a spring, the Oracle in which Belegir placed so much faith.

Why can't we sleep outside in the hall? Why can't we leave the door open? she wanted to ask, and didn't. She wasn't going to demand that Belegir change the recipe before she found whether the cake rose. Maybe there wasn't any Oracle beyond wishful thinking. But she owed the business a fair test, like it or not.

Belegir came back inside carrying the bedroll in his arms. He set it down, and then, just as she'd dreaded, pulled the door shut. The darkness seemed to rush in, pressing against her with a soft dry weight.

But once Glory got past the first sharp clutch of unease, she found the darkness's weight almost soothing, like a mother's hug. This was strange and just a little weird, but she felt the deep conviction, too, that nothing bad could happen to her here. She had the sensation of being safe, protected, watched out for in a way that people left behind with childhood. Slowly she felt herself relax, and as the tension drained from her body, exhaustion seeped in to take its place. She took a couple of steps back and leaned against the wall (and her sword), feeling things she'd been too keyed up to feel in hours. Her shoulders were hot and raw with sunburn, making the rock feel colder and rougher than it was. Her feet hurt. Everything under the corset itched, making her long to get it off and have a good scratch.

First things first. She set down Gordon and her bag, then unhooked the sword and sheath from her costume—an operation that required a person to be only slightly double-jointed, but she was feeling too lazy to go about the operation in the proper fashion.

As she struggled with her armor, Belegir moved

around the edge of the room, lighting fat white candles from a splinter of wood he'd lit at his lantern. Once several of the candles were lit, the little chamber was surprisingly bright.

"Here we will spend the night, drink the oracular waters, and take what counsel Erchane sends us," Belegir announced. He unrolled the pack and separated out the blankets: two for each of them. Well, she'd slept rougher. After today's hike, Glory felt she could sleep on the bare stone as comfortably as if it were an innerspring mattress. She spread the blankets out and sat down on them, pulling off her thigh-high boots and wiggling her toes with relief. A quick rummage through her purse found her enough pins to get her hair up off her shoulders, and then she pulled on the big logo T-shirt and proceeded with the delicate business of getting her costume off beneath it.

The corset came away from her skin with a sucking sound—it was lined in buckram, and they usually replaced the lining every week or so, or the thing went higher than roadkill in August—and she took a deep grateful breath. Then she squirmed out of the chafing leather panties and into her jeans, and dragged off the double bracers (she still couldn't bring herself to vandalize them, not quite), piling the stiff damp costume elements against the wall.

Then she rooted around in her purse for a hairbrush, tucked her legs under her, took down her hair, and began to brush it. She probably ought to braid it, if there were going to be further adventures, and elegance be damned.

But maybe there wouldn't be. Hadn't Belegir said that the Oracle might send her home?

This time tomorrow I could be home in Melbourne. Or at least in a hotel room somewhere in America.

It was an unsettling thought. She ought to have

been uncomplicatedly delighted by it, but oddly, she wasn't.

If I leave, I go knowing Belegir and all his mates're going to die.

But it wouldn't be her choice, now, would it? It'd be the Oracle's choice.

Did that make things better—or worse?

Daft cow brought me here in the first place. S'her problem, innit?

No. Now that Glory knew about the situation, it was her problem, too, in some fashion she hadn't quite worked out yet.

She glanced over at the pool, and blinked to see Belegir scooping water out of it into his tea-bottle in a rather cavalier fashion. The spirit-stove was already assembled and lit, the tea-things laid out around it. She'd thought there'd be more ceremony and reverence somehow, if this place was as important to the Allimir as Belegir had let on. Her stomach rumbled loudly, reminding her that it had been a long time since a small lunch, and a bit of something would be nice.

"A little tea and fruitcake to refresh us," Belegir said, smiling, "and then we will drink from the Oracle and dream her counsel."

"Happy days," Glory said. She pulled her henna-enhanced mane into a thick braid and tied off the end with a scrap of ribbon, then picked up Gordon and cuddled the stuffed blue elephant protectively. Vixen had Sister Bernadette, the Fighting Nun. Glory had Gordon.

The tea was thick and sweet, a different thing entirely than what they'd drunk at noon, and the fruit-cake was exactly that—cakes of dried fruit, mashed together with honey. Her head rang with sugar overload, but at least she wasn't hungry anymore.

"Belegir," Glory said impulsively, "what do you reckon will happen?"

"Whatever happens, it will be Erchane's will," the Allimir mage said firmly.

Glory bit her lip. She hated to ask the inevitable follow-up question—she *liked* Belegir—but she needed to know.

"And the rest of it? The reason I'm here? That, too?"

Belegir smiled sadly. "Erchane is not kind, though She is just. Her face is both dark and bright—ask the farmer who has lost his crop to drought or storm, his flock to wolf or lion. Ask the mother who has lost her firstborn to fever. Life feeds life. That is Erchane's way. But it is also the way of Life to struggle to live, and so we must. We are Her children, no less than the wolf and the storm. She favors none above the other. The beasts have fang and claw—the Allimir have magic, and the knowledge of Erchane's will. She will help us, if we will help ourselves."

Which seems to bring it right back around to you, gel.

"But wouldn't the Warmother be sort of against Erchane's will?" Glory asked, floundering through unfamiliar epistemological territory. Either chaining *Her* up or letting *Her* loose would have to be. Assuming, of course, *She* existed. That was the real question, now, wasn't it?

Belegir shook his head, not smiling now. "Perhaps a Great Mage could answer such a question, but there has been no such since Cinnas died. You ask questions no one thought to ask in all our long golden years of peace. And now there is no one left to ask them."

"Well, maybe we can find some answers anyway," Glory said with a defeated sigh. *Why do I keep trying to have these conversations?*

Belegir tucked the tea-things away again—she'd been

sure, for one apprehensive moment, that he'd been
going to wash them out in the spring, but apparently,
spiritual informality didn't extend that far—and then
circled the cavern again, dousing all the candles except
for the small glass lantern. When he came back to the
edge of the pool, he was holding a footed cup in his
hands.

It was most of a meter high. The bowl was of bone,
dark gold with age, the stem and foot of some darker
material, with the sheen of oiled and polished wood.
Belegir plunged it into the spring, submerging it completely, and then held it out to her.

Glory took it reluctantly. She'd seen a lot of magic
since she'd come here, but this was the first time she'd
been called upon to drink any.

Assuming, of course, that this Oracle business wasn't
all humbug and social engineering.

Whether it was or not, the water itself was pure and
numbingly cold, chilling her all the way down to the
pit of her stomach. She emptied the cup and returned
it to Belegir, who dipped it full again and drank, then
returned it to its niche and came back to his bedroll
carrying the lantern.

"Are you ready?" he asked, lying down.

"I reckon," Glory muttered, trying not to sound as
uncertain as she felt. She pulled out her sweatshirt and
struggled into it. Might as well be warm.

Belegir hooded the lantern, and the darkness fell like
a hammer. In the dark, Glory squirmed out of her jeans
and rolled them up into a pillow, then insinuated
herself between the two blankets, clutching Gordon to
her chest.

I'm not going to be able to sleep, she thought.

And slept.

CHAPTER FOUR:
Blood and Gold

It was the Duchess's castle in the North—many a work of fell sorcery had been accomplished behind its stark stone walls, with no one living to tell the tale. Vixen the Red, Scourge of the Night, Harrower of Hell, Doomslayer, had been here many a time before, and each time barely escaped, with Hell's own hounds snapping at her booted heels. Even the bravest freebooter would have thought hard before coming back, but Vixen had no choice. The two people she cared most about in the world—her doughty sidekick, Sister Bernadette, and Queen Gloriana's trusted adventurer-spy, the playwright Kit Marlowe—were in danger. She had to save them.

With the supernatural grace of her ninja training, Vixen scaled Castle Boleskine's outer wall. The Duchess trusted too much in the castle's terrible (and well-founded) reputation among the local peasants to bother with a regular guard other than the fierce, half-demon dogs that had the free run of the grounds after sunset.

With lithe pantherine grace Vixen sprang to the greensward below. Her sword left its scabbard in a rasping hiss and her red lips drew back in a feral smile as she heard the howl of the dogs in the distance. A little warm-up before the main event, when she would put an end to the Duchess of Darkness for once and all.

It's amazing what a little black makeup and some post-production CGI can do to tart up a Rottweiler, Vixen the Slayer thought happily.

The interior of the castle was oddly deserted. Torches burned with a weird green light, and for once the floor was blessedly free of camera tracks and electrical cables. She knew the Duchess was waiting for her somewhere up ahead, and she had to get there. If she didn't hit her marks in time, Megan would be furious with her. . . .

Something's not right.

Vixen stopped, shaking her head in confusion. What could be wrong? She was Vixen the Red, slayer of evil and all around badass. Somewhere up ahead was Lilith Kane, the Duchess of Darkness, her sworn enemy. She hefted her sword and strode on.

The Duchess was waiting for Vixen in Boleskine's Star Chamber. The floor was composed of a single slab of meteoric iron, inlaid with a Greater Seal of Solomon and edged in Cabalistic sigils shaped and quenched in human blood. The room was hung with draperies in glowing garnet velvet, and in the center of the demonic hexagram stood the Duchess of Darkness herself, a fragile-seeming blonde in a sweeping satin gown the color of freshly spilled blood. At her side, a dark shadow to her Satanic flame, stood the reptilian Fra Diavolo, the evil Jesuit who served her nefarious ends.

"Welcome, Koroshiya. How delightful that you have joined us at last. Shall I introduce you to our other guests? But I forget—you won't need any introduction. You're among friends here—old friends," the Duchess of Darkness purred throatily.

Vixen looked around. Her friends were chained against the velvet-covered walls. Plump and perky Sister Bernadette, in her short-skirted brown nun's habit and tights—Sister B's eyes went wide when she saw Vixen, as if she wished to shout a warning but didn't dare.

Beside Bernie was the tall and slender Marlowe—Wardrobe had only been able to give him one costume change for his episode, but the teal-blue velvet doublet (re-cut from one of the ladies-in-waiting's dresses from the series premier) showed off his craggy red-headed good looks to perfection. She did wish they hadn't had to kill him off at the end of his episode, but since he'd only been dragged off to Hell by demons, there was always hope.

"Undoubtedly, you will wish to know my plan," Lilith Kane said, stepping forward into her key-light. "Behold!" she said, with a sweeping gesture.

Fra Diavolo scuttled downstage, the skirts of his black soutane swishing, to fling back the curtain at the far side of the room. Lying on a tilted table, wearing a brief white shift and nothing else, was another Vixen, identical in every respect to the original but seemingly asleep. Startled, Vixen looked down to make sure she was still her.

The Duchess laughed, a pealing laugh like silvery bells. "Surprised? I sent to Cathay for the most perfect mandrake, and from it and a drop of your blood I had the foresight to save from our last adventure I

had my alchemists grow a homunculus indistinguishable from you in every degree. Soon I shall give it life,
and send it forth in the world in your place, where it
will undo all the good you have done in your short life
and make the name of the Slayer anathema throughout Merrie England! Only two people could possibly
see through this masquerade, and so I had them
brought here, where their blood will give my poppet
life—and seal the covenant of your doom and everlast-
ing disgrace!"

There was a pause.

"Oh, Jesus," Sister Bernadette muttered, sliding her
hands out of the manacles.

"Line!" Marlowe shouted, looking behind Vixen.

"Effing—goddamned—amateurs!" the Duchess
shouted, dropping the posh pear-shaped tones and
turning away. "Christ on toast, girlie, when I was at
Southland, your size-eighteen ass would have been out
the gate the second time you blew your line that way."

"Hey, Zorro, you just hit 'em with your sword, right?
I mean, it's not like they should expect you to *talk*,
too—"

Vixen whirled. Standing behind her was Count
Wolfgang von Blitzkrieg, Hentzau's ambassador to the
Court of Queen Elizabeth, and former Eurotrash
underwear model. He wove drunkenly toward her,
leering sloppily.

"Leave her alone," Julie Sluice said. Vixen's former
Olympic teammate was wearing her selkie costume
from Episode 18, and the silver makeup glistened in
the torchlight. "It isn't her fault she isn't any good.
When she was on the team with me in Seoul, she
always did her best. It wasn't much of a best, but . . ."

"Time is money here," Sister Bernadette said, walking forward. "How hard can it be to say 'Come,
camrado, evil wakes' or whatever it is this week? For

heaven's sake, Vixen, you've said it a hundred times. Just tell her she'll never get away with it, and—"

"Stop it!" Glory shouted. She threw her sword down on the stones, where it clattered ringingly. "I can't do this without a script! I don't know what to do! I'm not Vixen—I'm not even really an actress!"

"Well, we all knew *that,* didn't we, sweetie?" Lilith Kane vamped maliciously. She turned and began to walk briskly away, toward the back of the Star Chamber.

Glory followed her. She was angry enough to want to shake some manners into Miss High-and-Mighty Romy I-Was-A-Star-Before-You-Were-Born Blackburn, and somewhere deep inside she figured that Romy might know what was going on. The Duchess always knew what was going on—she was the one plotting all the plots, after all.

But somehow Glory didn't seem to be able to get any closer to her. She went from a walk to a run, from baffled anger to red, murderous fury, until all she could think of was getting that snooty bitch's lily-white throat between her fingers. She ran, and somehow never reached the back wall of the set, and Lilith floated on ahead, tauntingly just out of reach, her long blond hair (a wig, certainly, Romy's hair was nothing like that long) shimmering down her tight-laced red satin back beneath her lace-edged Elizabethan headpiece.

And then Glory lunged forward and grabbed a fistful of hair, and miracle of miracles, the wig held, and she snapped the Duchess back toward her like a bimbo yo-yo, panting with victory and rage.

She spun Romy around, and realized, to her horror, that the Duchess was *tearing,* that Lilith Kane was coming apart like a weird rubber disguise from which the contents had suddenly been removed. Suddenly Glory was alone, holding an empty dress, and the lights were going out.

"Hello?" Glory said. Her voice sounded small and frightened.

"I am the Dreamer of Worlds."

The voice seemed to come from all around her, soft yet definite. With each syllable, the world around Glory took on form, until she could see once more. She knew now that what had come before had been a dream, and that while this, too, was a dream, it was a dream of a wholly different sort—a *real* dream, as opposed to her mind's hermetic churning of memories and fears.

She was surrounded by stars. Beneath her feet, there was a softly glowing crystal plate a good hundred meters in diameter through which she could see more stars, though more dimly. She stood in its center, and so need have no fear of falling off, which was a good thing, because there were stars below as well as stars above, stars a thousand times brighter than anything she'd ever seen, even looking up at the sky last night from the Allimir encampment. So bright they shone in colors, unwinking and unwavering, stars all the way down to the edge of the crystal horizon and stars beyond.

There was no one else in sight.

"Ah . . . hello?" Glory said again.

"I have come to test humanity for its worthiness to be admitted into the Universal Dream," the disembodied voice said. It was cool and sexless—Glory thought of it as being female without being able to quite put her finger on any actual reason for why she thought that. Probably it reminded her a bit of a dental receptionist she'd used to know.

Glory was pleased at how well she was taking all this, all in all. It helped that she was quite certain she was asleep. On the other hand (as she belatedly remembered) she *was* supposed to be having an oracular dream just now.

"Erm, excuse me, but are you the, um, Oracle of Erchane?" she asked.

"I am the Dreamer of Worlds. I have come to test humanity for its worthiness to be admitted into the Universal Dream. This is your test."

"This here? Doesn't seem like much. Or what you did to the Allimir? Them having to go looking for a hero is a test for ME?" The anger that she'd felt at the dream-Romy, suicidal though it might be in this situation, came seeping back, and Glory wished she still had her sword.

"If not the Allimir, it would have been some other. These misfortunes I do not cause, nor do I need to. Hear me now if you would save the Allimir people and your own," the cool dispassionate voice commanded.

"I am the Dreamer of Worlds, and I have come to test humanity for its worthiness to be admitted into the Universal Dream. Long have I considered the case of Earth. Until I have judged humanity worthy—or otherwise—the magic of Earth is withheld from your mages; your creatures of magic are absent from your sight. Magic and creatures of magic live now only in the imagination of your peoples, but should you fail my tests, you will be denied the Universal Dream forever, and even that tiny blessing will be lost to you. You, Gloria Emmeline McArdle, are the last I will take from your world to test. Know that all before you have failed."

"Well, that's comforting, innit?" Glory muttered to herself. She looked all around, but couldn't find any particular thing that looked like a Dreamer of Worlds to glare at. "So tell me why I care about this in particular, why don't you?"

"Is it possible you do not fully understand?" the Dreamer of Worlds asked itself. *"I will explain. Unless humanity passes this test, Earth will be sealed off*

forever from contact with all other races of the Dream—as an evolutionary dead end. All magic will be removed from Earth, and through that loss, your world and your people will dwindle away into extinction, like all failed experiments of the Master Dreamer. So choose well what you do here, Gloria McArdle."

"Wait!" Glory yelped. "You can't mean that the whole future of humanity depends on what I do here! That's stupid! What's the test? How do I pass? How do I get HOME? Come back here, you stupid pommy git!"

But there was no answer, only the slow inclination of the crystal disk beneath her feet, until she was first sliding, then falling helplessly into the sharp and merciless stars.

She floundered awake struggling and swearing, but only when she hit her head—*hard*—on the wall beside her did the real world of the Oracle's cavern separate itself from the terrifying fall of her dream. She sat up, running her hands over skin still sticky and clogged with the remains of yesterday's makeup. *Should have had a wash in the fountain outside when you had a chance,* she told herself wisely. Surreptitiously, she pulled up a corner of her T-shirt and scrubbed at her face, feeling tidier once she was done.

On the other side of the cavern there was sudden light as Belegir opened the lantern and the candle's flame rushed into light once more.

"Slayer?" he said, sounding much like any man awakened abruptly by a bellowing female.

"Okay. S'okay. I had a dream, I reckon." She rubbed her eyes, testing the memory of the dream the way you might probe a sore tooth. She'd dreamed she was standing on a dinner plate in the middle of the universe, while some invisible ABC Received type told her that the whole human race was going to live or die based on what she did here on the windy plains of Serenthodial.

Balls.

Just what *had* been in that tea she'd drunk last night, anyway? She sighed and stretched, trying to work out the kinks that came of sleeping rough, from her body if not from her mind.

"I, too, dreamed." Belegir's voice was low. "And lo, it is morning." From the sound of things, he hadn't had a much better time of it than she had.

She kilted her blanket carefully around her waist, grabbed her jeans, and groped to her feet, feeling every muscle cry out in protest. Feeling her way over to the door, she pushed it open. It swung outward, letting the pale rosy illumination of the corridor fill the room. She ducked through the doorway and stepped down into the corridor. The smooth stone was cold beneath her bare feet. She stepped out of Belegir's line of sight and dropped the blanket, stepping into her jeans and zipping them up tight. Dressed, or at least covered, she pulled off the sweatshirt and knotted it around her waist, then began her usual morning warmup: a series of kicks, stretches, and backbends, all the while trying to get her mind to settle as well.

Kick. Kick. Step. Lunge. Turn. Bend. Her sunburn reminded her of its presence every time she flexed.

Her dream couldn't have been a true dream. Not the way Belegir understood the notion. In the first place, it was too stupid.

Kick. Bend. Turn. Twist. Reach. Twist. Bend. Kick.

In the second place, it was about Earth, and it was the Allimir who were the ones who were in trouble.

Kick. Turn. Better now. She was feeling warmed up. She fell slowly forward onto her hands, then up into a handstand—slow, still, slow—then over into a slow backflip and up. She felt a little residual stiffness, but not too much, and a longer workout should eliminate that as well.

As for the dream, it was either a really compelling nightmare, a drug-induced hallucination (just what *had* been in that nightcap Belegir had so thoughtfully brewed?), or an attempt of the Warmother to undermine her confidence, Glory was almost sure. Because it just didn't make sense that the fate of Earth should rest on something Glory did here, particularly when she wasn't quite sure what that might be. You couldn't pass a test when you didn't know what the test was.

Right?

Right.

Therefore, there was no test.

She was about ready to go back inside when Belegir came out, the rest of his belongings in a neat bundle.

"We can make tea at the Pilgrim's Fountain," he said, sounding like he was hedging his bets somehow. "And make the animals ready for the journey home."

"Sure," Glory said dubiously. She'd thought there'd be more to this Oracle business than this—like maybe some answers—but it didn't seem like there were going to be any. And—it belatedly occurred to Glory—she was still here.

She didn't know what that meant, and from his face, Belegir was in no mood to be asked. She went back inside the wellspring chamber. Her things were waiting where she'd left them, but she really couldn't face the thought of getting back into the armor right now. Not without breakfast, or some of that ale that Belegir had mentioned yesterday. She shrugged, and spread out the blanket she was carrying. With a few deft motions, she folded boots, corset, bracers, slops, and sword into the blanket and rolled it up tight. It would make an awkward bundle, but not as bad as wearing it. When she'd made as neat a bundle as she could manage, she knelt by the oracular pool and quickly washed her face. She felt a faint twinge of desecration at doing so, but she really wanted to get the last of the makeup off from last night and she still felt slightly cheated by the bizarre nature of her dream. Scrubbing her face dry on her T-shirt, she scooped up several palmsful of the icy water, drank, and got to her feet. She tucked Gordon carefully into her tote-bag this time, and slung it across her shoulder before picking up her bundle. Her sneakers were in her bag, but she decided not to bother with them; the temple floor was as smooth as linoleum from here to the fountain.

Belegir was waiting patiently for her outside. She didn't know what he'd dreamed, but whatever it was, it seemed he'd taken it to heart. The hopeful optimism of yesterday was gone. Belegir had the look now of a man doing nothing but going through the motions. She guessed neither of them had dreamed anything particularly useful.

Her stomach rumbled, reminding her to worry about that after breakfast. She padded after Belegir in silence, back through the jeweled labyrinth that was the Oracle of Erchane.

But when they came out on the portico at the top of the steps in the large open cavern, there were no animals gathered around the fountain. Not Kurfan. Not the three ponies. If not for the piles of droppings, and the bundles of her and Belegir's remaining provisions, there'd be no sign the animals ever had been here, either.

"This is bad," Glory said aloud. Well-worked animals simply didn't go for a wander in the middle of the night, not with water and feed available—and wasn't Kurfan's job to keep the beasts from straying?

"But what can have happened?" Belegir asked blankly.

"Trouble happened," Glory said patiently. Her hard-won American accent welled up through her voice like underground water through the rock, turning it hard and edgy. Trouble. And since that was the case, the worst thing they could do was go charging right off into it. "So be a good mage and run and get breakfast started while I get dressed. I'm not chasing horses on an empty stomach."

Belegir stared at her for a moment and began to shuffle slowly down the stairs. Glory retreated behind the pillars to strip.

She wasn't really thinking past the moment, not in so many words, precisely, but if she had been, she would have been thinking about getting the Allimir artisans to run her up a slightly more practical set of armor. Something she could still do all her backflips and walkovers in, and that might have a fighting chance of . . . something . . . but there her imagination would have faltered, because she wasn't quite sure what sort of problem she was facing, beyond the obvious (and now apparently obsolete) one of a day's horseback ride in a corset and black leather hot-pants and thigh-high boots.

So far, she had addressed the problems as they had been presented to her, and not given up. There wasn't much more than that she could do. She knew what her ultimate goal must be, but did not have even the faintest notion of how to accomplish it, or if that accomplishment were even possible. Any time she tried to step back mentally and look at the larger picture, she simply found it impossible. The situation she was in was too stupefyingly improbable to deal with in any other fashion than one step at a time.

So she would. First, she'd get dressed. Slops and corset, boots and bracers, a big sword and a heavy layer of makeup, and Vixen the Slayer was ready to ride again. She tucked her civilian clothes away in her bag, tucked Gordon carefully into the top, and skipped down the steps, braid bouncing against her back.

Belegir was waiting for the tea to boil. Without comment, he handed her a large leather mug. Without comment, Glory drained it, letting the thick chewy high-octane Allimir ale blow away the last of the cobwebs. When the mug was empty she scooped it full again from the fountain and carried that over to sit beside Belegir.

"So. What d'you reckon happened to the brumbies?" she asked companionably.

"I don't know," Belegir said miserably.

"Your world," Glory pointed out with judicious fairmindedness. "What *didn't* happen to them?"

Belegir sighed, as though he were sick of answering stupid questions but couldn't think of a polite way out of it. "They did not wander further into the temple. They did not simply vanish. They did not wander back out into the forest of their own will and choice."

"And nothing bad came in and took them, because it couldn't," Glory said. "And it wasn't just some other band of Allimir, because why would they take the animals and leave the stuff?"

Belegir regarded her with grudging admiration. "And so it is something else. What?"

"We go find out." She took a sip of her water and wished for a hot breakfast, but at least there *was* breakfast—stale bread and apples and some dried fruit, but it filled the belly. From the look of things, they'd better find their way back to the *vardos* pretty soon though, or one of the two of them was going to have to develop hunting skills.

Belegir packed up everything once breakfast was done and looked at Glory. He was waiting for her to make a decision, she realized, and oddly enough, for once the thought didn't frighten her into a blue fit.

"We leave all this stuff here. Either we can come back for it, or we can't," she said with a fatalistic shrug. "Depends on what's out there."

Belegir nodded, grimly. She tucked her bag beside his baskets, and the two of them walked out of the Oracle's temple.

Almost immediately she could see the speck of daylight that indicated the cave entrance. The passage was empty. There was no sign of the animals. The sugar-fine sand underfoot was disturbed, but it didn't hold tracks well enough to tell her if something other than three ponies and a dog had crossed it recently.

This time she wasn't distracted by the murals and their teasing promise of answers to the Allimir riddle. There wouldn't be any more answer there today than there had been last night, only more questions. She concentrated on walking the stiffness out of her legs and back that had come from a long day's ride and a night of sleeping hard, stopping every ten minutes or so for some deep bends and stretches. Fortunately, the Vixen suit had always been less armor than costume, cut and gusseted to allow her the gymnastic moves that passed for characterization.

The corridor was shorter than she remembered it being. As the two of them got closer to daylight, everything about the Oracle's temple seemed to recede into the unreality of a dream, as if it hadn't quite happened, and only this was real. Glory was surprised to see that it was only an hour or so past dawn. The day seemed as if it had already been so full that it should be later than that.

She stepped cautiously out of the cave, Belegir close behind her. For a moment she saw nothing, then a flurry of movement at the foot of the steep spur-track they'd climbed last night in the dark caught her eye. Fat carrion-birds, disturbed by her sudden appearance, flapped awkwardly away from their feast, only to waddle back to it when she made no further move.

Something out there was dead, and that needed investigating.

"Stay here," Glory said in a low voice. She drew her sword.

Getting down the path was a more difficult proposition than getting up it had been, and she made it to the bottom in a controlled slide. Waving her sword like a giant steel flyswatter, she shooed the big black birds away from the body. They went, grudgingly, swearing and grumbling, eager to return.

It was—it had been—a dog.

Something had torn off its head.

Glory felt foolish angry tears prickle in the back of her eyes and fiercely willed them away. Not here. Not now. She prodded the headless body with the tip of her sword, trying to figure out what this meant. The beastie hadn't died of natural causes, or even normal ones, lacking a head as it did, unless there was something in these woods big enough to bite it off, and nothing like that had figured in Belegir's catalogue of predators of the night before. Was this Kurfan? There wasn't enough of the body left to be sure. The dirt was churned up, the earth scored by claws. She looked around, slowly, and barely choked back a scream.

It *had* been Kurfan. The thing that had torn the dog's head off had wedged it onto the stump of a branch. Birds had pecked out his eyes, and insects were swarming all over the head, blackening the dangling pink tongue and making the pale fur shimmer with their crawling.

Something that *thought* had done this. Something with *hands*.

She turned away and all of her breakfast came boiling up from her stomach in a rush. She bent forward and threw up.

"Slayer!"

Belegir's terrified shout interrupted her misery. Coughing and spitting, she turned around, trying not to see the impaled head as she did.

Something had come out of the forest. A monster-thing, covered in black fur but wearing clothes; its back hunched as if it were an effort for it to stand upright. It looked from Glory to Belegir, and in that flat amber gaze she caught the echo of the black wolf-dog's assessment in the village yesterday: *is this prey? Is this FOOD?*

And she knew what Kurfan had died trying to kill.

It was poised halfway between her and Belegir. She raised her sword. But it ignored her, turning toward Belegir, stalking him like a cat.

"Belegir—RUN!" she bawled at the top of her lungs.

But Belegir stood frozen. From fear, or because he would not lead the monster into the Oracle's temple, Glory didn't know. She only knew she had to get to Belegir before the monster did.

She reached the top of the spur-trail about the time the monster did. It was huge—a good foot taller than she was, outweighing her by at least twenty stone.

"Back off!" Glory shouted, and swung her sword as hard as she could. The flat of the blade connected with the monster's stomach with a resounding slap, and it backed up in surprise, giving her the space to step in front of it.

It bared its teeth and growled, releasing a scent like ancient sun-ripened garbage, and Glory realized with a thrill of frightened self-preservation that it *wasn't* going to back off, not for long. This wasn't something she could rout as easily as she could a flock of carrion-crows. She was going to have to kill it.

And there was no script in place that awarded her a guaranteed and bloodless victory.

It swatted at her and she ducked, but she wasn't sure of the countermove. This fight hadn't been choreographed in advance, so if the monster left her an opening, she didn't know how to take it. She was fighting on a steep hillside covered with slippery pine needles, and if she tried to decoy the monster to a better killing ground, there was no guarantee it would follow. It wanted Belegir more than it wanted her, or at least it seemed to.

Then she stopped thinking about things that didn't immediately matter, because it struck her a glancing blow on the shoulder, leaving deep bruising gouges down her left arm and refining all her desires down to one: to kill this thing the way it'd killed her dog.

It wasn't nearly that easy. But she did her very best. She was actually fairly good with a broadsword—and it was a real sword, forged and tempered—for the show she'd needed to be able to lift it and swing it with ease, so Bruce had taught her some katas, or whatever they were called. She knew the moves.

But the sword wasn't sharp. Why should it be, when it would never have to cut anything? And strong enough to put on a show was a far piece from being strong enough to do lethal damage with a dull piece of metal. She hurt the monster, bloodied it, did a certain amount of damage.

But not enough—and it didn't take the creature long to realize that she couldn't. It reached out, grabbing her blade in one enormous hand and squeezing until its own blood flowed between its fingers. Immobilizing the blade.

And then it hit her with its other hand.

She didn't lose consciousness. She felt a jarring shock—no pain, not then—and a sort of discontinuity, a sense of distraction as she rolled down the hillside and crashed to the bottom, lying stunned for a moment, unable to remember who she was and what she'd been doing a moment before. There was a ringing in her ears, and beyond it she could hear nothing.

When she tried to get to her feet she fell, and so she crawled, knowing she had to be somewhere other than where she was. A rush of heat roared through her body, centered in her face. Fresh sweat oozed suddenly from her skin, running into her eyes, and then the pain came, pounding hotly in time with her heartbeat, but she was already climbing back up the side of the hill.

The monster was leaning over Belegir. Her sword was lying on the ground behind it, the monster's bloody hand-print halfway up the blade.

She picked it up. She didn't think. She stepped back and took a stance, swinging the blade back over her shoulder. It wasn't a swordsman's stance, but something from the long ago summers of her life. And then she brought her bat forward, using the edge, not the flat, driving an imaginary ball past the wicket, driving the thin edge of metal into the vulnerable place where the skull met the spine in anything that walked upright, using all her anger, all her fear.

There was a crunch.

In the end, the sword in her hands was no more and no less than a long steel club. And that was enough.

The monster fell forward onto Belegir. Glory dropped the sword and grabbed the creature, dragging it off. The fur against her fingers was greasy and coarse, undeniably the creature's hairy skin, and revulsion filled her. Pain thrilled through her arm and back as though there were wires under her skin and someone was pulling on them. The monster's yellow eyes were wide and fixed, already starting to take on the glassy crystalline cast of death. She'd killed it, and with that certainty she was filled with a strange mixture of dread and glee.

She turned to Belegir and forgot those feelings utterly.

He was covered in blood. His face was bruised and torn, his robes ripped open down the front. There were deep claw-marks down his chest, and his throat was bruised. But he was breathing.

Glory moaned, deep in her throat. She knelt beside him. What should she do? What would Vixen do?

No. That wasn't any help. What would *Sister Bernadette* do?

Sister B would use her nursing skills to take care of the wounded, then use her detective skills to find out who'd attacked them, then explain everything to Vixen so the viewers would understand it.

"Belegir?" Glory whispered hopefully. To her vast relief, his eyelids fluttered. He tried to draw a deep breath and coughed, whimpering with pain.

"Where I come from, werewolves don't come out during the day," she said, forcing a bravado she was far from feeling. "Don't worry. It's dead. I killed it."

"One of *Her* creatures," Belegir whispered, and this time Glory didn't have the heart to disagree. That thing she'd killed had been evil—evil in the way that terrorists and serial killers were evil; a thing that took a personal delight in cruelty, in harm.

"I've got to get you back inside where it's safe, Bel. If that thing could of come in to the cave, I reckon it would've, so in there must be safe." *Mustn't it? Please let the answer to that one be "yes."* "How bad is it?"

"I can walk," the little Allimir whispered through his damaged throat.

Glory doubted it, but she *knew* she couldn't carry him, at least not far. She got to her feet, using her sword as a cane—everything was starting to hurt—and lifted Belegir to his feet.

The Allimir were useless in a fight, but that didn't mean they weren't brave. The guts it took for Belegir to get on his feet and stay on them without complaint made Glory feel small and ashamed. His face was grey with agony, and fresh blood welled from every wound, but he made no sound. He leaned heavily on her, and the two of them shuffled the few feet to the cave mouth.

Even that much exertion had Belegir gasping and choking for air. There was no way he could walk as far as the fountain.

"Is this safe? Belegir—is this safe?" Glory asked urgently.

"What?" he mumbled. She leaned him gently against the cool stone wall to take some of the strain off her own back and shoulders.

"Is this far enough for the Oracle's magic to protect you? Are you safe here?"

"Safe," he croaked, but she wasn't sure if he understood.

It would have to be safe enough. Because she couldn't carry him any farther, and he couldn't walk. She lowered him gently to the stone floor, placing her sword beside him—little use though it would be to him if this place *wasn't* safe—and took off running.

She had to get him back to the fountain. There was water there. Their supplies. Safety.

The night before on her way to the Oracle's spring, she'd passed chamber after chamber stuffed full of stored tat. What were the odds that in one of them, the cart or sledge used to bring them in was still there? And if she couldn't find one quickly, she could at least make up a travois from some of the mattresses, ropes, and blankets in the sleeping rooms. They could survive here. They might go short of food, but with all that water, they could run on scant rations a few days.

It was a long leisurely walk from the cave opening to the Pilgrims' fountain. She reached it in twenty minutes, every step jarring stars behind her eyes and making her head throb with the mother of all migraines. She stopped to drink and duck her head, rinsing the sourness from her mouth. Her shoulder was starting to stiffen, and the gashes, clotted with blood and dust, looked hot and angry even against a ripe sunburn. Her back hurt and her head and face throbbed with a dull headachy pain from the blow she had taken.

Best broker me a miracle, then, while I'm here.

"You hear that, Old Woman?" she said aloud, flipping her sopping braid back over her shoulder. It hit her back with a wet slap. "Dream-catcher, Oracle, whoever you want to be. You give us a fair shake. Or I'm climbing back up on that dinner-plate of yours and ripping your gizzard out, you nasty old bat!"

It hurt to talk.

She ran up the shallow steps to the temple, something nagging at the back of her mind. *Cistern. The big cisterns in the Presence chamber. You saw how far away the Wellspring was. You want to be the one carrying bucket after bucket all that way by hand? Bet they have a wagon. Have to have.*

It didn't take her long, after all, to find it. There were only two sorts of places it could be: near the spring or near the cisterns, and she already knew what was stored near the spring. Near the Presence Chamber she found a series of rooms that were obvious storerooms, holding everything necessary to the life of a well-dressed Temple acolyte. One room held nothing other than several small flatbed carts of carved and polished and gilded oak. There was a swag of velvet-covered rope on the front, but Glory suspected the carts were mainly designed to be pushed. Their wheels were wood, bound with what looked suspiciously like gold. Each was designed so that two large square ashwood vats could be fitted into its bed, and the sides of the vats could be hung with golden buckets. Glory sighed and shook her head. All the treasure of El Dorado, but what she wanted was the cart to use as a gurney. She dragged one of them out of the room, and by dint of main force and using several words she hadn't known she remembered, got the cart itself into the Presence Chamber. Getting it around the narrow turn scraped the crust off her wound and got her shoulder bleeding again, and after that she left long smudgy red commas on every wall she staggered into. She wept, and swore, and howled in frustration, glad that there was no one to hear. But she got it done.

She stopped at the sleeping cubbies to load the cart up with mattresses, then hauled it out onto the portico. She looked down the long flight of stairs. No sense just giving the cart a push and letting it jounce down, when it might crash to flinders at the bottom. She sighed and backed it around, holding onto the velvet rope and preparing to use herself as a brake. The cart was all wood and heavy. Fortunately the steps were wide and shallow.

There was a tense moment near the end as the velvet rope, never designed to support the whole weight of the cart, tore free, but the cart was most of the way down the steps by that point, and all it did was bounce noisily the rest of the way down and roll gently into the middle of the floor.

Glory sighed, shaking with exhaustion and pent-up

emotion, but she couldn't stop now. Belegir was counting on her.

She was counting on herself.

She riffled their supplies and found the mead he'd
mentioned yesterday. She took that and filled a
waterskin at the fountain and added all of the blankets, loading everything on the cart, and, on inspiration, added the coil of rope that Belegir had used to
lash down the pack. Then she began to push the cart
through the corridor.

Across the stone floor it was fine, and across the
crushed gravel as well.

When it reached the soft sand, the wheels stopped
turning entirely. Pushing the cart became like pushing a sledge. If the sand had been any deeper, this
might have been impossible. As it was, it was only
nearly so.

She didn't stop, though the struggle was a new and
particular species of hell. She desperately needed to
reach Belegir, not knowing whether he was dead or
alive, and she was reduced to this Tantalusian crawl.
She put her head down and her shoulder down and
pushed, stubbornly. Her feet slid in the sand, blurring
the patterns further. Any tears she might have had left
were burned away by sullen fury. And she didn't stop.

Eventually the wheels crunched across gravel, then
ran free on stone once more, the lack of resistance
driving her to her knees as the cart rolled fluidly away
from her.

"Belegir?" *Don't let him be dead he can't be dead
if he's dead I'm climbing up to the top of your magic
mountain and cutting your guts out whether you're real
or not you poxy bitch—*

But he was breathing, still, she could see it, and
Glory whimpered in relief.

She grabbed the water and a blanket and hurried

over to him. Moistening the edge of the blanket with the water, she dabbed carefully at his swollen blood-caked face with it, then pulled the blanket up over him.

His eyes opened slowly, then widened in fear.

"It's okay. You're safe," Glory said soothingly. "We're going to get you back inside and get you all fixed up, and everything's going to be fine. . . ." She was blowing smoke and she knew it, though she hoped Belegir didn't. She didn't know if he'd brought along whatever passed here for a first-aid kit, but she did know she didn't know how to use it if he had. Without Belegir, she couldn't find the rest of the Allimir again, either, and she doubted any of them would come looking for them when they didn't make their rendezvous.

Think about that later.

She raised Belegir carefully to a half-sitting position and offered him the waterskin. He drank, thirstily, and when he started coughing again, there wasn't as much blood as there had been before. She wanted to be hopeful, but she felt too sick and terrified to think straight. She was exhausted with pain, and wanted nothing more than to crawl into a corner and sleep until the world went away.

"I wasn't sure—" Belegir whispered.

"Had to go whistle up a taxi," Glory answered in Vixen's flat American drawl. "Brought the mead back with me. Figure with a bellyful of that, you won't be in a position to complain about my driving."

Belegir smiled, painfully. The monster had hit him in the face and by now the bruises had the time to ripen; his nose and one eye were purple and swollen, distorting his face to unrecognizability. His lip was split, puffy and blackened. "Slayer, what then?" he asked.

Glory smiled, even though it hurt. "Then we figure out who sent tall dark and hairy. And I go explain to them why they mustn't do things like that, I reckon."

Belegir seemed to believe her—which was more than Glory did, if the entire truth be told—and when she brought him the mead, he drank until the skin was nearly empty.

"I will sleep now," he whispered.

"I hope," Glory muttered, easing him down again. Getting him into the cart wasn't going to be a picnic for either of them, and she didn't even want to think about the return trip.

She waited, kneeling beside Belegir, until she judged he was about as relaxed as he was ever going to be. Then she moved the cart as close to him as she could, remembering to turn it around so it was facing the way it would need to go. She stretched, limbering up as much as she dared, and squatted beside Belegir. She got an arm beneath his shoulders and one under his thighs, pulling him gently toward her.

I hope he isn't too broken up inside. I hope his ribs aren't cracked and one doesn't go into a lung. I hope I don't blow a disk or anything else I'm going to need.

Then she stood up, pulling him with her in a dead lift.

The world went white, and she couldn't breathe. She hugged him tightly against her, terrified of dropping him to the hard stone floor, of falling. Pain snaked down her spine and into her legs, wrapped her skull in a hot crown of barbed wire.

But she did it.

He gasped and choked, clawing weakly at her chest with the arm that wasn't pinned against her. She walked—tiny, staggering baby steps—toward the cart, Belegir cradled in her arms. She laid him down on the mattresses, leaning forward to do it and feeling every muscle she possessed tremble and scream. His legs dangled over the end, but only by an inch or two. Not enough to count.

She took his hand.

"That's it. That's all. That's the worst, I promise. No more. No more pain. Belegir, I'm sorry. I'm so sorry, mate. This is my fault."

His hand tightened over hers.

"Cinnas said—" His voice was very faint, almost impossible to hear. She leaned over. "Cinnas said . . . there was a glory in war. The worst . . . outweighed the best, but . . . without war, there were no heroes." His eyes closed again.

Heroes.

"Some hero," Glory muttered, in an angry shaken whisper. Her eyes stung with tears, but she was too tired to cry. She covered Belegir with three of the blankets and used a fourth to make a pillow for his head. The cart was facing the temple. All she had to do now was get it there.

She glanced back at the cave opening. That thing— safely dead—was still out there.

What would Sister Bernadette do?

She'd go look for clues. There was nothing Glory could do for Belegir just now. And he deserved a bit of a breathing space before she started jouncing him back toward the fountain.

She took a deep breath and another careful stretch, and absently scrubbed at the blood trickling down her arm where the monster's claws had gashed her. It hurt and itched at the same time—a good trick, that. She stopped and picked up her sword, and cautiously headed back outside.

The monster was still lying there, looking horribly real in the bright light of full day.

Crows had already been at the body, pecking and digging, and there was a black trail of insects swarming across the pine needles toward this feast of broken meats. Glory shuddered all over, but by now she was far beyond simple squeamishness. She advanced on the creature, waving and shouting hoarsely to displace the crows. At least now she could get a good long look at what she'd killed.

A good seven feet tall and muscled like a Russian weight-lifter. Covered with greasy, rank, greyish-black fur, but wearing clothes like a person—a vest and a pair of knee-length breeches, both of plain leather, dirty and stained and worn in patches. The skin on its palms and the soles of its feet was black, calloused to grey in places. It had long curved doglike nails, though its hands and feet were human-shaped, and the nails on its hands were pointed and sharp, as if they'd been filed. It had an inhuman head, more wolflike than ursine, but with a bear's short muzzle. It had the pointed ears of a wolf, though, set wide at the edges of the high-domed skull, giving it a gnomish aspect. Its teeth were long and yellow—a carnivore's teeth, designed to tear and rend, and gulp dinner down in large steaming chunks.

It wasn't something from the murals. It wasn't anything Belegir had described, or known to expect. It had killed Kurfan. It had turned its back on her, even though she had a sword, to go for the Allimir mage, as though Belegir represented the greater threat. Had it waited for them to come out, or had that been a coincidence? Why had the animals come out at all? Belegir'd said they wouldn't, and they had.

Too many questions, and not enough answers.

She didn't really want to touch it, but she knew she didn't have a lot of choice. She was looking for clues.

She knelt beside the body, gritting her teeth, and lifted the edge of the leather vest. Nothing there. No pockets, nothing concealed.

But in the fur on the chest, a glint of bluish light. She started to reach for it and thought better of it, pulling one of her Lucite "rowan" stakes from its sheath on her boot to poke the dead monster's chest with. When she did, she found it was wearing a pendant around its neck, a piece of oval glass about as long as her thumb that glowed with its own cerulean light. There was a hole bored through the top, and a leather cord ran through that. She used the stake to tease the pendant off over the creature's head, being careful not to touch the pendant itself. She might not be from around here, but by now she knew magic when she saw it. Only all the Allimir magic she'd seen was purple, so what was this aquamarine stuff?

She dumped the pendant into the pine needles and was about to turn back to the body when she saw motion out of the corner of her eye.

The pendant was moving.

Slowly—you could mistake it for the settling/sliding any object would do on a slippery slope, but it was more than that—the pendant was sliding away, like a needle being pulled by a powerful magnet.

"God's Teeth!" Glory gasped. In one smooth (and well-practiced for the cameras) motion, she hammered the resin stake in her hand down into the dirt, skewering the knotted leather cord and trapping the glowing pendant.

"I am not cut out for this, I am *so* not cut out for this!" she groaned aloud. What should she do now? Sister Bernadette would sprinkle the blasphemous thing with holy water and say a few prayers, but Sister Bernie wasn't here, and Anne-Marie Campbell wasn't a real Catholic anyway (nor, for that matter, was Glory), so that was no help. She watched in horrified disgust as the pendant slowly squirmed to the end of its tether and strained southward helplessly, then turned back to the monster's body.

What Glory *did* know was that she couldn't leave

something like this lying around loose, but it would take her a while to come up with the proper thing to do. Meanwhile, there were other chores to finish. She went on searching the body.

No pockets in the leather knickers either, and nothing under the leather except more monster. She couldn't just leave the body lying in front of the Oracle's cave like an invitation to every bug and carrion-crow in the forest, either. She was going to have to move it. Somehow. Glory sighed and got to her feet, staggering just a bit with weariness. It wasn't much past ten A.M., judging by the position of the sun, and it had already been a very full day.

She brushed herself off thoroughly, feeling imaginary and not-so-imaginary bugs crawling all over her, then used the tip of her sword to prod the monster's body over the edge of the slope. It rolled a good distance, but she'd rather have it where she couldn't see it. The heavy carpet of fallen pine needles that lay everywhere on the ground should make it easy for her to drag it at least a few yards, providing she could shift it at all.

There's always work in the Land of Erchanen for Vixen the Slayer, she told herself with gallows humor.

Before she followed the body down, she dug up a few handfuls of earth and used it to scrub her swordblade as clean as she could, then slipped the sword into its shoulder-sheath again. This time, the practiced flourish took her three tries to achieve; her hands shook, and every muscle ached and protested, sending shooting aches down her arms and back. Then she went down the hill again.

Seeing Kurfan's ruined head again made her throat ache with pity. The poor beast had done his very best for them, and died a hero's death. She went to the monster and stripped off its leather vest, then used it to lift Kurfan's head off the stump of the branch and wrap it tenderly.

She took the dog's head and set it on the monster's chest. Let the monster be Kurfan's honor-guard across the Rainbow Bridge. That done, she dragged the head and the body as far into the woods as she could, a hundred meters or so off the edge of the trail. Bigger things than birds would find both of them soon, and in a day or two everything would be reduced to anonymous bones. It was the best she could do.

She stood for a moment among the pines, working up the gravel to go back up the trail and start the long business of getting the cart holding Belegir down the corridor, when she became aware of a peculiarly familiar odor.

Smoke. Burning meat. And in this time and place, not a good smell.

Investigate? With Belegir hurt, she didn't know how bad, and only her to care for him, and herself hurting? Not one of her brighter notions, even if it were an inevitable scriptwriter's gambit.

But if she didn't, if she did the sensible Normal Person thing and turned away, she might be leaving a whole pack of monsters at her back to ambush the two of them at leisure. And she didn't know for certain that the monsters couldn't go into the Oracle cave. She only knew that she hadn't seen this one inside.

She sighed, sniffing smoke. She couldn't afford to ignore it. But the morning had shown her that she wasn't really equipped to fight monsters, either, at least not excellently. So she'd just go see if this was something really close—and by the smell, it wasn't far—and then run off and hide. Quickly. And maybe a miracle would occur and this wouldn't turn out to be some new problem after all. Maybe it was a rescue party.

Ha.

She checked the direction of the wind, and backtrailed the smoke as quietly as she could, moving through the forest. The smoke thickened the closer she got, until she was walking through low-roiling clouds of it thick enough to make her stifle a cough, and soon enough she saw why.

Somebody had left dinner on while they nipped down to the pub and never came back. And now dinner was burning.

She stopped, hidden behind a tree, and looked carefully over the scene, searching for trouble. Vixen would have charged right in with a battle-yell, but Vixen had a nice sharp sword and no hostages to fortune. And in fact, Glory realized with an unfamiliar pang of insight, Vixen had never played for stakes this high. If Vixen failed, if Vixen lost, there were always others to take her place in the battle against the Darkness. In this time, in this place, there was no one else to take up the fight. There was only Glory, and because that was so, Glory could not afford to take chances. And so she studied the situation before her very carefully.

It was a camp, one that had the look of long-usage. The fire-pit was well-dug, ringed and lined with large stones. The camp also had the smell of long-usage, the strongly ammoniac stench of something big that liked to mark its territory.

Two of the Allimir ponies were there, forelegs hobbled, and tied, for good measure, to a large log by nooses of coarsely-braided leather around their necks. They looked concerned, but not distressed enough to be making serious attempts at escape.

By the look of things, the third Allimir pony was the source of the smoke. A large portion of some good-sized beast had been spitted and left to roast over the fire, and when the fire's owner hadn't come back, the meat had begun to burn.

Gazing around, she sighted the rest of the butchered pony, wrapped in its hide, hanging in a tree out of the reach of other predators. The pony's head was jammed between two branches, just as Kurfan's had been, and now that she looked for them, she saw that most of the trees in the area were decorated with clean-picked skulls, big and little. The monster had been living here for quite some time. There was nothing much to the camp but the firepit and the horses— no bedding, no other food or drink. Just skulls, meat, and soon-to-be-meat.

And if she wanted the surviving ponies back she'd better work quickly, and hope the dead monster didn't have mates sharing its camp with it.

She went over to the spit, and heaved the joint off the fire. It must be twenty pounds of meat, maybe more. The fire was on its way to being a good bed of coals, and she looked around for something to smother it with, then gave up. It would burn itself out safely eventually. There was a large rusty iron blade beside the firepit that the monster must have used to chop firewood and butcher its meat. She picked it up and went over to the ponies.

"Now I'm going to say soothing things to you," she said to them, "and you're going to repay me by not kicking me to bits or bolting into the next county, right? It's just as well you're none too bright, or seeing your mate served up as the blue plate special here'd be in a fair way to making you pretty nervy. But you're completely oblivious, hey?" She held out her hand, and gently stroked each pony's muzzle in turn. The animals nosed at her hopefully.

"Well, let's get you out of here." *I hope.*

The hobbles were a simple loop-and-toggle arrangement of braided leather, easy enough to undo if you had thumbs. She shook them free, then used the heavy chopper in her hand to cut the braided leather ropes where they looped around the log. Dropping the machete, she grabbed the trailing ends and led the horses away as quickly as she dared.

The ponies followed her willingly enough, apparently on the theory she was going to feed them. Nothing followed them, but by the time the Oracle cave mouth was in sight again, Glory was so filled with unreasoning fear she could barely force herself to move forward. Only sheer luck had gotten her through that little adventure alive. She could not imagine what bold spirit of idiocy had impelled her to go wandering through the forest in search of freelance ogres to slay: if she had managed to find one, she'd be dead now. Tripping over the two surviving horses, and rescuing them, was such a stroke of undeserved good fortune that she knew it would have to be paid for with even more terrible future horrors.

She was moving by sheer will alone by the time she reached the cave entry. As before, the horses hurried to enter the narrow cut in the rock.

She dropped their leads, letting them forge on ahead, the blue flash in the dirt reminding her of something she'd managed to forget, as rattled and shell-shocked as she'd been.

The wolf-man's talisman. It was still there, still straining to get to . . . something.

She picked it up—carefully—by the end of the cord, and tucked her faux-rowan stake carefully away in its boot-sheath. As the jewel swung from her fingers, it was easy to pretend that it had never exhibited that strange pseudo-life.

But she still wasn't going to touch it. Or let it touch her.

She sighed wearily and followed the horses into the cave. In the doorway, she felt a tug. She looked down at her hand. The jewel was hanging straight sideways, as though there was some force keeping it from entering the Oracle cave.

Glory pulled. There was a weak pop, as though someone had put a lightbulb under a pillow and stepped on it. The gem came through, its light fading away.

So much for finding anything out about what it is or where it came from, I reckon, she thought sourly.

Glory shook her head. Some days were like that—just one damned thing after another. Now she supposed the thing was useless from a forensic standpoint.

The ponies were wandering up the corridor in a leisurely but determined fashion. Glory ran after them and grabbed the trailing lead-ropes—dropping the pendant in the process—and led them firmly back to the cart. After she'd gone to all the trouble of getting them back, she had no intention of losing them again.

Belegir was conscious again when she got there.

" 'Lo, Bel," Glory said. "How's tricks?"

He tried to smile, and winced instead. "Water," he whispered.

She knotted the two lead-ropes together and hooked her arm through them, then got the waterskin for Belegir and held it for him as he drank. His color was better now.

"This is one of the lustral cars," he said, in a faint voice.

"Had to put you in something."

"And you've brought the horses."

"Two of them. Monster killed the other." She took back the waterskin and drank thirstily. The water was tepid and tasted faintly of leather. It was delicious.

"Slayer, forgive me."

Glory lowered the waterskin suspiciously. "For?"

"I doubted you. When the Oracle spoke to me—"

"Well, you don't have to believe everything you read in the newspapers," Glory said hastily. If the Oracle had told Belegir she was going to fail, she really didn't want to hear it. Not when she was starting to believe in the lot of them: the Oracle, the Warmother, maybe even in the Dreamer of Worlds. "We heroes have a way of coming through in the backstretch, y'know. It isn't over till it's over. Now all we have to do," she said with a sigh, "is get you back to the fountain, and take stock."

The ponies tugged at the lead again. Probably they were thirsty, and could smell the water. Too bad she couldn't hitch them to the cart. That would solve several problems at once.

Or maybe she could.

"Wait here," she told the surprised Allimir mage. "I'll be right back. No worries." She took her sword out of its sheath and laid it in the cart with Belegir. It weighed close to four pounds, and by now she felt every extra ounce.

"No worries," Belegir echoed, a smile in his voice.

It took a bit more doing than before to get a leg up over the back of one of the ponies—the beasts felt they'd been ill-done-by, and wanted everyone to know it—but she managed. It took very little urging to get the two of them moving toward the fountain, still linked together by the awkwardly tied braided leather rope. All she had to do was hang on.

When they got there, the ponies headed straight for the fountain. Glory slid off, and staggered over toward the supplies.

There was, as she'd hoped, more grain with the supplies, and several more of the compressed fruit cakes. She took some of each to use as lures while the ponies occupied themselves at the fountain, wolfed a fruit cake down herself, and turned her attention to the packsaddle. It was a simple device: a thick sheep-skin pad, two cinches, a light framework of curved ash spokes to hold a pack in place. She didn't have a horse collar, and the cart didn't have any kind of hitching tree, but if she could get one of the ponies strapped into this, she bet she could use pony-power to pull the cart back here.

She went over to the fountain and pulled the horses away from the water—she didn't know how much water was too much, but they'd get another crack at it soon—and began the ticklish process of getting one of the ponies buckled into the packsaddle. She didn't even know if Marchiel was one of the two survivors, or if this animal had ever done anything like this before—but she managed. She did know that however tight she thought the cinches were now, she'd have to tighten them again later. She tossed the two saddle-pads up onto its back and added the coiled leather reins that the Allimir favored, and the basket filled with equine bribes. She wasn't going to bother to try to ride the other horse back, but all that leather should come in handy. Then she led the animals back down the cor-ridor one more time.

Her feet hurt. Her back hurt. Her head hurt, and the gash on her shoulder was hot and swollen now to the touch. Sleep had rarely seemed so desirable. But short term temporary conditional victory was nearly within her grasp.

She used one of the saddle-pads to make a chest-pad for her designated carthorse, and ran a length of the rope over that as well. Then, if nothing broke, if the pony didn't kick the whole arrangement to flinders, she'd just re-invented the horse-drawn cart. She untied the two ropes, and lashed its mate to the back of the cart, hoping the beasts were still as docile and gregari-ous as they'd seemed the day before. Belegir was asleep again, which was probably the best possible thing, all things considered.

"Come on," she said, taking a handful of mane in one hand and holding out a palmful of grain in the other.

The pony started, and stopped when it felt the unfamiliar pull of the cart and heard the noise behind it. Started again at Glory's urging, trying to turn to look behind it. After a few minutes of that, she got the inspiration of bringing the second animal up and tying it to the packsaddle instead of the cart. Finally, after an eternity of coaxing, both ponies moved forward, and the cart followed. And she wasn't the one dragging it.

Though short, it was not a journey she would care to repeat.

There were probably a dozen useful things she ought to have done, once she finally got the cart to the fountain, but she didn't do any of them. She got the makeshift harness off the ponies and watered them again, then tied them up to the cart once more so they didn't either wander off or go rummaging through the supplies, giving them a bit of grain to sweeten the deal.

Belegir was asleep again, or at least unconscious. His breathing sounded steady, but his skin was hot. She wasn't sure whether it was a fever, or if it was normal with the Allimir—it wasn't like she'd spent a lot of time feeling up the little people before the balloon went up. Either way, there wasn't much she could do, and right now she was so tired she was stupid.

She filled all the waterskins, and had a big mug of water with a splash of ale in it, then she squirmed out of her costume again, sopped her T-shirt in the fountain, and used it to give herself a nonce-bath all over, scrubbing until her skin (fishbelly here, sunburned and starting to peel there, bruised and bloody elsewhere) felt a little cleaner. It wasn't enough of a bath to scrub away the smells and memories of the morning, or the feel of the monster's fur on her hands, or the way it had looked at her, but it was all she could do. Then she laid her T-shirt over the side of the fountain to dry, pulled on her (by now rather grubby) jeans and sweatshirt, got Gordon out of her bag, and curled up with her back to the fountain and her stuffed elephant in her arms, trying to summon up the strength to go up those stairs one more damn time and look for something useful. Clothes, or supplies. Something to keep them alive.

She should have brought the butchered horse with them. Meat was meat. She ought to go back for it now. In a little. When it was safe to leave Belegir. She would. In a little . . .

She woke from a confused dream of a surreal courtroom and a stern justice in wig and robes thundering down sentence upon her—or Vixen, she wasn't sure—and was unable, for a moment, to remember where she was. Then it came swirling back to her with dizzying force. The Allimir. The Oracle temple. The Warmother, and her furry little friends.

Groaning, she got to her feet and stretched, feeling the kinks and knots go off like a string of firecrackers along her back and limbs. Stiff and sore, and the side of her face ached like a broken tooth.

Belegir was awake, and trying to get out of bed.

"What do you think you're doing?" Glory snapped, hurrying over to him. She put an arm around his back and helped him sit up. That brought on another spate of coughing, and more fresh blood. She wiped his face with the edge of the blanket.

The monster had hit him in the face to knock him down, and ripped open his robes, leaving deep gashes in his chest, but what it had mainly been doing, from the look of things, was strangling him, fortunately for Belegir.

"I need . . . to get up," Belegir gasped, blushing.

"Oh. *Oh.*" This might be Middle Earth, but the human body was no respecter of crises. Glory thought quickly. "No you don't. You wait right here. And if you move while I'm gone, I'm going to come back and make you wish you hadn't. You got that?" she said fiercely.

"Yes," Belegir said faintly, holding on to the edge of the cart.

When she was sure that he *could* stay where he was put, Glory left him, moving faster than she really wanted to. Back up the steps of the temple, back to the cart room to where the little golden buckets were.

"Here," she said when she got back. "Use this."

Belegir looked at her, horrified.

"Look. I don't know where the latrines are in this place, but I do know you can't walk there. Erchane will cut you a break. We'll throw it out afterward, okay? And I won't look."

Belegir managed a weak smile. "Cinnas warned us about heroes," he said, reaching for the golden bucket.

When he was finished she took the bucket and set it down beneath the cart. "Can you stand, do you reckon?" she asked. "You ought to get those tatters off. There's some robes and things up there. Thought I'd do a bit of scrounging, for new clothes and bandages and suchlike. You could do with a new outfit."

"My mage-robes," Belegir whispered sadly. "Yes, Slayer, you are right. And . . . I think I can stand." Carefully she lowered him to his feet and peeled him out of the filthy and tattered mage-robes and his tall felt boots, discovering in passing that Allimir mages were pink and hairless all over. She didn't like the angry look of the gashes on his chest—God knew what that monster'd had under its fingernails—and tried not to think about her own wound. Afterward, she rearranged the mattresses to keep him elevated—better than lying flat if there were something wrong with his lungs— and helped Belegir back into the cart, covering him up warmly with the blankets.

"Belegir, what do your folk do when someone gets hurt?" she asked, hoping her question sounded idle.

"We call for the healers, of course—or, if it is not a great injury, for the herb-doctors," Belegir said slowly. He looked at her shoulder—blood had seeped through the grey sweatshirt fabric—and sighed. "I am not a healer."

"You *need* a healer. I was wondering . . . do you reckon . . . do you think the Oracle's water would help? If we poured it on you?" Glory asked.

"By Erchane's Will," Belegir said listlessly. Even the short conversation had tired him, though he managed to rally a bit. "But Slayer, please . . . use a different bucket."

She grinned. "No worries. You just get some rest."

She put one of the full waterskins in the cart with easy reach, and tucked Gordon up beside him—she didn't know why, it just made her feel better. When she was sure he was asleep, she eased the bucket out from under the cart and looked inside. As she'd feared, there were dark threads of blood mixed in with the urine.

This is not good. This is so not good.

But there was nothing she could do about it.

She took the bucket to the far end of the cavern and dumped it on the floor, then sluiced down the spot with clear water from one of the waterskins—piss-poor hygiene (to coin a phrase), but the best she could manage. Then she emptied out her gym-bag and her purse, and took a quick inventory.

Logo flashlight (reasonably useless). Cigarette lighter (wonder of wonder and miracle of miracles—hot tea later!) Gordon. A copy of the script for the MTV special (useless unless you wanted kindling). Her sneakers (she stopped to put them on). Her purse: wallet, with her passport, Melbourne drivers license, Access card, and a lot of funny-looking American currency. Tissues. Comb. Lashings of makeup. Hair-pins and a couple of ribbons.

Aspirin.

Not quite a miracle drug, but it could reduce a fever and cut minor aches and pains.

Could Belegir swallow them?

She'd worry about that later. She emptied the tote, stuffed everything she could into her purse and piled the rest beside it, and slung the empty tote over her shoulder in case she found something she wanted to carry back. Ready to go.

But something made her hesitate, and finally she came back and picked up her sword.

She wasn't sure why—there was nothing here in the temple that could harm her—but by now she'd learned to trust her hunches. In the here and now, they were all she had to go on, and so far, they were working about as well as anything else.

Then back up the stairs again—she'd lost count of how many times today that made—with all the muscles in her calves and back screaming a chorus of protest.

Her first stop was the sleeping rooms, where she grabbed a couple of mattresses to make her bed for tonight and carted them back to the top of the stairs. Next, the robing room, where she added an armful of shapeless fluffy white wool robes. They'd give Belegir a new frock, and the rest could be used for bandages, and what she wouldn't give for a pair of scissors, or even a sharp knife, right now.

The easy parts done, she grabbed one of the golden buckets, and wandered through the rest of the Temple, looking for anything useful. Unfortunately, anything useful to two bushwhacked adventurers was something of use to embattled fleeing refugees as well, and she didn't really have the time to turn the lumber rooms inside out, or the mother wit to recognize something clandestinely useful when she saw it. She saw large amounts of gold and silver Objects; paintings and tapestries, porcelain and glassware, books and scrolls; but nothing that was offhand valuable in the current situation. And she didn't really dare wander all that far from the main drag, not really. It would be too easy for her to get lost in a vast underground Temple of unknown size, and then where would they be? Bad enough that they were going to be starving soon enough. Her stomach was already rumbling, reminding her that one handful of dried fruit in about two days and a breakfast that went by twice in under an hour was not the equivalent of three squares, and no chance Belegir was going to be able to ride out of here any time soon, not with him pissing blood the way he was.

If it isn't one damn thing it's another.

Giving up on the side rooms—Allan Quartermain might have had a field day here, but he would have come with a pack full of food—she headed for the Oracle's wellspring, sword in one hand, bucket in the other. Best get the water and head back.

Everything was just as she'd left it. It was only a few hours ago that she and Belegir had woken up here after an eventful but useless night, but it seemed like that had been another lifetime. And somewhere along the way between then and now, almost insensibly, she'd developed a Plan.

Belegir said the Warmother was on the top of

Elboroth-Haden—or at least that *She* had been. Glory was going to go see. And then she was going to kick the bitch's ass from here to breakfast. She was tired. She was pissed. And she was fed up with oracular bitches coming along and telling her she was some kind of test case and not telling her what they meant by it.

All she had to do was get herself and Belegir out of this mess alive, first.

Glory removed the bar and opened the low door to the Oracle's spring.

The cavern was still dark, and cold rolled out of the little room like the breath of the Earth itself. Glory shuddered, unaccountably reluctant to go in. But nothing bad had happened to her in there before, and Belegir said the water might help. Probably do him as much good as the aspirin, any old how. She pushed the door open wide, propping the bar and her sword against it just in case, and went in.

She knelt down at the edge of the spring. It seemed like a good time for a prayer, but Glory wasn't sure who she ought to be praying to. She'd never been a very religious person back home—she'd always felt that if God tended to His business, she'd tend to hers. Prayers and bargains always seemed a little like cheating somehow, and besides, Erchane wasn't *her* god.

She dipped the bucket into the spring. The water was numbingly cold. Remembering how Belegir had filled the chalice the night before, Glory plunged the bucket in as deep as she could manage, and held it there for a minute.

"All right, you," she said aloud. "Belegir's always been straight with you. He stood by you even when it didn't look like you were paying much attention. Now it's your turn to do something for him. That's all."

She felt a little silly once she'd said it, but there was

no way to take the words back. She lifted the bucket out of the water—it was much heavier now—and set it carefully by the side of the spring.

And just in case there *was* something in Belegir's belief that the spring could do something about the infection, she pulled off her sweatshirt, unsticking it gently from her shoulder, scooped up several handfuls of the water, and washed out her own gashes thoroughly, pinching and prodding until they bled freely again. The cold made her shoulder feel better, if nothing else. She also washed her face, and rinsed the blood-spot out of the shirt as best she could. *Going to have a pretty bruise in the morning, if the heat on that cheek is anything to go by.*

She got to her feet, pulled the damp sweatshirt back on, picked up the bucket, and left the grotto, collecting her sword on the way. She realized she was going to have to set something down to bar the door again— not that it was really necessary, but it was the way she'd found it, so it was the way she'd leave it—when she realized that something had changed.

The door to the armory was open again, the violet light flooding out of it as if it were a high-end designer boutique on the *Bois de Expensive*.

She knew they'd closed it the last time they'd been down here.

She was pretty sure it'd been closed when she'd gone in to the Wellspring just now.

She knew what was in there.

"God's Teeth," Glory groaned tiredly, setting the bucket down again. Cinnas' gods-be-damned Warmothering sword was in there, with all its freight of can-be-carried-by-the-One-True-Hero and all that happy hoo-hah.

She bet it was sharp, though.

Sharp enough that if she'd been carrying it this

morning, Belegir need never have gotten hurt at all.
She could have cut the monster up like a breakfast egg,
made it bleed, ruined it with a blow or two, enough
to take it out fast and sloppy. Nobody hurt. Nobody
dying by inches, and her with no way to help.

That decided her.

She set down her sword, closed the door to the
Oracle spring, and picked up her sword again, then
walked into the armory, giving the floating glowing
sword a wide berth.

She might as well look around here for something
useful before getting herself into trouble meddling with
magic. Fortunately, she found something, which
improved her temper a bit. On a table in the back,
there was what was obviously a maintenance kit of
some sort, picks and rasps laid out on a chamois square,
including several small hooked knives, sharpened on
the inner side, for shortening the straps that held armor
in place. The leather straps were nowhere in sight but
the knives were still sharp, and there was a small stop-
pered pot of what was obviously leather cream—Belegir
had said this stuff hadn't been used since the Time of
Legend, but she bet someone had still got the job of
cleaning it regularly, back when the Oracle Temple was
full of Acolytes. She worried the cork out and stuck
a finger in it, sniffing, smelling beeswax and lanolin.
What would do for leather would likely do for skin as
well. She added both knives and leather dressing to
her bag, and the chamois square as well, then returned
to the hovering wizard's blade.

Unless she dragged the table over, she couldn't climb
up to it, and even if she did, there was no guarantee she
could pry it loose from the air. Magic, Glory told herself sagely, on the basis of no information at all, was
funny that way. And if the blade was as sharp as it
looked, she didn't want to grab the end she could reach.

She reached up with her own sword and prodded at the other blade tentatively. It didn't even wobble, but the sound the two blades made when they connected was like hitting a tuning fork.

A very big tuning fork.

Hit really, really hard.

She winced, staggering back from the high sweet ringing. It faded quickly, and Glory had the odd feeling that Cinnas' sword was laughing at her. In a fond paternal way, but laughing at her nonetheless.

"I am not amused," she said aloud.

She couldn't knock it down, she couldn't yank it down, what did that leave?

She looked down at the sword-blade-shaped slot in the stone on the floor, and then at the sword in the air, and then at the one in her hand.

They say King Arthur got his way by pulling a sword OUT of the stone, but he was a Pom. Let's see if things go by opposites.

She flipped her sword up and dropped it, point-first, into the slot in the stone.

It had been quiet before, but suddenly it was as if a sound she'd gotten used to hearing had suddenly ceased. She jumped back with a startled yelp as The Sword of Cinnas fell down out of the air like a startled rock and clattered on the floor, bouncing and ringing on the stone floor like a crowbar flung from a speeding car.

When it was lying perfectly still, she approached it warily. The bright neon glow had faded, though the jewels set in the hilt were still rather bright, but the whole thing still looked weird as hell. Eldritch, that was the word. The sword looked *eldritch*.

She went back over to her prop-sword, and gave it an experimental tug, but it was now welded fast to the stone. She nodded, obscurely satisfied. Give a sword to get a sword. It made sense. She only hoped that the next bright laddie who came along needing a good blade would appreciate what she was leaving for him, and would have the mother wit to be able to winkle it out of the rock. But that wasn't her problem.

The armory was darker now, the background glow slowly fading, as if the Temple itself were telling her she had no more business in this room. She turned back to Cinnas' blade and reached for it cautiously. It seemed to be finished with signs and wonders, though, because it was nothing more than a sword in her hand, if a bit lighter than the one she'd given up. She touched the edge of the blade gingerly. And sharp as she'd thought. That was a plus. She swung it experimentally and felt herself smile. Hairy buggers beware. This time when she hit them, she'd split them for sure.

Carrying the sword carefully away from her body, she left the armory, picked up her bucket, and headed back for the front of the temple.

She didn't look back.

Getting her loot down the stairs took her a couple of trips, and by the time she wrestled the mattresses down, Belegir was awake again. Fortunately, she'd gotten the sword down on the first trip—no sense in giving the old fellow heart failure when she didn't have to. She'd tell him about the sword later.

"We'll give you a nice wash-up straight from the Oracle," Glory told him, with the spurious cheerfulness of the sickroom matron, "and then pop you into one of these lovely angel-robes and I can brew you a nice cuppa. How's that?"

Belegir had a strange look on his face, not entirely due to his discovery of the close proximity of Gordon.

"Slayer, I have no magic. And I did not think to bring flint and steel. I am sorry."

It took her a moment to figure out what he was

getting at, and when she did, she smiled in relief, even if it did make her face hurt.

"No worries. For once, I brought something useful along with me. I've got a lighter. I can make the fire. We'll have tea, no worries. Now let's get you squared away. Do you think you could get a couple of pills down you?"

She got out the bottle of aspirin and shook some tablets into her hand. Two for her, two for Belegir. She thought it over, then dissolved his in one of the tea-mugs with a bit of the mead. It'd make a nasty-tasting drink, but probably easier on his bruised throat than the whole pills.

"This is going to taste foul," she said, bringing over the cup, "but it might help."

He swallowed it down without complaint, though he did shudder at the taste. She followed it with as much as he could hold of the Oracle-water—if it worked, it would probably do as much good inside as out—then sorted through the robes, selecting the largest two for Belegir's use. The hooked knife made short work of another two, converting them into large bandage-squares and a number of long binding strips.

About half the bucket was left. She dipped her rags into it, daubing off the blood on his face and chest as gently as she could.

"You are . . . very efficient," Belegir said in a breathy voice.

Glory smiled to herself.

"I grew up on a— well, I guess you might call it a farm. Sheep station. Dad's still there, but Mum was a city girl at heart. Out in the country, you have to do for yourself. No one to do for you."

With the blood gone, the bruising was spectacular, and to her concealed dismay, the gashes on Belegir's chest were already bright red and puffy and starting to ooze a straw-colored fluid. She wrung out a cold compress for his bruised face and sopped up a couple of wooly squares to cover his chest.

"Now you just let that perk for a while. I found a nice pot of goose-grease in the back to make a proper dressing with. Not all according to Hoyle, but it should make you more comfortable." *If it doesn't kill you outright.* She covered him up with the blankets again. No sense him catching pneumonia while she was trying to save his life.

The most important thing done, she returned to their meager supplies. There was some grain left, a couple of the fruit-cakes, a little of the mead, another skin of ale, and of course the sugar and the tea. That was all.

She sighed, and shook her head. A steely eyed adventurer would consider the horses as extra provisions, and it wasn't that she was averse to eating a horse—well, not exactly—but she had no way to kill one of the ponies cleanly and no idea of how to butcher it, and even if she did, there was no way inside the Temple for them to cook it afterward, and she definitely drew the line at eating one of the damned things raw—which pretty much put paid to her notion of going back for the rest of the other pony, even if she was willing to risk the trip.

As for the protein on the hoof . . . they couldn't eat them, they couldn't ride them, and the cart was pretty useless outside of the temple, so there was no point in even trying to make a go of hitching the beasts to it and going on from there. All that being the case, the logical thing to do was to turn the beasts loose to fend for themselves and hope they survived.

But if she was going to do that, she might as well do it in the morning after they'd had a good meal, or as much of a good meal as she could field them. A

couple of handfuls of grain wouldn't make much difference for her and Belegir in the long run. She shook
her head. Soft-hearted, that's what she was.

She divvied the grain up into two neat piles, widely
separated, then led the horses over to their meals one
at a time. Afterward she watered them, then tied them
to the packsaddle, several yards away from Belegir and
the supplies. No sense leaving them to wander loose
and get into trouble.

The area around the Pilgrim's Fountain was starting to reek strongly of stable, and Glory told herself she'd be just as glad to be rid of the nasty
smelly beasts, but she knew she'd miss them, especially since she knew they'd probably fall down the
first rabbit hole going and break a leg, or be eaten
by another of those pants-wearing nightmares, or by
something else just as horrible. Still, they'd have a
chance, which looked like more than she and Belegir
did.

She changed Belegir's compresses. Was it her imagination, or did the gashes look a little better? *Please,
let it be so.* Then she got to work setting up the little
tea-boiler.

She picked up the round pottery bottle and her
lighter, and got the wick alight with a few snaps of her
thumb, then set up the rest of the tea-boiler around
it. When they'd had their tea, she could boil down a
couple of the fruit-cakes in the pot. She didn't think
Belegir was up to chewing, but the thing ought to be
willing to turn itself into soup with a little encouragement.

Belegir was lying back on his improvised hospital
bed, watching her. His color was better, and despite
the purpling bruises, and the white cloth laid over half
his face, he looked pleased.

"Here now, Bel, how much of this tea-stuff do I add

to the water?" Glory asked, shoving her braid back out
of the way and waving the canister.

"Come here, and I will show you," he said.

Obediently she carried the canister over to him,
and watched as he measured an amount out onto his
hand, looking to see that she understood. He poured
the dry leaves back into canister and beckoned her
close.

"I think you are a very great hero," he said, smiling.

"You're demented," Glory said, not unkindly. "The
water's boiling."

After the tea had brewed and she'd poured it into
mugs, she washed out the pot in the fountain and
refilled it to stew two of the shredded-up cakes of fruit.
Before bandaging Belegir, she tried the salve on her
arm, changing back to her now-dry T-shirt first. It
didn't hurt, and it might help. She wound some of the
wool bandage firmly around her arm, and tied it in
place as best she could. At least she wouldn't have to
look at it now.

Bandaging up Belegir was an awkward and messy
process, leaving her slathered with goo to the elbows
before she got the dressing firmly tied in place. But
once she got a new robe over his head, both of them
felt better.

"I have not worn something like this since my days
as a novice in the temple," Belegir said ruefully,
smoothing down the pale creamy wool. "And that was
long ago."

At Glory's quizzical look, he continued.

"Those of us who feel Called to be mages serve at
the Temple, so that we may become used to Erchane's
presence. Sometimes it will happen that there will be
no place for a new apprentice for many years, or a
Mage and an apprentice will not . . . suit."

I reckon there's a whole story in that, Glory thought sagely.

"So until the day comes when an apprentice may leave the temple to serve his Mage, he serves here. I served here a long time, until Acoril chose me."

"What was he like?"

"She. Very strict, very . . . all that I am not. She said I was the burden Erchane had called upon her to bear, and that she had chosen me only so that no other Mage would be so terribly afflicted." He smiled at the memory. "She did not wish me to study the Old Texts. But she chose me when no other would, and for that I honor her memory."

He sipped his tea.

"I'm going to turn the horses loose tomorrow. We can't feed them. Maybe they'll find their way home," Glory said.

"You should go with them. Ride east. You will find the wagons easily enough," Belegir said.

"You know I don't ride as well as all that." Not with the Allimir idea of a saddle and bridle, not with all of Serenthodial to get lost in. Not that either of those things made any difference to her decision. Belegir had called her a hero, and she guessed she was going to have to try to be one. And heroes did not leave their wounded behind them to die alone.

She got up to stir the soup, pleased to see that the fruit had dissolved into a sort of sweet mush by now.

Had she come all this way to die here just for a run of bad luck? She didn't believe it. But maybe that was what all fools told themselves, until it was too late to say otherwise.

Never mind. They'd have dinner and a good sleep, and she'd think about what to do next in the morning.

After they'd eaten there was nothing to do but sleep, in the endless magical twilight of the enormous cavern, and she was more than ready for it. She took one of the last of the white robes, and with some merciless plying of one of the harness-knives, tailored herself a passable nightgown. A little tight across the chest and hips, but worlds better than either her armor or another night spent in her grubby jeans. After Belegir was settled and she'd performed her final ablutions, she examined her face in the small compact mirror. Yes, a lovely bruise, right along her right cheekbone. It gave her a rather dangerous appearance, the battered hero in the last reel of the summer actioner, sallying forth to kick butt and take names.

She wished it were true. She wished she'd brought a gun with her, instead of a bag full of licensed tie-ins and makeup. Or a bar of soap and some shampoo. At least she had her toothbrush. Thank heaven for small favors.

But what she had was what she had. And hey, at least now she had a magic sword. That was something.

She unbraided her hair and spent a long time brushing it, thinking of nothing, the purple sword lying unsheathed at her side.

If only she'd brought her cell phone. If only there was someone to call. If only Belegir weren't hurt, so *he* could be a cell phone. If only the monster hadn't been out there this morning. If only the horses hadn't wandered off in the first place. If only they'd brought more food. If only there'd been food stockpiled here.

If. Only. If only somebody'd listened to Belegir in the first place, and the Warmother hadn't gotten loose.

Brush—brush—brush— Until finally she was tired of it, and her red hair shone, crackling and curling around her brush and her hand with every stroke. Then she braided it up again, this time loosely, and curled

up under the blanket Belegir had insisted she take—
Gordon under one arm, the hilt of the sword loosely
clutched in her other hand.

Sleep was instant and deep.

Glory woke to a confused clatter of sound. She was
too tired to come instantly awake, but she was up and
moving without true wakefulness, knowing nothing
more of who and where she was than that she must
hold onto the sword.

The shouts—of fear, of surprise and dismay—
galvanized her further, without bringing her very much
closer to consciousness. She swept her sword before
her in a threatening gesture, trying to force her eyes
open, knowing she had to move toward the right without remembering what was there that she needed to
protect. At the best of times, Glory McArdle had never
been a morning person.

People. Strangers. Horses. *Belegir!* She got her back
against the cart that held him and prepared to sell both
their lives dear.

"Slayer! Slayer! They are friends—*friends!*" Belegir
gasped hoarsely, before collapsing into another coughing
fit.

She lowered the sword quickly and went to help him
sit upright, ignoring the others completely. Slowly,
Belegir's spasm eased. Only then did she look back at
the others.

It was Ivradan—Helevrin's other son—and two other
Allimir she didn't know, leading half a dozen fully laden
pack horses and staring at her as if she were the
Warmother incarnate. She could have kissed them all
out of sheer relief.

"Well?" Vixen the Slayer growled. "He's hurt. Aren't
you going to help him? I hope to God you've brought
coffee with you." She lowered Belegir gently down

again and stalked off to the other side of the fountain, her mood abruptly darkening.

She should be happy they were here. Their presence meant she and Belegir were going to live. But instead she felt unreasonably irritated, angry without understanding why. She leaned over the fountain, splashing water on her face, finishing the job of bringing herself awake.

Ivradan and the others had clustered around Belegir, talking in low voices. The new arrivals were darting her quick worried looks. As happy as she'd been to see them a moment before, she wished them at the devil now, and she didn't know why.

Best to get out of their way until she was feeling more human, then.

She gathered up her Vixen costume, slipping Cinnas' sword into the sheath—it fit as if it had been made for it—and bundling the lot (and Gordon) under her arm. She slung her tote-bag over her shoulder and made a determined—if not entirely dignified—exit up the temple stairs. No one tried to stop her. Probably all quaking in their fuzzy little felt boots, that lot.

She went back into the Presence Chamber and sat down on one of the benches, dumping her gear at her feet. Away from the others, her black mood lifted, and she was able to reason her way to the bottom of it.

When it was just her and Belegir, well, he'd seen her pretty much at her worst. She didn't have to pretend for him. But the others . . . they'd be expecting Vixen the Slayer, not Glory McArdle, and she felt obligated to put on a show for them, like it or not. And she *didn't* like it, while knowing it was something she had to do.

No rush, but she'd best get on with things before they came looking for her.

She prodded at her shoulder, and was relieved to

find that while it was sore, it wasn't much worse than
it had been the night before. She peeled off the wool
shift and went through her complete routine of morning stretches, ending with a slow walkover that assured
her that everything still worked as well as it ever had.
Now that she knew Glory was in good working order,
it was time to add the fancy dress.

The Vixen costume was like an old friend, with its
friendly false promise that she knew how to go on in
the world.

She took out her compact and inspected her face.
The bruises had ripened in the night, a glorious
black and green welt along her cheek, and her freckles had disappeared beneath a new coat of tan,
making her eyes, even without makeup, almost as
gold as Vixen's.

Oh. Nice. No wonder they turned tail and bolted.
Well, that's why God made Max Factor.

She daubed pancake gingerly over the bruise until
the worst of the damage was covered, trying to blend
it into her newly darkened complexion—the puffiness
was still there, but they'd all have to live with that. A
little kohl, a lot of mascara, some blood-red lipstick,
and Hell's Own Harpy glared back at her out of the
mirror. She smiled.

"I don't know if you scare the enemy, but by damn,
you scare me, mate."

She unbraided her hair and brushed it out, using
the mirror to inspect the roots critically for lighter
growth. A few weeks yet before her own natural color
became obvious, and by that time . . . well, maybe there
was henna somewhere here in the Land of Erchanen.
Belegir had been wearing mascara when he'd first
showed up in her dressing room. These people weren't
barbarians, after all.

Time to face the music.

She stuffed all her leftover bits and pieces back into her tote-bag and walked back out of the temple.

The Allimir had been busy while she'd been gone.

The horses, including her two survivors, were all picketed at the far end of the cavern, watched over by a couple of random dogs and one of the Allimir riders. A small fire under a portable cooking tripod was heating something that smelled a great deal like breakfast. Ivradan was tending to that, while the remaining Allimir fussed over Belegir in a reassuring fashion. They'd moved him out of the cart and onto a pallet onto the ground while Glory'd been gone, and she—at least Glory thought it was a "she"—had opened a large pack full of businesslike jars, tins, and bottles, and was re-dressing his chest-wounds. There was a large whiffy dressing covering his face as well—Glory could smell it from the foot of the stairs; something swampy and astringent, with just a hint of mint.

Glory approached Ivradan, who got warily to his feet. Remembering her lessons in dealing with Belegir, she did her best to look cheerful and nonthreatening, while feeling anything but. She realized Ivradan wasn't staring at her, but past her, and after a moment, she realized why. The Sword of Cinnas, with its hilt full of purple neon magic Erchane power crystals, was highly visible over her left shoulder.

So much for subtlety. On the other hand, he *had* seen it earlier, when she'd been waving it at him half-awake.

"Good morning, Ivradan." There was a pause. "Ivradan?"

"Good morning, Slayer." With a great effort, Ivradan transferred his gaze from her sword-hilt to her face.

"I'm glad you got here," Glory continued with teeth-gritting bland patience.

"I— That is, we— Helevrin thought— When you didn't—"

"Helevrin sent you after us?" she suggested.

"Yes," Ivradan said with relief. "She said that the Warmother was waiting for you at the Oracle. I found this in the Hall of History—" He reached into the pocket of his smock and pulled something out, holding it out to her.

It was the pendant the monster had been wearing, the one she'd dropped. In all the confusion, she'd forgotten about it until now.

"Yah!" Without thinking, Glory swatted it out of his hand. It went skittering across the floor.

Ivradan cowered back, terrified, and all her good work was undone.

"No— Wait, look, Ivradan, I'm sorry," Glory said quickly. "But that is very bad magic. It was around the neck of a monster I killed. It's *Her* magic."

Ivradan stared down at it in horror, and then at his hands. "I touched it," he said in a frightened whisper.

You aren't making things better.

"Well, I don't reckon it can do anything in here," Glory said hastily. "It was glowing when the critter was wearing it, but when I brought it in here, it stopped glowing. I forgot about it until now."

Ivradan was staring at her as if she'd just grown another head.

You FORGOT about it? Are you listening to yourself, Gloria Emmeline McArdle?

"Bring it here," Belegir said. His voice was stronger now.

Glory went over and picked it up—by the cord, she still wasn't going to touch it without a damned good reason—and carried it over to Belegir. The Allimir girl who was tending him backed away as if Glory were radioactive.

Glory knelt beside Belegir, holding the pendant toward him gingerly. She was a little bit shocked to see him grasp the pendant itself as if it were nothing much out of the ordinary, holding it up close to his good eye.

"You say the creature was wearing this?"

"I didn't see it until I searched the body. But it glowed. Blue. And after I took it off him, it . . . tried to get away, so I stuck it to the ground with one of my stakes while I went looking for the horses." She looked at Belegir. "I forgot about it," she said defensively. "I was going to show it to you. It stuck, sort of, in the doorway, and when I pulled it through, it popped, and then it stopped glowing. And then the horses were getting away, and well, I just forgot about it. . . ." she finished lamely.

"This is very bad," Belegir said. "Far worse than I'd feared, if *She* is twisting our own magic against us. As we have Called you to us to be our Defender, so She must have Called others to be her allies. The creature will have used this to Call the animals out to it in the night. If we had not slumbered in Erchane's embrace, we would have fallen prey to its foul casting as well."

There was a murmur of frightened agreement from the others.

Glory sighed in exasperation. "Yes, but Belegir, what does it *mean*? Is this blue stuff some kind of voodoo? What?"

"*She* uses it to enslave the will of lesser creatures and bend them to Her will, as well as lending them Her power," Belegir said. "As our magic is a link to Erchane, so this—and others like it—is a link to *Her*. You must destroy it," he finished firmly.

"Just promise me it doesn't involve a long trip to the top of an active volcano," Glory muttered grumpily.

"No. Nothing so distant. You must drop it into the Oracle's spring."

"But— Crikey, Bel, don't you reckon Erchane'll *mind*?" Glory sputtered, nonplussed.

"It must be done," Belegir said somberly. "If it is removed from the Temple it will come to life once more, and *She* will know all that has been done here."

"Well, we can't have that, now, can we? But d'you reckon it could wait until after breakfast?" Glory said hopefully.

"Yes. Of course. And you must let Tavara tend your injury, so that it does not grow poisoned," Belegir told her.

Tavara was the Allimir girl who had been seeing to Belegir—shy as a fawn she was, but judged against Belegir, all of the Allimir commonfolk were timid little things, ill-at-ease with the magic that Belegir lived with as a matter of course and that even Glory had come to take for granted. With trembling fingers, the girl peeled away Glory's makeshift bandage. Her eyes filled with tears at the sight of the gashes, though Glory was relieved to see they didn't look much worse than they had yesterday.

"You should see the other guy," Glory said encouragingly.

Tavara blushed hotly, too tongue-tied to speak, but her movements were quick and deft as she cleaned away the greasy salve and carefully prodded the flesh around the gouges.

"The wound is clean," she pronounced. "It will heal well." From one of the containers at her side she took a small handful of greenish dough, first rolling it into a ball, then working it into a thick patch big enough to cover the whole area. This she bound into place with a long strip of what looked like homespun linen. "You must leave this in place until it is dry. When it begins to itch, then you may take it off." She sounded as stern as a Public Health Nurse, and Glory stifled a smile.

"Gotcha. Belegir—he's going to be all right, isn't he?" She'd rather have had this conversation somewhere out of Belegir's earshot, but doubted her ability to get Tavara off somewhere private without giving the girl heart failure.

"He is old, and weak, and badly hurt. It will be many days before he can ride even as far as the edge of the forest," Tavara said matter-of-factly.

"But the day *will* come, right?" Glory insisted.

"If Erchane wills it," Tavara said, casting her eyes demurely downward.

Fortunately, Ivradan chose that moment to appear with the local version of a McDonald's Happy Meal— a big bowl of boiled grain spiced with raisins and cubes of smoked meat, a thick slice of buttered bread, and a wooden mug full of tea. Glory accepted all three with avaricious gratitude, and wolfed the bread down in a few short bites.

"You lot came prepared, I'll give you that," she said around bites of bread, reaching for the tea. It was scaldingly hot, but she had no complaints. It was food, and there'd been little enough of that in the past day or so.

"Helevrin told us we must. If only her True Dream had come sooner—!" Ivradan agonized.

" 'If only' gets you nothing in this life, Ivradan," Glory said with rough kindness. "You came, and you came in time to save our bacon. That's more than enough. I'm sorry about the other horse. And Kurfan. He died game." She blinked back unexpected tears. "I wish I could have saved him."

"You saved Belegir," Ivradan said, putting an awkward hand on her shoulder.

"I hope." She glanced over her shoulder. Tavara and

the other Allimir were sitting beside Belegir, having their own breakfasts. Tavara was feeding Belegir sips of gruel from a small spouted cup. "She says he'll be okay?"

"When I was younger, I fell from the roof of our barn at haying time, and spent the whole season in bed. But I am here today. When he can ride again, Tavara will release the spell that Helevrin sent with us, and the Allimir will come to bear him away."

"But you and I will be gone by then," Glory guessed, looking straight at him.

Ivradan didn't flinch. "Helevrin said that also."

Glory sighed and ate weird oatmeal. It wasn't bad, particularly if you couldn't remember the last time you'd had a full meal.

"That's why you brought so much stuff."

"She said the Oracle would speak to you."

Only it *hadn't* spoken to her, and apparently it'd told Belegir she'd go toes-up at the first opportunity. All she'd had was a wacky dream she couldn't quite remember any more. Well, bugger that for a game of soldiers. She was going to muddle on as long as she could, and damn anybody who got in her way.

After she'd eaten, Glory got carefully to her feet. She'd eaten too much too fast, and in combination with the corset, felt like she'd swallowed a young pig, trotters and all. Still, she'd rather be full than empty.

"So, Ivradan. Want to come see the Oracle?"

She could tell from the look on his face that he'd much rather not, thank you very much. But if he was going to be her native guide to the wonders of Elboroth-Haden, the former Grey Arlinn, it'd be just as well for him to get his feet wet with some nice friendly magic first.

So, Glor, just when did you get so ruthless?

"C'mon, mate. Y'wanna live forever? Besides, there's a map in there I want you to see."

Looking as if he'd been told off to be hanged, Ivradan followed her up the stairs into the temple. She was actually getting used to the treachery of the stairs, after all this time.

He was on familiar ground as far as the Presence Chamber, but once she took him through the back wall and into the Old Temple, Ivradan's eyes bulged, and he stared at everything at once.

"Belegir says this is the part they used to use a long time ago. The floor's a map. Look. We're here." She pointed at the purple triangle on the floor that represented the Oracle. "And we need to go . . . here."

Ivradan gulped, staring at the red glyph set into the floor. If the Allimir'd had the gesture, Glory bet he would have crossed himself. As it was, one hand groped toward something hanging around his neck beneath his clothes.

"There?"

"That's right."

"Ah . . ." he said, sighing resignedly. "Thus it must be, if Erchane wills."

"I reckon you're right there. Just get me close enough that I can find my way. I'll do the rest."

And who in God's name was writing her dialogue this morning? Glory wondered. It was bad enough to say things like this after a pint or two of overproof Allimir ale, but on tea and oatmeal it was nothing short of criminal.

Must be the water.

After giving him enough time to gawk, she led the way back down to the Oracle spring. After so many trips this way, it had begun to seem like her morning commute. She carried the blasphemous trinket by its cord—she'd be glad enough to get rid of it, and surely Belegir knew the proper means of disposal if anyone did, but it still seemed a touch impertinent to go tossing it into a sacred well as if it were a rubbish tip. Still, she'd rather think about that than the fact that the Warmother (whether she existed or not) had apparently gotten up the brains to rope in a cadre of extra-dimensional bad guys to help her out. Apparently *She* hadn't had any trouble getting people to show up when she wanted them.

It wasn't fair, that was what it wasn't.

"You can wait out here," Glory said when they reached the door to the spring. "Unless you want to come inside?"

"No," Ivradan said, taking a step back. "No. Thank you, Slayer. I will remain here."

"Suit yourself." She lifted the bar, opened the door, and stepped inside, wondering—and not for the first time—just what it was these people were worried would get *out*. You didn't bar doors that weren't going to open, after all, did you?

A fine time to think of that!

She leaned over the pool, trying to see down inside, but as always, the surface of the spring was nothing more than a smooth black mirror. She leaned out over it, and dropped the pendant in as close to the center as she could manage.

She'd thought it would float, or at least sink slowly. It sank as if it were made of lead, disappearing instantly.

She'd expected more drama, somehow, but except for the floating sword, Allimir magic didn't seem to be the flashy sort, really. More results oriented. Just as well for her fragile nerves, Glory told herself wisely.

She went back outside, dropped the bar into place again, collected Ivradan, and walked back to the Pilgrim's Fountain.

"Let's go outside," she said, when they got there. Tavara was sitting beside her patient, and the young chap—Ivradan said his name was Cambros—was off grooming the horses. Obediently, Ivradan followed her.

By now, the sand paintings were muddled past all recognition. Glory thought about the hordes of Temple acolytes who must have spent hours every day putting them together, just to see them trampled by pilgrims the moment their backs were turned. Once upon a time, Belegir had been one of those acolytes, and Helevrin, and even Englor. She supposed that outside of those three, there wasn't anyone alive who knew how to do these paintings any more. She sighed. Deep thoughts for a half-talented actress and former Phys Ed teacher whose biggest qualification for either post was being able to turn three backflips in rapid succession.

"Where are we going?" Ivradan asked diffidently.

"I want to get a look at the outdoors. And I want you to get a look at that monster that came after Belegir yesterday. Maybe you'll see something I missed."

"I don't think so," Ivradan said cautiously.

It was late morning when they got to the cave opening, and Glory took a deep appreciative breath of really fresh air. She hadn't minded being inside the temple cave while she was in there, but now that she was back in the free air, she couldn't imagine how she'd stood it. She slid her eyes sideways, looking over her shoulder at Cinnas' sword, and wondered uneasily how she could have accepted the whole setup—magic and monsters and ancient temples—so effortlessly. There was something unnatural about it, as if it hadn't occurred to her until this very moment how *bizarre* it all was. As if magic had picked her up and moved her about like a chess-piece, for its own needs, suppressing her own sense of self-preservation, and only now, when its necessities had been fulfilled, did it release her to feel the proper fear and unease she should have felt all along.

It was creepy. She'd always thought you'd notice magic when it showed up, that it would appear in a sudden grand display that would stop everything for miles around dead in its tracks like a New Years' fireworks display, that it wouldn't be a case of looking back and realizing you'd been bathing in the stuff as obliviously as a trout in milk. It was like all those Greek myths where you couldn't see a thing unless you looked in a mirror. If you looked at it straight on, you couldn't see it at all.

She sighed. No wonder Vixen was grumpy all the time, if she had to put up with magic morning, noon, and night. Glory concentrated on her blessedly magic-free (or so she hoped) surroundings. It was a nice day. You could tell that fall was coming, though there was a long stretch of warm yet to get through; there was just something about the air, the same promise of cold to come—without anything really palpable about it—that in spring was turned to the affirmation of coming summer heat. Now, the air seemed to say, was the time to be getting the harvest in, fattening everything up for winter.

Only nobody was much getting the chance to do that, this year, were they?

She stopped and sniffed, suspiciously.

"Smell anything?" she asked Ivradan.

Ivradan obligingly sniffed. "No."

"You should, I reckon. Okay, so it's pretty cool under the trees, but I whacked that critter about a day ago, and the weather's been warmish. He should've gone off at least a little, and I didn't drag him all that far. Let's go see."

For that matter, she'd left most of Kurfan a good sight nearer to the trail, and she didn't see those remains either. Their absence could be chalked up to scavengers easily enough, but it would have to be a pretty big and a pretty determined scavenger to take on the task of moving the amount of meat the dead monster represented.

She led Ivradan down the trail and off into the wood. Her drag-marks from the previous day were still there—hard to cover your trail in a pine forest—but when she got to the spot where she'd left the body, she found that what she'd been afraid of had happened.

The monster was gone.

Kurfan's head was still there, wrapped in the leather vest, wedged between the roots of a tree, as though it had been carelessly rolled away when whatever had come for the monster's body had shifted it.

And there were no drag marks. No drag marks at all.

"This," said Glory, "is not good." She looked at Ivradan. "Something came and took the body." *I hope. I hope it didn't just get up and walk away.* She looked around. "I don't see any tracks. Do you?"

Ivradan considered the question carefully, looking around the clearing. "None. Not even deer have been here."

For one fey wild moment Glory thought about going back to the monster's campsite and seeing if it or something like it was there, and firmly quashed the notion. She'd gotten far too much luck yesterday to squander it today on an idiot gesture designed to impress someone who was already terrified of her anyway.

"Let's go back and spread the good news. Belegir isn't going to like this. And . . . when do you want to leave, and how long will it take us to get there?" *And do you reckon there's any possibility—any at all—that we'll arrive alive, with things like that bear-wolf out there in the dark looking for us?*

"We could leave tomorrow at first light, if that suits you, Slayer. From the Oracle to Great Drathil is not far—half a day, if that, and a good road to follow. From there . . ." his voice dropped, "I do not know the length of the path that leads to the Forbidden Peak."

"Well, maybe Bel will know. He knows a lot of things," Glory said philosophically.

CHAPTER FIVE:
Smoke and Mirrors

According to Belegir and Ivradan, Great Drathil had once been a sizeable stone-and-timber city in the foothills of the High Hilvorns, surrounded by sprawling fields and orchards.

That was then.

Great Drathil was now a sizable charcoal-and-large-rocks wasteland surrounded by scorched earth and tree stumps, with only a few bits of wall to get in the way.

She and Ivradan sat a-pony on a rise at the edge of the forest, overlooking what used to be the city. They'd left Cambros, Tavara, and Belegir behind them at the Oracle early this morning, and on Felba and Fimlas (it was Marchiel who'd been the blue-plate special after all, so said Ivradan, not that Glory could tell any of the ponies apart), and leading another pack-pony, she and Ivradan had taken the supply road that had once connected Great Drathil with the Oracle of Erchane.

And now they were here, at what had once been the Allimir's largest city.

Once.

It was an area at least as big as downtown Melbourne, and it wasn't there any more, just charcoal and grey mud and pieces of buildings, but not quite enough of them to let her guess what the living city had looked like. There wasn't even green on the mountainside beyond the city—just bare rock and more bare rock and a few hundred million kilos of lab-sterile potting soil, all in shades of grey. The surrounding hills were nothing but bare mud, deep-cut with the erosion-furrows of five years of rain.

What the hell had happened? The city looked as if it had been firebombed. Supposedly it had been the first place in the Land of Erchanen to feel the Warmother's wrath, and that was five years ago. Surely there ought to be weeds and vines by now. Something to soften the look of utter destruction.

There was nothing. It looked like somebody had drowned the place in weed-killer and kerosene and then set it alight. Grey, and grey, and more grey, as bleak and sterile as something Glory couldn't think up a good comparison for. Not the mountains of the Moon, not even the death-camps of the last big war: the Moon was empty and neutral as a glass dish, and the death-camps had been the ultimate expression of human monstrousness. This was different than either one, disturbing where it ought to be terrifying, as though it were something so far beyond merely human comprehension that the human mind couldn't get a good hold on it.

But she'd better. Because this was where the danger was, and if she couldn't recognize the danger when it came, she was going to be buying a quick ticket to the boneyard, with the Allimir to follow her in pretty quick order.

And you might even be able to take a step back out of your own skin and look at that from a philosophical point of view, were you so inclined (it was amazing, as a noted Outback philosopher had once said, how much mature wisdom resembled being too tired), except that Glory had the sneaking suspicion that the nastiness wouldn't stop here. She already had ample evidence that the Warmother's magic didn't confine her to this world alone. Why should *She* stop here, once she'd turned the whole place into a bigger version of Great Drathil?

She wouldn't, would she? Glory bet that all those heroes who'd been "too busy" to come to the Allimir's aid would find time to pitch in against the Warmother once she wandered off her own patch, right enough. And Glory also suspected it would be too late.

So screw the consolations of philosophy.

She adjusted the sweatshirt she'd tied around her shoulders (and around her sword), shivering in spite of it. The day had dawned overcast, and even now was still grey—just as well, all things considered. Glory didn't think she could face the looks of this place in full daylight.

"Well, *this* is cheery, I must say," Glory muttered under her breath, getting ready for what came next.

It wasn't so much that she had an actual plan, as that she knew what she had to do. Whether that conviction stemmed from heroism or lunacy, she didn't know, and she certainly didn't think that the Oracle had provided the inspiration. All she knew was that she was entirely fed up with this Warmother, and she was going to go and tell her so.

"Which bit's . . . it?" Glory asked Ivradan.

Ivradan pointed at the tallest of the peaks. She had to crane her neck to look at it. The top, fittingly enough, was shrouded in clouds. Great Drathil had been built directly into the base of Elboroth-Haden, the mountain on which the Warmother had once been imprisoned—not where she would have put her largest city, if she'd had a seriously taboo mountain to contend with, but what the hey?

"And the path?"

Ivradan pointed again, lower. Blinking and peering through the ruins of the city, Glory could make out a smooth stone path leading toward the mountain. At one time, it looked as if there'd probably been a set of rather nice iron gates barring the way—at least until they'd been mashed, crumpled, and generally wadded up like a couple of balls of waste paper in a rather petty-minded fashion by something large enough to do the job.

Not good.

"There's something moving down there," Ivradan said in a tight voice. The Allimir horse-master wasn't a happy camper, but Glory gave him points where points were due: he neither grizzled nor whinged, and he'd come along without complaining. He did his job, and if he wasn't happy about it, who was she to blame him? She wasn't happy herself.

"Where?"

Then she saw it. Someone moving around down in the ruins, just stepping out of the shell of one of the buildings. Not a monster. A man.

There was something familiar about him . . .

"Hup-hup-hup!" A better horsewoman than she'd been this time last week, Glory chivvied Fimlas down the road into the city, leaving Ivradan behind.

The little beast was a showoff at heart, happy to leap the fallen timbers that stood in its way. Its unshod hooves clattered over the paving stones of the city proper as it moved into a gallop, and Glory found herself giving tongue to Vixen's trademark battle yell: "Hi-yi-yi-yi! Come, camrado! *Evil wakes!*"

She didn't even feel silly about it.

By the time she reached the place where she'd seen him, the man had disappeared. The building must have been dead impressive once, whatever it had been: the ground floor was made of large blocks of the local granite, which was why most of it was still here now. The side and back wall were almost intact, though blackened and fire-glazed, and enough of the second floor was still in place to form a roof of sorts, making the structure dark and shadowy inside. A nice place for spiders and snakes, not that she'd seen many of either since she'd got here.

Not that she'd put it past the Warmother to import either by the boxload, just for grins.

She swung down from the horse and pulled her sweatshirt off her shoulders, dropping it to the ground and drawing her sword. The blade flashed, an absurd spot of cheery color in the grey desolation.

"Come on out, you! Better now than later!" she shouted.

There was a scuffling sound from inside the ruins, and a figure emerged.

"Dylan?" Glory stared in slack-jawed disbelief. Dylan MacNee, a cutting-edge vision in black from his Versace loafers to his collarless Prada linen duster, stepped gingerly over the broken rubble and gawped at her in turn. Defrocked priest, hedge-Satanist and black magician (at least he played one on TV), she could have kissed him on the spot.

His resume claimed he was five ten, but Glory towered over him even in flats, and thought five eight was being charitable. Like most actors, he lied about all his vitals. He was slender and pale, with black hair and (thanks to colored contacts) startlingly green eyes, his narrow beard carefully trimmed and waxed into a properly Satanic point for his role as

Fra Diavolo, minion of Lilith Kane, the Duchess of Darkness. He had the usual resume: East End, a little Shakespeare, a few episodes of *Dr. Who,* some commercials. One of that legion of eternal journeymen, their lives unchanged from the Bard's day, whose entire epitaph might well consist of the single line: "He always worked." Like the rest of the *TITAoVtS* cast, Dylan had been shipped to America on the promo tour, but his part in things had ended earlier than hers had, and Glory hadn't seen much of him after New York.

"Glory?" When he wasn't putting on side as the cultured Castilian, Dylan's vowels were pure working-class Britain. "What the hell are . . . ? That's not your sword!"

She'd used to think the stereotypes about actors never carried over into real life until she met Dylan.

"I reckon it is now," she said with magnificent simplicity. "Dylan, what are you *doing* here?"

"I was in the men's room at the Waldorf Astoria," he said with an expression of hurt dignity. "Then I came out again and they'd bombed the place or something. I'll sue, I swear I will. But what's going on? I thought you were out in the land of sun and hardbodies, doing vapid telly for luscious bronzed young persons. My God, you *are* a mess, aren't you? Ooh, Tricia is just going to *kill* you when she sees what you've done to your leather! And where's your sword? Your proper sword? Our Brucie won't be best pleased if you've gone and lost it somewhere, now, will he?"

"Dylan, did three short people in strange costumes show up and ask you to come and save the world?" Glory demanded in exasperation, cutting short what promised to be a lengthy catalogue of her lapses. Dylan's ability to ignore everything that didn't revolve directly around Dylan was legendary on the set, but this was excessive, even for him.

He fluttered his lashes at her sweetly. "Well, I *am* staying with some *dear* friends down in the Village, but . . . no. Now *what the hell is going on*?"

Glory sighed. "It is a *very* long and *very* complicated story. I'll tell you everything I know—"

"That shouldn't take long."

"—but first I want you to wait right here while I go take a look at something."

"Suppose I don't feel like it?" Dylan said sulkily.

"Do you see any taxis around here?" Glory said. "Or Craft Services, for that matter? Stand about. There's things that come out at night here that make the jackbooted Family Values crowd look like something you'd want to meet. Hold this," she added, thrusting Fimlas's lead-rein at him.

For once, Dylan didn't have anything to say. He didn't even criticize her delivery. Glory strode past him, sword out, stepping into the ruin.

She wasn't sure what she was looking for—the men's room door of the Waldorf-Astoria, maybe. But there wasn't anything. She got as far as the back wall of the building, and found nothing more than a curious absence of debris. No mages, good or bad. No glowing crystals in any color, or eldritch runes, or anything in the least peculiar. Assuming she could identify, any longer, what peculiar consisted of.

But . . .

If Belegir had recruited Glory to aid him because he was looking for a hero and had gotten her confused with the part she played, why was *Dylan* here? He didn't look all that much like Sister Bernadette, assuming The Powers That Were had decided she needed a sidekick. And if they'd wanted a Bad Guy, why wasn't *Romy* here, not Dylan?

Though anybody who tangled with Romy Blackburn got what was coming to them, and then some.

She shrugged. She had *no* clue. But even assuming they were after Fra Diavolo instead, anyone seizing upon Dylan as a henchweasel of evil had some unhappy surprises coming. Dylan wasn't willing to exert himself that much.

"The explanation?" Dylan demanded waspishly, when she re-emerged. He'd dropped the rein, and Fimlas had wandered away, looking for something to eat. She hurried after the pony and collected it, then sheathed her sword before returning to Dylan. She picked up her sweatshirt, trying to figure out what she was going to say. No point in trying to convince Dylan of the reality and the gravity of the situation. If Great Drathil itself couldn't convince him, nothing she could say would help. Best to stick to simple facts.

"When I was in Hollywood, a bunch of wizards from another dimension came and asked me to save their country from this villain called the Warmother. She lives up there," Glory added, pointing toward the mountaintop. "They'd got me all confused with, you know, *Vixen*, but before I could sort them out, their magic went off and I ended up here. Since she's going to do the lot of us whether I help or not, I thought I'd see what I could do."

"That's the stupidest pitch I've ever heard," Dylan said after a long pause, speaking with the surreal self-possession of the entirely self-involved.

Glory didn't say anything.

Another pause, then: "Are you out of your flaming little mind, dearie?"

Glory shook her head wearily. "This isn't a pitch, Dylan. This is real life. And do you have a better explanation? Or an idea?"

"Run like hell," Dylan said smugly.

"Where?"

"Well, there's got to be somewhere," Dylan said uneasily. He looked around. "Even assuming I believe your idiotic story."

"Come up with a better one," Glory said reasonably. She turned and began to lead Fimlas back up the path toward Ivradan.

Dylan grumbled something barely audible and followed her.

"But look," he said, though he was forced to address this cogent argument to her back. "Even were I to accept this utterly shopworn tale at face value: why me? *Galaxy Quest* is hardly a fresh new idea. If someone wants a hero for their gladiatorial games, well and good, but why me? I'm a henchman, Glory, dear. Second villain and all, supporting frightener— though I must say, my Mercutio has been rather well received, and—"

"I don't know," Glory said bluntly, stopping to look back at him. "I want to know. I reckon I'd better know. But right now, I don't." She did manage to feel a bit sorry for Dylan. He'd been dropped right into the midst of things, and that none too gently. She'd be happy to send him off to the sidelines if she could, but where? The only possible place was the Oracle.

Maybe she could send him back with Ivradan. Who'd be worrying just now, and who would at least be easier to explain things to. She led Dylan back out of the ruined city, up the gentle rise to the edge of the forest to where Ivradan waited with the other two ponies. She only hoped he wasn't as familiar with *TITAoVtS* as Englor had been, or she was going to have a lot of fast talking to do to explain the presence of Fra Diavolo.

Ivradan's eyes widened when he saw Dylan. "Mind your manners," Glory told Dylan in an undertone. "His mum's a wizard who can turn you into a hatstand if you look crosswise at him. S'okay, Ivradan," she said, pitching her voice a little louder. "He's my, um, camrado. Dylan comes from back home. Where I come from."

Ivradan inspected the newcomer warily, taking in Dylan's wildly inappropriate but *very* fashionable outfit.

"Is he a wizard?" the Allimir horse-master asked at last. Dylan smirked.

"Not exactly," Glory temporized. But if she'd managed to kill an eight-foot-tall monster with a dull sword, who knew what Dylan might not be able to accomplish if he had to? She considered how best to explain to Ivradan that he was to take Dylan back to the Oracle with him, and how to persuade Dylan to go peacefully.

"More of your little friends?" Dylan asked idly, pointing out across the plains.

Glory turned and looked, and her heart sank.

A mass of marching figures. There were a lot of them, as many as *TITAoVtS* would lay on for a superdeluxe big-budget crowd and battle scene, say eighty to a hundred. They were, by the most generous estimate, five kilometers away, too far to make out the individual details clearly, especially in the diffuse grey light of the overcast day. She could not even tell whether they were entirely human. But the blades of their pikes or spears or whatever they were were clearly silhouetted against the sky, and they were wearing some kind of armor, and here and there in the mass of determinedly marching figures, she thought she could see a toxic gleam of blue, as from the glow of an amulet.

Ivradan watched them come with the worried incomprehension of a man who knows the news can only be bad, but still has no idea of what it is he's looking at.

The marauders were heading straight toward the ruined city, which meant straight toward them. The three of them couldn't hide and couldn't fight. And their directions for running away were decidedly limited. Glory took a deep breath.

"Ivradan," Glory said gently, "that is an army, and I reckon they'll be unkind to us if they reach us. I'm not sure we can outrun them, and if we try, we'll just lead them back to the Oracle. I'm afraid all three of us are going to have to go up the mountain. How fast can you get the pack off that pony?"

"An army?" Ivradan abruptly went greyish under his all-weather tan. "*Her* army?" He swayed on his saddle-pad, causing Felba to shift uneasily beneath him.

Glory growled a flavorful Elizabethan profanity under her breath—one that had slipped right past the Standards and Practices review board when it had made it into the script for the pilot episode—and went over to the pack-pony. She pulled at the forward cinch's double-ring closure, growling under her breath. Maybe there was some way over the mountain that didn't involve tromping down the Warmother's throat—and even if there wasn't, that was still better odds than standing here while an army of rogue bushrangers and freelance nightmares marched over them. The three of them could take the beer and whatever food they could carry with them, but the rest would have to be left behind.

The cinch loosened, and Ivradan, bless Erchane for what backbone he did have, was there to take the weight of the sliding pack and work the second cinch free faster than Glory could have managed.

"Can the wizard ride?" he asked, letting the pack-saddle slip to the ground and worrying its waterproof covering loose.

"Like a sack of turnips," Glory said succinctly.

"Let Fimlas take him, then. You ride Felba, and I shall have Heddvi here." He tore through the contents of the pack with ruthless efficiency, winnowing its contents into three bags small enough for them to carry. She heard things break.

"Do you mind if I ask what's going on?" Dylan demanded, coming over to look. The first sack was full, and Glory thrust it at him, pointing back over his shoulder.

"*That* is an invading army. *We* are running away from it as fast as we can."

"On what?" Dylan asked, in tones that rather suggested he knew.

Glory looked at him.

"No," he said, backing away, still clutching the canvas sack. "No, no, no. I don't *do* horses. You remember— when that damned Adrian of yours stepped on my foot I was lame for a *month!*"

Adrian the Wonder Horse had been a joy to all who knew him, but trick-horses weren't so thick upon the ground that Full Earth could afford to pick and choose, and Adrian, ham and prima-donna though he'd been, was a great big gorgeous beast, far less easy to replace or do without than any of the human cast. And he'd known it, too, more the pity.

"Then stay here and die," Glory snapped, losing what passed for her patience. If the errant gods of whimsy wanted to supply her with missing cast members, why couldn't they have sent her Adrian? He'd have been a bit more use at the moment. "I don't have time to argue with you, and I'm not going to carry you. But I reckon you ought to know that that lot coming are probably cannibals."

Dylan looked back toward the army. "I'll fall off," he whined, as if that made any difference to the facts.

"Try not to," Glory advised. "And don't drop the bag. It's got your dinner in it." She hoped.

Taking pity on him, she took one of the spare cinch straps out of the wreckage of their pack and buckled it around Fimlas, apologizing to him as she did. It would give Dylan something to hold on to, at least. The pony regarded her with wise sardonic eyes and shook its head energetically.

She got Dylan aboard Fimlas and mounted Felba, and Ivradan handed her tote-bag up to her and passed her one of the bags of supplies and a blanket, then mounted Heddvi, not bothering to rig what passed for a bridle here. Glory dug her heels in, and the pony headed back down the path toward Great Drathil. As she'd hoped, Fimlas followed of his own accord, and the sense of urgency was enough to keep even Dylan momentarily quiet.

The ridge cut them off from the sight of the enemy army almost immediately, though it was closer now, and Glory could hear scraps of sound carried toward them by the freakish acoustics of the ruins. A cry; something that might be part of a marching song. The most disturbing thing of all was that everything about the advancing horde wasn't alien. Although she didn't know for sure that they weren't human, they certainly weren't Allimir. And if the marauders *were* human, she had an even better idea of what would happen if the villains caught up with them, though it hardly mattered *how* dead they got, or what happened to their bodies afterward, if they were killed. Dead was dead.

She headed Felba toward the ruined gates and the path that lay up the mountainside. On their way here this morning, Ivradan had described Great Drathil as a walled town surrounded by a ring-road and a moat used primarily for drainage and sewage purposes. Glory had reason to be grateful for that now: the moat had probably been full the night the city burned, and its presence had kept the destruction from spreading across the road, with the result that their headlong flight was reasonably unimpeded now. Glory led, urging the pony to a ground-eating trot, and Ivradan brought up the rear, making sure that Fimlas and Dylan stayed essentially together.

She'd lost sight of the gate when they reached the ring-road, though she could see the higher bits of the path up the mountain now; a set of switchbacks leading all the way to the top. The army would be able to see it too, and probably the three of them on it, but there was literally nowhere else for them to go. They couldn't hide in what was left of the city—even retreating back into the forest wasn't a real option: if her eyes hadn't been fooling her, and those blue gleams she'd spotted were real, the magic the enemy was carrying would be enough to track the three of them down—or call them and their mounts to it, the way the monster had called Kurfan and the ponies out of the Oracle-cave.

Glory shuddered. Maybe they wouldn't look up and see them on the mountain path. Maybe they had other marching orders. Maybe the magic of the Sword of Cinnas was more powerful than their little talismans and would shield the three of them somehow. Maybe the bad guys were afraid of Elboroth-Haden, too.

Why do I always come up with perfectly good plans and then come up with perfectly good reasons why they won't work? She'd liked it better when she thought the Warmother was a figment of the Allimir's collective imagination.

At last the gates that had once barred the way to the Forbidden Peak came into sight. She could imagine they'd been pretty impressive back in the day. They'd probably looked like the gates on Skull Island, the ones the natives put up to keep King Kong out of the potato salad. Allimir teenagers probably snuck out here on dark nights and dared each other to touch them, then ran off giggling. That sort of thing.

Not any more.

They'd been made of wood and gold and iron. The wood had been reduced to a black spray of charcoal, as if someone had thrown paint on the rocks. The gold and iron had run all together, and the iron had rusted red with the rain of passing seasons, while the gold, annealed to utter purity, gleamed as bright as if it were still molten, running in threads across the dull rusted surface of the iron. The metalwork had been softened until it had sagged like moist potter's clay in a rainstorm, melting and slumping and sliding away, pulled by the patient force of gravity.

Then something, angry and impatient, had taken that soft hot malleable metal and forced it open, tearing it like an unbaked piecrust and crushing it against the bones of the mountain. There it had cooled, its form halfway between shapeless slag and the careful work of art it once had been.

Glory took this in during the seconds it took her to approach the gates and make her way through them at a trot. She'd have preferred a gallop, or a flat-out run, but Dylan couldn't stay on Fimlas at that gait, and they couldn't use the ponies up now when they'd need them later. Besides, they weren't going to win this one by speed. There was no way to outrun this enemy. Only to outwit him, ill-prepared as she was for that kind of fight.

What I need is a miracle, true enough. And this place has been running scant on those for a long time now, hasn't it?

The path began to incline sharply upward, and the pony, no fool, slowed from a trot to a walk. Glory wasn't sure what she'd expected to see on this side of the gate, but what she did see was a wide path, narrowing as it rose up the mountain, that seemed to have been cut directly into the rock as if with God's own butter knife. It ought to have been covered with the natural accumulation of the dirt and debris of a thousand years, but at the moment it was scrubbed as bare and clean as if someone had been through here with a new broom and one of those industrial steam-jets they used to de-grime skyscrapers with. The ponies' hooves clicked on the stone as if they were walking down Bourke Street back home. Even the rock around her held no shadow of moss, no fugitive weed making its home in a handy crevice.

Ivradan pulled level with her, and Felba took the opportunity to slow to a meditative walk. The horsemaster's face was grim, set in an expression that suggested he never expected to hear good news again.

"What now, Slayer?" he asked in a low voice.

"We go on. Maybe this path curves around the mountain. If we get round the side before they think to look up, we're home free."

"We're on Elboroth-Haden," Ivradan pointed out unnecessarily.

"Maybe the trail branches out up ahead and we can go somewhere else," Glory said soothingly. "Come on." She urged Felba into a faster walk, glancing back to make sure Dylan was still back there. He was. He looked rumpled and irritated, clinging to the cinch strap. She wasn't in the least surprised to see that he'd dropped both the bag and the blanket she'd handed him, and she was just as glad not to be able to get into any conversations with him just now. Ivradan dropped back to keep pace with him—and also, Glory rather thought, to allow her to be the first to face anything the mountain had to throw at them.

But that left her with nothing to do but brood, and keep the pony moving. Had she made the right decision? It had all happened so *fast*. Maybe they could have gotten out of there on foot ahead of the villains and kept all the supplies—it occurred to her she'd just sent the three of them haring up the side of a mountain at the end of summer with nothing more than the clothes on their backs and a couple of blankets.

Dammit.

But for that matter, what was an army—or a raiding party, or whatever it was—doing coming in this direction, anyway? They couldn't be looking for Allimir. All the Allimir were out on the Serenthodial, cowering in their *vardos*. There were only two things in this direction.

The Oracle.

And the top of the mountain.

"Oh sod and bleeding buggering bugger all," Glory groaned feelingly under her breath. What if the raiding party was going *home*?

But no. She knew she was grasping at straws, but still. There'd never been raiding parties before, only the invisible *something*, striking under cover of darkness, that none of the Allimir had ever seen. That certainly wasn't a description of that mob the three of them were fleeing from now. Ergo, the Warmother did not, in the normal course of business, have job lots of villains heading back and forth to this particular mountaintop. So while the odds weren't against them heading in this direction, they weren't especially in favor of it, either.

Back to Square One. And back to this being a waiting game, or as much of one as you could play while ambling up a mountainside on ponyback at a brisk clippity-clop.

Fortunately, it was in the nature of mountain trails to curve, and eventually this one did, but unfortunately she'd been wrong about it going around the mountain. Instead, it turned at a right angle to itself and sent them parallel to the city, several hundred yards above it. Instead of sheer walls of granite on both sides of them, the one on their left was gone, and by now the trail had narrowed appreciably. They proceeded single file along an uncomfortably narrow path with a sheer cliff to their right and a sheer drop on their left, more-or-less in plain sight of anyone who cared to look up.

But the view was magnificent.

Beyond the burnt scar that had been Great Drathil, the vast prairie of Serenthodial the Golden stretched outward to meet the sullen sky. Somewhere out there were the last of the Allimir, counting on her to save them. The more fool they.

Closer at hand were the enemy nightmares. They'd reached the city and were swarming over the ruins as if searching for something. She could hear them shouting at each other angrily, and wondered what they were looking for. Unfortunately for her curiosity, she still couldn't see them very well. Great Drathil itself seemed to be their goal, any how, which was some small relief.

"I am going to be sick," she heard Dylan enunciate crisply behind her, and recalled guiltily that Dylan wasn't terribly good with heights.

"Sorry," she said, half turning on Felba's back to talk to him. Dylan's face was a greenish color and he clung to the leather strap about his mount's ribs like grim Death. "Just close your eyes and try not to mind. We'll be at the top soon." *I hope.*

Dylan followed her advice and addressed several feeling remarks to the ambient air, of which "insensitive Colonial trollop" was perhaps the most complimentary.

Glory spent the rest of the ascent worrying. She started with the probable and likely perils: the enemy forces, the weather, the state of their supplies, and then with enforced leisure, moved onward and outward: the possibility that one of the ponies would slip and hurl itself and its rider over the cliff, the prospect of a sudden ice storm or monsoon, the chance that they would be set upon by giant killer eagles or radioactive mutant bats. Somewhere in the middle of her worries she dug around in her bag and pulled out Gordon. Cuddling the stuffed elephant made her feel better, and it hardly mattered if she looked ridiculous.

When she had exhausted all the possible and improbable disasters that could happen during their ascent, she prepared to start in on what would happen when they got to the top of the mountain, but then she realized she really didn't need to. Her imagination was exhausted. When they got to the top of the mountain, they were all going to die. She believed that absolutely. She was certainly going to give interfering with that outcome her best shot, but she knew that so far she'd only seen the Warmother's warming-up exercises, and even those were good enough to squash her like a bug.

Still, giving up wasn't in her. You went out there and tried—and tried your best, because anything less was cheating yourself and your opponent. Winning wasn't as important as doing your best—the lessons of a thousand gymnastic competitions, drummed into her from the time she could barely walk, came back to her now. Outgunned, but never outclassed, that was what her coach Ross always used to say to her. *"C'mon, Glory-gel, y'wanna live forever?"* And the answer she'd learned to give—if only inside her head—as she grew was always the same: *"I choose glory over length of days . . ."*

They'd been climbing steadily for what seemed like ages, but with the switchbacks and the angle of the trail, it was impossible to see any distance ahead, and hard to tell how much farther they had to go. It was only when she reached the last of the switchbacks that she realized it was the last one, or near it, because ahead the trail was blanketed with a dense fog. Clouds. She remembered that the top of the mountain had been shrouded in mist.

She hoped Dylan still had his eyes closed.

She reached out her left hand and let her fingers brush against the rock. It was wet. They ought to dismount and lead the ponies, but the trail now was too narrow and much too slippery even for that. She didn't know if Felba would walk on if he couldn't see the trail in front of him, or how slippery the mist would make the bare stone beneath his hooves, but this was no time for second-guessing. She wound her free hand in the pony's mane, clutched Gordon tightly against her side, and held on, wishing she could pray, but she couldn't bear to close her eyes.

Felba walked on into the mist at the same placid unhurried pace at which he'd covered the rest of the ascent. The mist settled around her, wet and chill, until she could see nothing—not her outstretched arm, not the animal beneath her. The sound of the ponies' hoofbeats, so clear and sharp a moment before, jumbled and faded away into an echoing arrhythmia.

"Glory!" Dylan's voice boomed out of the mist somewhere behind her. She heard something else—maybe Ivradan—but couldn't make out the words.

"It's all right," she shouted back, though to her own ears, her voice sounded flat and muffled. "I reckon we're near the top. Hang on!"

As if he'd do anything else. Fair strangling the poor beast, he probably was.

Water beaded up on her skin and began to run down it in rivulets, trickling beneath her corset and soaking the lining. Glory shivered as the chill of the sodden fog began to make its presence felt, and spared a wistful thought for all those other blankets they'd had to abandon. Her hair was braided back, but even so, she could feel it getting heavier as it wicked up moisture from the air around her just as if it were raining. She hoped that whatever that purple sword was made of, it wasn't something that could rust.

Through it all, the little pony plodded on doggedly.

Glory didn't know how long they spent in the cloudbank—it was strange how the destruction of all visual referents destroyed the time sense as well—but suddenly she was aware of a peculiar brightness ahead. Then the mist thinned further, and she realized it was sunlight. Bright afternoon sunlight.

As simply as that, they were through the fog. Somewhere back in the mist the trail had widened, or ended, or whatever. They were here, at the top, in daylight, looking down at the tops of clouds.

The top of the mountain was absolutely flat, as though someone had decided to construct a king-size scenic car-park in the middle of nowhere. It was large—you could drop Melbourne Cricket Ground in the middle of it and have elbow room to spare—and completely covered with short, velvety, utterly weed-free lawn.

And in the middle of it there was a genuine size-extra large Mad Enchanter Stronghold. It looked like it had been designed by Perky Goths, or maybe by Martians who'd seen one too many episodes of *Beverly Hills 90210*. It was at least five stories tall—the towers were taller, and there were a lot of them—and apparently chiseled out of one giant piece of mother-of-pearl. It was carved and ornamented over every inch of its surface, and polished to a fare-thee-well. It flashed and glittered iridescently in the sun, and the whole thing gave Glory a headache to look at it. Banners and pennants flew from every place a banner or pennant could fly from, all of them as soap-bubble glistery as the palace itself.

"What the bleeding 'ell is that?" Dylan demanded, reverting to the vowels of earliest youth. He slid stiffly off Fimlas' back and staggered toward Glory, giving his inoffensive mount a backward look of venomous dislike.

Ivradan made a sound very like a groan of despair, slipping easily from Heddvi's back. Both animals stood stolidly, neither dipping its muzzle to browse at the greensward.

"Turn them loose," Glory said in a low whisper. She stroked Felba's neck, stripping cloud-water from the coarse hair. She didn't like this place. She liked it less with every passing moment, and she didn't know why—other than the obvious. It was storybook-pretty; cloyingly, exuberantly sweet, like a Precious Moments version of Middle Earth. It shouldn't leave her feeling the way Ivradan looked.

"Turn them loose," she repeated. She swung her leg over Felba's rump with some difficulty and stood up, letting her tote-bag slip to the ground. "Send them away, if you can."

She was here by choice. Ivradan and Dylan hadn't exactly had a choice, but they were able to consent. The ponies could neither choose nor consent to their involvement, and Glory wanted to save them if she could.

"That won't be necessary."

She'd been looking toward the others. The voice came from behind her. Glory swung around.

She was staring at a woman who might even be taller than she was. The woman was wearing a long heavy robe of turquoise blue gold-shot silk that

resembled the robes of the Allimir mages the way a
showroom-new Maseratti sports car resembles a battered old Ford truck. Her hair was entirely hidden
beneath a silk caul in the same color, and she wore a
high elaborate jeweled headdress with sheer floating
veils that brushed the grass at her feet. Her eyes were
brilliantly blue, her beautiful face serene in the way
of a statue's or a saint's.

"If you want them gone, then they shall go." Her
voice was like low music, kindly and amused.

Before Glory could say anything, the woman raised
one arm in a sweeping gesture. The rings on her fingers flashed: the stones were a rich and toxic azure,
a brighter blue than the sky. The robe had long batwing
sleeves; they fell back as she gestured, revealing a tight
undersleeve as brightly gold as if it were made of the
liquid metal itself.

The horses were gone.

Glory stared numbly at the place where Felba had
been, unwilling to look back and see that the other two
were gone as well, though she knew they were. Even
her tote-bag was gone. She clutched Gordon tighter.

She'd be a thousand kinds of fool not to know what
was happening here. This was the Warmother, up close
and in person. This was the monster the Allimir had
sent her to whack. She was pretty—more than that.
Beautiful. Glory wasn't deceived. She was entirely
certain the Warmother needed whacking, no matter
what the bitch looked like.

But what she couldn't do was just haul out her sword
and start swinging, because that wasn't what heroes did.
There were rules for being a hero, and Glory knew very
well what they were (especially after a whole season
as Vixen of playing straight man to Lilith Kane), even
if she wasn't altogether fond of them. The rule in this
situation was very clear: the villain had to attack first.

Glory could reproach her with her wickedness, but she couldn't just walk in and clobber her. That just wasn't what the hero did.

And nothing less than textbook heroism would save the Allimir. If she wasn't a hero, she'd at least better try to be what she was—an actress—and act her part. Act like a hero, suck it up and do this according to Hoyle, and maybe when she bought the farm it would make a difference.

"Just what did you—" she began.

"Well, now, I'd say you've got something going for you a good deal better than smoke and mirrors," Dylan said, striding forward. He bowed to the Lady with a Shakespearian flourish. "Dylan MacNee—artist, thespian, student of the Bard. And who might I have the pleasure of addressing, dear lady. . .?"

The woman smiled, a cool smile of utter self-possession, and looked at Glory. "*She* knows. But for now, it pleases me for you to address me as . . . Charane."

She said the name as though it ought to have meant something to them, and Glory glanced back at Ivradan, but he was plainly and simply terrified, not up to fielding the in-jokes of Hell Incarnate. She stepped back and put a hand on his arm. She could feel faint shudders coursing through him, a trembling he could not control, though he kept his face impassive.

"Gracious lady, *dear* Charane," Dylan cooed ingratiatingly, and Glory realized what all this tiger butter was in aid of. Dylan might not have grasped much else about the situation he found himself in, but he did realize that magic had gotten him here, and only magic could get him home. And the monster in the fancy blue hat was the likeliest source of it available. "You see before you a lost and weary traveler, a long way from home—"

"And so I have made plans to greet all of you

properly," Charane said gaily. "I bid you welcome to
the castle of Arlinn, where there is a great feast prepared in your honor. Come. Join us. Let me receive
you properly—and I promise you . . . *all* your desires
shall be fulfilled," she finished in a meaningful purr.

"Well, this is something like!" Dylan said happily.
Charane tucked her arm through his and led him
toward the castle.

Glory looked back at Ivradan.

As she watched, he sank to his knees with a low
moan of absolute terror, covering his face with his
hands.

Glory knelt beside him, still clutching Gordon. She
put her arms around him awkwardly, patting his back.
Everything she could think of to say seemed
inadequate—and worse, patronizing. Of course he was
terrified. He wasn't a hero. He wasn't even an Allimir
mage. If the Warmother scared *her*, what must
Ivradan be feeling right now?

"I know I told you I wouldn't bring you here," she
finally said, "but I couldn't leave you down there. The
army would have killed you. And they might have
made you do something that would hurt Belegir and
the others first. I can't leave you alone here, either.
I know you won't be safe. You won't be safe with me,
either, but I don't think she means to do anything
just yet. I think she wants to play." Now that the first
shock was over, Glory was starting to get angry again.
"Just like she's been playing with you lot all along."
She shook her head and went on stroking his back.
She could feel his muscles quivering, but Ivradan
made no sound.

Glory looked around. There was no one in sight
now—just the blue sky, the green grass, the white
clouds stretching out level with the top of the mountain, and that ridiculous fairy-tale palace smack in the

middle of everything. Like a deserted amusement park, or a stage set.

And it *was* a stage set, in a way. This was where the last act in the farce was going to be played out, wasn't it?

Glory faced it down, believing in her future enough to see it clearly at last. What if it had been the Warmother who had brought her here, all along? What if she'd done it to raise the Allimir's hopes, to make them think they'd found a hero, so that when Glory failed them, their disappointment would be all the more crushing? Like the cat that lets the mouse think it can escape, over and over again; that was how the Warmother was.

Glory gritted her teeth. *I don't care.* She regarded the glittering castle with narrowed eyes, a dull purposeful anger filling her heart to the exclusion of everything else. *I don't care who brought me here—Erchane Incarnate, or the Warmother, or that Dreamer of Worlds bimb. It doesn't matter. The end result is the same.*

She was here for the Allimir. It was just too bad for Earth, and whatever test Humanity was about to flunk for the eleven-hundredth time, but she'd been asked to this party by the Allimir, and now they had her. They had Vixen the Slayer, Vixen the Red, Scourge of the Night, Harrower of Hell, Doomslayer, Koroshiya, Hell's Own Harpy. And she had the Sword of Cinnas. *That* couldn't have been part of anybody else's plans!

Win, lose, or toes-up: she'd come to these games to compete. Stone the rules and stone the judges. She had the playbook. She was going to play.

Abruptly, Glory wasn't afraid, not the way she had been when she first saw the castle. She was still afraid of pain, and afraid of dying, certainly (though she hoped she was just a little more afraid to fail), but she wasn't afraid of the Warmother, not his/her/itself. You had to respect something on some level to be properly afraid of it, and Glory had never respected a bully. There was no self-discipline in being a bully.

She stroked Ivradan's hair. Poor little bugger. He didn't deserve to be here any more than the ponies had.

"I can't leave Dylan alone in there, thick as he is. And this is what I came for." *To be murdered in an alien dimension by a crazed demon just to get out of a publicity tour?* "To try to make her stop. So I reckon I've got to go in there after her. I can't say what's going to happen then. I'm sorry. I reckon I'm not too good at making other people's choices for them. I did my best, but maybe it isn't much of a best. I won't ask you to do anything you don't think you can do, Ivradan. I reckon you could try to make it back down the trail alone, if you want . . ." She stopped, unable to finish the sentence. She knew he wouldn't make it to the bottom alive, and if he did, the army would be there.

Either way—stay or go—he'd be dead.

"But you . . . you will go on?" Ivradan whispered, at last. He sat up, and brushed his hair back out of his eyes. His cap had fallen off, and his burnt-chestnut hair was as unkempt as the mane of one of his own horses. He looked hollow-eyed, like a man who had faced down Death and accepted his mortality.

"I'm stupid that way," Glory said with a faint wistful smile. She offered him her elephant.

"This is Gordon. Ever since I was a little girl, I carried him with me everywhere, especially when I thought I was going to places I wasn't going to like."

Ivradan regarded the stuffed blue elephant with an unreadable expression.

"A doll," he said at last.

"Hey! This is a genuine *interdimensional* stuffed

elephant from the world of Vixen the Slayer, which has accompanied her to the very wellspring of the Oracle," Glory said, desperately hoping to make him smile.

Ivradan regarded Gordon with more respect, and picked him up as he'd seen Glory do. "I will go with you, Slayer," he said, getting to his feet.

"No worries," Glory said automatically, standing as well. *After all, we're dead one way or the other, seems to me. Maybe we can really piss this Charane bint off before we die.*

She put her arm around Ivradan's shoulders, and side by side they started across the lawn toward the Warmother's castle.

Was this the worst idea she'd had in a long history of having not terribly good ideas? Glory wondered to herself. She knew a sane person would be peeing themselves in terror at this point, but the strongest feeling she was conscious of was irritation.

She had a lot of time to wonder about her own sanity in the time it took to cross the lawn and lead Ivradan up the steps of the castle.

The inside seemed to be much larger than the outside.

There was a short entry hall and the walls were mirrored. In their flawless reflection, Glory could see herself clearly for the first time in many days.

Though her hair was braided and still wet from the clouds, it still managed to be frizzy and unkempt, and it was several days late for a wash. The bruise on her cheekbone was fading to greens and yellows, showing through the pancake she'd hastily applied this morning. Her eye makeup was smudged and runny, ringing her eyes in a sloppy raccoon mask, and she'd eaten off all her lipstick hours ago. Her leather was scuffed and battered, desperately in need of a good polish and some decent care. She'd torn a couple of the chrome

studs off here and there, and the crushed velvet panniers were crumpled and dusty. Her shoulders were
peeling, and the bandage Tavara had put on her arm
was grimy and tattered.

Dylan had been right. She was a mess. A joke. A—

"Don't look," Ivradan said urgently. She turned
toward him. He was staring fixedly at the floor. "You
will lose yourself if you look into her mirrors."

They're only mirrors, Glory wanted to say, and
didn't. There was nothing "only" about any of this. Back
at the Oracle, she'd had one taste of how sneaky magic
could be. Who was to say that this wasn't another? She
nodded, saying nothing, and kept her eyes fixed on her
boots (not all that scuffed, not really) as she walked
forward toward a set of silver doors even larger than
the golden ones. They stood open, framing the entrance
into what was obviously the place Charane had been
taking them. The mirrors stopped a few feet short of
those doors, and Glory looked up.

As if some invisible bubble had popped, she suddenly became aware of what lay beyond. The sounds
of music, of talk and laughter and singing, the scents
of roasting meat, of flowers and incense, flowed out
of the great hall in a rolling wave of dazzling sensation. Framed by the silver doors as bright as mirrors
she could see intense colors in every possible shade
and hue; people and creatures talking, laughing, dancing; torches flaming, and bright banners waving lan-
guidly in the air of the windowless chamber. It was a
three-ring circus and a Roman orgy and downtown
Manhattan at high noon on a weekday. It was like
walking into the Ginza on a Saturday night after three
weeks in a sensory deprivation tank.

She stood where she was, stunned with the shock
of it. Living among the Allimir, being with Belegir at
the Oracle, had been . . . quiet. Restful, in a weird way.

This was noise and bustle and toxic craziness, like being dropped back into Real Life with a jarring, disorienting thump. It was like nothing she'd ever seen—and yet, somehow, it was familiar.

After a long moment, she shook her head and doggedly forced herself forward, dragging Ivradan with her. If all this brought her up short, it must bollix him up twice over.

Glory reached the doorway and stopped again, though she'd sworn she wouldn't. The enormous room was oval-shaped, windowless as she'd guessed, and constructed somewhat after the fashion of an old Roman arena, making her think once more of Roman orgies and decadent mad emperors.

I hope that isn't an omen. . . .

On each of several levels that terraced the room, banqueting tables were laid, with plenty of room for the feasters to move around them. Staircases between the tables led down to the floor, on which dancers were gathered. Though she could see little of the walls themselves, covered as they were with banners and tapestries, if she were to judge by the floor, the castle seemed to be made of mother of pearl inside and out.

The musicians she had heard were gathered in screened platforms hung high on the walls out of harm's way—Glory couldn't quite see how you could get in or out of the boxes—and there were also strolling players working the crowd here and there. Directly opposite the entry doors, set on the highest tier, was a table with only empty terraces gleaming pearlescently below it. The wall behind the table was hung with azure velvet, and there was a gold-fringed canopy above it, and beneath the canopy sat an enormous golden throne upholstered in white velvet, with two smaller thrones beside it, all out of the *Little Golden Book for Deranged Medieval Fascists.*

Charane sat upon the enormous throne, with Dylan seated at her left hand, looking very much as if Trish was going to rush in any minute and scold him for being out of costume on the set during a dress walk-through. A number of lesser seats were arranged along Charane's table. All those seats were empty, but every other seat here in the Hammer Hall of Horrors was full. As Glory stared at the High Table, a servant came through the draperies to pour wine for Charane and Dylan, so there must be at least one other exit from the chamber. The table was covered with a long white damask cloth (at least if this were a medieval romance it would be damask: it could be polyester for all Glory actually knew), set with plates and goblets of jeweled gold—but only three sets. It looked like Charane had only been expecting two guests for dinner—but which two? Her and Ivradan? Or her and Dylan?

She glanced back. Ivradan was one step behind her, clutching Gordon like grim death and not looking as if he found any of this in the least amusing or even faintly interesting.

Glory looked around the room, eyes narrowed. The Warmother had certainly been busy. Only some of the creatures here were what Glory could properly call human. But she'd gawk at them later. Right now she had an entrance to make.

"C'mon, Ivro. Don't ever let 'em see you sweat," she muttered to her companion in an encouraging undertone. Squaring her shoulders, she strode down the steps on her way to the High Table.

She knew how Vixen would play it, and so Glory played it the same way: head high, face a mask of disdain, looking neither to the left or the right as she made her way down the long flight of steps. Conversation came to a stop as she passed, until by the time she got to the bottom of the stairs the room was completely quiet. Even the musicians had stopped playing. She hoped Ivradan'd had the great good sense to follow her.

Everyone was staring at her, watching her, and at last she realized why this seemed so familiar. Seoul. The Games. Walking into the arena with her mates, and everyone staring. Her heart beat faster. She'd thought then that it was going to be the most important time of her life, the payoff, that what she did there would pay for all the rest. It hadn't been true then, but it was true now.

There was a rustle like pigeons' wings as the dancers moved back to let her pass, and for a moment Glory felt like the heroine in a fairy tale, one of the dark Northern ones that ends badly. She heard the scuffling echo of Ivradan behind her. Then the steps at the far side of the dance floor were before her and she began to climb.

Going up was harder than coming down. She made her mind a blank and concentrated on doing it well. There were no re-takes here. All live, all real.

She reached the top and hesitated. Behind her, the conversation had resumed once more, quietly, and she had the feeling it was all about her. The Hero's Manual did not have a single clear-cut answer to cover this situation. Should she sit down next to the bitch and pretend they were all taking tea at Government House? Sit down at this end where she could reach the stairs easily? Refuse to sit down at all? She supposed it all depended on which kind of hero you were being, and unfortunately Vixen had never been in this sort of situation. She shrugged, and walked behind the table toward the "special guest" chair. Refusing to sit down would be silly, and Charane could probably outrun her or outfly her or something.

Glory pulled the chair out with her foot and eased

herself into it as well as she could with the sword in the way. There was no way to really get comfortable without taking the sword off, and she didn't intend to do that. It was her only ace. She plonked her elbows on the long linen-covered table and stared out at the revelry without really seeing it.

The room was full, and only some of its inhabitants could rightly be called human. The Warmother had cast her net wide: there were more upright bear-wolves like the one she'd killed, but better groomed; androgynous golden-scaled bipeds with tall red crests; men shorter than Allimir, but blue-skinned and wearing furs; tall, hard-eyed Amazons in white tunics; bronze-skinned men who could have passed for human anywhere on Earth—in short, trouble in every shape and size and color, mercenaries and sellswords and villains all.

And all of them as out of place as she was. What had Charane told them to bring them here? Was it anything close to the truth? Would any of them rather be back where they'd started from?

She wasn't likely to get any of those questions answered.

Ivradan seated himself dolefully beside her. Glory looked sideways at the Warmother. *Charane.*

What was it about that name? Glory wished Belegir were with her, or even Englor. She bet either of them would know what it meant. She also bet Charane would have killed either of them outright, rather than playing cat and mouse with them here in Sorceress Barbie's Mystical Castle.

But Charane hadn't killed the Mages out on the Serenthodial. She'd only made a real try for Belegir when he'd gone back to the Oracle. Which meant— and wasn't it just the way, that she figured this out when it was too late to help?—she bet that Belegir could have done something at the Oracle that would have put a spoke in the Warmother's wheel. Too bad neither of the two of them had known it at the time.

But knowing that *She* had a few vulnerable bits left was comforting. If Ivradan got away—and knowing what Glory knew about Charane, she'd probably want someone to take the news back to the Allimir that their hero had failed—he might remember to tell Belegir what she'd called herself, and then—

Glory smiled a glassy and insincere smile at the amphitheater full of nightmares, groaning inside. She couldn't measure the Allimir by the standards of her mates back home. Even if the information Ivradan brought meant something to Belegir, he wouldn't do anything about it. He'd just curl up and wait to die. And she couldn't exactly blame him. There was something wrong with him—something wrong with all the Allimir.

Which didn't make what Charane here was doing right.

"So. When do we eat?" Vixen the Slayer asked the Warmother coolly.

Charane smiled her catlike smile. "Has the Allimir's precious hero found her courage at last?" she asked.

"Is the tucker here that bad?" Glory asked, still in Vixen's flat American accent.

"Do you think you can—" Charane began.

"Oh, for heaven's sake, Glo, you're not in front of the cameras now!" Dylan said hastily, leaning across Charane. "Save the *shtick* for your little fans and remember who you really are."

"Yes," Charane echoed meaningfully. "Remember who you really are."

Glory smiled. She hadn't missed the expression on Charane's face when Dylan had interrupted her, the moment when the mask of smiling serenity had slipped to reveal a flash of pure fury. Anybody who could get angry that fast wasn't quite as smug about things as they were putting about.

"But tell me what I can do to entertain you. I'd hate to think you'd come all this way just to be *bored*," Charane cooed with poisonous sweetness.

Glory stared at her blankly. As far as Glory could tell, the Warmother was the original Bad Hat, but there didn't seem to be any dignity about her evilness. Even supposing you said she was so powerful and so inhuman that she didn't care about the human suffering that she caused—why was she so interested in causing it? If she was that inhuman, how could she calculate the grief she caused to a tax accountant's nicety, killing the Allimir off by inches?

She couldn't.

And if she did know precisely what she was doing, and how much it hurt—and she must—all this pretending she didn't, and making them pretend along with her, was the mark of a particularly nasty, low-minded, *undignified* bully.

Glory hated bullies. They all knew Charane could kill her, and it was hard to get excited about anything less. And as a matter of fact, this part of things always *did* bore her, in books and movies and the like—the part where the villain paraded his or her superior might and boasted about his or her plans, showed off whatever Doomsday Machine might be knocking about the shop, and attempted to impress the onlookers with a sense of their vast futility and unimportance.

"Look," Glory said, a little desperately, "could we just skip all the stuff where you explain about how invincible you are and how nobody can stand against you and just get to the part where you try to kill us? Because if you really—"

"'Try' to kill you?" Charane said, standing up. "Do

you think that I cannot? I am War, and Darkness, and
the fear that comes for a man in the lonely places. Do
you think that I cannot destroy you if I please? I have
destroyed the Allimir—"

"Not yet," Glory heard herself say.

Charane stared at Glory as if she'd slapped her.

"They aren't all dead yet," Glory explained reasonably, still hoping they could skip the villain-talk. "So
either you can't destroy them, or you can, and you're
just toying with them when you know they don't have
any way of fighting back. And that isn't exactly the sort
of thing they write songs about, you know. It's petty.
Lilith Kane doesn't do things like that."

Dylan winced and said something under his breath.

"I will scour the Allimir from the plains of the
Serenthodial," Charane said conversationally. She
straightened to her full height and spoke to the room
at large. "You see here beside me the last hope of the
Allimir—the hero their precious Oracle has delivered
to them! You know what I am, as she does not: No
warrior born of woman, no weapon forged in the world,
can unmake my form, yet their Slayer has come here
to *slay* me!"

The room exploded with laughter—nervous and
fearful, it was true, but laced with enough mockery to
make Glory think that whatever the truth might be,
those here in this room believed Charane's words.

And that meant they might be true.

Had Belegir known this, or suspected it? Was this
a part of the dream the Oracle had given him? That
no matter how many fancy swords Glory had, she'd fail?

And would she have acted any differently if she'd
known that?

"But she shall be slain instead, and you, my chosen people, I shall turn loose upon this pleasant realm
to reap my red harvest. I shall populate this world with

my legions, until all the world runs crimson with War once more!"

There were wild cheers from the creatures assembled below.

"And then what?" Glory asked, getting to her feet as well.

The cheering for Charane continued, banging off the walls and filling the room. It was so loud Glory couldn't hear herself speak, but somehow Charane heard her. The Warmother's head whipped around; she stared at Glory with her blue, blue eyes.

Glory stared stubbornly back. "So the whole world runs red with War. What then? It's just one world."

"Many things," Charane said, though for the first time she sounded ever so faintly uncertain. Glory could hear her plainly, as though the two of them were the only people in the room. "But you will not live to see them, Vixen the Slayer."

Glory sighed, and wondered why it was that nobody here could keep her straight from her character. She'd given it her best shot, but they'd had the threats and exposition part of things after all. She guessed there was a Villains Handbook to go right along with the Heroes one. Someday she'd like to get her hands on the loon who'd written both of them. At least she knew what came next.

She reached back and drew her sword. The crystals along the hilt flared brightly enough to shine between her fingers.

"All right, then," Glory said. Her mouth was dry, but her voice was steady. The frenzied cheering was still going on—these people seemed to be the local equivalent of football fans, willing to shout for hours—and that was another thing that reminded her of home. It didn't matter that the cheers weren't for her. They never had been, not really, but she'd liked hearing them all the same. Somehow, in a strange way, it had always been the cheering that was the important thing, not who it was for.

"Kill her," Charane said simply. She stepped back behind Dylan's chair and spoke directly to him. "Kill her, and I will give you anything you want."

The Warmother reached into her sleeve and set a gun on Dylan's plate.

It was a Webley Mark 6. Her father'd had one like it, handed down from *his* father, who'd brought it home from the War. It was black and dangerous and utterly out of place in this frothy whipped-cream idiocy of a magic palace. And facing it, Glory might as well be holding a peacock feather as a magic sword.

Dylan stared at it in fascination and horror.

"Kill her?" he asked, as though he wasn't quite sure he'd heard the words correctly.

"You have seen my power. I can give you anything you desire. I can send you home," Charane said. "Just do this one small thing for me."

Dylan reached for the gun, then drew back. He looked at Glory, and she saw honest, naked emotion on his face.

Terror.

In that moment, Dylan MacNee looked every day of his age. A man in his late forties, claiming mid-thirties, who thought youth and illusion was the only thing he had to sell. Who knew that the only relationships in his life would be transactions, and measured his viability by what he had to sell.

"Don't do it, Dylan," Glory said quietly.

"Do, by all means, listen to the golden girl," Charane advised cordially. "She's taken such tender care of you so far, hasn't she?" She leaned over, and spoke into his ear. It was a whisper, but somehow, Glory could hear it clearly, even over the shouting and cheering from the rest of the room.

"Just kill her. No one will ever know. You can go right back home, just as if today never happened. It will all seem like a dream. I'm not asking you for so very much. Haven't you really always wanted to wipe the smug smile off that arrogant no-talent bitch's face? Walking into a starring role that she wouldn't have except for *you* . . ."

Dylan picked up the gun, shaking his head. He looked miserable.

"I'm sorry," he said to Glory. "I just want to go home."

Glory was still standing flat-footed, still unable to believe he'd fire. The first shot caught both her and Dylan by surprise.

Dylan had been raising the pistol, squeezing the trigger at the same time. It went off unexpectedly, making a sound like the loudest cherry-bomb in the world. The gun jerked up with the force of the shot, and Dylan dropped it.

The bullet passed Glory several inches to the right. She jumped back, turning to look behind her just in time to see Gordon jump up and fill the air with whitish fluff as the bullet passed through him. Ivradan shrieked and went over backwards with his chair.

"You shot my elephant!" Glory screamed.

The quality of the sound in the room changed, but she didn't dare look around. Dylan was down on his hands and knees, searching for the gun among the billowing blue velvet draperies. Glory raised her sword and started forward, knowing even as she did so that she couldn't hit Dylan with it.

She looked for Charane—if she threatened her, could she make this *stop*?—but Charane was gone.

And Dylan had found the gun again.

He swung around, holding it with both hands this time. Between the shouting and the gunshot, Glory's ears were ringing. She shook her head to clear it, knowing it wouldn't help. She took another step, passing him.

Glory ran.

She didn't know where she was going. She just knew that she didn't want to get shot, and she didn't want Ivradan to get shot, so she ran away from him. Only six bullets in the Webley. Dylan would run out sooner or later. Then she could beat him senseless with her bare fists.

Dylan fired again. A piece of the wall dissolved into a spray of sparkling chips beside her head, and she realized that the roaring in her ears had been replaced by the angry shouts of a mob, not an audience. She darted a quick glance across the room. With Charane gone, her pet mercenaries were off the leash. They were on their feet, reaching for their weapons, moving in all directions. Some—not all—were heading this way.

Glory reached the end of the terrace. Dylan was behind her, ready to fire again. There was no place to go but down, but the first of the villains were already at the foot of the steps. She heard a crash, and saw one of the tables go over, trapping struggling bodies beneath it. She heard screams soaring above the shouts, and the high pure clang of steel.

Dylan fired three shots in quick succession. He was rapidly losing his gun-shyness, though fortunately his aim hadn't yet improved. How many rounds did that make?

The terrace directly below was still clear. It was an eight-foot drop. Glory turned away from the stairs and jumped.

They hated having her do her own stunts on

TITAoVtS, because if she got hurt, production stopped dead, but in fact she was damned good at it, and the stuntpeople had taught her a few helpful tricks. She held the sword well out from her body and threw herself into a forward somersault, landing on her feet, crouching to absorb the impact—just like the vaulting horse, that—and backing up quickly against the wall. If Dylan was as rattled as she was, it might take him a second or so to figure out where she'd gone.

The noise was deafening, and the floor beneath her feet shook. She looked out over the room, catching her breath and trying to think of what to do next. What had been orderly moments before was . . .

There really were no words.

As if Charane's presence had been the only thing keeping them in order, her creatures had turned on each other. If they'd all been trying to get to the High Table, she, Dylan, and Ivradan would be dead now, but they weren't even that orderly.

Some were trying to get out, fighting their way up the long steep staircase to the only door they could see. The chamber might have been designed to trigger a bloodbath, and with a distant clinical thrill of horror, Glory wondered if it had been. The ones who had already gotten out were trying to push the doors shut to keep the others inside (why?), but the doors were jammed open by the fallen bodies of the dead and dying. Others were simply fighting, as if for the sheer joy of it, slowing those who were bold enough to rush the High Table.

There was blood everywhere. A swampy smell, sulphurous and meaty, rose up from the floor below. The liquid on the floor—wine and blood and ichor commingled—stood in pools. More trickled down the edges of the white stairs in absurdly cheerful candy stripes. Men and creatures slipped in it, and fell, and died, and all for no reason that she knew. It was bedlam, this chamber a proving ground designed by a master sadist, being put to its intended use.

She heard screaming that brought tears to her eyes, and turned her head resolutely away from the direction of the sound. She would not look.

Ivradan. She had to get to Ivradan.

She forced herself to shut out the distractions, to focus, to *move,* clutching the sword so hard her fingers hurt. She had no doubt now that she could use it on anything that got in her way. She was terrified, and filled with a cold unemotional purpose all at the same time. Here, in this room, was the reason Cinnas had chained the Warmother.

The stone at her feet exploded in a shower of chips. She looked up. Dylan was standing at the edge of the terrace above.

"It never runs out of bullets," he shouted happily. She could barely make out the words. He aimed out at the crowd and pulled the trigger half a dozen times, with the relieved look of one who knows that nothing matters because this is all a dream. Then he pointed the gun at her again.

"Dylan—no! Don't do what she wants!" Glory shouted, though she knew it was useless. He probably couldn't even hear her. And he'd already made up his mind.

The javelin caught him neatly in the chest, just below the breastbone. It appeared as if it had suddenly teleported there. To throw a javelin twenty feet into the air with enough force that it will pierce a human body upon its arrival is no small matter; someone down there was skilled. There was no blood; the javelin plugged Dylan as neatly as a cork in a bottle.

Dylan stared down at it; Glory saw him blink in surprise. He reached up to it with the hand that held the gun, but never completed the gesture. He went limp, collapsing at the knees and falling forward to land at Glory's feet. The impact drove the shaft through his body in a red rush. It wavered, teetering upright, tapping out sketchy wet hieroglyphs against the pristine wall behind him.

Numbly, Glory bent down to pick up the pistol. She was still clutching the sword in her right hand, precious little use though it had been to her so far. At last she turned and looked in the direction from which the javelin had come.

Standing in the middle of the floor, surrounded by her warriors, was one of the tall grey-eyed Amazons, a still point in the chaos that surrounded her. She held another of the slender throwing spears in her hand. The woman was bloody to the knees; even the edge of her short fringed tunic was red. For a moment their eyes met.

Not knowing why she did it—it seemed somehow fitting—Glory tossed the gun down to the woman. The Amazon queen caught it easily and stared at it curiously, then looked back at Glory. Glory pantomimed squeezing a trigger. The woman nodded, smiling grimly, and turned away, raising the gun.

Glory turned back to the wall, the moment already forgotten. If this was shock, it was a damned useful invention, a small part of her mind said perkily. She had to get to Ivradan, and straight up the wall was the fastest way.

Behind her, she heard the sound of gunfire.

She reached up, setting the sword on the level above her, then jumped as high as she could. She managed to get her elbows over the edge. The cloth puffs around her elbows slipped on the slick surface, and she swore, but the studded leather on her forearms gripped the floor, and she squirmed up, fighting hard for every inch.

At last she dragged herself over the edge, grabbing the sword and rolling under the table without thinking.

It was dim under the cloth, and gave the illusion of safety. She blinked, willing her eyes to adjust, and began to crawl forward. If he'd panicked and run— If Charane had taken him somewhere—

Then she saw the huddled figure, curled into a tight fetal ball in front of the tumbled chair, still clutching the ragged remains of the blue elephant.

"Ivradan!" she gasped. The word came out in a husky croak. She wriggled forward, dragging the sword, and reached out for his hand.

And the world went dark.

CHAPTER SIX:
Stone and Clouds

For one sickening, surreal, disorienting instant, she thought she was back on the set. A number of other equally plausible alternatives presented themselves in quick succession.

She was blind.

She was dead.

She was in yet another godlost alternate universe.

Then she moved, and the sense of her body returned to her. She could feel weight on her wrists, and emptiness beneath her feet.

She was hanging in chains.

She'd been in this situation before, only then she'd been standing on a box (placed outside of camera-range, of course) so that her full weight didn't dangle from her wrists. Now there was nothing beneath her feet but air. The bracers protected her wrists from the full brunt of the shackles, but her arms were stretched wide, and all her weight was pulling her shoulders taut. She kicked back, and felt the wall at her back. Getting her feet behind her and pushing out helped a little, but not much, and she had no idea where her sword was. It had been in her hand. It wasn't now.

She felt dazed and battered, off-balance. The absence of the chaos of a moment before was as much of an assault on the senses as its presence had been. Her heart was still hammering, making it hard to breathe, and she struggled uselessly against her chains, fighting against a threat that wasn't there any more, the horrors she had seen playing themselves out inside her mind.

Dylan was dead. She'd barely registered the fact at the time, but now, in the darkness, she saw it again too clearly: the spear sticking out of his chest, the moment of shocked surprise, the awful, utter, deadness of him when he fell.

And what had she done? She'd given his gun to the woman who'd killed him. How heroic was that? She'd rewarded his killer.

She choked on a sob.

"Slayer?"

Ivradan's voice came out of the darkness. No, not darkness. Her eyes were adjusting now. Dimness. She blinked, realizing she could actually see him looking up at her.

He was alive and whole. Scared to death, but that was a sane and wholesome response to the situation. She took a deep breath, forcing herself to relax, settle down, focus.

"G'day, mate."

"I don't know what happened," Ivradan confessed, as if it were somehow a failure.

"Neither do I," Glory admitted. "Fine pair of heroes we make."

"Hero?" Ivradan sounded outraged at being given such a title. It made Glory smile, though she'd never felt more like bursting into tears.

Her feet slipped on the wall, and she fell to hang full length in her shackles again. The jolt of impact dragged her hands halfway through the cuffs, and that gave her an idea. If they were that loose . . .

"Say, Ivro, how chipper are you feeling?"

He came over and stood at her feet, still holding the decidedly more slender Gordon. She could now see that she was hanging only a few feet off the floor, but a few inches or a few yards, it didn't make much difference to her shoulders. It did make a difference to what she wanted to try.

"'Chipper,'" he echoed warily.

"Can you lift me up a little? I think I can work loose from these cuffs if I can get a little leverage."

Ivradan stepped forward and set Gordon down carefully. He bent down and hugged her firmly around the knees. Then he straightened up.

Glory felt the release of the strain as a thousand tiny needles of fire along her shoulders and back, and the resulting cramps in her legs as she fought to balance in Ivradan's grip. But now she could hear the chains clank, and feel their weight, and she could lift her arms enough to make the manacles slide on her wrists.

But that wasn't what was going to get her out of them. She pulled down, carefully, twisting her wrist back and forth as she did and inventing new curses for the costume designers at the same time. She folded her thumb into her palm as hard as she could, and strained against the metal, and hoped . . .

Her right hand slipped free of the shackle. And at the same time Ivradan dropped her.

She had just enough warning to point the fingers of

her left hand. There was a wrenching strain as all her weight hung suspended for a moment from one wrist, and then the cuff simply slipped off. She dropped to the floor and fell sprawling, more or less on top of Ivradan.

She rolled out of the tangle, and it seemed like too much trouble to get up, so she didn't. She lay there, wishing all her problems would go away. If she hadn't killed Dylan (and she didn't feel quite guilty enough to shoulder the blame for that one, not quite), at least she hadn't saved him, and that was bad enough. He was a pratt, certainly, but he was *her* pratt, and he hadn't deserved killing.

Only now he was dead, no matter whose fault it was. A lot of people were dead, each of them the stars of their own lives, butchered like bad cattle—and for what? Window-dressing in the Warmother's set-piece? Was she that . . . wasteful?

If she was (as she claimed to be) War Incarnate, the answer to that was a resounding "Yes," and the real question became, why in Heaven's name didn't everybody run screaming the moment they heard of her instead of sticking about?

But people were funny that way, even blue people, or gold scaly people, or people in any of the other odd shapes and designs she'd seen today. People were funny in general, when you came right down to it: Glory'd even heard there were such things as Satanists, and if you wanted to talk about unprepossessing targets for fealty . . .

The Amazons didn't seem to fit in with the rest of the Warmother's crew, somehow, though—maybe they'd manage to get shut of Charane while her back was turned, or something, though why they'd followed her to Erchanen in the first place . . .

Glory sighed, realizing she'd really better pay attention to the problem at hand instead of letting her mind wander off down pathways that were more interesting simply because they weren't related to the matter at hand. Item: one dungeon, constructed for the reception of neither Australian nor Allimir, to judge from the size of the shackles.

If there could be cement here (and she didn't actually know there couldn't be), she'd say this place was made of cement. It was damp and cold. There were several sets of rusty shackles set into the wall above her head; she watched the set she'd recently vacated swing slowly to a stop, bouncing back and forth along the wall with a dull clanking and scraping. The ceiling itself was too far away to see. Set into the wall at her feet, maybe fifteen or twenty feet up, was a line of narrow windows, horizontal slits really, that let in the remains of a pallid, wan, grey, overcast entirely unprepossessing day. The air, like the dungeon, smelled wet and cold. It was probably raining somewhere.

She sat up with a groan, then stood (reluctantly), looking around. She spied her sword over in a corner, under a bench, and went to fetch it, inspecting it carefully. It seemed unharmed and untampered with. Was it so irrelevant and harmless that Charane didn't think it worth bothering with, or so powerful that she couldn't touch it?

I wish I knew—that among other things. She slipped it back into its scabbard.

"Let's get out of here," she said aloud.

"How?" Ivradan asked simply.

And Glory took another look—a really good look this time—at their prison. *All* of their prison.

It had windows and manacles and chains and benches, high smooth walls and a distant vaulting ceiling. All the things you'd expect to find in a high-class dungeon.

But it had no door at all.

⁂   ⁂   ⁂

Half an hour later she knew more than she had before, none of it encouraging.

Even if Glory could lift Ivradan up far enough to reach the window-slits—and she couldn't—they were too narrow for him to get through.

The Sword of Cinnas, fine magical item though it was, could not chop through the walls, or even dent them.

The benches could not be removed from the walls.

There was no way out.

It bothered Glory, and she wasn't exactly sure why. It seemed that the two of them were going to have plenty of time to think about it, though.

"It just doesn't *work*," she said, pacing the cell. It was nice that there was plenty of cell to pace in: the floor of the cell was at least twenty feet by forty, and Glory was using every foot. Back and forth, and all she could come up with was the conviction that this would make a lousy episode of *The Incredibly True Adventures of Vixen the Slayer.* Meanwhile, the light from outside slowly dimmed. Eventually, it would be entirely dark.

Bummer.

"She likes to play. Helevrin said that about her, Ivradan. Cat and mouse. Never too much all at once," Glory said. Thinking out loud—or at least trying to. She wasn't having much luck so far.

"That is so," Ivradan admitted, watching Glory warily. The Allimir horsemaster lay full-length on one of the stone benches, looking utterly spent. But Glory was too keyed-up to rest.

"But why this? It's like she's *quit*. Where's the fun for her in just locking us up somewhere in a magic dungeon to starve to death?"

"Perhaps," Ivradan said in a peculiar voice, "in that we could get out if we would."

Glory stopped pacing and stared at him.

"Slayer, I have been thinking," Ivradan said, still looking as if he'd suddenly swallowed a live carp. "About the horses."

"Yes," Glory said quietly. If she startled him now, she'd never hear what he had to say, and it might well be important.

"You remember the mist on the trail, and how they walked into it without changing their gait? And how, when they reached the summit, even though there was green grass all around, they would not graze?"

"I remember," Glory said.

"That is not how horses behave, and it has puzzled me, but now I think I have found an answer. I do not believe they saw either the mist or the grass, though we did, and felt them, too. Could it be that they were not there at all? And if such things could be illusion, could not this prison be illusion as well?"

"Oh, sure," Glory said flippantly, and then thought about it. Hard.

If Ivradan said the horses didn't react to the mist and the grass because they were illusions, he probably had the right of it. And if the two of them were stuck in a dungeon that wasn't really here, that would be enough of a giggle to keep Charane amused, wouldn't it? Watching them commit suicide in a prison that wasn't one?

"If it is an illusion, how do we make it go away?" she asked.

Ivradan sat up and looked at her hopefully. Glory sighed. He was right. It was the sidekick's job to come up with the fool notion, and the hero's job to make it work. Division of labor. Only she hadn't the faintest idea of how that was to be accomplished. The dungeon certainly looked—and felt—real.

As real as the grass—and the mist—had.

Not much to go on, that.

She walked over to the wall and leaned her forehead against it, concentrating on its not being there. The wall remained stubbornly solid.

"Slayer—" Ivradan said in an awed whisper.

She opened her eyes. Bright violet light illuminated the wall, casting her image upon it in sharp black shadow. The Sword of Cinnas had woken up, glowing as brightly as it had back in the Temple.

"Oh, silly me," Glory said weakly. "I've been using the wrong end of the sword."

She stepped back from the wall and—feeling just a bit as if she were playing Joan of Arc—drew the sword and grasped it below the crosspiece, where the blade was dull. The violet crystals set in the hilt glowed as though lit from within, almost too bright to look at directly.

"Ivradan—come here."

She could wield the sword, she could play the hero, but she couldn't *believe* in this as much as the Allimir could. And what they needed right now was belief. Whole cartloads of it.

Reluctantly, Ivradan approached, still clutching Gordon. The bullet had blown the back of the stuffed elephant open, and most of its stuffing had escaped, so Gordon was now a rather saggy baggy elephant, but that didn't matter. If they got out of here, Glory promised herself she'd get him the best new innards money could buy.

"This is the Sword of Cinnas, with which he chained the Warmother back in the Time of Legend. It is full of Erchane's magic, and it is strong enough to destroy this illusion. Put your hand over mine," she said in Vixen's ringing tones.

She felt Ivradan's hand tremble as he placed it over hers. And then, slowly, keeping her mind studiously blank, she moved the glowing crosspiece of the sword toward the wall, trying not to expect failure.

As the power crystals neared the wall, she felt resistance, the kind you'd get if you tried to push two magnets together the wrong way. Glory became enormously heartened by this, suddenly believing it all herself. This *was* an illusion. The sword *would* get them out. She wasn't thinking beyond that, to actually getting *away*.

It became harder to push the sword forward, and she felt a pang of alarm—suppose it was destroyed the way the bear-wolf's talisman had been when she brought it into the Oracle-cave? But even with all the jewels dark, the sword would still be a sword, its blade still sharp, and they had to get out of here.

They *had* to get out of here.

The hilt clattered against the wall, and Glory felt a sharp pang of cheated disappointment. It hadn't worked. The wall was still there.

But wasn't the sound of the sword's impact a little wrong, the feel of it hitting the wall not quite right? She forced herself to notice those subtle things, to believe them, to keep pushing as if there were someplace for the sword to go, because the wall mustn't be there, the dungeon couldn't hold them. It was all false, unreal, a thing of illusion, and an illusion that had just been routed by superior firepower, at that. She told herself that fervently, demanding that it be true, because she *needed* it to be true. For Ivradan's sake, and Belegir's, and because she wasn't dead yet, and she'd promised to destroy the Warmother. . . .

And suddenly she realized that the wall wasn't a wall at all. It was mist, and wet cardboard, and old mopstrings. Glory could see nothing, and instinctively closed her eyes. She reached across herself with her free hand and grabbed Ivradan's wrist fiercely, making sure he held fast to the sword, and pushed forward.

Suddenly they were in the middle of a storm. Wind and rain tore at her, knocking her down, pulling Ivradan away from her. She had an instant to choose between holding onto him or the sword, and with a pang of grief, she chose the sword. The wind knocked her sprawling; she fell and rolled, clinging to the hilt and trying to force her eyes open against the freezing, soaking gusts of rain-heavy wind.

Then, as if the storm had only been another wall to pass through, it, too, was gone. She shook the water out of her eyes and stood. Her braid hung down her back like a wet snake, heavy and clinging.

"Ivradan!"

She was back where they'd started—the top of Grey Arlinn. But nothing else was the same. It was twilight; that meant a couple of hours of light left at this altitude. Stone-colored thunderheads were piled among the mountains, and the setting sun shone between them; a spectacular view, not that she cared. Her leather was soaked through—still flexible, but she was shivering with cold. She looked around quickly.

The fairy-princess castle, the lawn, all the silly-bugger trappings, were gone.

Except for one.

In the center of the flat open space stood a huge cantilevered slab of smooth black stone. Manacles were set into it, and Ivradan was locked into them, spread-eagled as though he were waiting for a vulture to come and tear out his liver. He'd dropped Gordon, and the little elephant was a blot of bright color at the foot of the stone, like an offering of flowers to a sacrificial prince.

Glory ran across the mountaintop toward the stone.

The whole set-up looked remarkably like one of the concept-sketches from *TITAoVtS's "For Whom the Belle Trolls"* episode they'd been supposed to shoot next season. In her hand, the Sword of Cinnas was vibrating madly, as though somebody had flicked a switch inside it.

"No worries, mate," she said breathlessly. "I reckon I can get you out of there, and—" As she reached out to touch the stone, Ivradan's face went . . . strange.

::Have you come to chain me once more, little mortal?:: a voice said inside Glory's head.

She froze, not turning, part of her mind waiting for someone to call out and tell her they had the shot, fine, cut for lunch. The twilight faded from the sky as someone had shut off the lights, and then it went right on getting darker. At the same time, cold rolled toward her as if someone had opened a freezer.

Ivradan gazed at her hopelessly for a moment, and then closed his eyes in surrender.

Glory turned, slowly, telling herself desperately that it didn't matter what she saw, she wouldn't scream, she *wouldn't*.

The sound she made instead emerged as a desolate moan.

Charane had gotten tired of playing. This was her true form at last, it must be—and it looked like every nightmare Ridley Scott'd had for the past twenty years.

The monster towered over Glory in the greenish dusk, a few meters away, but close enough that it only had to bend down to bite off her head. Its hide was a crusty glistening tarnished black, and there was something horribly serpentlike about its movements. *Dragon—dragon—dragon—* her mind babbled idiotically.

Glory's stunned gaze stumbled over its unfamiliar

contours, unable to figure out what she was seeing. A dragon. A monster. A nightmare. Something that could not possibly exist. She took a step backward and bumped into the stone, and Ivradan's body. She could feel the rough homespun of his trousers, the warmth of his body, through the bare flesh of the top of her thighs. He was still alive.

Meant to be. All this. A set-up. The last act. Her thoughts were a disjointed commentary that even she wasn't listening to. She desperately wanted to run, to be anywhere that wasn't here, looking at that. If she threw down the sword and ran, the dragon would let her go. She knew that—or at least it was worth a try. Better that— Better that—

The sword was blazing in her hands, as hot as the rest of her was cold, vibrating so hard she was afraid she'd drop it. She could see it wobble, its movement only partly because her hands were shaking so hard. If she took a single step, her knees would buckle and she'd fall. She couldn't remember a single thing Bruce had ever told her about fighting, and even if she could remember, it would do her no good against something like this.

But she would not run. She was too terrified to think clearly, but Ross, her gymnastics coach, had spent hours and days and years training her to go beyond thought. Her mind blank with an emotion too profound to be called fear, Glory wrapped both hands around the hilt and raised her sword.

The Warmother . . . recoiled.

And suddenly Glory *knew.*

"Father?"
"Only a little farther, Charane."
"Where are we going?"
"Only to the top of the mountain. . . ."

✳   ✳   ✳

"Charane was his daughter," Glory said hoarsely, stunned. Cinnas had brought her here, chained her just as Ivradan was chained now, and enchanted the spirit of War into her body, trapping the Warmother for a thousand years.

The spell had killed her.

He'd killed his own daughter.

And now Glory could do the same thing. Kill Ivradan, and chain the Warmother again. Because Cinnas had left the spells behind. The sword-blade wasn't the true weapon. It was the gems in the hilt, the spell-gems that were the magic of Erchane in solid form, just as Belegir had been telling her all along.

::Well?:: the Warmother said. The dragon opened its mouth. Black teeth glistened with venom. It spread membranous wings, blotting out the light.

Glory threw herself sideways out of sheer expectation, and a moment later a fine mist of venom sprayed the ground where she'd been standing, just missing Ivradan. Glory brandished the sword threateningly, gripping the hilt tightly.

::No warrior born of woman, no weapon forged in the world, can unmake my form, for I am made of all warriors and all weapons. Prepare to die, Vixen the Slayer!:: the Warmother cried gloatingly.

The gems blazed, leaking light in a thousand directions. Its demand to be used was so insistent it nearly distracted Glory from the creature that was trying to kill her. She could feel the ghost of Cinnas in the purple light, trying to take over her body and make her do as he had done before.

The Warmother must think she didn't know what to do with the sword, but she did. She could see it all so clearly in her mind. The day had been fair and bright. There had been a young girl in a blue dress, crowned with flowers. Blue flowers. She'd loved her father. She'd *trusted* him.

USE THE SWORD, came the voice inside her mind. The sword's voice. A voice she thought she knew.

"*Silly me. I've been using the wrong end of the sword.*"

Sacrifice an innocent. For an ideal.

No!

Slowly, she backed away from the dragon, moving slowly, as if that would keep it from striking at her. Its eyes glowed blue, blue as Charane's magic. Blue as the flowers in a child's hair.

Was Dylan *Her* last try at tricking the spell? Or someone's? Chain Dylan there instead of Ivradan? But it would have made no difference to Glory. Dylan or Ivradan, either one would have been an innocent victim. Neither could be sacrificed.

Who comes UP with these ideas?

The Warmother reared back, and its body seemed to stretch, its contours crawling and changing until it resembled an insect rather than a reptile: a mantis. It was the size of a city bus, its body the color of tarnished copper, its giant faceted eyes a glowing glittering blue. Glory stared in amazement, her terror dissolving in the face of this fresh impossibility. Then the monstrous head dipped toward her, mandibles flexing, and she scrambled back out of the way. No matter what shape the creature took on, the Warmother was still trying to kill her.

She ran backwards, dragging the balky sword with her, pulling the fight away from the rock where Ivradan was chained. The Warmother was fast, but Glory had plenty of room to move, and adrenaline to keep her faster. And she thought the Warmother was still a little afraid of the sword, which was all to the good. In fact, Glory was getting to be afraid of it, too. If it could take her over— If it could make her do what it wanted—

If she threw the sword over the edge of the cliff she'd break Cinnas' attempts to bespell her. And the Warmother would kill her and Ivradan both, and then everyone else. *One life for the many*, the sword whispered, *is that such a bad trade?*

No!

Heroes did not kill the innocent.

She could hear the little girl Charane had been inside her head. Charane was screaming, the high disbelieving screams of an abandoned child.

He'd chained her to the rock. . . .

This is no way to persuade me!

The mantis-thing scuttled forward and she slashed at it. The blade struck the creature across the top of its skull and bounced, as if Glory had struck stone. The mantis reared back and pounced, but Glory wasn't there. You could cover a lot of ground with a series of standing back-layouts, and she did. The mantis-thing sprang after her, but Glory had room to manoeuvre and plenty of incentive.

The wind was picking up again. It was getting harder to see, but there wasn't much up here to trip over. And the sword provided plenty of light. It was magic, after all—magic that had trapped her, tricked her, lied to her. Kept her from asking any of the right questions, until it was too late.

But she could still be a hero. She could still win.

All she had to do was *let go*. . . .

Let the magic take over.

Believe.

And hit the Warmother with the *other* end of the sword.

Chain her again.

And kill Ivradan to do it.

He could have died anyway, right? Any time this past five years. Any time today, in fact.

She could be a hero. . . .

No!

The sword twisted in her hands, desperate now to fulfill its purpose. She could feel sharp pieces of metal working their way loose in the hilt, cutting her hands until they bled. She gripped it tighter, ignoring the pain. She'd been an Olympic-class gymnast. Pain was an old friend.

There has to be another way!

The mantis looked fragile. Cut its head off, and maybe it would go away, at least for a while. If she could get back to Belegir—tell him what she knew—get his advice—

Then the monster darted forward—much faster than it had moved until now—and plucked the sword, blade first, from her hands, flaying her palms raw as it tore the hilt from her grip. Even over the sound of the rising storm, Glory could hear the faint pinging as the Warmother crumpled the blade in its mandibles. The hilt, with its cargo of magic, went spinning off out of reach across the stone. It burned like a beacon. Easy to spot. Impossible to reach.

As she stood, dumbfounded at this sudden disaster, the Warmother lashed at her with one barbed foreleg, and Glory flung herself out of the way, automatically catching herself on her hands. But they were slick now with her own blood, and instead of going into a forward rollout, she slipped and fell heavily onto her right shoulder, knocking herself breathless.

She'd lost.

I guess I wasn't the right sort of hero after all, she thought bitterly. *I'm sorry.*

Nothing happened. She raised her head. The Warmother was waiting, still chewing on the blade as if it were a stalk of grass. Waiting for her to get up, so it could chase her some more.

Slowly, Glory got to her feet, but she didn't run. There was no point. She was damned if she was going to exert herself just to amuse that thing. She straightened up and stood waiting, wiping her bloody palms down over her bedraggled velvet panniers. Nice to know they were finally good for something. Fresh blood welled up almost immediately from a thousand tiny cuts.

::*I don't need this form to destroy you*:: the Warmother sneered. It began to melt away, dwindling until it had taken the form of a naked woman, impossibly old. Her mottled skin hung in folds on her emaciated body and only a few wisps of white hair clung to her waxy scalp. Her face was fallen in, her cheeks were slack and hollow over toothless gums. She drooled. Only her eyes were alive, black pits of malignant fire.

::*This is what you fear most.*::

Age. Death. Incapacity.

"Everybody dies," Glory said flatly. And everybody got too old to be what they wanted to be. It was the prevailing fear of an actor, but Glory had already faced it as a gymnast. And in comparison to what had just happened, it seemed like such a petty thing to be afraid of.

You've won. And it's not enough for you. You still want to play around. The resignation of a moment before vanished, replaced by cold fury and a desire to at least piss the Warmother off before she died. *Think, stupid! What would Vixen do? She's lost her sword before. Lots of times.*

And the sword wasn't Vixen's only weapon. . . .

Moving as slowly as she dared, Glory let her hands drop to her sides as the hag walked slowly toward her.

She groped along the side of her boot for one of the row of stakes—Genuine English Rowan (not)—sheathed there. *I guess I'm not through fighting after all.* While her sword had been some kind of magic wizard metal, these stakes weren't even wood. They were cast plastic. They wouldn't do any better than the sword had, but at least she'd go down fighting. Her fingers closed painfully over one of the stakes and eased it gently from its sheath.

The Warmother reached for her, a gloating smile on its hideous crone's face.

::But you will die NOW, Vixen the Slayer.::

Its flesh was colder than snow where it touched her, even through her costume, and Glory felt her heartbeat slow as she was gathered into the hag's embrace. She gritted her teeth, and raised her arms to embrace the Warmother in return, filling herself up with all her anger, all her hatred of petty bullies and pointless cruelty.

"Up yours, Granny," Glory whispered in helpless defiance, gripping the stake.

And thrust inward as hard as she could.

She felt a *crunch*. The stake had gone in. But it wasn't supposed to do that, was it? It was supposed to just bounce off, the way the sword had.

There was a yelp of astonished pain right in her ear, and something hot and thick and nasty spurted over the back of Glory's hand. It burned caustically where it touched her open wounds, and she hissed with the bright pain of it. The cold reptilian embrace slackened, and Glory recoiled, jerking free and staring at the thick black blood on her hand, wondering if she were poisoned.

::No warrior born of woman, no weapon forged in the world can unmake my form!:: the Warmother said in disbelief. The hag took a staggering step backward, still staring at Glory in shock.

Glory kicked her in the face. The impact sent the hag sprawling onto the prop-stake in her back, driving the point through her ribs in front, but Glory wasn't willing to settle for that. She'd already pulled a second stake from its boot-sheath, and dropped to her knees beside the hag's squirming body. With a practiced gesture, she hammered it down through the sternum, driving it home with the heel of her hand. Black goo, thick as watery gruel, pushed up out of the hag's mouth and ran down the sides of her face. Glory reached for a third stake, ignoring the burning in her hands, talking as she hammered it home beside the other.

"I'm a Phys Ed teacher, mate, not a warrior. And that's a prop, not a weapon. Didn't anybody think to tell you?" Cast, not forged, and in another world than this. Tailor-made for the circumventing of prophecies, as a matter of fact.

She reached for a fourth—Vixen carried six—but the Warmother had stopped moving.

As Glory stared, the ancient hag withered away to a skeletal mummyish bundle, then began to *melt* like a chunk of dry ice, a thick mist rising skyward from her huddled form.

The Lucite stakes were dissolving along with the body, leaving only melted stubs and ends behind. Seeing that, Glory tore the cloth panniers loose from her costume and scrubbed her hands furiously with them, tearing the shredded flesh further, until there was nothing left on her skin but her own blood.

It began to rain. Thick, fat, cold drops of honest water, hitting her on the back of the head, on her raw back and her bare sunburned shoulders, trickling down into the lining of her leather corset. Glory had never been so grateful to be cold and wet in her entire life.

::*You'll live to regret this, Vixen the Slayer!*:: came

a faint disembodied whisper, fading even as the words were uttered.

"Yeah, yeah, yeah," Glory muttered, not paying very much attention. *I guess bad villain-dialogue is the same everywhere.*

She was jittery and exhausted at the same time, giddy with relief, watching as the creature dissolved. *I won? How could I have won? It can't be that easy. . . .*

"Slayer!" came an irritable shout.

Ivradan.

Irritable?

Wearily, Glory got to her feet and walked carefully over to the altar rock. It was raining in good earnest now, and the smooth granite mountaintop was as slippery as polished marble. Puddles were gathering in places where the surface wasn't quite as even. Soon it would be completely dark.

But the Warmother was dead.

They'd won.

Ivradan was struggling against his shackles. "Get me *out* of here!" he demanded.

"Um . . . sure, mate," Glory said, surprised. *Look here,* she wanted to say, *I've just put paid to your chief villain for you, and all you can think to do is yell at me? How about the thanks of a grateful nation, and all that, hey?* "Any ideas?"

She wanted to sleep. Right here, right now. In the rain. On the rock. Her hands hurt. She leaned against the slab, wincing. She thought she'd done something not very nice to her shoulder in that last fall. Not that anybody around here seemed to care. Her eyes prickled hotly. In another moment she was going to start bawling out of sheer self-pity.

"Use the sword. Or what's left of it."

Ivradan sounded downright pettish. She supposed

he might have a right, since he'd been the one about to be the dragon's lunch and all, but it didn't really seem *fair,* somehow. . . .

And suddenly the penny dropped.

Belegir: "A terrible power has been unleashed in the land of Erchanen. Long was it prisoned upon the peaks of Grey Arlinn. . . ."

Charane: "No warrior born of woman, no weapon forged in the world can unmake my form."

Long was it prisoned . . .

No weapon can unmake . . .

Not "kill." *Unmake.*

"Uh-oh," she whispered guiltily. Cinnas might have been called the Warkiller, but he hadn't killed the Warmother. You couldn't kill War. Cinnas had *bound* her into corporeal form, removing the threat of war from Erchanen by removing War Herself. And then he'd chained her up.

And what had Glory done?

Only a hero can chain her once more, Belegir had said, but that wasn't what Glory had done. Glory had unmade Cinnas' binding, forcing the Warmother to return to her original form from eons before, the form out of which she'd been summoned by the Mage Cinnas so that she could be chained.

"Well, bugger all," Glory said inadequately. And began to laugh.

"What are you laughing at?" Ivradan demanded.

"I've violated the bloody Prime Directive! Hoo!" Glory told him gleefully, giggling harder. *James T. Kirk, where are you when we really need you?* The giggles turned to guffaws, then great roaring whoops of laughter that made her sides ache. She'd solved one problem, and set up a thousand new ones. The peaceful pastoral Allimir were now the old warlike Allimir again. She'd been out to do a good deed, and it looked like

all she'd done was re-introduce the concept of not-very-
original-sin into a world that had managed to get rid
of it.

Of course, alternatively, they could all be dead.

She found the notion insanely funny. It was raining, they were stuck on top of a mountain, Ivradan was
shouting at her in a red-faced fury—thanks to her—
and every time she looked at him it set her off again,
until Glory was lying helplessly on the ground at his
feet, clutching Gordon to her and whimpering helplessly because her ribs hurt from laughing so hard.

"Don't you see, Ivro?" she finally managed to get
out. "War's *back*. She's back in all of you, just like
before."

There was a moment of silence.

"Back? But you killed her, Slayer. I saw it." He
sounded halfway between impatient and worried.

Wearily, Glory pushed herself to her feet again. She
realized she was stiff with cold and soaking wet and
if they didn't get down off this mountaintop, there'd
be nobody to bring the good news about this day's work
to the home folks.

"You can't kill War," Glory said, figuring it out as
she spoke. "Cinnas reasoned that out back in the
day. He *bound* her into corporeal form. She got
loose of her chains, but she was still in one piece
and one place, as it were. What the sword was
supposed to do was chain her up again." She
thought she'd leave out the part about Ivradan getting killed in the process. Belegir could have the
whole story. Let him decide how much the rest of
the Allimir needed to know about what their great
hero had *really* been like, and what he'd done to
gain them their thousand years of peace.

"But you didn't do that," Ivradan said.

"Nope. I reckon I unmade her, back the way she

was before old Cinnas did all his spells to make you lot into pacifists. So I guess you've got a lot to re-learn."

And fast, if any of Charane's imported frighteners were still wandering around loose.

"I . . . see," said Ivradan, who obviously didn't. "*Now* will you unchain me? I'm cold."

"Cut. Print. Save it for the day, kiddies, we'll go again tomorrow," Glory said to nobody in particular. She looked around for the sword—or what (as Ivradan had so kindly reminded her) was left of it. It was still glowing, making it easy to spot. She could wrap her hands up in the pannier-cloth so she wouldn't have to actually touch it. She walked over to the glowing sword hilt, wrapping the cloth around her hands.

It wasn't glowing as brightly now—and was it her imagination, or did it look just the least bit pissed off?

"Sorry, mate," she said to it. "But where I come from, we don't do things like what you did. Heroes don't, any how."

Captain Kirk would have made a fine speech about how cultures needed to change and grow and overcome their warlike natures naturally the way Earthlings had, but Glory was tired and she didn't have a scriptwriter handy anyway. She bent over—stiffly, everything hurt— and picked up the sword by what was left of the blade. Her hands hurt, and every finger-twitch seemed to start fresh bleeding.

What if this didn't work? What if the sword wouldn't open the shackles? Neither she nor Ivradan would survive a night spent here on top of this mountain. She wasn't even sure they could get down it in the dark.

But they had to give it a try.

She carried the sword back to the slab, moving with a slow shuffle an arthritic tortoise could have bettered. The gems in the hilt glowed faintly, as if they were slowly going out.

Hurry up, damn you! she told herself.

She reached the slab, and as she did, her foot skidded in a puddle of wet. She fell forward, catching herself automatically on her hands, slamming the sword-hilt into the stone and falling full-length against Ivradan. He grunted as the breath whooshed out of him.

There was a sort of a crackling sound, as though someone were crumpling cellophane next to her ear.

"Get off me," Ivradan said, pushing her away.

Pushing her away.

"Hey," Glory said, pleased, surprised, and irritated all at once. She rolled away, looking and then feeling for the sword-hilt. "I liked you the other way better," she muttered under her breath.

It was gone. Metal hilt, jewels, everything. Gone. *"Returned to Erchane's embrace," I reckon, just like the one in the staff. And good riddance, if you ask me.* Where the iron shackles had been, there was nothing more than rusty stubs set into the rock.

Ivradan slid down the rock and stood, hugging himself against the chill and the wet. "Now what do we—"

"Why ask me?" Glory snapped. "Seems to me you're the bossy-boots with all the ideas around here! 'Slayer, get me off this rock!' 'Slayer, you broke the magic sword!' 'Slayer, go find the *rest* of the magic sword and undo my shackles!' 'Slayer, I'm wet,' 'Slayer, I'm cold,' Well, *I'm* the one who just slew the damned dragon, and does anybody think about how *I'm* feeling? Oh, no, it's all Me—Me—Me. Well, you can just—"

Ivradan put a hand on her arm.

"Slayer, I'm sorry. I was afraid," he said humbly.

Glory smiled, feeling chagrined at her burst of temper. "Fine pair of heroes we make."

It was too dark to see, but she thought he smiled back. "We *are* heroes, aren't we?"

"Damn right," Glory grumbled, obscurely mollified. "Think we can make it down off this rock in the dark?"

"We can try," Ivradan answered.

CHAPTER SEVEN:
Truth or Dare

There were two good things about descending Elboroth-Haden in the dark during a rainstorm. One of them was that they couldn't see how far they had to fall if they slipped. The other was that at least moving kept them warmer than standing still.

It still wasn't fun.

Ivradan led, being in marginally better shape than Glory was. She kept close behind, one hand on his shoulder, the other pressed against the cliff wall, Gordon tucked tightly under her arm. He was a wet and soggy bag of elephant, but he'd made it this far, and she wasn't going to abandon him now.

She told herself that her work was done, that it really didn't matter whether or not they got down alive: the Warmother would stop coming after the Allimir—from outside at least. She told herself that the trail had been wide enough going up for the ponies, so it had to be wide enough going down for two people on foot.

She wished it would stop raining.

She hadn't thought it could be possible to sleep while walking, but she must have, because she didn't remember very much about the descent at all until the part where Ivradan stopped and shook her gently to rouse her.

"Listen!"

Glory blinked and looked around.

It had stopped raining at some point. The night was clear, and the moon—*moons*—were out. The two of them were standing on the flat, and the sky gave just barely enough light for her to make out their surroundings. Ahead lay the ruined gates to the mountain path.

They were down.

She rubbed her bare upper arms with her wrapped hands—she'd lost the bandage somewhere along the way—trying to clear her head. After a moment, she heard what Ivradan had heard.

Singing.

She nodded to Ivradan and crept forward as quietly as she could. Her leather creaked, and the empty scabbard on her back jingled faintly. Might as well get rid of it now. Nothing to put in it.

She reached back to unhook it, and a lancing pain in her shoulder stopped her. She winced, shaking her head in disgust. She'd definitely done something to that shoulder up on the mountain. The scabbard would have to stay.

"Can't you be quieter?" Ivradan whispered.

"Only if I go naked, mate," she whispered back. She started forward again, and reached the edge of the gate. From there she could see the city, and beyond.

Serenthodial was pale in the moons-light, stretching

off into the distance. Nearer to hand stood the black ruin of Great Drathil.

And here and there, among the ruins, fires. Camp fires. She could smell the smoke, too, now that she was sniffing for it. Her stomach rumbled, reminding her of the long gap between meals. Sometime soon there'd come a day when she got breakfast, lunch, *and* dinner all within the same 24 hours, and wouldn't *that* be a minor miracle?

Just now she had other things on her mind.

It would have been too much to ask that all of the Warmother's good works vanish with her, Glory thought irritably. The mercenary band of nightmares that had chased them up the mountain in the first place was still there, and somehow she didn't reckon that striding into the camp and announcing that she'd killed their boss was likely to improve anybody's temper. She thought about the slaughter back in the castle of Arlinn when the Warmother had simply left, and shuddered. No.

"What do we do?" Ivradan whispered.

"Let me think," Glory answered.

She knew they had to get back to the Oracle where Belegir and the other Allimir were waiting. It was barely possible that they could use the ring-road to sneak around the edge of the mercenary camp and reach the trail through the forest. There was no way to get into the forest any sooner. The ring-road was cut down into sheer rock, and neither of them was in any shape to try to scale the ridge any place short of where the forest road cut into it.

She worked her right shoulder, trying to decide how bad the damage was, as she listened. From the singing, it was clear everyone wasn't asleep down there. How many guards did they have out and how alert were they? How far was the camp spread out? Had anyone made it out of Charane's palace alive this afternoon and brought news of what was going on?

And did any of these people care?

One good thing—or bad, depending on how you looked at it—was that the Warmother's magic wouldn't be working any more. But if they noticed that, they might notice that *She* wasn't around to keep an eye on them anymore . . .

"We don't know where they are, and we can't tell from here. Let's see if we can sneak back to the Oracle trail and get back to your mates without putting the wind up anybody, hey?"

"What if that doesn't work?" Ivradan said dubiously.

"Then we try something else," Glory said, with far more confidence than she felt.

"Before we go . . . " Ivradan said, hesitantly.

"Yes?"

"Give me the magic doll. You can't hold onto him and fight at the same time," Ivradan said.

"Oh."

Reluctantly, Glory extricated Gordon from beneath her arm. She wrung him out carefully before handing him over to Ivradan. Ivradan tucked him just as carefully into the front of his tunic (lucky Ivradan, to be wearing proper clothes, and layers at that, even if they were wet) and cinched his belt tight. "There."

Glory smiled. "'Come, camrado,'" she said, consciously quoting. And hoped Evil was taking the rest of the night off.

This time she led, trying to remember what the road had looked like during the day. It would have been too easy if the ponies Charane had magicked down off the top of the mountain were waiting here for them. Maybe they weren't dead, wherever they were. That had been the Warmother's style, hadn't it, really? Not to kill outright when she could make things miserable instead?

Maybe she'd sent the ponies back to the Allimir just to make Belegir's lot unhappy, bad cess to her.

As they got closer to the raiders, Glory began to wonder if *anyone* in the mercenaries' camp was asleep. There seemed to be entirely too much drinking and carousing going on for anybody to get his head down in the middle of it. And what could they possibly be drinking? From what she'd seen of them earlier, they hadn't been carrying much with them.

Unless Great Drathil'd had vast untapped wine-cellars that had escaped the original fire . . . ?

She looked around. The ring-road had dipped. They were out of sight of the fires, and from the sound of things, the mercenaries were still some distance away. "Ivradan?" she whispered, stopping him. "When this place burned, did anybody ever come back here?"

"What?" He stared at her as if she'd lost her wits.

"Did any of the Allimir come back? To salvage anything?"

"Of course not," he whispered back. "It is a cursed place."

And everything above ground had been burned by the Warmother. But from what she'd seen when she'd been mucking about in the ruins today, there'd been a lot built in stone, and the ground itself hadn't been too badly damaged, just . . . sterilized, like. The city had burnt from the top down, not the bottom up.

"Were there cellars? Deep cellars?" she asked.

"Are you feeling all right?" Ivradan demanded incredulously.

She gritted her teeth and held on to her temper with an effort. "Cellars? *Wine* cellars?"

Finally he saw what she was getting at. "Yes. Of course. Wine—beer—mead—the vineyards of Great Drathil stretched for miles, and its vintages were famous. Why?"

She patted him on the shoulder with relief.

"Because every soldier I ever heard tell of went looking for the pub first. And from the sound of things, I'd say this lot found it."

It took a moment for Ivradan to work that through. "The— They— You mean they're *drunk*?"

"I *hope* they're drunk. They sound drunk, anyhow. What time is it—how long until dawn?"

Ivradan looked up at the sky, judging the time from the position of the stars and moons. "Nearly midnight."

It had been around noon when the mercenaries had arrived at Great Drathil. Say four or five hours to find the cellars and get at least some of the stock out, and by now the party should be well underway. If she were lucky, at least half of them were legless with drink by now.

"Come on."

Moving faster now, they continued along the road. The Oracle was north of the city, and the entrance to the forest road was on a ridge overlooking one of the main city gates. Anybody who cared to look would be able to see them at that point, and there was no cover, but with only a little luck they were too drunk to notice.

Glory and Ivradan were walking close beside the ditch-moat—she had a vague back-up plan that involved jumping in and hiding if they spotted anyone—when up ahead, she heard the unmistakable sound of someone retching.

Glory froze. Then, to her own astonishment, she began to move forward quickly, giving Ivradan a hard shove in the chest so he'd stay put.

Something that was puking like that had to be human-shaped, didn't they? And with so many different kinds of imported talent around here, who was to say she looked out of place?

She hoped.

She could see the sufferer silhouetted against the road. It was one man, alone, sicking his guts up, leaning on a spear for support. He didn't even notice her approach. And he reeked of vomit and wine.

Glory yanked the spear away, wincing at the weight in her hands and the pain as her cloth-wrapped palms closed over it. It was a footman's weapon, heavy as a pool cue from Hell.

The drunkard was turning toward her, staggering off-balance, mouth open to yell. Glory hit him in the side of the head with the spearshaft as hard as she could. Her bad shoulder made her pull the strike a little, but it was still hard enough. There was a sound like a cricket-bat hitting a ripe melon. He went down, and he didn't move.

She was looking down at him, trying to decide if he was still breathing, when a sound out of the farther darkness stopped her cold.

"You shouldn't a' hit Bakar like that."

Two more shadowy shapes came forward out of the night, moving with the ponderous unsteadiness of the far-from-sober. Bakar's mates, come to make sure he got back to his drink okay, and just her bad luck. She swung the spear around, grounding the butt with a thump. It had a wide leaf-shaped head, sharp and gleaming.

"I reckon you don't know who I am, mate. I'm Vixen the Slayer. I kill gods as a warm-up routine."

"You shouldn't a' hit him," repeated the one who'd spoken first, too drunk to take much notice of what she'd said. She doubted his friend was in much better shape, but it wouldn't take much competence for the two of them to kill her. All they really had to do was yell.

She heard a rasp as the one who'd spoken pulled his sword and started weaving toward her. It was a short sword; all three of them were wearing studded leather tunics and sandals, making Glory think of the Roman legions. His mate moved sideways, so that they'd be coming at her from two directions. It was a bar-brawl move as old as time, and no less effective for all of that.

She backed up, away from Bakar's body and the drainage ditch, moving to get the rock wall at her back. She had the longer weapon, and there were things you could do with a quarterstaff. It was too bad it was dark and she didn't know most of them.

The second one didn't have a sword. But he had a bottle. She heard it smash against a rock, and knew he'd be coming in close with a fistful of broken glass, and her armor didn't cover all that much. She swept the spear at them both, jabbing, driving both of them back, but it was only a matter of time before they found a way to get to her.

"Hey," said Broken Bottle, in tones of aggrieved and very drunk discovery. "It's a girl. D'you suppose she's one a' those— One a' those— You know. *Those.*"

"She shouldn't a' hit Bakar," said Swordsman, who was apparently a man of few but very fixed ideas. "Let's kill her."

Broken Bottle lurched forward again, and Glory swung her spear toward him. Swordsman rushed in, trying to take advantage of her lapse, and Glory kept on swinging. The butt-end of the spear came up and poked him in the face, not hard enough to do any real damage, but it confused him at least. He reeled back and sat down hard, dropping his sword. It went sliding away up the road.

It would all have been funny, if it hadn't been so real. They were trained professionals out to kill her, and only the fact that they were drunk and it was dark had saved her from dying immediately.

Broken Bottle was still on his feet, the jagged neck of the wine bottle in his hand. Glory thrust at him with the spear, and discovered why spears were often impractical on the field of warfare. It went sliding in through a gap between the studs on his leather armor and sank into the flesh along his ribs—not a lethal wound, but bloody and painful—and then it stuck. The head twisted and the studs held it fast. She couldn't pull it free.

Broken Bottle screamed, a full-throated bellow of disappointment, pain, and surprise, dropping the bottle and clutching the shaft of the spear. Glory shook the spear furiously, but she couldn't pull it free. She gave up and shoved as hard as she could, knocking him sprawling. They'd have the whole camp here in moments.

She turned.

Ivradan was standing in the road, holding the other mercenary's dropped sword. The man was getting slowly to his feet, looking far more sober than he had a moment before.

"Give me that, little man, and I won't hurt you. Much," Swordsman said.

Glory stared for a frozen moment, unwilling to shout and distract Ivradan. What could she do? What would Vixen do?

She pulled one of her last remaining stakes from her boot, forcing her stiff clumsy fingers to fold themselves around it. Not long, but sharp, and his neck was bare. She could hurt him with it. Badly.

"Why don't you pick on somebody your own size?" she shouted to Swordsman, running toward him.

He was on his feet, advancing on Ivradan, but he stopped when he saw her. "Tadmar! Get up off your dead ass and be some use!" Swordsman bellowed, backing away.

Tadmar must be the one she'd stuck. She wished she could see what he was doing, knowing she didn't dare look. But over Swordsman's shoulder she could see the lights of the camp coming closer. Torches. And that meant people to carry them.

They were seriously screwed.

But she meant to take a couple of them with her if she could.

"Get behind me!" she shouted to Ivradan. "And watch out for Tadmar!"

She advanced on (the former) Swordsman, thinking of nothing but the best way to take him apart. She smiled, and something about her expression made him turn and run. She watched him for a second or two, obscurely satisfied, and turned back just in time to see Ivradan cut Tadmar's throat.

"Hey," she said weakly, just as if she hadn't been hoping to do the same thing to Tadmar's mate a moment before. She watched as Ivradan set the swordblade beside the spear, cutting the gash wider until he could work the spearhead free.

I reckon you lot won't need that much help in getting back to your old habits after all, she thought uneasily.

"C'mon," she said urgently. No need to whisper now. She could hear hoofbeats along the road, heading their way. Big horses, too, not the little Allimir ponies.

Ivradan came trotting back, spear in one hand, sword in the other. There was blood on his face.

"What now?" he asked, offering her the sword.

"How far to the trail?" she asked, as she took it. Automatically she slipped the stake back into its sheath. She might need it again later.

"Too far."

"Let's try."

Ivradan dropped the spear—too heavy to carry—and

they ran full-out. Get far enough away from the bodies, and they still might be able to trick the rest of the army for long enough to get away. At least now she had a sword.

They got back past the first gawkers without difficulty—either they were too drunk to notice the two of them, or were following the old soldier's dictum of not asking questions. But then there were more—a milling, disoriented mob of creatures and the more-or-less human—all drunk, belligerent, and demanding to know what was going on, waving sputtering pitch-soaked torches about with a fine disregard for the faces and hair of their companions. There were even some of the bear-wolf things in with the mob, towering over the rest by a good foot and more. None of them looked particularly worried about being attacked. The Warmother must have told them this place was easy pickings.

Glory grabbed one of the wobbling torches from its owner and held it high with her free hand, trying to work her way through the crowd. For a few moments, she thought the two of them were going to get away with it; slip through the mob and get away.

"Hey! Who're *you*?"

It was one of the lizardly things she'd seen up in Charane's palace. It stepped right in front of her and grabbed her by the wrist that was holding the torch.

Glory stared back blankly. What could she say? She didn't feel a lot like Glory McArdle at the moment, but if she told them she was Vixen the Slayer, they might recognize the name.

"Koroshiya," she said after a moment.

"*I* don't know you," the lizard-man said, tightening his grip on her wrist until she was glad of the bracer's protection.

Glory brought the point of her sword up between

his legs and pressed. He might not keep the family jewels there, but she reckoned he wouldn't fancy being sawed in half just the same.

"Just how well do you want to know me?" she said, her voice hard and flat.

But she'd attracted too much attention. Everybody was looking at them, and Ivradan didn't look like anything but an Allimir. Things were about to get ugly. Glory could feel it. The mob pressed closer, and she felt something sharp dig into her back, cutting into the leather. The lizard-man smiled, showing pale yellow gums and a pair of long bluish fangs, and reluctantly, Glory lowered her sword.

Then there was a different kind of disruption, and people were looking away from the two of them, behind her. The mob that had been pressing up against her from all sides drew back, and even Lizard-Man let go of her wrist and stepped back, raising his hands in a gesture of submission.

With a sinking heart, Glory turned and looked.

It was the Amazon queen.

She was riding a white horse, and there were six more Amazons behind her, also riding white horses. All seven of them looked stone cold sober, and none of them looked particularly pleased to be here.

The queen dismounted. She tossed her reins to Glory as though she'd expected her to be there just to hold them, and as she strode past her on her way to Lizard-Man, she whispered one quick phrase from the corner of her mouth:

"Take my horse."

Glory turned to Ivradan, trying to pretend she was Romy on a Bad Hair Day: pissed with everyone in sight and looking for someone to run errands. She threw her torch at the feet of the nearest mercenary—the man danced back, out of range of the shower of sparks—

and passed Ivradan the reins. "Get up," she whispered. He was the better horseman. He could get them out of here if anyone could.

"What's going on here?" the Amazon queen bawled, in a voice that would wake the dead on battlefields six counties over. "Where's the commander of the Night Watch? Is that *liquor* I smell on you?"

Bluff. It was all sheer bluff, and they had a bare instant to use it.

Ivradan was up. The stirrups were far too long for him. He reached a hand down to Glory and hauled her up behind him with surprising strength. She got her feet into the empty stirrups and held on one-handed, still clutching the short-sword.

Ivradan drove the mare forward with a sudden lurch. The mercenaries scattered.

"Stop her!" the Amazon queen shouted a moment later. "She's stealing my horse!"

Glory looked back. For some reason, the other six Amazons had all lost control of their mounts at the same time. The animals were plunging back and forth through the mob of drunken sellswords, scattering them and completing their disorganization. Not one of the women reached for her quiver of spears.

Then they were past even the stragglers, out of the glare of the torches, with only the light of the moons to steer by. Ivradan was leaning over the mare's neck, stroking her and talking to her in a low voice. Glory's eyes, still dazzled by the torches, saw only darkness, no matter how hard she strained. The wind whipped tears from her eyes, blinding her, until she gave up and closed them. She leaned over Ivradan's back, holding onto him tightly and concentrating on not falling off.

Then the mare slowed from a gallop to a trot, and lunged up the embankment to the ridge. A few minutes more, and they were under the trees of the forest road. The mare slowed to a walk.

We made it, Glory thought in disbelief. She looked around, but there wasn't much to see. The trees had shut out what little light there was from the stars and moon, and there was nothing to see but darkness. She twisted around in the saddle to get a better look behind her—everything hurt, and her bad shoulder was a sullen constant ache as the adrenaline wore off, but she guessed it didn't matter much now—but she saw nothing behind them but darkness, and heard nothing but the sound of the horse's hooves on the leaf-strewn trail, the jingle of her tack, and the creak of her own leather.

It had all happened so fast. From the moment she'd first hit Bakar till now was . . . what? Ten minutes, if that? She had no way to be really sure. But she knew it hadn't been as long as it seemed.

Ivradan pulled the mare to a halt.

"I'd better lead her the rest of the way," Ivradan said, slipping down from the saddle. "Poor lady, she is lost and far from home, and these paths are strange to her."

"And how do you know all that?" Glory asked, shifting forward in the saddle. She laid the sword across her thighs, so as not to drop it in the dark, and gripped the front of the saddle with both hands. Gingerly. Her palms felt puffy and swollen, like a combination of a bad burn and a fresh bruise. Funny how she hadn't really noticed it back there while she'd been fighting for her life.

"She told me," Ivradan said simply. "Her name is Maidarence."

"Yeah?" Glory said intelligently. Ivradan began to lead the mare forward at a slow walk.

"I'll get down and walk," Glory said reluctantly.

"No," Ivradan said firmly. "She can carry you without trouble, and you are weary from your labors."

Got that right, mate, Glory thought with guilty relief. Killed a dragon, climbed down a mountain, fought a mercenary army . . . it might all be in a day's work for Vixen the Slayer, but it was damned tiring work all the same.

And she'd killed someone, she remembered with a belated pang of realization. At least, Swordsman thought Bakar was dead. And she'd been trying to kill some others when they'd been rescued—by a woman whose name she didn't even know. Not to mention Ivradan's contribution to the evening's festivities. Slitting Tadmar's throat as cool as you please. And Glory hadn't even blinked.

God's teeth, what am I turning into here?

Best to leave off wondering about that until the sun comes up, she decided wisely.

"Think they'll come after us?" she asked, after a few minutes of silence.

"Erchane protects Her own," Ivradan answered.

Not noticeably, Glory thought, but then she wondered. It was true that they'd gotten out of all of these scrapes by the skin of their teeth, but they *had* gotten out. No thanks to Cinnas and his magic, though. It was Cinnas who'd made this whole mess in the first place, him and his great idea to get rid of War forever.

That's not the way it works, chum.

Maidarence's rocking walk was soothing, lulling her, if not to sleep, then at least into a comfortable absence of thought. They were going home, if nothing killed them first, and soon all the Allimir could go home, and if it wasn't going to be quite the happily ever after anybody'd been looking for, it was better than the alternative.

Right?

"Slayer?" Ivradan said, after another long quiet while.

"Um?" Glory said fuzzily.

"Why did she give you Maidarence?"

"What? Who?" Glory asked, struggling further awake. She looked around. She didn't know how Ivradan could see to find his way—it was as black as the inside of a coal mine at midnight out here. It even *smelled* late: three or four o'clock, say, a couple of hours before dawn. If she ever saw a bed again, she promised herself she was going to sleep for a week.

"The woman in white. Why did she help us? She was one of the Warmother's allies."

Glory thought about it. "You know, mate, I don't reckon she was like the others, her and her girls. I don't guess you saw much of what happened up there in the palace?"

"The wizard betrayed you." Ivradan's voice was flat with anger.

"No, Ivro," Glory said sadly. "She tricked him, and he didn't have someone like you to let him know what she was on about. She tricked him and she scared him, and she didn't give him time to think."

And now that it was all over, she found that she could actually be sorry for Dylan as well. He hadn't asked for any of this, God knew. Fra Diavolo had been just another acting job to him, not even a chance to play out a wonderful game of make-believe, the way Vixen was for her.

She sighed, and brought her thoughts back to the present. "Anyway, that thing Charane gave him was a gun—a weapon from my world. And he went a little bit troppo with it—started shooting at everybody, not just me. So the Amazon queen—that's the Woman in White to you—put a spear through him. Killed him dead. And I gave her the gun. Guess she used it to shoot her way out of there."

"So the wizard is dead?"

"I reckon."

"And the— the *Amazon queen* was grateful to you?"

"I reckon," Glory said again. "Or something close enough to it so that we're here now, any how."

"Good," Ivradan said comprehensively. "What will happen to her now? They will not be grateful to her for allowing us to escape."

"I don't know," Glory said honestly. "It depends on if they sober up enough to figure it out. But I know I wouldn't want to get on her bad side."

A while later the first birds began to call out from the tops of the trees, and a little after that, there was enough light that Ivradan mounted up in front of Glory again.

Glory wasn't sure which of them the others were more stunned to see: her and Ivradan, or the enormous white horse they rode in on. Unlike the Allimir livestock, Maidarence had no opinion of the Oracle cave, and both Glory and Ivradan had gone on foot to coax her along through the cave passage.

"They've returned! Tavara—Mage Belegir! The Slayer has returned to us!" Cambros shouted when he saw them.

His voice echoed weirdly through the cavern of the Pilgrim's Fountain. Maidarence, at last seeing something she understood and approved of, was pulling Ivradan across the floor toward the water. Her shod hooves clicked loudly on the smooth stone.

Glory stopped where she was and let them go on ahead.

Belegir was lying on his makeshift bed beside the fountain, with Tavara sitting beside him. The Allimir healer had gotten to her feet at their approach, and was standing uncertainly, looking almost as if she wanted to fend Glory off. Belegir looked pale and worn, ground down by his injuries, but alive and obviously on the mend. It was only when she saw him, when she was standing once more in this place that all her instincts told her was a really safe place, that Glory could honestly feel that her task was over, the battle ended.

She'd won. Vixen the Slayer had won.

She walked over to the fountain and knelt, stiffly and awkwardly, beside Belegir. Her leather, only faintly damp now, creaked loudly as it flexed.

"It's over," she said simply. "The Warmother will come to trouble you no more."

Belegir closed his eyes in relief, but the tears Glory had somehow expected of him did not come. The Warmother's unbinding had changed everything, everyone she'd known here in Erchanen. Even him.

"There is more to tell?" he asked, after a moment.

"A lot," Glory said. She glanced back over her shoulder. Cambros and Ivradan were fawning on the white mare, like boys with a flashy new car, and Tavara was regarding Glory warily from a safe distance. All of them seemed somehow more *normal*, more *there*, as if some missing ingredient, like salt in stew, had suddenly been supplied. "I don't think I did what you wanted. What Cinnas wanted. I'm sorry for that."

"It is the way of heroes," Belegir said gently, reaching out to take her hand. His eyebrows rose at the sight of the makeshift bandage. "I think you must hear now what the Oracle told me, Slayer."

Glory's eyes opened wide in apprehension. "Oh, no, Bel, I don't reckon—"

But Belegir was strong enough now to argue. "Leave us," he told Tavara firmly.

The young healer bobbed an unwilling curtsey and walked away toward the others.

"It cannot harm you now," Belegir said to Glory. "You have done what you came to do, have you not?"

"I . . . yes," Glory admitted. Still holding his hand, she moved from her knees to a cross-legged seat that was a little less uncomfortable. She had the woozy, light-headed feeling of too many hours awake on too little food, and hoped to be able to sleep soon. But she owed it to Belegir to listen to what he had to say.

"That night when the Oracle came to me, it said that you would bring to the Allimir such sorrow and disaster as our people had not known for a thousand years. I did not know what to think. I thought then that Erchane meant you must fail in your task . . . but She did not, did She?"

"No," Glory said reluctantly. *But you're all still alive! You've got a chance now!* she wanted to protest. "You know what Cinnas did, don't you?"

"He bound the Warmother upon the peak of Elboroth-Haden of the Hilvorn, then called Grey Arlinn," Belegir said. "He bound her by binding her into mortal form."

Glory squeezed his hand gently with her fingertips— it hardly hurt at all—and then released him. She rubbed at her eyes. "She was all of you, first. He took her out of all of you—the spirit of War—and gave her a single form. His daughter, Charane. *That* was what— that was who—he chained to a rock up there. I had a chance . . ." She stopped, staring off into nothing. "I could have killed Ivradan, and he would have taken Charane's place, and everything would have been just like it was. But I couldn't do that."

Couldn't kill Ivradan to save the rest of the Allimir, but she could drag him into mortal danger without a backward glance, couldn't she? And found it easy enough to try to kill anyone else that looked at her cross-eyed, didn't she? She *knew* she'd done the right thing—but it didn't seem very logical, somehow.

She shook her head wearily.

And what, she suddenly wondered, would have happened to all those mercenaries the Warmother had imported if she had taken the easy way out, and chained War up again? Would they have all gone back to their own places and times just as if *She* hadn't summoned them up in the first place? Or would they still have been here, with the Allimir as helpless as before against them?

Did I make the right choice after all?

"So I guess I undid Cinnas' original spell," she said, after a long silence. "You're back where you started. Back in the Time of Legend."

And now the tears she'd been expecting did come. Only they were hers.

She scrubbed at her eyes angrily with the tips of her fingers—if anybody here ought to be grizzling, it was Belegir. "Sorry," she whispered. "Sorry."

Belegir patted her knee. "Do not weep for us, Slayer. It is Erchane's will, and a problem to be faced another day. Now you must rest, and have your own wounds seen to. Tavara, attend us!"

The healer came hurrying back as if she'd just been waiting to be called—as she undoubtedly had been.

"See to the Slayer's injuries, taken in honorable battle," Belegir said decisively, "then let her sleep undisturbed."

Too exhausted to resist—or even think straight—Glory allowed herself to be led off.

The Allimir rescue party had packed in quite a lot of gear on their string of ponies, or else had gone out shopping while Glory's back was turned. One corner

of the cavern had been set up as a combination surgery and supply dump, concealed behind a standing
screen that must have come from somewhere inside
the Temple complex, as it was far too large to have
been packed in.

Tavara took Glory behind it and seated her on a
makeshift stool, then disappeared again. When she
returned a few moments later, she was carrying Glory's
other clothes—the jeans and T-shirt she'd left behind.

"If you will remove your armor, Slayer . . ."

"Easier said than done," Glory muttered. She managed to unlatch the clasps down the right side of her
corset, but could not manage to twist around to get
at the ones on the left. Tavara came forward and helped
her, peeling away the filthy, clammy leather shell that
was glued to her with an accretion of sweat, mud,
blood, and other things best left unremembered.
Fortunately, a girlhood spent in gymnastics had pretty
much erased any trace of body-shyness Glory might
have been born with. Tavara draped a blanket around
Glory's shoulders, and waited.

Glory looked down at her boots, up at Tavara, and
shrugged.

"Sorry," she said simply. Between her hands and her
back, there was no way she could get those boots off.

Tavara knelt before her and tugged. First one boot,
then the other, came loose with a grinding, sucking
sound. Glory wiggled her feet, sighing in relief. *Hello,
toes.* She stood—carefully—and pushed the bedraggled
remains of her Elizabethan slops down over her hips.

"Any chance of a bath?" she asked hopefully. Now
if she could just get those damned bracers off. She
never wanted to see any part of this S&M rig-out again!

"Soon," Tavara answered, sounding like nurses everywhere. "What did you do to your hands?"

Glory looked down at them. They were mittened in

the black velvet panniers she'd torn from her costume, and only the fingertips showed. The dye had run, staining her skin a greyish black—at least, she hoped it was the dye. She'd torn a couple of fingernails. The fingers looked swollen, and her hands felt stiff.

"Ripped them up pretty good, didn't I?" she said disinterestedly. "Just help me get these bracers off," she added, "And then you can bandage to your heart's content."

The leather bracers that covered her arms like opera-length gloves laced for fit, and normally Glory just slipped them on and off like bracelets, trusting friction to keep them in place, but they'd been soaked through and dried several times since she'd put them on last, and by now they'd shrunk a bit. After struggling with them for a few moments Tavara got a knife and sliced through the lacings. She pulled them open, freeing Glory from the last vestige of Vixen the Slayer.

Only . . . not. She's me now, and I'm her. It's not the clothes, or the makeup, or the sword. It's all the rest. It's what's inside.

Tavara brought another blanket and let Glory stand to wrap it around her sarong-style—apparently this was going to take a while—then started to unwrap the makeshift bandage that covered her hands. It was soon apparent it was stuck to the flesh (a happy thought, that), so Glory got to balance a bowl of green-tinged water on her knees, soaking the cloth on her hands free (the dye ran, turning the water black; a relief of sorts), while Tavara gave her a makeshift sponge-bath and exclaimed over each of the various cuts and bruises she discovered as though Glory had gotten each one of them just to make extra work for Tavara.

Glory wasn't really looking forward to seeing what was underneath the velvet. She could still feel the way the hilt of the sword had dug into her flesh with a thousand tiny needles. And then the Warmother had bled all over her.

"You tore the bandage on your shoulder loose," Tavara said accusingly.

"Hurm?"

"Here. On your shoulder. I told you to leave it there until it fell off, and you didn't. Does this hurt? There's a bruise."

"Bleeding *hell*!" Glory yelped, as Tavara dug her thumb in just below Glory's right shoulderblade. "Of course it hurts, you fool girl—I sprained it!" And a little quarterstaff practice on top of things hadn't helped any.

She glared over her shoulder at the little Allimir in a fashion that would have had the healer cowering under the furniture a few days before, but now Tavara stood her ground.

"I'll strap it for you so you can rest it, once you've dressed. There's bruising and some scrapes, but it doesn't look too bad."

"That's because it isn't *your* shoulder," Glory muttered under her breath. The jolt of pain had roused her to full wakefulness again, and she started picking at the wet cloth, pulling it away from her hands. Whatever was in the water seemed to numb the pain, or else she was used to it by now. Tavara didn't object as she peeled her hands free and dropped the wet cloth to the floor. She held her hands up, inspecting them critically.

Both palms were starred with dozens of bloodless wounds, covering them from the heel of the palm all the way to the middle of the second finger joint, all the places where her hands would have touched the sword. They looked like razor cuts, and where they intersected, there were pits in the skin where chunks of flesh had been torn away. Both hands were swollen, as if from a burn, but her right hand—the one that had held the stake—was puffiest, covered with tiny broken blisters.

All things considered, Glory was just as glad it had been too dark to see clearly up there on the mountaintop.

Even Tavara didn't have any smartmouthed nursery rejoinder to make when she saw Glory's hands.

"What did you touch?" she said in a small voice.

"Something poisonous," Glory said. "But they bled a lot."

"Then that— That's good. It will have washed the poison away."

I hope, hovered unspoken between them.

Tavara bandaged her hands with a thick black foul-smelling salve that felt cold and gluey, followed by yards and yards of bandage going halfway up her arms until her hands resembled thumbless boxing gloves. She daubed Glory's other scratches with something that simply burned, and then finally relented and helped Glory into her jeans and T-shirt. It was something of a shock to confront once more the image of her *doppelganger*— painted, coiffed, and immaculately armored, glaring menacingly up at her from her own chest.

"Live the Legend." Ah, if you only knew . . .

True to her word, Tavara put Glory's arm into a sling to immobilize the shoulder, then bound the arm against her side with more strips of bandage, covering up the Vixen-image.

"Do not, I ask you, Slayer, destroy more of my handiwork," the little healer said scoldingly.

"Do my best," Glory said, her words slurred with exhaustion. "An' if I starve because I can't hold a spoon, it's on your head."

"You will not starve," Tavara said, smiling now. "Come."

She led Glory back to the fountain. Her bed was

laid out beside it, and Ivradan was waiting for her, scrubbed up and dressed in fresh clothes. He looked tired, but pleased with himself, and was holding a steaming mug in each hand.

"Felba and Fimlas and Heddvi are here," he said happily. "All well."

It took Glory a moment to place the names.

"The ponies *She* . . . ?"

"She only sent them away," Ivradan said happily, "and so they sought the nearest place where they knew they would be fed. They came here, arriving before night fell."

No wonder the others had been so stunned at the sight of them, showing up the morning after their horses did. It hadn't been Maidarence at all. It had been them coming back from the dead.

"And it's all right?" Glory said fumblingly, not quite sure of how to ask the right questions.

"No harm can enter here," Ivradan said soothingly. "Come. Sit. I have brought soup for you. You will sleep—we will both sleep, and tomorrow Belegir will tell us what we must do."

She was too tired to pick holes in his logic. She managed to get herself down into a sitting position one-handed—awkward, with the bed so low—and let Ivradan hold the cup for her. It held a thick broth, with a faint undertaste, but tired as she was, Glory hardly cared if Tavara had been spiking it. She was asleep before she finished the mug.

She half-woke a few times, just far enough to remember there was no reason to wake up, and went back to sleep, wallowing in unconsciousness as in the ultimate self-indulgence. Once somebody pulled her hair, but after a while they stopped. She cuddled Gordon tighter and ignored them, her face buried in the toy elephant's mold-scented dusty plush.

Eventually hunger—and more pressing needs—roused her to full consciousness again. She pried open her eyes, and bopped herself in the face with a large bandaged mitt when she tried to rub her face. There was something under her arm.

Gordon.

Sometime while she'd slept, someone had taken Gordon away, and cleaned him, and put him back together again. He'd been restored to his original roundness; the bullet-holes had been carefully patched before they'd brought him back and tucked him in with her again. The color and the fabric didn't match, but it was at least blue, carefully oversewn around the edges to hold it in place against the well-loved plush. She kissed him gently on the forehead, working the tips of her left-hand fingers to the edge of the bandage so she could touch him. Good old Gordon. A real trouper. Not many stuffed elephants could say they'd faced down a demon-queen and survived.

She sat up cautiously, and looked around. Everything was quiet. The others were all asleep. She didn't know how long she'd been out—long enough, obviously, to get herself turned around from all of them. What she needed now was to find the jakes.

Aside from the bum shoulder, and her hands, she wasn't in too bad shape, all things considered, though she wouldn't be in competition condition any time soon. She got to her feet without much difficulty, leaving Gordon on her pillow, and went padding barefoot toward the temple steps. She knew she could find something to make do with up there—better than wandering around down here until she woke somebody, anyway—and besides, she knew she could be alone there. Now that all this was over, she thought she was entitled to a bit of a think.

As she got to her feet, she realized that the Allimir

had done more for her while she was sleeping than repair Gordon. Someone had brushed out her hair and rebraided it into two loose braids. *Must've been dead to the world and all found,* she thought, looking down at them. A nice gesture, even if a little unsettlingly intimate. She wondered which of them had done it.

Sore muscles protested as she went up the broad shallow steps, but it was no more stiffness than a little stretching would cure. She'd give the shoulder a couple of days rest and then see if Tavara had any liniment for it. If these people had horses, they must have horse-liniment, and that would do fine for her, too.

A few minutes later, having debased one more solid gold bucket and another acolyte shift, Glory sat down on one of the benches in the Presence Chamber and took stock of her life.

What happened now? She wasn't any closer to getting home than she had been the day the door fell off her dressing room, as far as she could see. The Allimir were in a little better shape—but now they were sharing the plains of Serenthodial with a job-lot of imported villains and frighteners, none of whom looked like good candidates for honest work—except maybe the Amazons, and Glory still wasn't sure how they'd got mixed up in all of this—and all of whom were likely to be just as much trouble for a bunch of farmers trying to get the crops in as the Warmother had been. The first thing the Allimir were going to need was an army of their own, and where were they going to come up with one? They might not be all that peaceful any more, but they still didn't know anything much about the arts of war. And she couldn't teach them.

Maybe Erchane'll send them a nice drill-sergeant next.

And there was one other thing still bothering her.

If Belegir's dream had been true, what about hers?
"Slayer?"

The voice behind her caused her to levitate with a shrill unheroic squeal. She spun around, cursing her awkwardness, to find Ivradan standing in the doorway.

He was undressed for sleep, capless, his long chestnut hair hanging down over his shoulders, barefoot as she was, wearing only his loose linen undersmock and calf-length trousers.

"I woke and saw you gone. I thought you might have come this way," he said.

"So I did," Glory said, taking a deep breath and trying to slow her racing heart. It seemed almost odd not to feel the springy resistance of the corset when she did so, but it was going to be a cold day in whatever passed for Hell around these parts before she put that outfit on again.

"My turn to ask you, I reckon: what happens now, Ivradan?" she said, when she was sure her voice was steady.

"Now we can return to our homes, and rebuild the Allimir nation," Ivradan said. "It will not be easy, of course."

"Not with a bunch of pissed-off mercenaries wondering where their meal-ticket's got to," Glory said. She sat down on the bench again.

"There will be . . . intemperance," Ivradan admitted reluctantly. "Peace-breaking. Even violence."

"Lots of that," Glory agreed. "Harsh language. People may even lose their tempers from time to time."

Ivradan blushed and hung his head, looking embarrassed.

"But you'll need all those things," Glory said urgently, wanting to comfort him. "They're what you'll have to have to survive. Maybe you don't have the

Warmother around any more, but she left you a whole world full of enemies."

"That is what I must go and tell them," Ivradan said. "With your permission, I will take your horse, and—"

"*My* horse?" Glory interrupted, confused.

"Maidarence," Ivradan said. "I know that the Amazon queen gave her to you, but she is wonderfully fast, faster than our ponies, and so I thought . . ."

"Take her, take her," Glory said, waving at him with her free hand and feeling unaccountably irritable. "I reckon she's really yours anyway. Likes you better than she does me, anyhow. When are you going?"

"As soon as it is light. Belegir has given me the authority to call the people together and tell them all that you have done for us, and what we must now do for ourselves. I will send others here to take my place, and in a few hands of days, when Mage Belegir is able to travel . . ."

He stopped.

"You braided up my hair, didn't you?" Glory said, getting to her feet again. So he was leaving. No reason for him to stay, was there?

Ivradan nodded.

There was another silence.

"Thanks for taking such good care of Gordon, hey? He looks good as new."

"I knew that was what you would want, Slayer."

Silence.

"I reckon you'd better shake a leg then. You've got a long ride ahead of you. Maybe— Well, have a good ride, then."

Ivradan turned and left. Glory watched until he was out of sight, then waited until she was sure he was out of earshot. Then she kicked out viciously at the nearest bench with the side of her foot.

Hot needles of protest raced up her leg into her back. The bench teetered and fell over with a loud and solid thud. Glory limped over to the one next to it and sat down on it, and stayed there until she was entirely sure Ivradan had ridden away from the Oracle.

The day after Ivradan left, Belegir was allowed to walk as far as the door of the cavern—Tavara and Cambros on either side—and Glory got her left hand rebandaged so that the fingers showed. That day's big adventure was moving the Allimir ponies down the hill to the old stables that once served the Oracle—visitors to the Oracle had always come on foot, so Belegir told Glory, but the Oracle's servants had kept some animals for their own use. Since neither of the invalids was any use in this under-taking, they were left to their own devices while the others were absent.

"You miss Ivradan," Belegir said.

"Doesn't matter," Glory answered shortly. Was it that obvious, or was Belegir just going all wizardly on her? "Every hero has to have a sidekick, and all. But I guess I'm out of the heroing business."

Belegir regarded her shrewdly. Though he still slept a great deal, and tired easily, the bruises were fading quickly and he was well on the mend. A new set of pink robes, a tube of Max Factor, and he'd be back in the Mage business. "Yet it seems to me that you have some unfinished business that disturbs you."

Glory sighed, shaking her head. "Yeah, well, you remember that night at the wellspring when you dreamed I was going to make a dog's breakfast of this whole business? I dreamed something, too."

As best she could remember it after so long, she told Belegir about what she had dreamed: about the

Dreamer of Worlds, who was somehow responsible for Glory's presence here in the Land of Erchanen. The more she told him, the more she remembered, but it still didn't really make a lot of sense to her. It all seemed a little too much like bad television.

". . . and she said I was being tested, but she didn't say what the test was, or how I'd know if I'd passed— just that if I *didn't* pass, everybody back where I come from would be toast, and that if I *did* pass, they'd all be admitted into the Universal Dream and have magic and wizards and unicorns up the wazoo—only that didn't sound so good either. And I don't even know if it was a real dream, Bel—maybe this Oracle-stuff only works for the Allimir, not for people like me."

Belegir considered the matter with careful deliberation, frowning as he thought.

"Yet you are here, and have held Cinnas' sword in your hands, and unmade the Warmother, so I think we must believe that Erchane smiles upon your people as well as upon my own. Still, this sending you speak of contains much to puzzle me. It is true that Erchane wears many names among her peoples, but never is she needlessly cruel. And never in all the ancient texts that I have studied have I seen any mention of such a being and such a test as you name—yet if such a test were true and real, the Allimir must have faced it and passed it in the long-ago, for all of Erchane's gifts are ours to wield. I cannot help you, Slayer, but there is yet one who may. Erchane herself, if She so wills, do you but seek Her counsel."

And look how well that turned out the last time, Glory thought sourly.

"Whether you would accept Erchane's counsel in that matter is your own decision, yet there is one more matter upon which you would do well to consult

Erchane—and soon," Belegir said, breaking into her thoughts.

Glory looked up at him guiltily, hoping her opinion of the uselessness of Erchane's Oracle wasn't as obvious as she was afraid it was.

"Will you go home—back to your own people? Or will you remain here—with us?" Belegir said gently.

Unfortunately, there was no way around that one. Glory wanted to go home, she told herself—of *course* she wanted to go home; who wouldn't want to go home?—and that meant going off to see the Oracle again.

She put it off as long as she could.

Three more days. Her shoulder had been unbraced, and she had Tavara's permission to exercise it gently. She was down to a light bandage on her left hand and an only slightly heavier bandage on her right, she could wiggle all her fingers, and had even gone back to doing parts of her morning warm-up routine. She'd nagged Cambros about the importance of watching for smoke to give them warning of the mercenaries' possible approach, especially with the horses stabled so far away (though she had to admit that the cavern did smell better now) and had taken to going to the cave-mouth several times a day to look herself, but she'd seen nothing.

Maybe they'd all killed each other. Maybe they'd all marched up to the top of Grey Arlinn and jumped off. Maybe they were all still getting drunk. But wherever they were, they hadn't come this way.

She wondered where Ivradan was, and what he was doing.

Tavara was the one who had mended Gordon, and she'd also resewed a couple of the acolyte's shifts so that Glory would have something to change into besides

her jeans. Glory'd managed something close to an
actual bath, and washed her hair, but aside from her
jeans and T-shirt, everything else she'd brought to the
land of Erchanen was gone: it had been with the horses
when the Warmother had magicked them off the
mountaintop, and hadn't survived the trip. So—no
makeup, no mirror, and no aspirin. She wasn't sure
which—if any—she missed.

She was standing in the cave-mouth, watching the
afternoon—more for something to do than because she
believed, by now, that any trouble would come—when
she saw a bright flash of red among the trees. At first
she thought it was a bird, but when she saw it over
and over again, coming closer, she realized it was one
of the spellbirds that Helevrin had loosed the first day
she'd come here. It flashed by her, arrowing into the
cave.

Glory ran after it, arriving panting and out of breath
to find Belegir consulting with Tavara. The little healer
had grown quite proprietary toward her charge just in
the time Glory had been here. She wondered if Mages
married—or whatever Allimir did to produce little
Allimir. They were going to have to do something to
fill up all those deserted cities.

"You got a bird," Glory said, when she could speak.

"Mage Helevrin sent word," Tavara said importantly.
"She will come with a party to the Oracle tomorrow—
for counsel. Just like— Just like Before!"

Belegir looked past Tavara's shoulder at Glory,
regarding her with as much sternness as his round pink
face was capable of. They both knew that she'd put
off what she needed to do for long enough. There was
no more time.

After dinner, Glory trudged up the steps to the
temple, lantern in one hand, Gordon in the other. She

carried the lantern carefully, because it was already lit. She was going alone, and she wouldn't have Belegir to light it for her once she got to the Wellspring.

But this time she was damned if she was sleeping on bare rock, and too bad if it took away from the purity of the whole experience. She wheeled one of the lustral carts out of its chamber, hooked the lantern on the side and propped Gordon jauntily up among the red velvet ropes, then went back to the sleeping alcoves beside the Presence Chamber and grabbed a mattress and several blankets and loaded them on the cart. The cart wheeled easily down the hallway to the Oracle—it was designed to, after all.

She felt a twinge of unease as she neared the armory, but the door was shut tight, just as she'd left it the last time. She thought about opening it to see if she could get her own sword back, and decided against it. If she got it back, something'd probably show up that she had to use it on, and she'd rather stick with her perfect record of victories. War, someone had once said, was hours of boredom punctuated by moments of stark terror. Well, she'd had enough terror. She was ready for several hundred hours of boredom.

She turned away from the armory and faced the Oracle

I don't want to go in there again, she thought, looking at the barred door. *What if it shuts and won't let me out?*

Then Belegir will come looking for you, she told herself pragmatically. Belegir knew she was down here. Cambros and Tavara knew she'd come down here to do some sort of mysterious hero thing. And even if something weird and peculiar happened to all three of them, Helevrin was coming tomorrow with a whole gaggle of people who'd need water fetched from here, and *she'd* get the door open. There was no possible way for Glory to be trapped here.

But her reluctance to go inside was strong.

God's teeth, gel, y'wanna live forever? Ross always used to ask her that—at least the last part—as if the obvious answer should be "no." And when the stakes were high enough, when people were counting on her, that *was* the answer, the right answer, the answer she gave.

But somehow, right here, that didn't seem to be the answer she felt like giving.

Growling under her breath, Glory strode over, jerked the bar out of its brackets, and swung the door open. It swept back fluidly, offering no resistance at all, and banged against the wall, the sharp reverberation of its impact against the stone making Glory jump nervously.

A regular bundle of maiden twitches, that's our Glor.

She wheeled the cart up against the door, hoping she could trick herself into believing she was going to leave it there all night to brace the door open, knowing deep down inside that she wouldn't. Sighing at her own perversity, she unhooked the lantern and went inside to place it into its niche. It was the one Belegir had used: slide the outer sleeve up, and everything was dark. Leave it down, and you saw the flame. She thought she might leave it down. The Oracle wouldn't mind her having a night-light, would it?

She was pleased to feel only the very faintest twinges of foreboding as she dragged the mattress down off the cart and laid it beside the Wellspring, making a second trip to arrange the blankets on her bed. It would be too short for her, but for one night, it wouldn't matter if her legs hung off the end. At least she'd had a proper dinner before she'd come, this time.

Dinners and breakfasts, baths and clean clothes—she was turning into a regular hobbit.

And here was her hole in the ground.

At last, reluctantly, she realized she couldn't stall any longer. She pushed the cart back from the door, climbed the steps for the last time and leaned out to pull the door shut.

It was dark. Every time, the quality of the darkness took her completely by surprise.

She fought down the moment of automatic panic, and, just as it had done before, it subsided, leaving behind the sense of peace and comfort. Nothing bad could happen to her here in the dark. This place was her friend. She was in the presence of Erchane the Mother—who, like all good mothers, let her children go free to make their own mistakes, no matter how disastrous those mistakes might be.

"Pity you couldn't've dropped a word in Cinnas' ear though, hey?" Glory said aloud. "How could he have done something like that to his own kid?"

But she thought of what she'd seen in Charane's great hall, the blood and the slaughter, and thought of seeing things like that every day, of horrors taking place everywhere in all the world you knew, to the people you knew, and thought that Cinnas had probably gotten, well . . . lost. The way Dylan had lost himself at the end.

That doesn't excuse it! she told herself angrily. But maybe it explained it, just a little.

And maybe, if the Allimir knew the whole story about Cinnas, and how his plan to save them had come out in the end, maybe they wouldn't make that same mistake again.

Always assuming they get the chance.

Not my department.

Her eyes had adjusted to the light from the one

small candle now, and she found the cup in its niche on the wall. She took it down carefully and squatted beside the spring to dip it beneath the surface, remembering just too late that her hands were still bandaged.

"Oh, well," Glory said with cheerful resignation. A little wet wouldn't hurt them. Might even help.

She held the cup underwater until the cold made her hands ache, then brought it up again full to the brim, holding it carefully so as not to spill any. Still crouched there, she chugged it down in one go, then got up to put the cup back in its place.

As she turned, her foot slipped.

Off-balance, Glory took a step backward, and fell into the spring.

She plunged straight down, deep beneath the surface, the water filling her nose and mouth, choking her. The water was icily, numbingly cold, and she could feel herself sinking. Desperately, she struggled to keep from inhaling. Her lungs burned with the need for air, but there was nothing to breathe here—only water, freezing and lightless.

The spring seemed to have no bottom. Her eyes were open, but there was nothing to see—she was blind in the darkness, and as she flailed, she could not feel the sides of the spring. All sense of up and down had deserted her; the cold and the blackness was as disorienting as a blow, and she was no longer sure which way she was oriented. Her lungs burned for air, and her vision was fogged with false stars. In the room above, she could almost step across the spring, but down here, not matter how desperately she struggled, she could not reach the sides, as if the small opening above were only the entry to some vast and stygian underground lake . . . or worse.

Don't panic! she told herself. *Just relax. You'll float*

up. But would she? Or was the Oracle spring more like
an underground river than a well? Was she being swept
along beneath the rock even now, carried away from
the only air-hole for miles, to suffocate and die in the
dark? Belegir wouldn't even grieve for her—when she
didn't return in the morning he'd think she'd been
magicked back home—

And Ivradan—

No!

That thought was too much to bear. She could feel
her mind going fuzzy around the edges as she greyed
out, and clasped one hand over her nose and mouth
to keep herself from breathing in water for as long as
she could. Kicking upward furiously—please, let it be
up—she reached out with her other hand. If she could
even touch rock above her head, she could pull herself back to the opening of the Wellspring and get back
to the cave. . . .

At last, when will alone kept her hand clamped over
her nose and mouth, she felt her questing hand break
the surface of the water, felt it slap down on the edge
of the spring in the free air, felt hard stone beneath
her palm. Frantically, she thrust her way to the surface and hung halfway over the edge, gagging and
sputtering, sucking in air in deep furious gulps between
wracking coughs. Her nose ran, and she coughed hard
enough and long enough so that most of the water
she'd drunk—and her dinner with it—came up to
decorate the rock. Glory felt a small vindictive surge
of triumph.

"Oh, no, you don't, you old besom. You aren't getting rid of me that easily," Glory gasped at last, her
voice hoarse with misuse.

Thoroughly cold and wet—and entirely out of temper with the Oracle—she dragged herself out of the
spring again and sat weakly beside it for several

minutes, panting hard. She struggled out of her foul wet T-shirt and jeans—losing her bandages entirely in the process—and towelled herself dry with one of the blankets.

What a mess.

She supposed she couldn't just leave the place looking—and smelling—like that. Using her T-shirt as a mop, she swabbed the stone clean, and then gave her shirt a thorough washing in the spring. The Oracle deserved it, after what she'd put Glory through, and the water should be clean again for drinking by the time Helevrin's lot came tomorrow. When she was done, she wrung out the T-shirt and her jeans as best she could, knowing they'd still be damp in the morning despite her best efforts, and spread them flat on the rock at the far side of the cave.

Just to remind me of why—and how much—I hate magic. Now where's that damned cup?

For a moment or two she thought she might have dropped it into the spring—and wouldn't that have made a pretty tale to explain in the morning?—but she finally found it. It had rolled over against the wall of the round chamber. She picked it up and put it back in its place, then picked up the lantern.

Oh, I'll sleep like a baby after this. No worries.

She brought the lantern back over to her sleeping pallet, warily avoiding the puddles on the floor, and set it down at the head of the bed. Her heart was still hammering with the narrowness of her escape when she sat down on the mattress to blot her braid dry with the damp blanket she'd used for a towel. If she'd hit her head going in— If that *had* been the entrance to an underground river after all—

But you didn't, and it wasn't, and you're here.

Finally her hair was as dry as it was going to get unless she unbraided it and combed it out with the comb she hadn't thought to bring. Reluctantly—alert for any further tricks on the Wellspring's part—Glory lay down and cocooned herself in blankets, tucking Gordon tightly under her arm and staring up at the candle's flame. She'd never felt less like sleeping in her life.

It was an accident, she told herself. *Sure it was. Course it was. That's just a big puddle of water, that. So maybe it's deeper than it looks—and wider underneath than on the top. That doesn't mean somebody pushed you in. You just scared yourself green, is all.*

After a while she sighed, giving up, and reached out to slide the sleeve up on the lantern, plunging the small chamber into darkness. *Might as well take the whole E-Ticket ride while I'm here.*

She was walking along the road, through the Victorian countryside where they shot most of *TITAoVtS'* exteriors. It was the winter season, and everything was green. She could pick out the familiar landmarks up ahead—Camrado Oak, and Slayer Rock—but none of the usual production company equipment was here— sound trucks, equipment vans, trailers for cast and crew. She didn't even see the standing set, though she should certainly have reached the village and castle set by now. She knew she was late for something— why else would she be in costume if they weren't shooting today?

She looked down at herself, at all her gleaming black leather, buffed and shining and fresh from Wardrobe.

Thought I'd mucked this up, she thought in faint surprise. Then she realized she must be dreaming, that the water had worked after all. Well, she'd swallowed enough of it, even if she'd tried to sick it all up again. But why was she dressed like this for a dream? She looked back over her shoulder. Even her sword was here—her own sword, the one she'd given up for the magic one. *And look how well THAT turned out. . . .*

She stopped and looked around at the familiar landscape, then shrugged to herself and started walking again. Might as well get on to where she was supposed to be. If this was a dream, it was a lot more solid than dreams usually got. But it didn't really look like the sort of place that the Dreamer of Worlds would choose for a return engagement—or Erchane's Oracle either, for that matter.

But someone was waiting for Glory, all the same.

The woman was leaning against the tree the *TITAoVtS* crew had named Camrado Oak. She was wearing a chain-mail shirt, split for riding, that fell to her knees. The mesh was so fine it almost looked like heavy cloth, and over it she wore a leather belt and baldric that held a sword hanging from a scabbard on her back. Below the chain mail she wore high boots over tight leather trousers, both black. She was also wearing gloves, their stiff flared gauntlets reaching almost to her elbows, and so heavily studded with metal above the wrist that it was hard to see the leather beneath. The glove part must be flexible, though, because she was holding a large red apple in her hand, and as Glory approached, she bent to pull a knife from her boot and began to peel it.

There was something oddly familiar about the gesture. Startled, Glory looked up into the woman's tiger-yellow eyes.

She was looking at Vixen the Slayer.

Yes. No. Or was it Vixen as she might have been, if she'd been dressed for practicality and not for ratings? The outfit looked practical, anyhow. Easy to move in. The woman's hair was as long as Glory's own, braided snugly back and wrapped with soft leather.

Glory saw it swing free as the woman straightened, still peeling the apple.

"Going to gawk all day?" Her voice was Vixen's too, the flat American drawl Glory had worked so hard to master. It was like looking into a distorting mirror of a different sort than the kind she'd faced in the Warmother's castle—one that made things better, not worse. With all her heart, Glory yearned to be the woman she saw.

"I . . . I . . . What are you doing here?" she stammered.

"Could ask you that. Ask yourself: what are you doing here?" Vixen said.

Glory set her jaw. If this was going to be another clever symbolic dream in a fancy hat, she might as well go along with it as far as she could, because bugger her if she was going back to the Oracle to spend the night a third time.

"I came to find out about the Dreamer of Worlds. What does she want? Did I pass her test? What happens now?"

Vixen went on peeling the apple in silence for a moment, removing its skin in the narrowest possible unbroken curl.

"The thing about gods, camrado, is that you can never be sure about them. They're always showing up and making pronouncements and wandering off again. Also, they lie. By the time she shows up again, your folk might not need her any more. Or she'll have forgotten you were supposed to be her last candidate. Or maybe the test's still going on. Some tests take a really long time, you know. God's Teeth! But you'll see."

"That's not very helpful," Glory said crossly.

"Sorry," Vixen said, not sounding very sorry at all. "I'm not good at questions. Solving problems, now . . . But seems to me you don't have many of those just now."

"But what am I supposed to *do*?" Glory wailed.

Vixen smiled, as though that was actually the question she'd been waiting for.

"Well there, camrado, I'd say you've got two choices. Whether you've passed the Dreamer's test or not, you've done pretty good in the hero line, and the Allimir are going to need one. Seems to me you could stick around and do some heroing. Or head on back to where you came from. Your choice."

But I already made my choice, Glory realized. *Back at the spring—I could have come up anywhere. That was my chance.* She remembered how hard she'd fought—not just to breathe, not just to get out, but to get back to the same place she'd fallen in—to Belegir, and Ivradan, and even Englor and Helevrin, bless their hearts. Back to the Allimir, and Erchanen, and the plains of Serenthodial. Once again magic had snuck up on her when she wasn't looking—but if she'd been truly homesick, she'd have been thinking of home while she was drowning, not Ivradan.

Glory smiled reluctantly. She'd been given a fair chance, even if a sneaky one.

"But they don't need me. They need you. I'm not you," she protested.

"'Course you are," Vixen asserted inarguably. "If not you, who? God's teeth, gel, who d'you think you're looking at? Someone has to take the dream and make it real. What were you doing in front of those cameras all those months? Or up on Grey Arlinn? Knitting?"

Glory stared at her, slack-jawed. *It can't be that easy.* But it could. She knew it could. Just that easy—and that hard. Embrace an ideal, and be willing to die for it. Live the legend, because people needed dreams as much as bread. And don't look back.

"But you'd better get yourself a proper sword. None of that tawdry magic. I hate magic. And nothing that breaks." Vixen's amber gaze roved over Glory's showgirl costume at length, and her lip curled eloquently. "And cover yourself up. You'll die of sunstroke and give your troops heart-failure if you don't."

"I . . . all right. I will." Glory squared her shoulders.

"Good girl. Do us proud." The last of the apple peel dropped to the ground in an unbroken coil. Vixen took a step away from the tree. With one smooth gesture she tossed Glory the peeled fruit.

Glory caught it, neatly, in both hands. She looked down at it, and it seemed as if by looking away from Vixen, she'd unmade whatever dream-world Vixen existed in. Suddenly it was dark, and Glory was awake enough to know she'd been asleep, or . . . something.

Darkness. She smelled wet wool and wet rock and burning candle, and realized she'd been asleep for a long time.

There was something in her hand.

She squeezed it, her head still fuzzy with dreams, and smelled apples. Suddenly she was entirely awake, rolling onto her stomach to slide the shutter on the little lantern down to expose the candle. In the abrupt brightness, she could see what she held.

An apple.

A freshly peeled apple, its white flesh only now starting to darken with exposure to the air.

And there was only one place it could have come from.

Magic.

True magic, real magic, miracle enough to hang a lifetime on. She sat up in her bed, grinning to herself. No fear she was going to forget what she'd dreamed this time! She'd remember it for the rest of her life.

But she wouldn't tell. Not even Belegir. No one needed to know, as long as she knew.

"Do us proud."

"Damn right I will," Glory said aloud. She bit into the apple. She'd better get moving. She had a lot to do today, and all the days to follow.

There's always work in the land of Erchanen for Vixen the Slayer.

VIXEN THE SLAYER:
The Episode Guide
(Season One)

COMES A SLAYER (1)

SUMMARY:

Vixen arrives in England just in time to investigate a series of mysterious deaths at the Convent of Sisters of the Holy Ghost, eventually exposing the Mother Superior as a fiendish (and very male) vampire in disguise. Along the way, she and Sister Bernadette join forces in what is to become one of the great partnerships in TV history.

COMMENTS:

Not bothering to waste time with an origin story, the series gets off to a rapid start, thrusting our heroine into mortal combat with the Undead even before the opening credits have run. Viewers are given only a few tantalizing hints as to Vixen's enigmatic past, some of which later prove to be extremely misleading. (The show's creators, the esteemed Slayer Staff, *claim* to have carefully worked out Vix's entire backstory in advance, but I have my doubts; how come Vix refers here to her years of martial arts training in "far-off Cathay" when later episodes clearly place her younger self in Japan, not China? And why is it she can read Latin here, but seems to mysteriously lose this ability in later episodes, presumably to give Sister Bernadette something useful to do?)

Still and all, a good beginning.

✳ ✳ ✳ ✳

BEHOWL THE MOON (2)

SUMMARY:
Who is responsible for a ghastly series of full-moon murders? The struggling playwright? The haughty contessa? The sinister Italian physician? The kindly beggar woman? Vix reveals deductive acumen to rival her gymnastic skills as she exposes the homicidal lycanthrope among the guests at Queen Elizabeth's surprise birthday party.

COMMENTS:
Okay, the true identity of the concealed werewolf is so obvious that she might as well have a pentagram tattooed on her wrinkled forehead, but this is still a fun episode, with many creepy scenes of the snarling man-beast stalking its victims through the foggy streets of old London town. This episode also marks the first use of Full Earth's notorious All-Purpose Creature Armature. Here it stands in for the Wolf of Westminster in all its hirsute glory, but foam-rubber facelifts would later transform the APCA into such

diverse (and economical) apparitions as the Grim Golem of Glastonbury and the demon Abraxodoceous.

Omens of Things to Come: Look carefully during the first funeral scene and you'll see that the service is being performed by none other than Father Diavolo himself, who would soon be seen again in far more incriminating circumstances.

Literary Alert! The title of this episode is lifted from Shakespeare's *A Midsummer Night's Dream*: "now the hungry lion roars, now the wolf behowls the moon." (Who says fantasy isn't educational?)

✳ ✳ ✳

TO HUNT THE HUNTER (3)

SUMMARY:

Lured to the secluded country estate of Lord Raptor, a celebrated big game hunter, Vix soon finds herself the quarry in the jaded aristocrat's latest blood sport. A gripping chase through foggy moors ensues, with Raptor's bloodhounds literally chomping at Vixen's leather-shod heels, but she eventually turns the tables on her relentless foe, so that she ultimately hunts the hunter of the hunter! (I think I've got that right.)

COMMENTS:

Just about every action-adventure series gets around to ripping off "The Most Dangerous Game" eventually, but it was a bit alarming that *TITAoVtS* was falling back on the old hunting-humans chestnut by only its third episode! Were the Slayer Staff running out of ideas already? Thankfully, this proved not to be the case, but one could be forgiven for fearing otherwise at this point.

On its own terms, "Hunter" is a briskly paced,

action-filled episode that gave Glory plenty of opportunities to show off her Olympics-caliber gymnastics skill. Interestingly, this is also the first ep to feature no overtly supernatural elements, although Lord Raptor is given a line or two about devil worship, no doubt to provide the episode a fig leaf of diabolism.

As for Sister Bernadette, Anne-Marie Campbell barely appears in this episode, showing up only briefly in the very first and last scenes. Her low profile here lends credence to the longstanding rumor that the Slayer Staff were initially unsure whether Vixen needed a sidekick at all, and even considered killing the character off! (Hard to imagine now, I know.)

Anachronism Alert! A stuffed gorilla is displayed prominently in Raptor's trophy room, despite the fact that the African gorilla was completely unknown to Europeans of the era. Oh well, what's a few centuries of zoological science between friends?

✳ ✳ ✳

WHAT LURKS IN THE LOCH? (4)

SUMMARY:
Vix takes the high road, and Sister Bernie takes the low road, but death—in the form of a notably gnawed-on corpse—gets to Scotland before either of them. The locals blame the legendary Loch Ness monster, of course, but Vixen soon pins the blame on a cannibalistic merman, recently escaped from a traveling carnival, who nearly makes a late-night snack of a skinnydipping Sister Bernadette before Vix feeds the greedy fish-man to the real Nessie.

COMMENT:
The Musgrave Range in central Australia doubled

(with mixed results) for the Scottish Highlands this time around, but much of the episode was actually shot in a leaky five-hundred-gallon tank located in a dank, chilly warehouse in Melbourne. Neither Glory nor Anne-Marie required lessons in Method acting to produce realistic-looking goosebumps during the episode's many aquatic scenes. One shot in particular, in which Vix and Sister Bernie's flimsy rowboat is capsized by a submerged menace from below, required so many takes that both stars were virtually water-logged by the end of the fourteen-hour working day. Guest-star Colin Piscatore (playing the voracious gill-man) fared even worse, nearly drowning when the hydraulically operated Nessie model went haywire and refused to release Piscatore from its mechanical jaws after diving back beneath the surface of the mock Loch. "Bloody hell!" he is reported to have hollered after being extricated (and none too soon) from the malfunctioning monster. "This is the twenty-first century, for chrissakes! Where's the goddamn CGI?"

In the end, "What Lurks" ran two days over schedule and nearly $25,000 over budget, inspiring the beleaguered Slayer Staff to vow, "No more sea monsters—ever!"

Or at least for awhile. (See "Sigh of the Selkie.")
※ ※

THE DUCHESS'S DELIGHTS (5)

SUMMARY:

When the aging Duke of Bleeksmore dies under mysterious circumstances, leaving his entire estate to his glamorous young wife, Vixen suspects foul play. At first, Vix suspects that the Duchess, who is seldom seen before sunset, is a vampire or succubus, but the truth proves far more alarming: Lilith Kane is the high priestess of a satanic coven who ultimate goal is nothing less than the total conquest of Europe! Already the Duchess has bribed, blackmailed, and seduced many prominent nobles into joining her cult, including trusted members of Queen Elizabeth's own court.

Our heroine almost ends up as a human sacrifice at a Black Mass, presided over by an unfrocked priest named Father Diavolo, before turning the tables on Lilith and her acolytes, and setting fire to Bleeksmore Manor with one of the Duchess's own monogrammed branding irons. Both Lilith and Diavolo perish in the resulting conflagration—or so we are led to believe.

COMMENTARY:
Enter the Duchess . . .
Every great hero needs a worthy foe, and, her apparent fiery death notwithstanding, Lilith Kane rapidly became Vixen's number one enemy. Irreverent, sardonic, and deliciously decadent, the Duchess is the antithesis of the Slayer's somber and crusading persona, yet their mutual antagonism is leavened by a grudging respect (and perhaps even an unspoken attraction) between them. Recognizing a good thing when they saw one, the Slayer Staff wasted no time bringing the Duchess back from the dead . . . again and again and again.

Romy Blackburn is clearly having a ball playing Lilith, chewing up the scenery, both dungeons and drawing rooms alike, and firing off one outrageously evil one-liner after another. Although her, umm, eye-catching costume is brazenly lifted from Emma Peel's "Queen of Sin" outfit from that old *Avengers* episode, Romy makes the Duchess a memorable character in her own right.

Previously glimpsed in "Behowl the Moon," Father Diavolo is revealed in this episode to be Lilith's most reliable henchman and sidekick. Like his unholy mistress, he can be counted on to die horribly at the end of every episode in which he appears, yet he keeps coming back, forever at the side of the Duchess herself. In a perhaps overly candid moment, Anne-Marie Campbell once remarked that actor Dylan MacNee was "ideally" suited to play the sniveling, venal ex-priest, but let's hope that was just a bit of sidekick rivalry speaking. One hates to think that MacNee would ever willingly ally himself with the Dark Forces . . .

✳✳✳✳

YO, HO, HO, AND A BOTTLE OF BLOOD (6)

SUMMARY:

Our heroine hits the high seas in search of a pair of curvaceous female pirates who have accidentally looted a priceless (and very dangerous) mystic artifact from a captured Spanish galleon. Unfortunately, an Undead privateer named Cap'n Cadaver is also after the Inquisition's spoils, putting him on a collision course with a certain seagoing Slayer.

COMMENTS:

Avast, ye maties! I confess, I'm a sucker for a good pirate story. Heck, I even wrote a young-adult pirate novel once (now woefully out-of-print), so I devoured this episode as readily as a buccaneer downs his daily ration of rum, despite a few glaring historical inaccuracies.

For instance: Mary Read and Anne Bonny, the distaff pirates Vix tracks down (and eventually joins force with), are genuine historical figures, but they actually plied their swashbuckling trade in the early eighteenth century, a bit after Vixen's time. Both women are said to have posed as men for much of their careers, which suggests that they probably weren't costumed nearly as provocatively (read: skimpily) as their TV reincarnations, who favor bare midriffs, tight trousers, and plenty of cleavage. Cap'n Cadaver, on the other hand, is strictly a product of the Slayer Staff's bloodthirsty imaginations.

If our favorite Slayer occasionally seems to resemble Geena Davis during the climatic sea battle, that may be because the producers frugally and shamelessly incorporated several minutes of footage from *Cutthroat Island* into the finished episode. Granted, they were probably safe in assuming that not many viewers (except us diehard pirate aficionados) had ever seen those shots before. . . .

✳✳✳ (for pirate buffs)
✳✳ (for everyone else)

CORSETS AND CATACOMBS (7)

SUMMARY:
Intent on ferreting out the last vestiges of the late Duchess's cult, Vixen travels to Rome in the guise of Lilith Kane herself. Little does she know that (gasp!) the Duchess is still alive, and impersonating Vixen as part of an elaborate scheme to steal the forbidden *Book of the Damned* from the vaults of the Vatican. Confusion, misunderstandings, and many titillating costume changes ensue.

COMMENTARY:
Silly, but fun. The coincidence-packed plot doesn't hold up to close examination (*why* exactly do Vixen and Lilith have to dress up as each other?), but it's undeniably amusing to watch Glory and Romy do each other's shtick. The general consensus among Vixites is

that Romy did Glory better than Glory did Romy, but then again, soap-opera veteran Romy does have the edge when it comes to acting experience.

It's also unclear why Truxton the Troll is lurking beneath St. Peter's Cathedral (or computer-generated facsimile thereof), but at least it gives the producers a chance to get yet more mileage out of the good old APCA, while guaranteeing a bit of action amidst all the mistaken identity nonsense.

Me, I'm waiting for the episode where Sister Bernie and Father Diavolo have to change places. . . .

✶✶✶

ENEMY UNSEEN (8)

SUMMARY:

An explosion in an alchemist's lab renders Vixen sightless, and not even Sister Bernadette can predict if and when the blindness will pass. This seeming handicap proves a boon, however, when the Goddess Kali dispatches an invisible assassin to destroy the Slayer and her sidekick. Forced to rely on her other senses, the blinded heroine makes short work of the transparent thuggee, ultimately running him through with her blind man's cane. (Eventually, of course, Sister Bernie's secret herbal treatments—or maybe her impassioned prayers—restore Vixen's sight. After all, we viewers could hardly been deprived of the heart-stopping sight of Glory McArdle's lambent amber orbs forever!)

COMMENTS:

The use of an invisible antagonist meant that the All-Purpose Creature Armature got a much-needed break this week, with Full Earth's SFX team resorting to a combination of computer-processed opticals and old-fashioned trickery to pull off a variety of "invisibility" effects. They do a pretty good job, given the financial and time restraints of episodic television, but if you look closely you can see the wires supporting the spiked mace that seems to float up behind Vixen of its own volition, as though grasped by an unseen hand. Having the invisible man take refuge inside a complete suit of armor also kept the SFX budget down, except for those shots where the armor's visor is lifted, revealing a seemingly empty helmet. (Naturally, this doesn't stop Vixen from using hot coals to heat the metal of the armor to such a temperature that the see-through assassin is forced to abandon his protective sheathing of steel.)

Meanwhile, despite her best efforts, Gloria herself was reportedly unable to maintain the fixed, sightless stare the script required, forcing director Dave Mack to hide the star's overly active orbs behind a strip of all-concealing linen, effectively rendering the actress as blind as the character she was playing. Reliable sources testify that the blindfolded star was something of a menace on the set, eventually taking out two stuntpersons and a $500 klieg light with her flailing cane.

Good thing Vix got her sight back, before the entire cast ended up in the hospital!

✹ ✹

NINJA NIGHTMARE (9)

SUMMARY:
Akira Okada, a valiant Japanese Samurai, arrives in London in search of the shape-changing ninja who slew his family. Thanks to the sort of misunderstanding that

always seems to occur when two heroes meet each for
the first time, he ends up crossing swords with Vixen
for two acts, before Slayer and Samurai team up to stop
the nefarious ninja from unleashing the Black Death
upon the city. Along the way, we also learn much more
about Vix's previously murky past.

COMMENTARY:
At long last, the Slayer Staff starts filling us in on
the Slayer's early years in the Far East, including the
fascinating tidbit that her real name is Koroshiya. Mind
you, as mentioned earlier, some of these new revela-
tions don't mesh exactly with what we were told back
in Episode 1, but I guess a super-heroine is entitled
to change her backstory along with her mind.

"Ninja Nightmare" is also a thinly-disguised pilot for
a spin-off series about a out-of-place samurai abroad
in Merrie Olde England, which explains the surprising amount of screen time Okada gets, occasionally at
Vix's expense, and why the nameless ninja gets away
in the end. So far, nothing definite has come of this
particular trial balloon, but who knows? If Gloria
McArdle remains MIA much longer, we may well end
watching the weekly exploits of Akira Okada, Samurai of London.

It just wouldn't be the same, though.
✳ ✳ ✳

MOTHER FOR A DAY (10)

SUMMARY:
Seems Sir William Webster, a successful and recently
knighted entrepreneur, promised the Dark Forces his
firstborn child in exchange for worldly wealth and fame.
Now the demon Abraxodoceous has come to collect,

and Webster, having experienced a change of heart, begs Vixen to help him keep six-year-old Rebecca from the demon's foul clutches. What's worse, Webster himself dies early on, sticking the manifestly unmaternal Vix with both a kid and a curse to deal with. Needless to say, our heroine soon finds dealing with the demon infinitely preferable to tending to a spoiled six-year-old. . . .

COMMENTS:

Look, if we wanted to see bratty kids cutting up, we could tune into any number of interchangeable family sitcoms. Fans want to see Vix kicking demon butt, not mawkishly bonding with a weepy orphan, which may explain why "Mother for a Day" is nobody's favorite episode.

It doesn't help, of course, that lil' Rebecca, played by the odious Molsen twins, is more annoying than ingratiating, although one can amuse oneself by trying to figure out which of the twins is the worst actress. No easy task! From what I could tell, Wendy Molsen appears to specialize in smart-aleck remarks, while sister Cindy handles the more saccharine moments, so I suppose it's ultimately a matter of taste.

According to Anne-Marie Campbell, the twins were holy terrors on the set as well, throwing tantrums, breaking props, and almost accomplishing what Vixen herself has never been able to do: send the All-Purpose Creature Armature to the junkyard for good. (Apparently, Cindy and Wendy mistook it for a climbing gym.)

By the end of the episode, Vix has sworn off motherhood forever. I wouldn't be at all surprised if Gloria McArdle felt much the same.

Literary Plagiarism Alert! Sister Bernadette's withering observation that "to lose one parent may be regarded as a misfortune; to lose both looks like care-lessness" is shamelessly lifted from *The Importance of Being Earnest* by Oscar Wilde. No surprise, it's the best and funniest line in the episode.

✳

THE BLOODY TOWER (11)

SUMMARY:

Is the ghost of Anne Boleyn really haunting the Tower of London, or are her shocking manifestations just part of a machiavellian plot to steal the Crown Jewels? To uncover the truth, Vixen must arrange to get herself arrested and confined to the Tower, cut off from everyone except "spiritual advisor" Sister Bernadette. No surprise, the so-called "Ghost" turns out to be yet another pawn of the ever-scheming Lilith Kane, but Vix manages to escape her rat-infested cell in time to keep the Crown Jewels out of the Duchess's avaricious grip. Oh yeah, she also gets a full pardon in the end.

COMMENTS:

One of the things I like most about *TITAoVtS* is that you can never tell whether the creature of the week is a genuinely supernatural phenomenon or just a cunning hoax. Other, more predictable shows usually choose one strategy and stick to it with numbing regularity, but *TITAoVtS* always keeps you guessing.

Strange but true: on the day of filming, the bird wrangler, who was supposed to deliver feathered stand-ins for the Tower's celebrated ravens, was nowhere to be found. Undaunted, the resourceful Slayer Staff threw breadcrumbs all around the set, attracting a sizable supply of pigeons, then painted the poor birdies black!

(Before PETA organizes a boycott, let me assure you that the paint was both non-toxic and water soluble!)

And, oh yes, Lilith dies again, this time by taking a fatal plunge from the top of the Tower to the murky Thames below. Was this at last the end of the despicable Duchess?

Of course not.

✻ ✻ ✻

BEYOND THE VEIL OF WORLDS (12)

SUMMARY:

A mystic mirror reveals a view of a parallel England where the Slayer is an exotic Asian woman whose fighting style resembles our Vixen's to an astonishing degree. Watching this other Ninja Vampire Hunter defeat a horde of fearsome *nosferatu* provides the real Vixen with the key to vanquishing a similar horde in her own reality.

COMMENTS:

TV producers are a notoriously frugal lot, so it's no surprise that the Slayer Staff eventually found a way to get some cinematic mileage out of the original *Ninja Vampire Hunter* pilot starring Doreen Liu. (If you look closely, you can also spot a pre-Vixen Glory McArdle lurking in the background of some of the crowd scenes, although most of Glory's footage has been surgically excised to avoid confusing the casual viewer *too* much. Watch for the striking, red-haired peasant wench grappling with the undead blacksmith in the tavern scene.)

At this point, it's hard to imagine anyone but Glory playing our favorite Elizabethan scourge of evil, yet "Veil" does give us an intriguing, if undeniably offputting, peek at What Might Have Been. In the end, the effect is not unlike watching one of those old

Batman episodes in which Catwoman is played by someone *besides* Julie Newmar: interesting, but not entirely satisfying.

(Internet rumors persist that Doreen Liu might someday make a genuine guest-appearance on the show, so that the two Vixens could actually fight side-by-side, but I'll believe it when I see it. Sounds more like fannish wishful thinking to me.)

❋ ❋ ❋

LONG LIVE THE QUEEN? (13)

SUMMARY:

Who needs plastic surgery when you have sorcery? At the Duchess's behest, Father Diavolo uses his black arts to transform Lilith into the Queen's identical twin (coyly referred to in the script as "Queen Elizabeth the Second"). When the imposter replaces the real Queen upon the throne, our heroines find themselves condemned as traitors and outlaws. While Sister Bernie cools her heels in the Tower, a fugitive Vix must rescue the real Elizabeth Regina before Lilith betrays England to the Spanish Armada. (Part One of Two.)

COMMENTS:

Gertrude Wallaby, the grande dame of Australian soap operas, gets a field day in this ambitious two-part episode, wherein she is called upon to play both the real Elizabeth and the disguised Duchess. A memorable comic high point is achieved when the bogus queen blows her cover by making a shameless pass at Vixen herself, something the actual Virgin Queen would *never* do (or so we assume). Certainly, any doubts Vixen may have had about what was going on were thoroughly dispelled by this ill-judged (if perfectly understandable) lapse on Lilith's part.

Devout Romy Blackburn fans were probably disappointed by her unavoidable lack of screen time this go-round, but otherwise it's hard to complain about this entertaining and ingenious episode. The cliffhanger ending, with the Armada approaching even as Sister Bernie faces the headman's axe, made for a long and suspenseful week as Vixites throughout the country waited avidly to find out what would happen next.

Trivia alert! As it happens, this is the *only* episode featuring Lilith Kane in which the Duchess doesn't appear to meet an untimely demise at the end—if only because her inevitably fatal comeuppance was postponed until next week's show!

✻✻✻✻

SINK THE QE2! (14)

SUMMARY:
While Sister Bernie stages a daring escape from the Tower, Vix must overcome a hulking Golem to rescue the real Queen. But can the Slayer and the monarch get back to Buckingham Palace before the treacherous Duchess spells England's doom?

COMMENTS:
One suspects that this particular adventure was stretched out over two episodes in order to get maximum value out of Full Earth's impressively computer-generated Armada, even if the final battle shipboard battle between Vixen and the counterfeit queen was filmed in that now-familiar 500-gallon tank in Melbourne.

The infamous All-Purpose Creature Armature gets

another workout, too, this time providing support for the stony Golem that (briefly) stands between Vixen and the Queen. Too bad Vix doesn't realize that she's fighting the same monstrous skeleton show after show; otherwise she'd probably make sure the darn thing was reduced to ashes before leaving another vanquished monster to rot upon blood-soaked cobblestones or a misty mire.

To be honest, Part Two of this saga is not quite as fun as the preceding installment, mainly because the mistaken identity/evil Queen angle was pretty much milked for all it was worth in Part One. Still, it's undeniably satisfying to see Lilith revert to her usual seductive self just in time for the big finish, even if the Duchess ultimately goes to a watery grave . . . or does she?

✳✳✳

FROM PRUSSIA WITH LOVE (15)

SUMMARY:

Count Wolfgang von Blitzkrieg, a charmingly dissolute Prussian nobleman (complete with a highly decorative dueling scar) arrives as a special envoy to the court of Queen Elizabeth. Despite herself, Vixen finds herself attracted to the handsome young rake, only to discover that his public vices hide an even greater duplicity. To pay off his enormous gambling debts, Wolfie plans to steal top-secret military secrets from the British crown and sell them to the highest bidder. Not only that, his dueling scar is a fake!

Overcoming her brief infatuation, or so it seems, the Slayer recovers the precious papers, but "accidentally" allows Wolf to escape more or less unscathed, albeit with a genuine scar upon his cheek. Vix claims she did her best to apprehend the young scoundrel, but Sister Bernie, frankly, has her doubts.

COMMENTS:

The Slayer Staff originally intended the roguish Count to be a recurring villain and/or love interest for Vixen, providing an overtly heterosexual counterpoint to the subtextual undercurrents running through the Lilith Kane episodes. Unfortunately, any hopes for a long-running battle of the sexes between Wolfgang and the Slayer were dashed by the palpable lack of chemistry between Gloria McArdle and Bruno Carlino, a talent-impaired former underwear model, whose week-long stint on the series is remembered with loathing by just about every member of the cast and crew.

Asked at SlayerCon 2000 why the character of Wolfgang had never returned, McArdle diplomatically mumbled something about "creative differences" and "scheduling conflicts." In fact, evil rumors paint an unflattering picture of spoiled, temperamental boy toy who showed up late every morning, fumbled his lines, misread cue cards, and didn't even seem to be quite clear on which TV show he was guesting. (Outtakes exist of him addressing Vixen as "Buffy," "Xena," and even "Zorro.")

In retrospect, Anne-Marie Campbell had the easiest time of it filming this episode. Those dirty looks that Sister Bernadette keeps giving Wolfgang probably required little or no acting at all!

(Trivia alert: the original script for this episode, which was posted on the web, had the count plotting to steal the Crown Jewels instead of classified documents. Wisely, someone on the Slayer Staff remembered "The Bloody Tower," and realized that *two* jewel-heist episodes would have been one too many.)

✳

A MIDSUMMER NIGHT'S MASSACRE (16)

SUMMARY:

Following a frenzied battle with an unusually hard-to-slay vampire, an exhausted Vixen collapses in a moonlit glen on Midsummer's Eve, only to wake in the Land of Faerie, where she encounters Robin Goodfellow, a.k.a. Puck, who explains that he has recruited her to save Oberon's fairy kingdom from a *coup d'etat* organized by the scheming yet seductive Titania (who bears a suspicious resemblance to the Duchess). Thanks to a powerful love potion, Vix briefly falls under the spell of Lilith . . . I mean, Titania . . . but snaps out of it in time to cut a swath through hordes of pointy-eared extras and foil the Fairy Queen's diabolical plot, before waking to find herself back in the real world again. It was all just a dream—or was it?

COMMENTARY:

Even today, months after this episode first aired, you can still get a decent flame war going on the internet regarding just how much of "Midsummer" *actually* happened. Was this all just an elaborate dream sequence, or did our favorite Slayer really go traipsing through Faerie? The cast and crew have only fanned the flames of the debate by issuing contradictory explanations in various interviews and public appearances. Glory herself insists that the whole thing was just a goofy lark, taking place entirely in Vixen's fevered imagination, but Romy Blackburn (who, of course, plays Titania) maintains that the Fairy Queen was as real as any other character, and fully capable of making as many return appearances as the fans will (hint! hint!) demand. The screenwriter, an ink-stained wretch named Bryan Gregory Stephenson, has been no help at all, telling *Camrado!* that the (un) reality of the episode is up to each individual viewer to determine. A diplomatic, if weasely, response.

Still, let's face facts. This whole episode is just an excuse to finally get Glory and Romy into each other's arms, albeit with a layer of plausible deniability. As played by Blackburn, Titania is just the Duchess decked out in chartreuse greasepaint and sparkles. But is anybody complaining?

Not me.

Meanwhile, the producers once again displayed their budgetary genius by frugally leasing a bushel of pointed ear prosthetics from the *Star Trek* folks, rather than commissioning their own from scratch. So what if the armies of Faerie looked like they had just beamed in from the Romulan Empire? Did I mention that Romy and Glory had a love scene?

✳ ✳ ✳

THE TROUBLE WITH ANGLICANS (17)

SUMMARY:

A chance encounter with Sister Bernadette's childhood sweetheart, now the priest of country parish overrun with Undead, sparks an overlong flashback to the stalwart sidekick's early days as a young novice, when Sister Bernie briefly questioned her calling for love of a hunky, young seminary student. Ultimately, however, their nightmarish encounter with a satanic night-gaunt convinced the future Father to dedicate himself to the priesthood, breaking poor Bernie's heart. Now, years later, the former lovers finally lay their troubled past to rest, while Vixen rids the village of vampires (offstage).

COMMENTARY:

Suddenly, killing off Sister Bernie didn't seem like such a bad idea. I mean, I love the chemistry and clever repartee between Vixen and Bernie as much as the next Vixite, but who wants to spend a hour reliving some boring romance that happened before she ever met the Slayer? Did *Star Trek* ever waste time showing a young Leonard McCoy cramming for med school exams? Do we really care what Gabrielle was doing on the family farm before she hooked up with Xena? Of course not.

Also, to be brutally honest, all the wigs and soft-focus lighting in the world cannot make Anne-Marie Campbell look like a dewy young maiden, a glaring visual distraction exacerbated by the twenty-something Leonardo DeCaprio clone cast as her long-lost swain. She looks ridiculous in the flashback sequences, while, buried beneath a ton of unconvincing old age make-up, he looks fakey in the present-day framing scenes, thus guaranteeing that *none* of their scenes together work at all.

Add to this the conspicuous absence of Glory McArdle (who was off doing a press tour in the States), and you have an episode that makes one yearn longingly for a nice, exciting rerun.

✳✳

SIGH OF THE SELKIE (18)

SUMMARY:

For once, the Slayer must come to the aid of a supernatural creature when an innocent seal-woman, or selkie, is captured by an unscrupulous Scottish fisherman, who puts her on display in a caged metal tank. (Sort of the Elizabethan equivalent of SeaWorld, when you think about it.) Sister

Bernadette initially opposes risking their lives on behalf of such an "unnatural" creature, but eventually comes around as our heroines race against time to get the dying selkie back to the sea where she belongs.

COMMENTARY:

Glory's Olympic roots paid off here when the producers recruited her former Olympic teammate, bronze medal-winning swimmer Julie Sluice, to play the captive selkie. The scene where she reluctantly performs various aquatic tricks in exchange for fresh fish, while a jury of stone-faced judges hold up signs scoring her performance, succeeds as a hilarious parody of both the Olympics and trained dolphin shows, although, admittedly, the whole sequence is a good deal campier than the series usually gets.

Having learned their lesson from "What Lurks in the Loch?" (4), the producers wisely contrived a literal fish-out-of-water plot that takes place mostly on dry land, only attempting to simulate actual ocean conditions at the very beginning and end of the episode. Even still, Sluice is rumored to have caught a nasty cold from the frigid water within her enclosed tank, which may explain why she's been in no hurry to reprise the role, her old athletic ties to Glory notwithstanding.

Geographical Trivia Alert. The seaside village of Blackwaterfoot, where this episode is set, is a real place, located on the Isle of Arran, off the coast of Scotland. You don't think the Slayer Staff could make up a name like that, do you?

✳

A SLAYER IN LOVE (19)

SUMMARY:

At the request of Queen Elizabeth, Vixen must team up with Christopher Marlowe, dashing playwright and part-time secret agent to uncover Guy Fawke's nefarious plot to blow up the Houses of Parliament. Sparks fly between Marlowe and the Slayer, who ends up inspiring the warrior queen in his play *Dido, Queen of Carthage*, but their passionate romance ends tragically when she discovers that his most famous play, *Doctor Faustus*, is largely autobiographical; Marlowe has sold his soul to Mephistopheles in exchange for literary immortality. Despite a fierce battle, Vixen is ultimately unable to stop the Dark Forces from claiming her lover.

COMMENTARY:

Historical purists will no doubt point out that the real Marlowe died in 1593, a good twelve years before the notorious Gunpowder Plot, but who cares when an episode is this good! Clever, dramatic, and full-blooded, "Slayer in Love" has plenty of great dialogue ("Is this the face that stalked a thousand crypts?" Marlowe asks upon first meeting Vixen) and, for once, a genuinely moving love story that only the hardest hearts could resist. As the witty, doomed Marlowe, Canadian actor Malcolm Craigie makes a much better paramour for our favorite ninja vampire hunter than Count von Blitzkrieg ever did; even though he's ultimately dragged down to Hell, one hopes that the Slayer Staff will find a way to bring him back for a few more appearances.

Granted, Sister Bernadette doesn't have much to do in this episode, aside from clucking disapprovingly at Vix's growing infatuation with Marlowe, but I guess you can't have everything.

✳ ✳ ✳ ✳

THIRTEEN MINUTES TO DOOMSDAY (20)

SUMMARY:

An ominous prophecy from *The Book of the Damned*, which Sister Bernadette filched from Father Diavolo in Episode 14, hints that Armageddon itself is drawing nigh, in the form of a brilliant alchemist who is on the verge of discovering the secret of cold fusion—in 1592! Vixen must reach the reckless genius's secret laboratory, protected by all manner of ingenious boobytraps and pitfalls, before all of England undergoes a catastrophic meltdown!

COMMENTARY:

Not a lot of characterization or humor here, but plenty of nonstop action and suspense, that starts off with a bang in scene one, then just keeps accelerating towards the apocalyptic conclusion. Dr. Xavier Fell's steampunky gadgets and deathtraps are a hoot, too, although the candle-powered laser is a bit of stretch, and you've got to admire any show that has the chutzpah to do a nuclear countdown plot almost four hundred years before the Manhattan Project.

Unfortunately, "Doomsday" turned into a much more of a cliffhanger than intended when Gloria McArdle mysteriously disappeared while taping an MTV special in Hollywood, with the final scenes of the episode yet to be filmed, forcing the producers to tack a TO BE CONTINUED title over the truncated final scenes, and raising dire questions as to the entire future of *TITAoVtS*.

Will the missing star reappear in time to film September's big season premiere . . . or will it always be "Thirteen Minutes to Doomsday" for the show's devoted fans?

Let's cross our fingers and pray for the Slayer's safe return. Meanwhile, I wonder: what's Doreen Liu doing these days?

✳✳ (for now)